GIDEON
RESURRECTION

Grant Rosenberg

GIDEON
RESURRECTION

GOLDEN GATE BOOKS

Golden Gate Books
San Francisco

First Edition

ISBN: 979-8-9876126-1-3

Cover photo by John Berg

GOLDEN GATE BOOKS

PREVIOUSLY ON GIDEON…

Dr. Kelly Harper spent her days working alongside her father David at their urgent care clinic in San Francisco and her nights with her boyfriend, a Homicide Inspector with the SFPD. All of that suddenly changed when her father was murdered.

As Kelly tried to pick up the pieces of her shattered life, she received a visit from Matthew Benedetto, her father's lawyer. He revealed a shocking truth; that her father led a double life as *Gideon*, a shadowy hit man who targeted only the most depraved people in society. The elimination of his victims made the world a safer place. The money from those jobs kept the clinic running.

David Harper's alter ego was a tightly guarded secret, but his murder signaled that someone had discovered Gideon's identity and carried out a revenge killing. All the evidence pointed to a drug dealer named Tommy Moretti, and Benedetto feared that Moretti's next targets would be Kelly and her sister Jessica, who lay comatose in a long-term care facility.

Kelly was forced to make life-altering choices, cross moral and ethical lines and embrace her father's past in order to save herself and protect her sister.

The events that followed affected every aspect of Kelly's existence. In the aftermath of her homicidal deeds, she pondered two questions: would she ever be able to lead a normal life again, and would Gideon one day return?

GIDEON
RESURRECTION

PROLOGUE

She loped with the ease of a seasoned cross-country runner despite the fact she'd just turned sixteen. The only sophomore on the varsity squad, she was already gaining notoriety in the Bay Area, and track coaches from Cal Berkeley, Stanford and Oregon followed her progress with interest.

Running was her escape; from anxiety, from reality, from her mother. Life at home had never been idyllic. For as long as she could remember there'd been an undercurrent of tension between her parents, simmering like an active volcano that at any moment would spew molten bitterness and fiery accusations.

She'd hoped things would improve when her parents divorced. Cohabiting as a couple had become unbearable, so living apart might douse the flames of anger and the vituperative verbal sparring. Unfortunately, when Dad moved out, Mom needed a new outlet for her terminal indignation, and turned on her two daughters.

When Dad remarried, the stress levels at home soared.

And so, she ran.

Crystal Springs Reservoir was only ten minutes from her house and offered miles of jogging options. Her normal route took her along the San Andreas Lake trail, where she did the seven-mile lakeside run, then doubled back, weaving among the fragrant eucalyptus trees, keeping pace with the music coursing through her earbuds. Fourteen miles was usually enough to clear her head, but this afternoon she needed more. The strain between her and her mother had hit a new level of intensity after she'd announced she was moving in with her father.

For both of their sakes, she had to get away.

The sun was low in the sky and shone directly into her face. The next mile was a familiar straightaway she'd traversed a hundred times. She knew every gradual rise and well-worn rut, so as she ran, she closed her eyes, letting the golden warmth wash over her.

Her thoughts drifted to a happier place. A place where things weren't so complicated. A place where she felt loved and felt safe.

As her endorphins kicked in, she turned up her music. She was in the zone where her mind was on autopilot and her legs took over. Everyday pressures melted away, and the outside world ceased to exist. She never heard the rustle of dry leaves, the snap of branches, or the swish of the blade that severed her carotid artery.

1

Tuesday

The Mission Street Clinic in San Francisco was humming at full capacity and every molded plastic chair in the waiting room was occupied. The facility didn't offer a complete line of medical services, but the doctors were friendly and efficient, and their fees were extremely reasonable. The clinic was the go-to for locals in the Mission District who suffered from bee stings, broken arms, scratchy throats, or embarrassing rashes in places where rashes caused maximum embarrassment.

Dr. Kelly Harper had inherited the practice two months ago after her father's murder. Dr. David Harper had been a brilliant physician, but a somewhat less brilliant businessman. When he left his previous job as Head of Surgery at St. Francis Hospital, he personally funded his new endeavor. Unfortunately, the clinic was an ongoing financial drain. On top of that, David's oldest daughter Jessica was a fulltime patient at Peninsula Oaks, a facility that specialized in traumatic brain injury. She'd been there for over twenty years, and her extravagant bills were only partially offset by insurance.

Kelly had not only inherited the clinic, but the substantial debt that went along with it.

David's policy had been to treat any patient who needed care, so the medical staff frequently ended up providing services free of charge. For David, this meant personal sacrifice, which included simplifying his lifestyle, taking out second and third loans on his house, and occasionally doing some "work on the side."

It was this "work on the side" that resulted in David's untimely demise.

3

He'd moonlighted as a shadowy assassin known as *Gideon*, targeting the most immoral and depraved people in society. David used his medical acumen to meticulously design every death to appear as natural causes, common household mishaps, or the result of "sometimes, shit happens" (like poisonous spider bites, or accidental drownings). His modus operandi was to have no modus operandi. Most people assumed that Gideon was nothing more than an urban myth, which was precisely the way David wanted it.

Gideon's earnings kept the clinic afloat, and the elimination of his victims made the world a safer place. It was a win-win, unless you were one of his targets.

After David died, the killing continued...now, by the hand of his not-so-willing daughter, Kelly Rose Harper. Every time she closed her eyes, she was bombarded with horrific images from the past two months: *Tommy Moretti's look of terror when Kelly injected him with an overdose of heroin; Angelo Moretti suffocating from a lethal allergic reaction; Anthony Moretti engulfed in flames.*

Kelly's murderous exploits resulted in chronic bouts of PTSD, and she bore the psychological scars, including periods of depression, trouble sleeping, momentary blackouts, and recurrent mental flashes where she was forced to replay not only the repugnant acts of violence she'd carried out, but also the abhorrent acts she'd been subjected to: being drugged, bound and sexually assaulted.

Kelly found temporary refuge in alcohol, but the drinking only served to add guilt to her already fragile psyche. On top of that, her post-traumatic stress often led to anxiety, irritability, and hostility, which meant Kelly had to be constantly focused on remaining even-keeled, calm and reassuring. Her patients and her hardworking group of doctors and nurses deserved nothing less.

The clinic was staffed by three physicians, two RNs and a receptionist. The small team was barely enough to handle the flow, and today was one of those days when they were pushed to the limit.

Kelly had her hands full in bay One with a rotund middle-aged woman who'd used a needle to separate her over-mascaraed

4

eyelashes and accidently stuck herself in the eye. In her years as an ER doctor, Kelly had treated thousands of patients with a wide range of injuries and illnesses. Just when she thought she'd seen it all, someone like Ms. Bambury would waddle in, her eyeball red and watery because she wanted to look good for her blind date.

The irony of the "blind date" was lost on no one.

Dr. Viknesh Danabalan was in bay Two setting a fifteen-year-old skater's fractured radius. Vik had worked at the clinic for almost three years, and when Kelly took over, he became the de facto second-in-command. Because of his Singaporean heritage and Oxford accent, the immigrant community in the Mission District embraced him as a fellow transplant. As such, he was frequently invited to family dinners, weddings and the occasional *quinceañera*. Being successful, handsome and single, he was considered by many matriarchs to be a perfect match for their daughters. So far, Vik had artfully avoided any such entanglements.

Nurse Annie Egan was in bay Three treating a nine-year-old girl's allergic reaction from eating a PayDay bar. The girl knew she had a nut allergy, but evidently didn't associate the candy with peanuts, even though the exterior of the bar was a blanket of the toxic legumes. Fifty, cheerful, with an Irish lilt and smiling eyes, Annie was a beacon of light.

Bay Four was occupied by Dr. Ida Samuel, who'd only recently joined the staff. She had the face and physique of a high schooler, and despite being twenty-seven, she would no doubt be carded at bars and liquor stores for years to come. Ida was new to San Francisco. In fact, she was new to big city living. She'd grown up in Sugarcreek, Ohio, a town of 2,200 whose claim to fame was the world's largest cuckoo clock which played rousing Swiss polka music on the half hour. Ida graduated from tiny Hiram College and attended Northeast Ohio Medical University. To say she'd grown up sheltered was an understatement.

It so happened that Ida's father, Joseph, had been roommates with David Harper in college, and the two remained friendly over the years. While David had practiced medicine at the highest levels in San Francisco, Joseph had been content as a "country doctor" in Dover, Ohio, where he enjoyed a slow-paced, quiet life and raised his only daughter with down-home values and practical sensibilities.

When David Harper was killed, "Doc Joe" and his wife Betty had flown to San Francisco to express their condolences in person, despite Joseph being in the advanced stages of Non-Hodgkin's Lymphoma. Kelly was deeply moved by their effort and when she received a call from Betty Samuel asking if she knew of any openings for newly minted doctors, Kelly didn't hesitate to offer Ida the vacant position at the clinic.

Ida was bright, caring and eager but suffered from a shyness born out of a small-town inferiority complex. Relocating to a city of 875,000, which happened to be one of the most expensive cities in the world, felt like a tremendous weight pressing down on her, leading Ida to constantly question her decision to pull up her Ohio roots and transplant them in California soil.

Dr. Samuel was examining Gretchen Sadowski, a thirty-eight-year-old employee of the San Francisco Public Works Department. Gretchen was part of the street maintenance crew, spending her days filling potholes and resurfacing cracked asphalt. Her nails were permanently chipped, her hands were forever chapped, and the smell of nicotine was inexorably woven into her clothing. She was short but sturdy, with arms like a stevedore. Ida gently probed Gretchen's neck.

"Is there any pain when I do this?"

"Nope. Just hurts when I move my head around."

"How long have you been experiencing chills?"

Gretchen shrugged, which triggered an involuntary wince. "Couple'a days, maybe."

Ida shined a penlight in Gretchen's eyes, moved the light away, and then back into position. "Any sensitivity?"

"No, but I've been pretty nauseous. Yerked a few times last night."

Ida was unfamiliar with the term but understood it in context. "Is that normal?"

"Nah. I used to puke regularly when I partied too hard on the weekends, but I've cut way back on the tequila. Oh, and I barfed a couple of times when I was preggo, but I know I don't have a bun in the oven 'cause a few years ago I switched from first to third."

Ida tilted her head, taking on the bearing of a confused terrier. Gretchen elaborated. "Found out I liked women more than men."

"Oh," Ida said, her face reddening.

Gretchen smiled, "Where're you from, Doc?"

"A small town in Ohio."

"Ah," Gretchen nodded sagely, "I'm guessing there's not a lot of same-sex hookups there, huh?"

"I really have no idea." Ida was eager to get back to the matter at hand. "Your symptoms are quite general. I'll write you a prescription for Zofran, which will help with the nausea, and I recommend you take some time off from work, stay hydrated and get a lot of rest. Come back and see me in two days if things haven't improved."

"Will do. So, Doc…you got a boyfriend?"

Ida wasn't used to such overt lack of boundaries, "No. I thought you…"

"I'm not hitting on you," Gretchen said. "I just thought you might wanna come out with us some night. Loosen up a little."

"Thank you, but I, uh, don't, um, get loose."

Gretchen cracked up. Ida beat a hasty exit.

Kelly had just finished with her patient when she heard a blaring car horn, followed by the squeal of tires and the sickening thud of metal colliding with a body.

She sprinted outside, followed by Vik, Ida, and Annie. A Tesla SUV was silently idling in the crosswalk and a man in his sixties was sprawled out some eight feet away, his leg bent at a horrifically unnatural angle.

Ida and Annie turned to Kelly for instructions, but Kelly's mind had temporarily transported elsewhere...*a dark rain-drenched street awash with red lights from police cruisers. She saw herself ducking under yellow caution tape and lifting a tarp to find the mangled, bloodied body of her father.*

"Doctor Harper!" said Vik. Kelly snapped back to reality and took command of the situation. "Annie, get out there and divert the traffic. Ida, have Ramona call an ambulance and get me scissors, gauze pads and adhesive wraps." Vik had already removed his jacket and was using it as a pillow to stabilize the man's leg. Kelly joined him and began checking vitals.

"Sir," said Kelly, "try to remain as still as possible."

"I never heard the damn car," the man growled through clenched teeth. "Elon Musk can go to hell." The man was writhing, and every movement triggered another jolt of pain.

"Sir, your leg is broken, and we need to keep it stable."

"The ambulance is ten minutes out!" shouted Ida as she returned carrying the medical supplies.

Vik carefully cut the man's pant leg, exposing a compound fracture...the tibia sticking out through the skin.

The man craned his neck, "How bad is it?"

"Sir, can I have your name?" Vik asked, not because it was necessary, but because it provided the distraction Kelly needed to apply the gauze pads before the man could catch sight of his protruding bone and instinctively flinch or go into shock.

Ida was impressed with their teamwork. Theirs was clearly a well-oiled partnership, and she worried how, or if, she'd ever fit in.

The early summer light was beginning to fade from the San Francisco skies, and the throngs of patients tapered off. Over the last month Kelly had trimmed back the clinic's hours, and now they closed at 7:00 p.m. It not only saved money, it also gave her and the staff more personal time, which everyone needed and appreciated.

There usually wasn't much of an "after dinner crowd," with the exception of a few street people looking for a warm place to hang out, or naïve newcomers to the Mission who thought they could con a tired doctor into writing them some script. Both ploys were aggressively discouraged by Ramona Vargas, the Dominican receptionist who one minute could be as warm as your favorite grandmother, and the next, as frightening as a rodeo bull on steroids.

Kelly was in her office, chipping away at the mountain of paperwork that came along with running the clinic. She sought to finish a few more patient insurance reimbursement forms before closing up and meeting Pete for drinks. Kelly and Pete Ericson had been dating for two years, and it was once a foregone conclusion they'd eventually tie the knot. However, the shocking death of David Harper stalled those plans. And then, Kelly's subsequent forays outside the law derailed any thoughts on her part of walking down the aisle. That conclusion was compounded by the fact that Pete happened to be a homicide inspector with the SFPD.

Since her father's death, Kelly had spent countless hours ruminating on whether she'd ever again enjoy a normal life. A life that included a relationship with Pete. Could she somehow lock her secrets into the darkest recesses of her mind, walling them up like Fortunato? She didn't know if that were at all possible, but in the meantime, her hopes for a future with Pete led her to at least keep her options open.

Kelly was lost in thought when the final member of her staff, Nurse Sonita Morales, entered and informed her that a nice-looking young man was here to see her.

Five minutes later, Sonita ushered Carter Dane into Kelly's office. Mid-thirties and well-dressed, he strode in with a smile on his face and high polish on his Thom Browne loafers. Carter handed Kelly his business card and she invited him to have a seat.

"Thanks for seeing me."

Kelly was intrigued and slightly concerned. Why would a commercial real estate broker come calling, especially after six o'clock?

"Mister Dane. What can I help you with?"

"This is strictly a courtesy call, Doctor Harper. Our company recently finalized the purchase of this building, as well as the adjacent liquor store and beauty parlor. I'll be personally handling the new lease agreements and wanted to introduce myself to my tenants."

"New lease agreements? Our lease runs for another two, two and a half years."

His smile hadn't changed, but what appeared a few moments ago to be charming, suddenly took on the appearance of a hungry wolf about to devour a succulent rabbit. "Doctor Harper, there's a caveat in your contract that states if the value of said property increases by more than fifteen percent in any calendar year, the owner has the right to revise the lease agreement accordingly."

Kelly did her best to stifle her rising anger. "You came to notify me that our rent's going to increase?"

"Not for ninety days," he said with a reassuring look. "You'll get the official letter tomorrow by registered mail, but I was passing by and thought I could inform you in person."

"How...courteous of you." Her disdain was obvious.

"I realize this isn't welcome news, but please know that our company's a big supporter of the work you do here."

"Big supporter, but you're going to raise our rent."

"Only to the extent that reflects the considerable increase in the value of the property." Carter shrugged, which didn't help soften what came next. "We have a business to run."

"So do I, but by the sound of it, you'll be forcing me to close it."

"I certainly hope not. We'd love the clinic to remain as tenants. As I said, the increase won't take affect for ninety days, and we truly hope the new terms will be acceptable." Carter stood and was about to extend his hand, but the chill in the room was palpable, and he reconsidered. He flashed a quick smile, turned, and left.

Kelly felt like she'd been mule-kicked. The clinic's finances were already teetering on the rim of a deep fissure. A rent increase would push it over the edge much faster than she'd anticipated.

2

Pete sat at his desk. The same desk he'd occupied since making inspector four years ago at age thirty-three. He had a spotless record and was viewed by the brass as "someone to watch." Despite his blue-collar background, if Pete played his cards right, one day he could end up with captain's bars.

He'd clocked out an hour ago and was killing time before he was due to meet Kelly for drinks. Pete hadn't seen her for a few weeks, which fed into his anxiety about how tonight would go.

It was clear Kelly was troubled. She used to be chronically happy and optimistic, and now she was often moody and withdrawn. She was drinking more, and Pete wondered if she was also self-medicating. He kept looking for signs of the old Kelly to emerge from her damaged shell, but the layers of that carapace grew more impenetrable over time.

Like Kelly, Pete held out hope that things between them could turn around. He believed if he could tie up the loose ends surrounding her father's death, Kelly would find peace, so he spent every free hour poring over the details of the case. However, after months of digging, he still hadn't uncovered Tommy Moretti's motive for killing David Harper, or how the two of them were connected.

Pete grabbed his coat and headed out, not realizing he was about to have drinks with the very connection he so desperately sought.

Tuesday night at 7:30 p.m. and the restaurant was packed. *44 Degrees* was a contemporary Pacific Northwest eatery, named for the latitude of the owner/chef's hometown of Bend, Oregon. It was a hit the moment it opened five years ago and had recently earned its first Michelin star. Reservations were taken up to six months out, and no-shows defaulted their hundred-dollar deposit. No questions asked, no excuses accepted. And yet, Kelly could always get a table or a seat at the bar. It was one of the perks of being the beloved neighborhood physician who treated anyone who walked through her door, which included most of the *44 Degrees* kitchen staff.

Pete had hoped for a lighthearted night, but when he found Kelly already seated in their normal booth, nursing a tumbler of bourbon, he realized that "lighthearted" probably wouldn't be an apt description for the evening.

"It's great to see you, Kel," he said warmly. "How's everything going?"

Kelly looked up, a forced half-smile on her face. "It's hard without my dad."

A waiter dropped off Pete's usual Cutty Sark with a twist of lemon and gave Kelly a "want another?" look. She shook her head. A second bourbon and she'd be face down on the table.

"How's the new doctor working out?"

"Too early to tell. Ida's a country girl at heart, and she's having trouble adapting to the city. She's smart and kindhearted, but clearly overwhelmed. I owe it to her parents to give her a fair shot, but in the meantime, the rest of us are having to pick up the slack."

Pete raised his glass in a toast. "Here's to smoother sailing in the days to come."

Kelly raised her glass and sipped her drink. She closed her eyes as the amber liquid filled her with a false sense that everything was right with the world.

"One can only hope. Just before I came here tonight, I had a visit from the new owners of our building. They're raising our rent."

"Damn. Have you talked to Alexa? Maybe she could call them and see if there's any wiggle room."

"This *just* happened," Kelly said with an unexpected edge. She didn't know where the attitude was coming from, but she was too tired and frustrated for self-reflection.

Pete was taken aback by Kelly's sharp response, but let it slide. He'd been letting a lot slide lately in order to avoid a confrontation. As he searched for some safe ground to tread, Kelly leavened the mood by changing the subject.

"How's work with you?" she asked. In the past, she'd found the details of his investigations fascinating, but recently his job didn't seem quite as riveting.

"There was a shooting last night outside The Mission Social Club. A Norteño dealer was killed."

Kelly perked up. "Norteño?"

"It wasn't Oscar." Oscar Sanchez, known as "Spider," was an eighteen-year-old Norteño gangbanger. Two months ago, his ten-year-old brother Diego had been shot in a drive-by and lost his leg. Kelly was very close to the Sanchez family and dreaded the day when the news would be about Oscar's death. "The victim's name was Felix 'Gato' Molina."

"Was it the Sureños?" The Sureños were age-old adversaries of the Norteños, and the two sides were in a constant push-and-pull for territory. If this recent killing was Sureño-on-Norteño crime, it would surely ignite a firestorm.

"We don't think so. This is the third dealer to be killed in the past year. One in the Tenderloin last September and one in Chinatown a few months ago. The same weapon was used in both shootings. We're waiting on ballistics to see last night's homicide was the same guy. Ron and I found a witness who thought the suspect was Caucasian. We're hoping that's true."

"It's depressing when the best news to come out of this would be that the shooter was white." The conversation hit another lull, and Pete took a new tack.

"Hey, remember that house we rented last summer in Tahoe? It just went on the market for three-point-five."

"Three and half million dollars for a two bedroom, two bath house built in the Sixties with intermittent heating, leaky faucets, and no internet signal."

Pete grinned. "Despite all that, we managed to have a good time."

Kelly allowed the happy memory to bring a smile to her face as well. "We did."

"Maybe we could do it again."

Kelly's smile turned sad, knowing that a vacation at the lake with Inspector Ericson was unlikely.

Their conversation shifted to the benign, chatting about things like the soaring cost of living in the city, the increased traffic in the downtown core, and a new Malaysian restaurant in Noe Valley.

As the conversation petered out, Kelly checked her watch, and explained that Jessica was starting a new medical trial in the morning, and Kelly needed to arrive early to meet with the doctor.

"Good luck," said Pete. "I hope it goes well."

"Thanks." Kelly rose to leave, but the evening felt incomplete. Pete didn't deserve to be treated like that. "Listen. I know things have been strained between us. I've just got so much on my mind…"

Pete interrupted. "It's okay. Whenever you need to talk, about anything, I'm here to listen."

And therein lay the problem. The things that were troubling Kelly were the precise things she could never discuss with Pete.

Or, for that matter, with anyone else.

Kelly leaned in and kissed him on the check. He watched her weave her way through the restaurant and out into the night.

It was obvious Kelly was being evasive. What was she hiding? The two of them used to enjoy an open and honest relationship, and now that door appeared to be closed. Why? Was there another man? Something to do with money? Was it something darker? No, that was ridiculous. Kelly was a straight arrow. As straight as they came.

Pete shook his head to clear those thoughts. He'd been programmed to profile criminals for too many years…and Kelly was anything but a criminal.

3

Wednesday

Kelly loved her sister, but never truly enjoyed visiting her. None of the family members who came to see their relatives at Peninsula Oaks found the experience pleasurable. How could they? The sole purpose of the facility was treating patients who suffered from severe traumatic brain injury. Some were in a vegetative state, and others, like Jessica, floated in a gray cloud of minimal consciousness…caught in limbo between being alive and having no life at all.

Kelly visited once a week without fail. She came out of love and out of guilt.

The two were inexorably linked.

She strode down the hallway and inhaled the scent of lavender. Lavender oil was used to calm the mind and body and help with insomnia. Kelly wasn't an advocate of aromatherapy, but the smell of lavender was a nice change from the cloying scent of ylang-ylang that previously pervaded the corridors of Peninsula Oaks.

As she approached her sister's room, she was suddenly assaulted with memories: *thirteen-year-old Kelly impatiently waiting on a tennis court; walking home in a surly mood and arriving to find two police cars and an ambulance parked in front of the house; rushing inside and catching a glimpse of Jessica on a wheeled stretcher, her head wrapped in bandages, the floor awash with blood; someone pointing at Kelly and screaming, "Get her out of here!"*

Even though the attack on Jessica took place over twenty years ago, Kelly recalled it like it happened yesterday. Those memories would never fade.

She took a few measured breaths to steady herself, then entered Jessica's room to find a broad-shouldered man with a bush of wiry, untamed gray hair. He was checking Jessica's vitals and making notations on her chart.

"Dr. Papadakis?"

He turned at the sound of his name and greeted Kelly with a toothsome smile.

"Doctor Harper?" He spoke with a Greek accent, which was to be expected given that Constantine Papadakis was the head of the Department of Neurology at the Medical School of Patras, located on Greece's west coast. "Nice to meet you face-to-face."

Dr. Papadakis was well known in the field of neurology, and over the years had conducted a series of studies on patients who were in vegetative states (VS) or minimally conscious states (MCS). One of his previous studies focused on spinal cord stimulation, while another was based on intrathecal baclofen. This new study centered on the use of a complex blend of synthetic compounds.

After five years and hundreds of trials on lab rats, Dr. Papadakis and Futura Pharmaceuticals finally received FDA approval to begin human trials. Papadakis unabashedly used his initials and the number of the successful test batch to label the experimental drug CP247.

In his mid-seventies, Papadakis had the ebullience of a man half his age. While he commanded respect based upon his four decades as a medical scholar, he also had a reputation as a showman who often took acceptable but somewhat questionable creative liberties when summarizing the results of his studies. Papadakis was no stranger to self-aggrandizement. He took pride in publishing his papers in the most prestigious medical journals, and was constantly flying to conferences where, for a substantial fee, he'd stage a lavish presentation of his "seminal findings."

He knew how the game was played. Greater exposure and impressive results begat more opportunities for funding. More funding led to more testing. And the more testing, the better odds to one day find the breakthrough that would land him in the Blue Hall, delivering a Nobel speech to the Swedish royal family.

He was convinced that *this* set of trials would punch his ticket to Stockholm.

As was usual, Papadakis turned on the charm when dealing with family members of his test subjects. "Doctor Harper, all things considered, your sister's health is remarkably stable. She's been very well taken care of."

"We've done the best we can."

"I imagine how difficult it's been on you and your family."

"Jessica *is* my family."

"Ah, yes. I'm sorry. Ms. Spiro informed me of your father's passing. My sympathies."

Kelly still found it difficult to accept that her father was gone. Hearing a stranger talk about him felt oddly invasive.

Dr. Papadakis gently brushed aside a stray coil of hair that had fallen across Jessica's forehead. As he did, she followed his hand with her eyes. He smiled at her, and in return, she glanced away, staring blankly at the wall. Jessica was generally unaware of the world around her. Occasionally, her lips would form what passed for a smile and she'd mutter a word or two, but rarely in context.

"There are nine other patients in the study," said Papadakis. "Half will be getting CP247, and the other half will receive a placebo. Jessica is in the former group."

"I thought the identities of the individuals in the two groups weren't disclosed."

"Usually they're not, but your sister is a unique case. She's been in MCS the longest, and as such, she presents the greatest challenge. Even a small improvement in her condition would be monumental."

"I've tempered my expectations."

"As you should. We can't provide any assurances that the treatments will result in a positive outcome. Additionally, there are some inherent risks when altering a patient's routine and drug intake."

"That all was made clear when we agreed to take part in the study. Ms. Spiro also discussed with me the need to add a fulltime nurse to monitor my sister's vitals."

"The university and the drug company incur the cost of the trials, but unfortunately, we don't have funding to cover that added expense. I hope you see it as money well spent."

"Of course." Kelly repressed her concern about where that "well spent" money would come from.

As Kelly exited the building, she pulled out her cell phone to call her oldest friend, Alexandra Russo, who was a vice president and investment strategist for a hedge fund in San Francisco. Alexa was like a sister, and growing up, she and Kelly were inseparable.

Up until a few months ago, Alexa and Kelly shared their darkest secrets. Since David Harper's death, and the events that followed, those days were gone. Kelly could no longer share her secrets with anyone…but she could still turn to Alexa for advice.

Alexa answered on the second ring. She sounded happy, and a bit relieved, to get a call from Kelly. In the past two months, she'd tried on several occasions to get Kelly to open up and was frustrated by the emotional wall her friend had erected.

"Hey, Kel. What's up?"

"I wanted to know if you were free tonight. I'm picking up dumplings from Mama Ji's."

"That sounds tempting but unfortunately, I've got plans. How about tomorrow?"

"Tomorrow works. Eight o'clock?"

"Perfect," Alexa said. "Everything okay?"

"Yeah. I just have a lot going on and would love to get your take on a few things."

"I'm always here for you."

Kelly's smile didn't hide her pain. She missed being open and honest with her closest friend. "I know. See you tomorrow night."

4

Tomás Sanchez watched with sadistic pleasure as two teenagers beat the crap out of each other behind the barracks at the Stockton Youth Correctional Facility. They weren't fighting out of anger. They were fighting for dominance. Whoever stayed on his feet the longest would inherit the unofficial title of *jefe*. The title was currently held by Tomás, but after three years of incarceration he was walking out a free man.

Before his internment, he'd racked up an impressive record of juvenile offenses. Besides shoplifting, vandalism and selling small quantities of drugs, Tomás was keen on picking fights, especially with younger and weaker boys. He didn't do it for their lunch money or their new kicks. He did it because he enjoyed inflicting pain. Tomás had successfully avoided spending time behind bars until he went a step too far, stealing a councilwoman's Audi and crashing it through the window of Red Carpet Liquors because they wouldn't sell him a forty.

His transgressions could no longer be ignored.

Now, at age nineteen, he was deemed ready to be released back into the world. But not before seeing two seventeen-year-old Mexican gladiators kicking and punching each other for his enjoyment and the entertainment of a few dozen teenagers.

"I gotta pack of smokes on Diablo," said *Rato,* a skinny, pimply faced thirteen-year-old who earned his rodent moniker from his slight stature and prominent nose. He'd latched onto Tomás a week after arriving in Stockton. "Cisco's a little *maricón*, right *jefe*? Who you got?"

Tomás smiled. "I don't give a fuck who wins. I just wanna see more blood, you know?"

Right on cue, Diablo smashed an elbow into Cisco's mouth, bursting his lip, busting his teeth and bloodying his face. As Cisco reeled, a vicious kick to his groin brought a collective "oh shit" from the crowd. Cisco dropped to his knees, then rolled onto his side, cradling his crushed *cojones*. The teens cheered, and a new *jefe* was crowned.

"Five-0," one of the boys called out.

The inmates scattered as Mike Carrillo, the administrator of the Youth Correctional Facility, approached. He saw Cisco writhing on the ground and crossed over to help him up. "What happened, Cisco?"

"Nothin'," he moaned. "I tripped is all."

Mike nodded. He hadn't expected a more illuminating response, but he was required to ask. He extended his hand to help Cisco up, but the teen ignored the offer of assistance, struggled to his feet under his own power, then painfully limped away. He lost the fight, but he'd gained respect among the other boys. They lived by a code here, same as on the outside, and that meant keeping their business private.

Mike walked over to Tomás. "You all packed?"

"Don't take long to put a few T-shirts, a pair of shoes and a toothbrush into a paper bag, you know?"

"I'd like to believe your time here has had a positive impact on your life, and that you'll play by the rules once you're out."

"Sure, Mr. Carrillo," he said with an insincere smile. "I been lookin' into getting my GED and then applyin' to City College. Maybe take some classes in film production or somethin'. Get a job in Hollywood. That'd be cool, you know?"

"That would be very cool. My understanding is the film business has gone to great lengths to create more opportunities for minorities."

"I'll fit right in."

They were both aware this conversation was a complete crock of shit. Mike knew the instant Tomás walked out of the facility, he'd be back on the street hustling. The sad reality was juvenile youth camp rehab programs were a failure. Almost seventy-five percent of their "alums" were rearrested within three years of their release. However, if, or rather when, Tomás stepped out of line, he'd be NLOP...a jaded acronym that stood for "no longer our problem." The next time Tomás Sanchez got busted, he'd serve time as an adult in a facility that had steel bars, razor wire and gun turrets.

Alma Sanchez was enjoying a rare day off, cleaning her small rental house instead of someone else's. She was humming to herself while vacuuming the hallway and didn't hear the front door open. A moment later she felt a presence behind her and turned to see a tall, thin man.

She screamed.

"Good to see you too, Mom."

Tomás stood a foot taller than when he'd left, and his voice had deepened, but his self-assured stance and cocky attitude were the same as Alma remembered before he went away. In that moment she could tell nothing had changed.

Tomás started down the hallway. "Three years and not one visit. Not one card or letter." He moved with a slow, sinewy, gait that invoked images of a rattlesnake and inspired the nickname *Culebra*, which was inked on his forearm, along with a coiled snake. "No money for candy or cigarettes. Three fuckin' years and *nada*."

Alma instinctively took a step back. She recalled the time when Tomás was nine and had come after her with a wrench because she wouldn't give him money to go the movies. And there was the time when twelve-year-old Tomás, high on dope, wrapped his hand around a roll of dimes and punched her in the arm. It felt like getting hit with a steel bar. She still had the broken blood vessels to mark the spot. Mother and son hadn't parted on the best of terms and there'd been no extension of an olive branch while Tomás was incarcerated.

"What are you doing here?"

22

As Tomás advanced on Alma, he smiled. The smile was devoid of warmth. "This is my home."

"*No mijo. Mi casa no es tu casa.*"

The smile disappeared, and Tomás's expression turned dark. "Where am I supposed to go?"

"*No es mi problema!*" As Alma's anger kicked in, so did her ferocity. "You stole from me. From your brothers. You brought drugs into the house. And you hurt me! I will not have you here!"

"That last time, I said I was sorry. I was high and wasn't thinkin' right."

"Your apology was hollow."

A door in the hallway opened and Diego squealed in delight. "Tomás! You're home!"

Diego limped out as fast as his crutches would carry him. Tomás spread his arms and scooped up his little brother into a warm hug. "*Como estás, hermanito?*"

"I didn't know you were getting home today." Diego shot his mother an admonishing look.

"Yeah, well, I just came by to see how you're doin'. I'm not stayin'."

"Why not?" A frown of utter disappointment made Diego appear much younger than his ten years. He turned to his mother, "Why can't he stay here? We have room."

Alma showed no sign of giving in. "He knows why."

Tomás nodded at Diego's pant leg, which was empty from the knee down. "I heard what happened. One of the guys in the camp had a brother from the 'hood." Tomás smiled, "Took a bullet, little man. More than Spider can say, huh?"

Diego started to grin but caught his mother's disapproving look and shrugged. "Was no big deal."

"Yeah, it is. How's it feel?"

"It hurts. Doctor Kelly got me this cool blade, like the runners in the Olympics use, but I think maybe I left it on too long. So now I can't wear my fake leg. It hurts too damn much."

"Diego! Language!" Alma scolded him, then turned to Tomás. "Go."

"So that's it, huh? I spend three years in a fuckin' prison…"

"That was your choice."

"I screwed up, I know, but I didn't ask to be kicked out of the family."

"You were given chance after chance, but you wouldn't listen. I don't trust you, and you are a bad influence on Diego."

"Mom. *Por favor…*" Diego pleaded.

She shook her head. "One day, maybe." She turned back to Tomás. "You gotta prove to me you changed, which won't be easy. Until then, stay away."

Tomás stared down his mother, but it was a losing battle. He ruffled Diego's hair. "See you around, D."

He headed back down the hallway and slammed the front door on his way out.

Alma exhaled a deep breath. She knew this day would come. The day she had to turn away her own son, but she had no choice.

The return of Tomás meant trouble.

5

Pete Ericson was blessed with great fortune when he drew Ron Yee as his partner. A highly decorated veteran, Ron knew all the players in the Mission and was held in high regard by police brass and gangbangers alike. He carried himself with a confidence and bravado not usually found in slight, 5'8" people. He was partial to Vietnamese cuisine, custom made suits, and colorful language...the color being blue.

At the moment, Ron was questioning a skinny, bedraggled homeless woman who went by the name of Queenie. With her umber skin and eyes to match, she looked like an African version of the agonized figure in Munch's *The Scream*. No one knew her real name, and as was the norm with street people, no one cared. Months ago, Queenie had homesteaded a corner of Cypress Street, a stone's throw from The Mission Social Club.

"No, not last night," Ron said. "It was two nights ago. Monday." He was relatively certain that he wouldn't get anything helpful from Queenie, given her penchant for staying perpetually strung out on whatever brain numbing substances she could scrounge, but he was dogged about chasing down every potential lead.

"Oh, Monday. Yeah. Where was I Monday? I think maybe, uh...what time?" Queenie's body exuded a malodorous cloud, and when she spoke, the rancid stench of her breath made Ron's eyes water. He was careful to avoid inhaling while she was exhaling, and he couldn't help but wonder if he'd have to get his suit dry-cleaned after this encounter.

"Around eleven o'clock," Ron said. "It was a gunshot. You know, a really loud bang."

"Oh, yeah." She nodded. "A gunshot! Monday. Loud. Like a big firecracker or something. You got a cigarette?"

"I don't smoke, Queenie. Now concentrate. Monday night. Were you on this corner when you heard it?"

Queenie stared off into the distance. Ron may have well been talking to the nearby fire hydrant. He was ready to give up when a dim light seemed to flicker in Queenie's eyes, as if her memories were a pack of feral cats she was finally able to wrangle. "A white guy shot a Mexican dude. Shot him dead then drove away. Right?"

"You tell me."

"Uh, okay. Yeah, that's what happened. I'm mean, I'm pretty sure. Yeah."

"And you believe the shooter was a Caucasian male?"

She nodded, smiling ecstatically like she'd just solved the riddle of the Sphinx. "White, yeah. Total Cracker Jack. Is there a reward or something?"

"Any idea what kind of car he was driving?" Ron was reaching. There was no telling if her recollection was factual or simply a notion in her muddled brain, but if he and Pete could corroborate some of the disparate facts they were gathering, they'd have something to work from.

Queenie closed her eyes and scrunched her face up in thought, taking on the look of a Shar-Pei in distress. It was painful to watch. A moment later her facial muscles relaxed, and she shook her head in bitter disappointment. "No."

"That's okay. You did good." Ron slipped a five dollar bill out of his pocket and extended it between pinched fingers, hoping to complete the transaction without physical contact. Queenie was surprisingly fast. The moment she saw green, her arms darted out. The two scaly appendages had a life of their own. Before he could react, Ron was wrapped up in a grateful, repellent, scabby hug.

He immediately pried himself free, but the damage was done. Dry-cleaning was no longer a consideration. The only solution now was the nuclear option.

While Ron was trapped in Queenie's fetid vortex, Pete was questioning the manager of The Mission Social Club. The Club had a small restaurant, with a few tables facing the street. The manager, a vaguely attractive, tatted woman in her thirties, had been tending bar on Monday and remembered the gunshot, but by the time she got outside, there was no sign of the shooter or the car. Only Gato's bloody corpse lying in the street.

She recalled there'd been a scant crowd that night and only one customer in the restaurant at that hour. A girl, maybe late teens. The manager had never seen her in there before.

"After the gunshot, what'd she do? Go outside? Stick around? Did you two talk about it?"

The manager shook her head. "I went out, saw the body, and when I came back in, she was gone. Left some money on the table and split."

"Can you remember anything else about her?"

"She had a backpack and some books. They could've been textbooks, I don't know. She didn't order anything from the bar, so I didn't pay much attention to her. Oh…and her hair might've been tinted blue."

Pete walked out into the daylight to see Ron coming down the street, shaking his head in disgust.

"No luck?" asked Pete.

"Queenie had some info which may or may not pan out."

"So, what's the problem?"

"She fucking hugged me is the problem. I smell like a goddamned month-old corpse that's been exhumed then rolled in raw sewage. I've gotta go home and shower and probably cremate this suit, which I just picked up from Mr. Chan. Only worn it twice. Four hundred and fifty bucks."

Pete took a small step forward, sniffed, and quickly retreated. "It's not that bad," he said, trying to keep a straight face.

"Yeah, right. Fuck you."

27

Pete glanced over Ron's shoulder to see two bangers dressed in Norteño colors coming their way. "Company."

Oscar "Spider" Sanchez and his brother Tomás approached. It was clear from their body language that despite Tomás coming home after being locked away for three years, theirs was not a joyful reunion.

Oscar nodded to Pete and Ron. "Inspectors. You find the *pendejo* who killed our boy?"

"Working on it," said Pete. "You have any information you'd like to offer up?"

Tomás gave his brother the side-eye then sneered at Pete. "We got nothin' to say to you."

Ron stepped forward. "Tomás, right? Where you been? Ventura?"

"Stockton."

Ron nodded. "You got taller. Question is, you get any smarter?"

"Question is, that your aftershave or you step in dogshit?"

Oscar gestured for his brother to cool it. "This is Inspector Ericson and Inspector Yee. They're cool, so chill, *hermano*."

Tomás he was just warming up. "Looks like things got soft around here, you know? Used to be one of ours gets hit, the next day one of theirs is in the morgue." He snorted. "We take care of our own business. These are our streets."

"I got news for you. These streets aren't Norteño," said Pete. "There's one law in the city, and it's us. You don't want to be getting off on the wrong foot, especially on your first day out. Be a shame if your freedom was short lived."

"I'm not going anywhere, *officer*. Gonna enjoy the hell outta my freedom." He punctuated his comments with a smug grin as he and Oscar made their way around Ron and Pete. Tomás took a few sniffs. "That's fuckin' nasty, dude."

As they headed down the street, Ron turned to Pete. "He's a real charmer."

"Yeah, but he's right about one thing. That's nasty."

28

6

Kelly absently watched the families gathered on the Marina Green, picnic dinners spread out on blankets. Some children kicked around a soccer ball, while others attempted to launch a kite into the early evening sky. To her left, the majestic and stalwart Golden Gate Bridge spanned the bay, providing ingress and egress to a hundred thousand vehicles each day. To her right, Alcatraz stood as a stark reminder that crime didn't pay but did get you a hell of a view of San Francisco.

She checked her watch. It was time.

Kelly crossed Marina Boulevard. As she approached Matthew Benedetto's Mediterranean style home/office duplex, she was reminded of her first visit. It didn't seem possible that it was only two months ago that her life had been completely turned upside down...and it all started here. Her father had left instructions that upon his death, Kelly was to be told the truth about his double life. She'd refused to believe the outlandish stories until she read her father's journal, which laid out his rationalization for why he'd taken that perilous path. It also detailed his "assignments," from preparation to completion.

The journal was a shocking admission that shattered her world.

Cora Mathews greeted Kelly at the door. In her sixties, her short gray hair framed an oval face that always seemed at peace. It was the face of a person who'd found balance in her life. Kelly hoped that one day she might learn Mrs. Mathews' secret to tranquility.

Cora gestured toward Benedetto's door. "He's expecting you."

As Kelly entered the office, Benedetto rose to meet her with a welcoming smile. "I didn't know if you'd be hungry, so..."

A conference table had been transformed into a buffet with a sumptuous spread of cheeses, breads, prosciutto, chilled crudités, freshly cut fruit, waters and wine. Expensive wine. Benedetto took pride in providing his visitors with every courtesy, which included delicious local foods and hard to find vintages. Kelly got the sense he was a lonely man, and this was his outlet for socializing and entertaining. The offerings were always excellent.

Benedetto opened a 2014 Jarvis Finch Hollow Estate Chardonnay and casually asked, "How's your hand?"

Kelly glanced down at the burn scar on her right palm, which triggered a cavalcade of memories: *being tied to a chair as smoke and flames rapidly spread throughout an abandoned garage; a streak of fire racing toward her face; her hand reaching out and grabbing a razor-sharp knife from the inferno, instantly searing her palm.*

She looked up from her hand, blinked a few times, then flexed her fingers. "It's coming along. A regimen of steroids, massage and silicone gel sheets have helped the healing process."

Benedetto carried two glasses over to Kelly who stood at the large window that looked out to the bay. "I think you'll enjoy this."

She took the glass with a grateful nod. "I don't doubt it." A sip was all it took for even an unsophisticated wine drinker to realize this was liquid gold, and probably worth its weight in the same.

"I was surprised to get your call," Benedetto said. "How are you holding up?"

"To tell you the truth, not well."

"That's understandable. I assume you're here to talk about your finances."

Kelly reacted as if she'd been slapped. "What do you know about my finances?"

Benedetto realized he'd overstepped and downplayed his comment. "Just that the clinic is a constant drain and Jessica's new treatments will result in additional costs."

Kelly shouldn't have been surprised that Benedetto had the audacity to pry into her life. Gathering information was his forte. When she'd requested a meeting, he would've gotten an updated dossier on her that included everything from her bank balances to her most recent purchases on Amazon.

It made total sense. But still…it pissed her off.

"My father may have given you entrée into his personal life, but that doesn't extend to me. I don't want you, or anyone who works for you, poking into my finances, my sister's medical records, or my nonexistent social life."

Benedetto held up his hands in surrender. "Fair enough. I apologize and it won't happen again."

Kelly glared at him for a moment, then her features softened. Whether or not she wanted to admit it, she and Benedetto would be forever linked. He was the only person who knew about her father's double life, as well as the two murders *she'd* committed. Kelly needed Benedetto on her side, and his being aware of her money problems was inconsequential compared to his knowledge of her more ominous secrets.

"As you obviously know, my financial outlook isn't exactly sunny," she said. "The clinic's in the red, and the new landlord is raising my rent. On top of that, I have added expenses for Jess. I believe you're still holding some money, and I came to find out how quickly I can get my hands on it."

Benedetto had not only brokered Gideon's services, he'd also washed the money through a series of shell companies before depositing it, squeaky clean, into the clinic's account. "I've already made arrangements to funnel additional funds into your account. Tomorrow morning you'll see two deposits; one for $9,650 and the other for $8,325. The remaining money can be held or paid out in cash." Making the amounts of the transactions random, and under ten thousand dollars, was critical to avoid raising red flags with the IRS.

Kelly exhaled a small sigh of relief. "I appreciate it."

"Now that business is out of the way, are you hungry?"

Kelly hadn't realized just how hungry she was, and then recalled she'd worked through lunch. As they ate, Benedetto gave her an update on the Gideon rumors circulating in the ether. A month ago, a message had been posted on one of the Dark Web marketplace boards that "John Smith" was specifically looking for Gideon to discuss a potential "business opportunity." A man claiming to be Gideon responded. They'd adjourned to a private chat room where a deal was struck...twenty grand to take out "John Smith's" wife.

A week later, the woman's body was discovered by her housekeeper. She was lying at the foot of a long staircase, her neck broken. It appeared that she'd tripped and fallen down the stairs. At least that was the intention of the faux Gideon. However, the coroner noted that the woman hadn't died from her tumble, but rather, was manually strangled. Additionally, she'd put up a fight and managed to scratch her assailant, whose skin was found under her fingernails. A DNA analysis led the police to a small-time crook named Otto Lingendorf, who'd recently been released from his third stint at SF County.

When he was picked up, he immediately rolled over and gave up "John Smith," who was currently registered in a seaside resort in San Diego with his twenty-three-year-old girlfriend. Lingendorf was charged with murder; "Smith" was charged with murder for hire. It was widely acknowledged in the clandestine chat rooms that Otto Lingendorf was not the elusive assassin Gideon.

Benedetto went on to casually mention there'd been no shortage of requests for Gideon's services, some of them intriguing. One involved a nurse in nearby Mill Valley who was suspected of "helping along" wealthy terminal patients and stealing their jewelry.

He had more information if she was interested.

Kelly didn't take the bait. Actively seeking another "assignment" was not a consideration. Her life was already a mess and the past two months had been a living nightmare. She wore the criminality of her actions like a shroud, and guilt permeated her everyday life.

"Despite my financial needs, Gideon is officially retired."

"I understand. Just thought I'd let you know."

"I can't fathom how my father was able to compartmentalize what he did as Gideon and go about leading an otherwise normal life."

"You read his journal. He was convinced his actions were justifiable, and in some cases, necessary."

"I don't how he kept the secrets bottled up."

"There was no one else in his life, other than you. No real friends, no romantic partners."

Kelly hadn't thought about her father in that way. She knew he didn't date and had no close friends. He didn't play golf or tennis. He didn't play poker or hang out and watch football games with buddies. She'd assumed he eschewed female companionship because he never got over losing his wife. Kelly didn't consider that the reason her father remained single was because he found it impossible to become involved with someone if he couldn't be honest with her. After he'd taken on the mantle of Gideon, he'd purposely avoided developing friendships of any kind. It made his life easier, just as those things made Kelly's life all the more difficult.

Her inability to open up and be truthful was costing Kelly her relationship with Pete, and she wondered if it would ever be possible to take Alexa into her confidence and tell her what she'd done. Kelly was desperate for someone to talk to. Someone to whom she could bare her soul. Someone who would understand the pressures she'd faced and not be judgmental. The question was, how would Alexa react? Would she be empathetic, or would she insist that Kelly go to the police?

Kelly wasn't ready to find out the answer. Not just yet.

7

By the time Kelly arrived home, she was feeling the effects of the alcohol. She knew she should've refused that last glass of Chardonnay, but with all the things going on in her life, she'd figured "what the hell." Plus, the wine was extraordinary.

She crossed to the built-in bookcase, reached behind a row of novels, and pulled out her father's leather-bound journal. Kelly lived alone and had no reason to hide the journal, but paranoia drove her to take special precautions. If the journal was ever made public, not only would her father's glowing reputation be ruined, but it would put Kelly and Jessica in the crosshairs of every vengeful family who believed they'd lost a loved one at the hands of Gideon.

She had read the journal from cover to cover, and at various times considered shredding or burning it, but it was written in her father's hand, and the idea of destroying it felt sacrilegious. She loved "hearing" his voice, even though she was stunned by his admissions.

Her father's first kill had been driven by vengeance. He'd hunted down and terminated Clarence Musselwhite, the man who'd murdered Kelly's mother and destroyed Jessica's life. David's decision to take on "freelance jobs" after that was made for a variety of reasons. As Benedetto stated, her father was able to justify his actions.

Kelly didn't share that mindset, and yet there she was, about to relive his Gideon narrative. Was it to solidify her decision to walk the straight and narrow, or was it to see if she'd be tempted?

The journal was a faithful but disheartening account of David Harper's "greatest hits." He laid out in detail not only how he went about each of his assignments, but also why he took those jobs. This time through, Kelly didn't care about the specifics. She was only interested in those passages that shed light on her father's evolution from virtuous doctor to paid assassin.

(David's Journal)

Nothing could change my mind about flushing all sense of morality (and legality) down the drain. I've spent my entire career helping others. I swore to embrace the Hippocratic Oath to uphold ethical standards. In any definition of the word, assassination falls well outside the bounds of ethical standards.

But the reality of life has once again come knocking. It's the reality of the clinic being on the verge of defaulting on a score of overdue bills, and Jessica's ongoing medical treatments being threatened by my inability to cover her expenses.

Kelly paused, allowing that statement to sink in. Her father's dilemma, both morally and financially, mirrored her own. She continued reading…

The more I think about it, the more I see how hypocritical I'm being. I voluntarily killed a man. There are thousands of people just like Musselwhite who are committing terrible offenses against innocent people. Do those miscreants deserve to die as well? If the answer is yes, who should be the one to mete out the punishment? Certainly not me. Why risk everything to bring an unknown criminal to justice, regardless of how reprehensible his or her actions are? I'm not a superhero. It's neither my responsibility nor my desire to act like one.

And yet, thought Kelly, in some circles, you became one.

After my last meeting with Benedetto, I came away convinced I could make a difference. I decided to take on an assignment. I don't know (nor do I want to know) who was offering the bounty on this individual, but I didn't pass judgement on them.

However, her father *did* pass judgement on the assignments. According to Benedetto, there were hundreds of requests for Gideon's services over the years, and her father was extremely selective about the ones he undertook.

The next excerpt came from a journal entry written after Gideon had been active for years and had recorded a dozen kills.

Taking on the role of Gideon has provided me with a clear and unique perspective on life. I've learned what's important and necessary to be productive and truly happy. It doesn't take a lot, just appreciation for those you love and caring for those who need. There will always be a huge hole in my life left by the death of Mary, but her death has set me on a path that might be making me a better person (if becoming a killer can possibly make you a better person).

I'm not proud of what I've become, but nor am I ashamed. I haven't gotten to this place easily, and I don't underestimate the consequences of my actions. I've unsuccessfully attempted to put aside the moral ambiguity of "right vs. wrong."

I've become a murderer.

Kelly's eyes welled up as her father's admission hit her hard. Even after all this time, seeing the words, "I've become a murderer," was a shock to her system. She turned to his final entry…

The eighteen people I have killed brought me no sense of joy. They were abhorrent individuals who had done terrible things to innocent people, and they deserved death, but the vengeance was for others to celebrate. I firmly believe that over the course of my work as Gideon, I've saved lives and spared future victims from acts of cruelty.

I've come to the conclusion that I have an important, if not critical, role in the grand scale of things.

Gideon is needed more than ever.

Kelly reread that last line, slowly shaking her head. "Gideon" had died along with the Moretti cousins. The final chapter of her father's journal had already been written.

She closed the journal. Tomorrow morning would come early, and she needed to be well-rested for another long day of caring for patients, as well as whatever unexpected curves life chose to throw in her path.

She'd come to expect the unexpected.

8

Thursday

Early Thursday morning, ballistics came back on the shell found at the scene of Gato's shooting. It was match to the weapon used in the two previous dealer homicides. Suddenly, the case took on more importance, and Pete and Ron were determined to catch the suspect before he could kill again.

Their investigation led them to the Theatre For The Arts, which was directly across from The Mission Social Club. The theatre had a CCTV camera mounted atop the building, but the manager said the camera was "kinda glitchy." That said, the police were welcome to whatever footage they had.

Ron and Pete watched the faulty camera's playback. "Kinda glitchy" was being overly generous. There was hour after hour of ghosted images, interspersed with video static. Nothing useable.

The manager suggested they try "The Bart" just down the street.

The Bartholomew Center was a non-profit rehab facility that took in teenagers with alcohol and drug abuse problems. The residents were all live-in, and the length of their stay was either thirty, sixty or ninety days, depending upon two factors: the depth of their addiction, and the level of support available to them at home. The Bart made it clear to the teens and their parents/guardians that the facility was not a jail, and if residents in the program decided to bolt, that was their prerogative. However, if they left early, they would not, under any circumstances be welcomed back, and there was a long waiting list to fill the forty-eight beds. Between that tough-love posture, the positive atmosphere, and the better than average meals, almost all the teens rode out their full terms, and most were reluctant to leave when their program was finished.

Still, many of these at-risk teens had an itch that needed scratching, and they could be quite creative when it came to fueling their desires. Recognizing the ingenuity of their residents, the facility managers took the necessary precautions, which included installing a security system with a buzzer entry and a high-res video cam.

The Bart's program director was a lovely middle-aged woman named Joanne Eckels who radiated a sunny compassion rare among people who worked day in and day out with troubled youths. The pay was modest, the hours long, and the recidivism rate was high, but being around Jo for even a few minutes, you could sense she had the innate ability to find positives in any situation, regardless how dire.

Ms. Eckels was happy to assist the police and cued up the security footage from the night of the Gato Molina shooting. Unfortunately, the camera was only activated when somebody buzzed to be admitted. Between the hours of 10:14 p.m. Monday and 6:04 a.m. Tuesday, the camera had been idle.

It was another dry well, but Jo wasn't the type to give up that easily. Her days were marked by challenges, and her personal success was measured by small victories. She called one of the caseworkers and inquired if any of her charges had mentioned the incident from Monday night. It turned out that a fourteen-year-old named Tamika Jones had been bragging to her friends that she'd witnessed a murder.

Five minutes later, Tamika was ushered into the office. She was reluctant to answer questions, since curfew had been in effect an hour before the shooting took place, and her room didn't face 24th Street. And yet, she'd told everyone that she'd heard the shot and seen a car drive away. Jo was quick to point out the obvious flaws in the teen's story. Either she'd been in someone else's room, or she was lying. Which was it?

Tamika had no choice but to fess up, admitting she'd been visiting another girl, but swore she'd only gone there to finish their homework assignment. Jo sighed. She'd heard it all before, and Tamika knew Ms. Eckels could smell bullshit from a mile away. The teenager turned to the cops and helpfully added that the driver never got out of his car, but she thought he had blonde hair, and the vehicle was some kind of SUV.

It wasn't a lot to go on, but it confirmed what other witnesses had mentioned. As Pete and Ron were about to leave, Ms. Eckels asked Tamika if she'd had a cell phone with her on Monday night. The use of cell phones was limited to outgoing calls from 4:00 to 5:00 p.m., at which time the phones were collected and held until the next day. However, it was well known that most of the residents had backups stashed away.

Tamika squirmed in her seat. It was already established she'd broken the rules, so one more small violation wasn't a big deal, especially if she could help the police. Did she happen to take a photo of the vehicle? She shook her head. Ron shrugged. Photographic evidence would've been too much to hope for. And that's when Tamika added, "but...I did get, like, a really short video."

Ten minutes later, Ron and Pete walked out with a download from Tamika's phone. The video was only eight seconds long and the images were shadowy. This had all the makings of one more dead end. However, the department had recently hired a young tech who was one of the rare computer nerds that found police work more satisfying than toiling in the communal spaces of Google or Facebook.

The eight seconds of muddy video would put him to the test.

While Pete and Ron were collecting evidence at The Bart, Kelly was pulling into the parking lot at Peninsula Oaks. When she entered Jessica's room, she was shocked by her sister's ghostly pallor. Jess usually had at least a hint of color in her face. This morning her complexion was alabaster.

A stout Germanic-looking woman was taking Jessica's pulse. Kelly correctly assumed this was her new full-time nurse. She turned, gave Kelly a quick once over, and nodded toward Jessica. "You're Jessica's sister." Her voice was surprising soft and warm.

Kelly nodded, "Is she alright? She looks..."

"Cadaverous, I know." The nurse, whose name was Ingrid, continued, "But not to worry. The doctor was here this morning and said this was an anticipated side effect to the initial doses of her new medication. Jessica's body will take another day or so to adapt to the treatment."

"Have you worked with Doctor Papadakis before?" What Kelly actually wanted to know was if this woman who was taking care of her sister had the appropriate training. Ingrid read between the lines.

"No, but I've had training in neurology, with a particular focus on patients who are in a state of minimal consciousness. This area of medicine is near to my heart because my mother lingered on in a similar manner for years. As for Doctor Papadakis, I'm quite familiar with the results of the clinical trials he's published in the Harvard Health Journal and the New England Journal of Medicine. The doctor can be flamboyant, but his findings are impressive, and his credentials speak for themselves."

Ingrid passed the test.

"Doctor Harper, I realize how difficult this is for you...not knowing if the treatments will work, or how your sister will react. Jessica's been here a long time, which is not easy on the family." Ingrid didn't mention the death of Kelly's father, but it was clear by the sympathetic look in her eyes she'd been informed.

She continued, "I'm not just here to take Jessica's temperature and change her linens. I'll take very good care of her."

"I'm sure you will." Kelly's mind was racing in several different directions. She was confident that Jess would be in excellent hands, but she couldn't help but wonder how much those excellent hands cost.

9

Tomás kicked back, enjoying a morning beer and spliff with Luis *"Toro"* Echavarria. In his mid-thirties, Toro was the OG of the 24th Street Norteños, which numbered anywhere from a few dozen to upwards of fifty if you included the shorties (underaged runners and spotters). As befit the boss, he lived in the house that the gang used as their hangout. The rank-and-file members kept the fridge well-stocked, the joints tightly rolled, and the *entertainment* available at a moment's notice. A Liga MX soccer game played on the eighty-five-inch Sony that happened to find its way to the house a week earlier.

It was good to be *El Jefe.*

"I want to start earnin' for you, Toro."

"You just got out, homes. Chill for a while. Enjoy the benefits."

"I have," Tomás said with a grin. "Last night, the Espinosa twins."

Toro laughed. "And you can still walk today?" He reached out his beer and they clinked bottles. "Chico gave you some spending cash, right?"

"Yeah. I appreciate it, *jefe.* So, who's runnin' Gato's corner now?"

"Gizmo."

Tomás shook his head. "Gizmo? He new?"

"Francisco Ramos. His brother, Eduardo, is doing time down in Lompoc."

"Oh, yeah. Eduardo. I remember him. Who's this Gizmo workin' for?"

"*Tu hermano.*"

Tomás snorted. "Don't Spider have enough corners?"

Tomás knew he had to tread lightly. On the one hand, he didn't want to openly question Toro's decisions. On the other hand, he wanted to carve out his place, and if he ended up screwing over his brother in the deal, so much the better.

"He does a good job."

"Gimme a chance, and I'll double what he's bringing in on Cypress."

"You'll get your opportunity. One day, I'm either gonna get tired of this shit or end up sharing a cell with your brother Rodrigo in Pleasant Valley. *La familia* Sanchez has paid their dues to the Norteños. Spilt their blood, and the blood of the Sureños. When I'm gone, someone's gotta take charge, you know? It could be a Sanchez, yeah?"

Just then, the front door opened, and Spider entered. He sized up the cozy meeting between Toro and Tomás and didn't like what he saw. For the past three years, Spider hadn't needed to look over his shoulder to avoid the thrust of the blade.

Now, he was on constant alert.

Spider handed Toro a thick envelope with the day's collection. Toro hefted it and nodded. He opened a drawer in a side table and casually pitched the envelope in, then grabbed a beer out of the cooler at his feet and tossed it to Spider. "We were just talking about you."

"Yeah?" Spider twisted off the cap and downed half the bottle. He hated the taste of beer, but it was critical to keep up pretenses. Any sign of perceived weakness would be exploited by others in the gang. Especially his brother.

"*Tu hermano* says he could move more merchandise than you over on Cypress Street."

Spider leveled his gaze at Tomás. "You don't even know what I'm pulling in."

"Don't matter," Tomás said with a cocky smile. "I know *you.*"

Toro smiled at Spider. "Nice to have Culebra back, right? Man's got some serious *huevos*. He's gonna stir up some shit, *verdad?*"

Spider held his emotions in check. "No doubt, Toro."

43

"*Niños,* I want the motherfucker who killed Gato. I'm hearin' it could be the same guy who hit those other dealers. Whoever ices him, gets that corner."

"*Jefe,*" Spider protested, "that's my territory."

Toro flared with intensity. "NO…it's *my* territory! It goes to who I say. *Comprende?*"

Spider nodded and didn't give his brother the satisfaction of looking over to see his smug face. "Can I talk to you in private, Toro?"

"You got something to say? Say it."

Spider weighed his options. If he said what was on his mind in front of his brother, it could cause problems. If he said nothing, he'd come across as a *maricòn.* Screw it.

"I don't think Tomás deserves a piece of the street."

"Fuck you, *hermano,*" said Tomás.

"No, fuck you!"

Toro held up his hands, and the brothers were instantly silenced. "Spider, why you taking a hard stand against your brother?"

"He can't be trusted."

"You don't know nothing about me, *puto!*" Tomás got to his feet and started to move in on his brother when Toro shot him a look that froze him in his place.

"*Basta!*" Toro turned on Spider. "You talk about trust. Your brother did three years in that shithole in Stockton. I got ears inside. He never said a word about the supply chain. I heard they offered him short time for info, and he told them to suck his dick. Did his full ticket instead of getting off easy. You know what that buys you, Spider? Membership. Culebra has the same rights as anyone else here. So, put aside this family bullshit, and just worry about pulling your weight. You start coming up light, one day you be working for your brother. *Estás escuchando?*"

On the inside, Spider was seething. He knew his brother would lie, cheat and steal to get ahead, but if Spider argued the point, he'd end up on the wrong side of the boss. His best strategy was to be the good soldier and play along. Sooner or later, Tomás would succumb to his voracious greed and overplay his hand.

When he did, Spider would be there to capitalize.

10

Ida Samuel was having trouble adjusting…to everything. The commute, the cramped apartment, the weight of responsibility of a real job. She had dark circles under her eyes that she'd tried to cover with makeup. On her way into work, she stopped for a double espresso. She added two packets of sugar, then dug into her purse and came up with a small, tubular pill case. She shook out a single, orange triangular pill. Dexedrine. Ida downed it with a sip of coffee and took a deep breath. In less than thirty minutes, she'd be ready to face the day head on.

Her first patient of the morning was a twitchy twenty-three-year-old named Erin Casey. She'd relocated to San Francisco from Tucson four days ago and was living with her sister and her sister's four cats in a tiny guest house in San Bruno. She now found herself perched on an exam table in an urgent care clinic with puffy eyes and a sore throat that made it near impossible to swallow. Erin long ago accepted the fact she was a Grade A hypochondriac, but she considered the inability to eat or drink without considerable pain a suitable cause for alarm.

Ida shined her light into Erin's throat, probed her tongue with a wooden depressor, and lightly ran her fingers up and down her neck. "Your uvula is swollen and inflamed."

Erin instantly teared up, certain this medical assessment was the forerunner to a much more alarming diagnosis. "Why? Is it like a virus, or like cancer or something?"

"It's called uvulitis. It's generally due to severe dehydration or an allergic reaction."

"Is it serious? It sounds serious."

Ida smiled, which helped to calm Erin down. "It sounds scary, but it's not at all serious. I'm going to give you Benadryl and a steroid shot, and the swelling will come down in a few hours."

As Ida prepared the shot, she asked if there were any recent changes in Erin's environment. When Erin mentioned she'd just arrived from the dry climate of Arizona and that her sister Shannon had a herd of housecats, the cause of her outbreak was glaringly obvious.

Ida gently administered the shot and told Erin it might be a good idea for her to explore alternative lodging. Erin did what she did best...panic. Where was she supposed to go? She didn't know anyone else in the city, and San Francisco was way too expensive for her to live on her own.

"I know," said Ida sympathetically. "I just moved here from Ohio, and the housing prices blew me away. I ended up finding a tiny studio apartment in South San Francisco. For what I'm paying each month, I could rent a three-bedroom house back home."

"This sucks. I mean, I thought everything was gonna be so cool, living with my sister and hanging out in the city, but first she comes down with some kinda flu, and now I've got this uvu-whatever thing."

"Your sister's sick? What are her symptoms?"

"I don't know...she's got a temperature, and she's throwing up and feels like roadkill. I've been taking care of the cats, and to tell you the truth, I don't even like cats. This whole thing blows."

"Erin, I'm going to have one of the nurses come in and get some details about your sister. Is that alright?"

"Yeah, I guess. Why?"

"It's a public health survey we do," she said with a reassuring smile. A moment later there was a commotion in the main area. Ida excused herself and came out to find Alma Sanchez pushing Diego in a wheelchair with rusted spokes. The boy would've been humiliated if he wasn't in so much pain.

Vik intercepted them, a look of concern on his face. "*Señora.*"

"Is Doctor Kelly here?" Alma asked.

"She had an appointment this morning. Let's get Diego into one of the bays."

Alma hesitated for a moment. She trusted all the doctors at the clinic, but when it came to care for her favorite son, she wanted her favorite doctor. Diego's moan made her reconsider. "Of course. *Gracias*, Doctor."

Moments later, Diego was up on an exam table. His stump was fiery red.

"Tell me how you're feeling," said Vik.

Diego's voice was barely above a whisper. "It hurts. All the time."

"Is it a sharp pain, or throbbing?"

Diego looked at his mother. He didn't know what "throbbing" meant. *"Palpitante,"* she said.

Tears came to his eyes as he shook his head. *What's it matter,* he thought. *Just make the pain stop!*

Alma pleaded with Vik. "Can you give him something?"

"Of course. Did you bring in his prothesis?"

Alma shook her head. "He says it hurts too much to put on."

Vik's voice was soothing, trying to calm both the boy and his mother. "We can take care of his discomfort."

Ida was a step ahead. "Five milligrams Oxycodone?" she asked.

Vik nodded and Ida was off to the meds lockup.

She entered the small room where the pharmaceuticals were kept. As she grabbed the Oxy, the Dexedrine she took earlier choose this moment to kick in, and Ida felt the rush, along with a momentary dizzy spell. She took a deep breath, collected herself, then tapped an Oxycodone into a small plastic cup. She was about to head out but reconsidered.

Ida did a quick inventory and found what she was looking for. She glanced over her shoulder, then grabbed a bottle from the shelf, shook four Dexedrine into her palm and slid them into her pocket.

Out in the treatment area, Vik was explaining Diego's situation to Alma. *"Señora* Sanchez. Diego has what's called cellulitis. We'll get some hot packs and start him on antibiotics. I'll need to draw labs and get a blood culture."

Alma suddenly beamed. "Doctor Kelly!"

Kelly made her way over to Diego, placed a reassuring hand on his cheek. "Looks painful."

He nodded.

Kelly examined the stump and turned to Alma. "We'll keep Diego here for a little while. When he goes home, he's going to require rest and a lot of fluids. No prosthetic until the redness is gone. Keep the stump clean and dry. Come back and see us in two days."

Ida returned with the pill and a cup of water. Kelly gave Diego a reassuring smile. "It'll take a few minutes to feel the effects, okay?" Diego nodded, holding back his tears.

Kelly slid open the curtain around the bay, then took Alma's arm and led her away to talk in private.

Ida handed the pill cup and the water to Diego. As Diego was bringing the pill to his lips, Vik suddenly snatched it from his hand. The ten-year-old was stunned, as was Ida. Vik held the pill out for her to see. Ida's eyes grew wide. The pill was pink, which meant it was twenty milligrams. Much too strong for a child.

She stammered. She wanted to apologize but couldn't find the words.

"Doctor, please bring me a *five*-milligram tablet," Vik said calmly.

"Doctor, I'm so…"

"We'll talk about this later. The important thing right now is to give Diego some relief."

"Of course."

Ida hurried out of the bay.

Kelly and Alma were in Kelly's office, the door closed. "I'm sorry you're having to deal with this, Alma. How's he managing?"

"It's hard. Diego just wants to be normal, but he doesn't know how to do it with one leg. He tries to fit in with the other boys, but..." She just shook her head.

"He's sensitive. You told me yourself that he's special, and he is. I know it's difficult for him, for both of you, but he'll get through it. Has Oscar been around?"

Oscar had cut ties with Diego when he'd betrayed Oscar's trust by telling Kelly an explosive family secret.

"No. But Tomás came home yesterday."

"Tomás? Your son who's been...away?"

"You can say it. My son who's been in juvenile detention. I told him he couldn't stay in the house."

"Where is he now?"

"*No sé.* I told him to keep away from me and Diego."

"And what's Diego relationship with him?"

"Diego loves him because he's the fun one in the family. Oscar is so serious, but Tomás always made jokes. Always made Diego laugh...and always made me cry."

"Did the pain in Diego's leg get worse after you asked Tomás to leave?"

Alma hadn't considered any correlation between the two events, but now that Kelly mentioned it, she realized it was true. She nodded, feeling a pang of guilt. "Diego missed Tomás. Talked about him all the time, but I can't trust him. It's a terrible thing so say about your own son, but he was better off where he was, and so were we."

"Families can be very difficult, Alma."

The old woman smiled. "If only I could be so lucky to have a daughter like you, *mija.*" Alma wrapped her arms around Kelly and gave her a hug. "Someone so smart. Someone so *pura.*"

Someone so pure, Kelly thought. If Alma only knew the truth.

Ida took a few moments to pull herself together. She'd made a terrible mistake, but she didn't have time to dwell on that right now. Her next patient was already waiting for her.

Abelino Lopez was a skinny nineteen-year-old with a wispy mustache who'd recently arrived from El Salvador, along with his cousin and his cousin's wife. They owned some kind of food truck, while Abelino worked as a dishwasher in a Peruvian restaurant on the Embarcadero. He'd come to the clinic complaining of nausea and a headache and was running a high fever. With San Francisco's vast multi-ethnic population and the constant flow of people coming into the city, there was always some new bug to contend with. Just when the medical community got their hands around how to treat the latest disease, a new one reared its head.

When Ida shined a penlight in Abelino's eyes, he flinched. She took a swab culture, recommended he drink copious amounts of water and juice, and get as much sleep as possible. He definitely shouldn't go to work for a few days. Abelino nodded, but Ida knew he'd be back at the restaurant for the lunch shift. Most of these kitchen employees were immigrants who couldn't afford to miss a day's work, and odds were slim to none that he received paid sick leave. There was a good chance he'd spread his contagions to other workers or customers, which was an all-too-common occurrence in urban areas.

Abelino left and Ida was finishing up her paperwork when Vik entered the bay and pulled the curtain closed.

"Are you alright?" he asked.

Ida nodded. "I...don't know what to say. I completely screwed up, and I realize how bad that could've been if you didn't step in. I'm so, so sorry."

"Things here can get very hectic, but that's the time to slow down. We can never allow ourselves to be in a rush because that's when you make mistakes. Doctors don't have the luxury of making mistakes."

"It won't happen again. I promise."

"Double and triple check your meds. And if you have any questions, ask me."

"Uh, Doctor Danabalan. Are you going to discuss this with Doctor Harper?"

"No. I'll leave that up to you."

A short time later, Ida brought Kelly up to speed on Abelino, Shannon Casey, and Gretchen Sadowski from earlier in the week. Their symptoms weren't identical, but there were enough similarities to surmise they may be suffering from the same ailment. As Ida was about to segue into her admission about what happened with Diego, she heard Ramona over the intercom, saying a patient was waiting for Dr. Samuel in bay Two. Ida headed out, relieved to dodge the bullet…for now.

Kelly checked in with the city Health Department. They weren't aware of any recent flu-type outbreaks in the city. She expressed hope that someone from the Department would visit the Peruvian restaurant and send Abelino home, but it was unrealistic to think that was going happen. Every city agency had fallen victim to cutbacks, and despite best intentions, there just wasn't enough time in the day for municipal workers to handle all the calls or file all the reports that required their attention.

Kelly hung up and stared at the unopened registered letter on her desk. It came from the new owners of the building and, if Carter Dane was a man of his word, there'd be a revised lease agreement. Even a modest increase would be financially devastating and, based upon the skyrocketing value of land in San Francisco, she didn't think "modest" would aptly describe the bottom-line figure that awaited her.

For a moment, she considered slipping the letter into the shredder and pretending she never received it, but of course, that would have zero impact on the eventual outcome. Better to rip off the band-aid in one fast move. Kelly slid her father's teak letter opener into the envelope and pulled out the new contract. Her eyes went directly to the monthly lease figure. She had steeled herself for bad news, but not for this. Unless she could somehow convince the new owners to show some mercy and cut the clinic some financial slack, her father's dream would cease to exist in a matter of months.

Kelly was overcome with a wave of anger, followed quickly by an undertow of depression. She felt like her life was hopelessly spiraling downward and she was afraid that when she hit rock bottom, she'd shatter into a million pieces.

11

Suchart Thongsuk was first generation Thai American, born in Fresno, California. Charlie, as he was called, was the sixth of eight children, all of whom did a required stint in the family restaurant before heading off to college. He'd earned a partial scholarship to UC Santa Cruz, where he studied Computer Engineering and Applied Mathematics. His parents pushed him to graduate with honors in four years. Charlie graduated with difficulty in five and a half. Had he been a Stanford Cardinal, an MIT Beaver, or even a California Golden Bear, his diploma would've carried enough weight to assure him a job in Silicon Valley. Being a Santa Cruz Banana Slug didn't have quite the same allure for potential employers.

After spending a few years as an IT consultant and writing code on the side for a Gameplay developer, Charlie heard about an opening with the SFPD. He was a sucker for true crime shows and spent far too many weekends binge watching documentaries on HBO and Netflix. Particularly those that dealt with homicide. He was fascinated by murderers and what made them tick, and had an encyclopedic knowledge of killers, from the infamous to the obscure. On top of that, he'd seen his share of movies that featured high tech computer modelling being done by the FBI and CIA. If a job with the San Francisco police department would provide him the opportunity to be involved with cases, especially homicides, he was in.

Charlie was the youngest applicant for the job and had no previous police experience, so he wasn't taken seriously. That was, until he unveiled his ASUS ROG Zephyrus S15, one of the most advanced and powerful laptops on the market, favored by gamers and hackers alike. He flexed his fingers like Tchaikovsky, then put on a demonstration of graphic manipulation, the likes of which hadn't been seen before in the station house.

The interviewer gave Charlie a thumb drive containing some grainy surveillance footage and told him he had an hour to see what he could do with it. The interviewer stepped out for coffee, and when he returned ten minutes later, he found Charlie playing *Assassin's Creed Valhalla*.

"You gave up already?"

Charlie hit a few keys and brought up the surveillance video, which now, in comparison, looked like an award-winning short film. The picture was sharp and the images clearly defined. "It was the best I could do given the substandard quality of the original."

He was hired on the spot.

The department's equipment was not only antiquated, it was junk. It made Charlie's laptop look like the Oak Ridge Lab supercomputer. He patiently explained to his new bosses that he needed at least twenty grand to bring their system into the twenty-first century. His new bosses patiently explained to him that he wasn't working for Apple. They compromised with the department agreeing to pay Charlie a rental fee for his laptop.

Pete and Ron looked over Charlie's shoulder as he manipulated the eight second download from Tamika Jones's phone. He'd only been with the SFPD for a month and was the sole full-time video tech, so he worked with whichever department needed his expertise. Most of it was tedious, boring crap that could be knocked out by a twelve-year-old with a MacBook Pro, but some of the requests got Charlie's juices flowing. This was his third time working with the Homicide Detail, and when he was challenged to take useless footage and turn it into something that could help find a killer, Charlie kicked into high gear. This is what he'd signed up for. Catching the bad guys. Solving murders.

The visuals on the screen were in constant flux. Charlie ran the video through a dozen filters, culminating with the images breaking down into minute dots, and then reforming into what looked like an oversaturated video game. He sat back with a satisfied smile.

"What are we looking at?" asked Pete.

"Computer alchemy. I ran each pixel through a program that analyzed it and auto adjusted the exposure, contrast and black point, then reassembled them into a coherent image. Cool, huh? Now that I've stepped up the resolution, I can enlarge portions of the video without blowing them out to mush."

"It looks like the shooter's vehicle is a Range Rover," said Ron. "Can you pull the plate?"

"The best I can do from this angle is get you a partial." The screen zeroed in on the plate and only the first two digits were visible: 8R.

"We'll run that and see if we get lucky."

The driver in the Rover was facing away from the camera, so they couldn't get a visual on him, but they could make out a tangle of curly, blonde hair. The odds were strong that he was Caucasian.

"Great job on this, Charlie," said Ron.

"This reminds me of a shooting a few years ago in Chinatown," Charlie said with a gleam in his eye. "White guy scoring heroin from a Wah Ching gangster named Peter Quan. Things got ugly, probably haggling over price, and the white guy pulled a Taurus 856 and put three .38s into Quan. Only difference was the shooter was driving a beat-up 2015 Chevy Equinox. I don't think they ever found the guy."

Pete was impressed. "How do you know about that case?"

"I'm kind of a homicide junkie, and now that I have access to the department files, it gives me something to do at night."

Ron and Pete exchanged a look of mild surprise. "You know that murder books are confidential, right?" said Pete.

Charlie nodded and shrugged. "I figured since I was on the inside, it wasn't that big a deal. Am I in trouble?"

"No, but don't you have better things to do then read about old murder cases?" asked Ron.

"Not really. I mean, it beats watching reruns of *Unsolved Mysteries*. Anything else I can help you with?"

Pete leaned closer and pointed to a person sitting in the window of The Mission Social Club. "We could really use an ID on her."

"Her? You mean that tiny, amorphous blob in the building across the street?" He sounded incredulous.

"We think she saw the whole thing go down. Right now, she's our only hope for a credible eyewitness."

Charlie laced his fingers and cracked all eight knuckles. "I might be able to do something. Could take a while, though, and I've got a request to clean up some traffic cam footage for a hit and run."

Ron patted him on the shoulder. "I'll talk to your boss and clear your schedule for the rest of the day. In the meantime, we'll run that partial."

12

It was just after noon when Kelly arrived at Benedetto's office. He handed her two deposit slips and a thick envelope that contained $6,000 in non-sequential fifties and hundreds, which represented the remaining money in her "account," and suggested she bank the money in uneven amounts over the course of a few days to avoid attracting attention.

"Can you explain to me how this whole shell company thing works?" she asked. "Is it something I need to be concerned about?"

"You're wondering if it's legal."

Kelly nodded.

"The companies are legitimate entities and pay the appropriate taxes. More importantly, the money that's deposited into the clinic is clean."

"Even though the source of the income is filthy."

"At least ten percent of the world's economy is fueled by dirty money. Ours is a miniscule drop in the financial ocean. I set up this system twenty years ago, and I register a few new companies each year. The remunerations paid to the clinic are labeled as consulting fees, speaking engagements, travel reimbursements, et cetera."

"But it's all a lie."

"Yes, but one that your father and I agreed would be the most effective way to handle the proceeds from his outside work. Since all the taxes are diligently paid, there's never been a problem with the IRS. Kelly, this isn't an issue you need to worry about. You've got enough on your plate right now."

He was right, of course. A little financial sleight of hand was nothing compared to murder.

Kelly was about to leave when Benedetto asked if she had a few minutes to spare. She knew whatever he had to say was probably not something she'd want to hear. Then again, he had sources throughout San Francisco, from City Hall to the police department to backrooms where nameless people made shady deals with their faceless counterparts.

If Benedetto felt a need to talk, Kelly felt a need to listen.

"I heard what you said yesterday about not taking on an assignment…"

Kelly was both relieved and annoyed. *"That's* what you want to talk about? You may have heard me, but evidently you weren't listening. I don't know how to make it more clear that I'm not a contract killer."

"I was listening, and you've been *very* clear about your feelings on the subject."

"Then why do I think there's a 'but' coming?"

"Because you're extremely perceptive. If you choose to walk out now, I'd applaud your decision."

Kelly shook her head in disbelief. When she spoke, she couldn't hide her exasperation. "You say that, and yet, you still want to tell me about some *incredible opportunity*, or some *dire situation* that only I can rectify."

"Something rather unique came to my attention this morning, and I thought it was worthwhile to bring to yours. That's all."

"That's *not* all. You seem determined to lure me into taking over my father's double life." Kelly's indignation was turning to anger. "When you told me that my father was a killer for hire, I asked what was in it for you. You said it was personal. I've thought about that a lot, and the only thing I could come up with was you had some scores to settle and used my father as your very own avenging angel."

He shook his head. "I bore no personal grudge against any of the people your father killed. However, that's not to say I don't have a strong sense of outrage about people like Musselwhite."

"You want me to listen to this *unique* situation, fine," said Kelly. "In return, I want you to pull back the curtain. You know my secret…it's time to share yours. If I can understand what's driving you, maybe it'll resonate with me, maybe not, but at least we'll be on a level playing field."

Benedetto was responsible for Kelly's situation. He owed her the truth.

He rose from his chair, came around his desk and perched on the edge. "I spent twenty years defending some of the worst humans on the planet. I was very good at my job, which meant most of my clients received reduced sentences or no prison time at all. I was selective about who I represented. No child molesters, rapists, terrorists, and so forth, but that left an endless supply of immoral people who needed a lawyer.

"The question often posed to me was, 'Why did I do it?' Why provide legal counsel to such despicable people?"

Benedetto got to his feet and began to pace, as if he was presenting his case in a courtroom.

"High-profile defense attorneys have myriad politically correct responses to that question. 'It's every person's right to legal representation,' or 'If I didn't do it, someone else would,' and then there's 'Many people who are presumed guilty are actually innocent.' Those are socially acceptable rationalizations, but in truth they're mostly bullshit. The real reason many criminal defense lawyers go into that end of the business is because of the financial upside and the ego-feeding press coverage that comes along with representing someone truly evil. The larger the crime against humanity, the bigger the headlines.

"I was at the top of my profession. I had my own firm, with a dozen associates, all of whom were highly sought after. We were making money hand over fist, and there was never a shortage of clients looking for representation. It was all going well, until I agreed to take on the case of Vance Conway."

Vance Conway was a miscreant product of a broken home. When he was seven years old, his father was shot and killed during a carjacking...his old man being the failed carjacker. Up until then, life had been tough enough. Following his father's death, things spiraled downward, hitting new depths on a daily basis.

By the time he turned twenty-one, Vance had already been fired from a dozen jobs for a dozen different reasons. Petty theft, sexual harassment, damaging company property, violating drug policies, punching a customer. The list went on and on. He finally decided that his true life's calling was to be a porch pirate. He got himself a secondhand brown shirt and pants, bought a UPS patch on eBay, and he was in business. Stealing packages from people's doorsteps was adventurous, prosperous, and best of all, easy as shooting fish in a barrel with an Uzi.

Vance's "job" left him with a lot of free time that he filled by frequenting strip clubs, which is where he met Shawna.

It was a match made somewhere south of heaven. Two losers, desperate for love and settling for sex. It wasn't long before Shawna moved in. Their relationship was a rollercoaster, with substance-fueled highs and morning-after lows. Against all odds, their relationship worked, until Shawna's baby bump started getting in the way of her occupation.

Vance detested the idea of becoming a father. He couldn't fathom being responsible for someone else, let alone an infant. Feeding, burping and changing diapers in the middle of the night was not in Vance's desired wheelhouse. As Shawna's belly grew, Vance's interest in her diminished.

While Shawna was in the delivery room, Vance was on a flight to Cabo. Shawna had an eight-pound baby boy. Vance had eight shots of Myers's Dark Rum.

A week later, Vance returned home much the worse for wear. He'd given the whole situation due consideration and had come to a decision. He told Shawna to take the kid and hit the bricks.

A distraught Shawna called two of her fellow dancers from the club, and they arrived to find her in a brawl with Vance, who was using his fists to drive home his point. Shawna grabbed a knife from the kitchen to fend him off, but that only served to inflame Vance's temper. Her two friends jumped into the middle of the melee to protect Shawna, and Vance attacked them as well.

The dancers got Shawna to a hospital and the final tally was a black eye, a punctured eardrum and three missing teeth. When she was wheeled back out to the waiting room, two San Francisco cops were there to take her statement.

She initially refused to talk about what happened, but her friends had already given their statements. Regardless of what Shawna had to say, Vance Conway was going to be arrested and charged.

Enter a reluctant Matthew Benedetto. Even though this wasn't the type of case he handled, he'd received a call from an old friend, who was a judge in the County Superior Court. The judge was also a deacon at St. Paul's, and Vance's mother was a devout member of his congregation. While Benedetto already had a full case load, turning down a request from one of the highest-ranking judges in his county was unwise. It was a decision that Benedetto would rue for the rest of his life.

When Vance was put on the witness stand, he insisted he'd acted out of self-defense. He claimed he'd calmly explained to Shawna that it would be best if she and the baby had their own place, and she suddenly lost her shit and attacked him with a knife. He only struck her to protect himself. Vance did acknowledge that he might've gone too far, but once Shawna's friends arrived, he was afraid that they too would attack him.

The story was flimsy at best, but if they could convince just one juror...

The prosecution centered their case on Shawna's injuries and her testimony, which was gut wrenching. With tears streaming down her face, she said she still loved Vance and wanted nothing more than for them to be a family. But...she was afraid of him. He was often irrational and hotheaded and would fly into a rage for no apparent reason. This was the first time he'd struck her, but she feared it wouldn't be the last.

Benedetto didn't know if his client was guilty as charged, but that didn't matter. He was hired to represent Conway to the fullest of his ability, and he would, despite the reality that his client didn't have a prayer...that was until the prosecutor inadvertently introduced prejudicial evidence that affected Conway's right to a fair trial. It was a small misstep that most attorneys might have missed, but Benedetto wasn't most attorneys. He vehemently objected to the prosecutor's violation of Conway's rights and the judge had no recourse but to declare a mistrial and reluctantly release Vance Conway, pending the prosecution's decision to retry the case.

While awaiting word from the DA's office, Benedetto experienced a growing sense of guilt. Shawna had risked her own well-being when she agreed to testify against Conway, and Benedetto felt compelled to relocate her someplace safe. An hour later, he put down a deposit on an apartment in a building that had 24-hour security.

Until Shawna could get back on her feet and figure out her life, she and the baby were temporarily staying with one of the bouncers from the club. Benedetto arrived to give her the good news, but he was too late. Shawna had been shot in the chest and face. Lying beside her was the baby, who had been smothered.

They were dead because of Benedetto's manipulation of the legal system. He was overcome with rage, staring at the real-life consequences of his actions. Suddenly, he heard a crash coming from a room down the hall. He grabbed a ten-pound kettlebell from the corner of the living room, and the next thing Benedetto remembered, he was standing over Vance Conway, the kettlebell in his hand, covered in Conway's blood...his face mashed to an unrecognizable pulp.

Benedetto stopped for a breath. Kelly was astonished, not only by the story, but by his admission of guilt. They now shared a two-way sacred bond of trust. When she spoke, it came out as a whisper. "What happened? I mean, did anyone ever...?"

"Suspect me? No. I'd spent enough time around law enforcement and in the courtroom to know how to cover my tracks. The evidence at the scene, fingerprints and DNA, overwhelmingly proved that Conway was responsible for the deaths of Shawna and her baby. However, his murder was a complete mystery. The bouncer had been at the club at the time of Conway's death, and there'd been no evidence of any other people in the apartment."

"And afterwards, you...?"

"I dissolved my firm. Took a few months off to assess my life. According to the law that I practiced, and twisted to suit my needs, I should've been in prison. What I did wasn't a justifiable act of self-defense. It was an act borne out of the fury over my own shortcomings. I knew there were people out there, people like Shawna, who needed protection. I wasn't cut out to be the one to 'don the cape,' but hoped that maybe one day I could assist the person who was."

Kelly finally understood what impelled Benedetto, and to a greater extent, her father. They made quite a pair. Benedetto was facilitating Gideon to assuage his guilt, and her father was carrying out the "assignments" to avenge the dead and protect the innocent. Between the two of them, they made one neurotic hero.

"Now you know."

Kelly nodded. "I'm glad you told me. That's a lot to carry around."

"The bigger the secret, the heavier the burden. I can't change the past, but in a small way, I can do something about the future. So can you if you choose to."

"Haven't we already been down this road? You told me yourself I wasn't cut out for this. I take too many unnecessary risks. I'm not equipped to handle all the stress and emotional turmoil that comes along with 'the job,' and I'm still trying to recover from the mental and physical trauma I went through. The last thing I need is to add to that…which brings me to the question, why are talking about this again?"

"Because a young girl could be in imminent danger."

Kelly shook her head and sighed. "You really know where to hit, don't you?"

"I'm only passing along the information. I have no vested interest, other than to possibly save the life of a teenager."

"That's so not fair."

"Life isn't fair. We both know that too well."

Kelly took a deep breath then uttered the words she never thought would come out of her mouth. "I'll think about it."

"That's all I ask. The girl's name is Emma. Her mother, Lisa Reynolds is the potential target. Mrs. Mathews has all the information."

This would be a huge decision. One that was too important to make without getting the full story and then considering every ramification. Kelly craved input from the person she trusted most.

Despite the potential repercussions, it was finally time to tell Alexa everything.

13

The vehicle search on the shooter's car turned up five black Range Rovers in the San Francisco area whose license plates began with 8R. One belonged to a fifty-year-old female child psychologist, another to a forty-six-year-old African American stock broker. A third was registered to a nineteen-year-old girl with a Chinese surname. The fourth had been owned by a thirty-two-year-old software executive, but records indicated that a month ago the vehicle was demolished in a three-car pileup. The final Rover was leased by Middleton Holdings, Inc.

Ron and Pete were at an impasse, until Pete dug deeper and discovered that the CEO of Middleton Holdings was Jonette Middleton, an entrepreneur and major campaign donor to whichever party was currently in power. She was also the mother of a thirty-seven-year-old artist named Myles Spencer.

The family was extremely wealthy, but Spencer had no interest in traditional commerce. He started out a tagger and eventually advanced to painting large format oils and murals. In the early 2000s, he generated some buzz when a Bay Area TV station did a story on a controversial anti-government art installation he'd erected in an abandoned Army base. The publicity established him as the latest bad boy on the local scene, which eventually led to him getting commissioned to paint a mural in the lobby of the Googleplex in Mountain View. They paid him in stock options, which skyrocketed in the ensuing years. When he cashed out a dozen years later, he'd pocketed close to fifteen million dollars.

Spencer celebrated his newfound wealth by purchasing a loft in San Francisco to use as his home, his studio, and party central for a growing list of hangers-on. There was never a shortage of expensive liquor, cheap women and free drugs. He'd been popped several times on possession, but each time the charges were reduced to misdemeanors.

Ron and Pete went to see Inspector Danny Fuentes in Narcotics who had no shortage of opinions.

"Fucking Myles Spencer. Me and my partner arrested him three times. Turns out, his mother carries a lot of clout at City Hall, and with the wave of a gold-plated wand, our busts turned to dust. He thinks he's untouchable, and to a degree, I guess he is." Fuentes smiled. "I hope he's the one who pulled the trigger on those dealers. I'd love nothing more than to see him go down. That'd wipe the shit-eating-grin off his smug-ass face."

Spencer ticked a lot of boxes. Not only did he frequently partake of illegal drugs, he had access to a car that matched their search, and his mug shot showed a man who was hip/grunge with a full head of unkempt blonde hair. It was far from a sure thing, but they may have gotten lucky and found their shooter.

It was time to pay him a call.

Ron and Pete stood outside Spencer's loft and repeatedly rang the bell, but there was no response. They'd pulled his cell number off his booking sheet and Ron punched it into his phone. Finally, on the fifth ring, a groggy Spencer answered. Ron informed him that he and his partner were at the front door. Spencer informed him that they could go fuck themselves.

That didn't sit well with Ron, who made it clear that the next sound Spencer heard would be a battering ram turning his front door into kindling.

A few minutes later, Spencer begrudgingly cracked open the door. His hair was matted, his eyes were red-rimmed, and his skin was pallid. He looked like a man who'd long ago traded a doctor recommended lifestyle for a steady diet of cheap bourbon and pharmaceuticals.

Ron and Pete flashed their IDs. Spencer was not impressed. "What the hell do you want?"

"We have a few questions we'd like to ask," said Ron. "Can we come in?"

"Fuck no. I'm not answering anything."

Pete stepped up. "We can do this here, or we can do it at the station."

Spencer shook his head in annoyance. "What don't you get? I'm not going anywhere, and I'm not answering any goddamn questions. Talk to your cop pals. They'll tell you I'm on the do-not-disturb list. And right now, you're disturbing the hell outta me."

Pete looked over Spencer's shoulder into the living room beyond. Amidst a cluster of empty beer cans, wine bottles and overflowing ashtrays was a foot tall glass bong in the shape of a beaker. Combined with the heavy scent of marijuana that hung like a viscous cloud, Pete figured he was on solid ground when he pushed his way past Spencer into the loft.

"What the fuck? I didn't give you permission to come in!"

Ron followed behind, spying the evidence that allowed the police to enter a premises. "Looks like drug paraphernalia to me."

"It's a bong. It's not illegal."

"What about this?" Pete asked, holding up a bag of weed.

"So, I smoke a little cheeba. In case haven't heard, it's legal."

"Up to one ounce," said Pete. He turned to Ron. "What do you think? At least three or four ounces?"

"At least. I wonder what else Mr. Spencer's got lying around. Meth? Heroin?"

"You can't be in here without a fucking warrant! I'm calling my lawyer!"

"Fine," said Pete. "Tell your lawyer to meet us at the Mission Precinct."

"You're not taking me anywhere!"

Pete pulled a set off handcuffs from his belt. "Turn around, put your hands behind your back."

"This is total bullshit!"

As Ron placed the weed into an evidence bag, Pete laid his hand on the butt of his gun. "On the floor. Now!"

Spencer had other ideas, and took an ill-advised, wild swing at Pete, missing him by several inches. Pete did a leg sweep that would've made a Cobra Kai sensei proud. Spencer landed on his ass with a painful thud. A moment later, his wrists were cuffed, and he was forcibly jerked to his feet.

Before Ron and Pete carted him off, they allowed him to call his lawyer. It turned out she was on maternity leave. Spencer left an expletive laden message saying that he was being taken into custody and demanded that someone from the firm meet him at the police station.

When they arrived at the precinct, Spencer became increasingly belligerent. As was the case with all uncooperative and aggressive suspects, he was stashed away in "the box," a cramped interview room that perpetually smelled of stale sweat and vomit. To show that the department wasn't completely heartless, he was given a paper cup of tepid water.

Spencer was left to stew in his own juices until his lawyer arrived. He tried pulling the "*do you know who I am*" bullshit, but obviously they knew who he was, or he wouldn't be stowed in a stagnant, windowless room. The rich ones felt money gave them privileges that transcended the law. Rules were for the masses. Laws for the wealthy were more like vague guidelines.

Pete was surprised, unpleasantly so, when Deanna Frost strode through the bullpen and announced she was representing Mr. Spencer. Pete and Deanna had met once in court years earlier during the trial of Leonard Bach, a neo-Nazi who was charged in a grisly double murder the press dubbed "The Honeymoon Horror." At that time, Deanna was a rising star in the defense attorney ranks, while Pete was testifying in his first homicide case. During a cross-examination, she'd taken Pete behind the woodshed, leading him into making a number of contradictory statements which tipped the scale in favor of her client.   Bach was set free, but fate intervened three weeks later when he was gunned down in a gang shootout.

Deanna grinned when she approached Pete.   Her smile reminded him of Pennywise The Clown, preying on innocent children in Stephen King's *IT*.

"Inspector Ericson. I saw your name on the report. Nice to see you again."

He ignored the comment. "You client is in room three."

"The one with no air conditioning. Classy move."

"Had I known you were his lawyer, we would've booked him into the executive suite."

"Let's move this along. I'm sure he'd like to get home, and I have a dinner reso at Gary Danko at six."

Ron glanced at his watch. "I don't think you're going to make it."

She flashed a vulpine smile in his direction. "Inspector Yee. You've got nothing on my client. Two ounces of marijuana, confiscated during a questionable search? And the fact that his car matched a partial plate? This is a joke." She pulled a print-out from her purse. "There are five black Rovers with that plate in San Francisco proper, but when you widen the search to include the Peninsula and the East Bay, that figure triples. You're grasping at straws. We both know that, right?"

"Like I said, you should move that dinner *reso*, because he's not going anywhere until he answers our questions. We both know *that*, right?"

Deanna introduced herself to Spencer, who made it clear he was unimpressed with her inability to immediately spring him. She did manage to wrangle him a Diet Coke, for which he sarcastically thanked her. Pete covered the basics. Where was Spencer on the night in question? *At home.* Was anyone with him? *No.* Did he happen to order in food? *No.* Did he own a handgun? *No.* Other than marijuana, what narcotics did he use? Deanna decided it was

70

time to earn her substantial legal fees and informed Inspector Ericson that her client was not going to answer an obviously leading and inflammatory questions. She went on to declare that the interrogation was nothing more than a fishing expedition, and they weren't biting.

Ron and Pete left the room to confer. She was right, of course. They both liked Spencer for the shooting, but other than the partial license plate match, his hair color, his list of prior misdemeanors, and the fact that he was an asshole, they had zilch. It appeared that Deanna would make her dinner reservation after all.

As Spencer was collecting his belongings, Deanna took Pete aside. "Inspector, I know my client can be a handful, but behind all of the bluster, he's a decent guy."

"Do you really believe that, or are you paid to say that?"

"Is there a difference?" She inched closer and Pete could smell her perfume. "Are you still dating that doctor?"

Pete's face flushed, and Deanna chuckled as she turned to catch up with Spencer. "See you around, Inspector."

Pete and Ron ate dinner together once or twice a week and the choice of cuisine was always a negotiation. Pete favored Chinese food, was somewhat less enthusiastic about Greek, and could always tuck into a thin crust, wood-fired pizza. Ron refused to eat Chinese food, declaring it to be an American bastardization of his culture. Granted, Ron was born 6,500 miles from China, and had never set foot there, but Pete learned long ago that the argument wasn't worth the trouble. Ron's hands-down-favorite was Vietnamese food, but his go-to restaurant, Saigon Kitchen, had been cited three times in the past year for health violations. That's where Pete drew the line. They ended up compromising and decided on a Mediterranean "fast-fine" place in the financial district that boasted authentic shawarma.

As they were getting ready to head out, Charlie Thongsuk arrived in the Homicide bullpen sporting a satisfied grin. A few minutes later, they were watching the results of his video dexterity.

The enlarged image of the young woman in the window of The Mission Social Club was grainy but discernible. The camera angle didn't reveal her face, but now they could make out a San Francisco State logo on her hoodie and the writing on the spines of her books: *The Balance Of Personality* and *The Science Of Human Potential.*

"I checked the reading list for the Psychology Department at SF State and those books are used in Psych 303. They have classes Mondays, Wednesdays, and Fridays from eight to ten. I'm betting if you hit the lecture tomorrow, you'll be able to find this chick, unless she decides to sleep in."

Ron gave Charlie a fist bump. "You're a wizard, bro."

"Thanks, Inspector. 'Preciate it."

"Lunch is on us sometime," said Ron. "Do you like Vietnamese food?"

"I like all kinds of food, except Thai."

Ron looked over at Pete with a cocky grin, and then asked, "Because it's not authentic here, right?"

"Because I'm sick of it. My parents own a Thai restaurant in Fresno, and we ate it twenty-four-seven, three-sixty-five. When I was a kid, I had to sneak out to Mickey D's to scarf an occasional cheeseburger."

Ron's cell buzzed, and he checked the caller ID. "I've gotta take this. Meet you at the restaurant."

As Ron left, Pete loitered around Charlie's computer until he heard the elevator ding. He leaned and spoke in a quiet voice. "There's some surveillance footage I'd like you to take a look at. See what you can do with the images."

It was obvious that Inspector Ericson wanted this done on the down-low. Charlie was cool with that but hoped he wasn't going to get dragged into some office politics, especially if it was territorial bullshit between homicide inspectors.

Pete gave him a case number, and a moment later, Charlie pulled up video of a dark-haired woman inside a nightclub. She was having drinks with some guy, and her face was mostly obscured by her companion. The overall quality of the video sucked, but Charlie's face lit up.

"Is that Tommy Moretti?"

"What do you know about him?"

Charlie could barely contain his enthusiasm. He was like a kid on Christmas, wandering into the living room and finding it piled high with brightly wrapped presents. "I've read all the case notes on Tommy Moretti, as well as everything I could find on his cousins, Angelo and Anthony. I also looked up the reports about his uncle Arthur. It's a pretty bizarre coincidence that the entire Moretti clan died within a six-month period."

Pete was momentarily taken aback. Finally, someone who agreed with his assessment about the Morettis. Even though Charlie wasn't a detective, maybe a fresh eye could shed a different light on this conundrum. "The official position around here is the cases aren't related. Do you have a take on it?"

"With all due respect to your department, that's an extremely myopic point of view. You can't convince me that these deaths aren't somehow connected. Starting with the old man. He was electrocuted by turning on a lamp. Now, that in itself might not appear to be suspicious, but when you add it to everything else…."

"Go on."

"Tommy Moretti died of a heroin overdose, and a few weeks later, Angelo died from an allergic reaction to food he'd ordered a dozen times from the same restaurant. You're telling me that doesn't sound kinda fishy?"

"It's fishy alright."

"And then the kicker to the whole thing was Arthur's son, Anthony. The Army listed him as killed in action, but the guy appeared out of the blue and set himself on fire? I mean, who does that? I love this shit, Inspector. What's the saying? A riddle, wrapped in a mystery, inside an enigma?"

"Something like that."

73

"It kind of reminds me of a case in Denver in the early nineties. Some perp systematically murdered five people in the same family over the course of a year. One every few months. Granted, these were murders and not weird, accidental deaths like the Morettis, but the police kept looking for a link...a motive. Never found one. Never made an arrest."

"You're a walking encyclopedia of morbid facts."

"Some guys have a mind for NFL stats, some guys can recite dialogue from hit movies. Me? I can tell you all you'd ever want to know about Jeffrey Dahmer, John Wayne Gacy, Ted Bundy, and Morris Spitz."

"Who?"

"Morris Spitz, aka the Tennis Pro."

"Never heard of him."

"He never got the press he deserved. Spitz was the head pro at a club down in Irvine and one weekend he just snapped. Used tennis racket strings as garrotes. Killed five women and was working on number six when her husband, a county sheriff, got home early. That put an abrupt end to Morris's short-lived murder spree."

"You're a fun guy to have around, Charlie."

"I appreciate it, Inspector." He turned his attention back go the screen, which featured a freeze frame of the barely visible dark-haired woman. "Any other angles?"

"Not of her."

"Any other cameras catch partials or reflections?"

"I don't know. Everything we have is loaded into the system."

Charlie nodded. "You think this chick could have something to do with the whole Moretti mystery?"

"I have no idea, but if we could determine her identity, it could potentially help piece things together."

"I'll see what I can do, but I'm getting a little backed up. How soon do you need it?"

"Sooner the better, but it's a cold case. I don't want you getting in trouble with your boss if you've got other priorities."

"Copy that. I'll let you know when I have something. And I'm guessing this is not an official request?"

"You catch on fast. Thanks."

"No prob, Inspector."

"By the way, if my partner invites you to Saigon Kitchen, you might want to take a pass."

"Rats?"

"How'd you know?"

"Most urban restaurants have rodent problems. Especially Asian joints. Traditional cooks think refrigeration is optional, plus they don't bother to securely store their food or their garbage. That's an embossed invitation for infestation. You should've seen the rats we had in Fresno. You could throw a saddle on them."

"Thanks for the heads up." Pete started out, then turned back. "What do you know about Mediterranean restaurants?"

14

Kelly was packing up to leave for the night when Vik stopped by to wish her a pleasant evening.

"Have you heard from your brother lately?" Kelly asked.

Vik's brother, Dr. Krishan Danabalan, had filled in at the clinic immediately following David Harper's murder. He was a gifted physician and had gotten a spectacular offer from St. Luke's Children's Hospital in Boise, which was one of the finest pediatric medical facilities in the country.

"Krishan is doing very well. He loves the people he works with and feels incredibly fortunate to have such a wide range of cutting-edge medical equipment at his disposal. However, while the city of Boise has a certain kind of charm, he's finding it lacks urban sophistication, as well as cultural diversity."

"There's no getting around the fact that most of Idaho is fairly..." Kelly was looking for the right word.

"White?"

She nodded. "And leans heavily to the right."

"Krishan says when he walks down the street, or goes into a restaurant, he gets many curious looks."

"It's not always easy to fit into a new city. Speaking of which, how do you think Doctor Samuel is doing?"

"I believe Doctor Samuel will be a wonderful addition to the clinic once she gets comfortable. Much like Krishan, she seems to be experiencing some culture shock, but in reverse. Coming to San Francisco from a small medical school and an even smaller hometown, it's normal to be overwhelmed."

"That's my assessment, as well. I've known Doctor Samuel's family most of my life and they're good people. I'm hoping Ida can get her feet under her quickly."

"If I may, I believe she could be more assertive in her diagnoses and handling of her patients. She has a tendency to second guess herself."

"I've noticed," said Kelly. "I'm also worried that she's carrying a lot of stress, which is causing her to occasionally lose focus."

"I spoke to her today about that very thing. She accepted my observation with an open mind and promised to be more diligent when finding herself in the midst of chaos."

Kelly broke into a smile. "Thanks for keeping an eye on her."

"Absolutely, Doctor. I'll continue to do whatever I can to make her feel at ease."

An hour later, Kelly was home, absently picking at a takeout carton of leftover Shanghai dumplings while she awaited Alexa's arrival. As she ate, she skimmed through her father's journal, hoping to find guidance.

She'd been resolute that she would never kill again, but the fact that there was even the slightest crack in her fortitude preyed on her. She had to make a definitive decision, and get on with her life, one way or the other.

In anticipation of Alexa's arrival, Kelly had weighed her potential money-making options, none of which were particularly attractive. She could sell her condo and get an apartment, but after she paid off her mortgage, she wouldn't have enough left over to find a decent place in the city. She could shut down the clinic and most likely get a job with a hospital or a private practice, but the clinic was a symbol of her father's generous spirit. It had come to define her and her relationship to the community.

She had nothing to sell. Nothing to barter. She'd looked into taking out a personal loan but that would only rack up more debt. Alexa had offered her an interest-free loan, which was an attractive thought, but Kelly already had enough pressure to pay her bills, and the last thing she needed was the additional guilt of not being able to reimburse her best friend.

Which brought her back to square one. There was a potential "offer of employment" on the table. A way for her to solve her short-term cash flow.

All she needed to do was kill somebody.

A woman named Lisa Reynolds.

Lisa Harrington Reynolds was a forty-three-year-old divorcee currently living in the tranquil, upper-class town of Millbrae, fifteen miles south of San Francisco. When Lisa was twenty-three, she'd gotten a job as a secretary to Bob Reynolds, a fleet salesman at a Ford dealership in Hayward. Bob's first wife had died unexpectedly from an overdose of painkillers, leaving him with an infant daughter named Hattie. Within a year of his wife's passing, Lisa and Bob were wed.

Tragedy struck when three-year-old Hattie drowned in the backyard swimming pool. Bob had been out of town on business and Lisa, according to the police report, had left their daughter alone in the backyard "only for a moment." The death of Hattie weighed heavily on the couple. The resulting emotional trauma led to angry bursts of mutual blame, deep bouts of depression, and long stretches of self-pity. Their marriage was dangerously close to imploding, but somehow, they managed to stick it out and weather the pain. Two years later, Bob and Lisa had a baby of their own, who they named Sydney. Three years after that, Emma was born.

Life had taken a positive turn. Bob was promoted to district manager, and the family moved from Hayward to the Peninsula, or what Lisa referred to as "the better side of the Bay." Bob was a wonderful father, but his job often required him to be on the road. When Bob was gone, Lisa drank. She drank because she was anxious. She was lonely. She was depressed.

Alcohol soon gave way to pills.

Bob would return from his travels to find the house in total disarray. The girls, now nine and twelve, did their best to cover for their mother, but it was abundantly clear there was a problem.

When confronted, Lisa lied and denied. Bob finally gathered family and friends together for an intervention and Lisa was forced to face reality. She needed help. If she refused, she stood to lose everything, including her daughters.

She spent sixty days in recovery, not only drying out, but learning how to deal with her issues. She was put on a diet of mood stabilizers, antidepressants, and anti-anxiety meds, and she attended weekly sessions with a psychiatrist.

When Lisa was released, she was welcomed home to a household free of temptations. Bob and the girls had swept the place and found bottles of all sizes and shapes cleverly stashed for easy access. Lisa didn't mind. In fact, she appreciated it. She was a new person and vowed to stick with her treatment plan. She never again wanted to find herself in those dark chasms, contemplating actions that went from immoral to illegal.

Life went on, but not without more bumps in the road. Bob's career continued its upward trend, but simultaneously, Lisa's mental health and stability slowly eroded. She made one clumsy attempt at suicide, which was an obvious cry for help. It was common knowledge that slicing one's wrist was an inefficient way to kill yourself, but a damn good way to draw attention to a deteriorating state of one's grip on reality.

She ended up back in a recovery program, this time for ninety days. It was during those three months that Bob met Rachel Lund, a sales manager at a dealership in Modesto. Rachel was single, attractive in a wholesome way, had never been married, and most of all, was emotionally and mentally anchored. One thing quickly led to another, and Bob realized that for the first time in many years, he felt genuine passion for another person.

He also felt a tremendous weight of guilt. Lisa was in her fourth week of secluded treatment and here he was, entertaining thoughts of leaving her. The fact that Bob and Lisa hadn't shared a bed in over a year factored in, but that didn't make it right. His daughters could sense he was tortured, but assumed it was due to his having a difficult time being a single dad. It wasn't until Sydney overheard her father talking on the phone in hushed tones that she finally realized the truth.

She suggested they go for a hike. Sydney and Bob headed up to Crystal Springs Reservoir, a place very familiar to Sydney since she ran there most days. As they walked along the dusty trails, Sydney revealed just how bad things had gotten at home prior to Mom checking back into rehab. How Sydney took on the responsibility of being a surrogate mother to Emma when Mom couldn't function, which had become more frequent. How Mom had accused Sydney of trying to replace her. Not only that, but she'd gotten increasingly jealous of Sydney's cross-country success and the attention she was garnering, which led to fits of rage. Some of Sydney's medals were missing and her All-Conference trophy had "accidently" fallen off the shelf and broke into three pieces.

Bob was stunned. He knew Lisa had been troubled but didn't realize she'd deteriorated to that degree. Sydney admitted that she and Emma pretended things were fine because they were afraid if he found out the truth, he'd want a divorce and they'd only get to see him every other weekend.

He assured her that he wasn't thinking about a divorce. He hoped Lisa's current stint at the treatment facility would put her life back on course and they could once again have a happy, normal life. Sydney took her father's hand and said she knew he'd hadn't been happy in years. Even if Mom returned home clean, sober and sane, it wouldn't change the fact that Bob no longer loved her.

He deserved to be happy. It was his time to live again.

Lisa's three-month program ended, and she emerged a born-again Christian. She claimed to have found strength and peace in the Lord and occasionally tossed around a few over-used moral platitudes. That didn't make her any easier to live with. If anything, it was worse. Whereas before she vented her anger in profanity laden tirades, now her words were pointed like needles, designed to inflict maximum pain.

Four months later, Bob moved out of the house and took up with Rachel in an apartment in nearby Foster City. Against his lawyer's advice, he'd agreed to a lopsided settlement, where Lisa stayed in the house and received very generous spousal support, as well as child support. Until the divorce was finalized, the girls would continue to live with their mother, but Bob would have open visitation, with twenty-four-hour notice. He kept in daily contact with Sydney and assured her that at the first sign of her mother's relapse, he'd pick up her and Emma and whisk them away.

No one could've predicted how incredibly well Lisa handled this life-changing event. After she'd gotten over the initial shock, she'd settled into a Zen-like acceptance of the situation. There was no feeling of despondence. No outward anger. She credited her new shrink, her new meds and the Lord for giving her a strong and positive outlook on life. She'd faced her demons head-on and defeated them, or at least held them at bay, which gave her an aura of happiness.

Bob and Rachel felt like teenagers in love. Things were too good to be true, especially the fact that Lisa wasn't causing problems. As long as it was quiet on that front, Bob and Rachel figured they didn't need to put off their wedding. The week after the invitations went out, Rachel's new Explorer was keyed, and the tires were slashed. She got a loaner from work, and the next day, someone wedged a garbage bag of newspapers under the car and lit it on fire. Fortunately, the papers were stacked so tightly they didn't develop into an inferno. The police said they'd look into it, but they had their hands full with actual crimes, and Rachel's case file was shunted off to the bottom of a mounting stack of reports that would yellow with age before they were ever addressed.

The wedding was a small affair. Emma was a bridesmaid and Sydney was the maid of honor. The girls avoided talking about the wedding in front of Lisa, but she prodded them, wanting to know every detail. Who was there? What did the bride wear? How was the food? They were cautious and tried to shrug off the questions with typical teenage answers: "It was okay," and "Kinda cool, I guess." History had conditioned them to tread lightly around their mother, even though she now exuded a sunny disposition.

Bob and Rachel booked a weeklong honeymoon in Paris. They were on their third day of newlywed bliss, wandering around Montmartre, when Bob got the call that Sydney's throat had been slit from ear to ear.

15

Alexa arrived precisely at 9:00 p.m. She was never late. If anything, Alexa had an annoying habit of getting places early. Her other annoying traits were she was stunning, brilliant and incredibly successful. But Kelly loved her like a sister, so she cut Alexa some slack. They shared a bond that began in third grade and grew stronger each year.

The narrative that Kelly planned to share with Alexa would surely test that bond.

"I brought some new wine to try," Alexa said, holding up two bottles as she walked in. "The Kistler is zesty, with notes of pear and melon and has a toasty oak finish. The Paul Hobbs is richer and has suggestions of apple and lemon meringue. Which one do you want to start with?"

Kelly stared at her friend, expressionless.

"What?" Alexa said. "What's wrong?"

"In fifth grade we used to talk about our dreams for the future. All you wanted was to marry Chad Barager, have three children and live in a house with a big oak tree in the front yard. And now, here you are, talking about notes of pear and suggestions of lemon meringue. Who the hell are you?"

"Luckily for you, someone willing to share some astonishing wine. And by the way, have you seen Chad Barager in the past few years?"

Kelly shook her head. "Let me guess. Fat, bald and two ex-wives."

"I ran into him at a financial symposium in Zurich last year, and he's only gotten finer with age. But you're right about the wives. He's currently on number three. Enough with memory lane. Grab a corkscrew and some glasses, and let's crack these bad boys open."

Kelly and Alexa settled in front of the fire, sipping their wine, and letting the rigors of the day slip away.

"These new landlords are really putting the screws on," said Alexa. "What's your accountant have to say about your reserves?"

"Last week she gave her notice and informed me that she was taking her mother on a world cruise. Not only is she gone, but she's unreachable. By my rough calculations, once the new rent goes into effect, we won't last more than a month. Maybe two."

"I did some preliminary research, and there are few different options you could consider. There's something called the California Capital Access Program, which encourages banks to provide favorable rates to small businesses. You could also apply to healthcare philanthropies for grants. Some foundations will do what's called 'responsive grant making,' if the clinic is serving vulnerable people. Let me make a few calls tomorrow and get some specific information for you."

"That would be fantastic," said Kelly.

"Keep in mind it's a slow process, and even if something does come through you might require a bridge loan to keep the clinic afloat. In the meantime, have you considered raising your fees?"

Kelly shook her head. "Our patients have a hard enough time making ends meet."

"Think how hard it would be on them if the Mission lost the clinic altogether? Kel, I know I've mentioned this before, but my offer still stands."

"The clinic loses money every month. How would I pay you back?"

"Don't know, don't care."

"I care. If the ship goes down, I don't plan on taking you down with it."

"Well, the offer's there."

"You're incredible," Kelly said. She drained her wine, girding herself for what she was about to lay on her closest friend.

"What do you think of the Kistler?" Alexa asked as she opened the second bottle of wine. "Was it too oaky for you?"

"If I didn't think you were serious, I'd burst out laughing. Lex, my palate wouldn't know the difference between oaky, buttery and melony. All I know is the wine was delicious, and I'm looking forward to that lemon meringue."

"Fair enough." As Alexa poured, she casually mentioned, "We've had some drama at work lately."

"What happened?"

"Our CFO, Greyston Stefancsik, was arrested yesterday. He was diverting funds from the company into a personal account in the Caymans."

"Wow."

"Yeah, wow. Evidently, he'd been cooking the books for a few years, siphoning off tiny amounts here and there. Never enough to raise a flag, but add it all together, and it would fund a very comfortable retirement."

"And no one suspected a thing?"

Alexa shook her head. "He was a gentleman. Pretty wife. Two grown children and a few grandkids. Remembered everyone's birthday. Always the first to pick up the check."

"Sounds like he could afford it."

"It was a total shock. Nobody saw it coming."

"Did you know him well?"

"I thought I did, but I guess not. It hit me hard. After all these years, I felt totally betrayed. Like I'd been personally lied to."

"You shouldn't take it personally. He was scamming everyone. I bet his family didn't even know what was going on."

"A thing like that really makes you wonder about human nature. What would drive a man, who seemingly had everything, to brazenly break the law?"

Kelly shrugged and took a long drink of her wine.

Alexa continued. "It's not like he killed somebody, but still...I have a hard time understanding what makes some people tick." She took a drink, then, "Damn, listen to me. You've got some serious issues and here I am going on about other people's problems."

"That's what friends are for."

Alexa raised her glass. "To friends."

Kelly clinked her glass and drank. She needed to seriously rethink her decision about baring her soul to Alexa. For now, her secrets would remain unspoken.

16

Friday

Early the next morning, Kelly sat across from Benedetto discussing Lisa Reynolds. There was no arguing that her history painted a grim picture. In the past twenty-four hours, Benedetto had obtained additional information, including police and autopsy reports, confidential doctor's records, and a summary from a private detective that Lisa once hired to follow her husband. The overall story was one of a woman who suffered from severe antisocial personality disorder.

In other words, she was a psychopath.

The first death in the family, the drowning of three-year-old Hattie, occurred while Bob was in Las Vegas at an auto convention. One of the many adverse traits of Lisa's personality disorder was a relentless paranoia. She'd been certain that people talked about her behind her back, which they did, and that her loving husband was cheating on her, which he wasn't...at least, not yet. As a result, she'd employed the private investigator. Bob may have believed that what happened in Vegas stayed in Vegas, but the PI had different marching orders. Included in his report were photos of Bob getting overly handsy with a willing saleswoman from Sacramento. The report stated that at the end of the night, the two of them retired to her room.

The next day, Hattie's body was found in the pool.

"The little girl's tragic death was labeled an accidental drowning," Benedetto told Kelly. "The officer who wrote the report stated that Lisa showed no outward signs of mourning. She seemed much more concerned with how her husband would react than with the loss of her child."

"People's reactions under severe emotional stress vary greatly," Kelly replied. "If Lisa is sociopathic, it would follow she lacked empathy. Was she ever a suspect?"

"The police considered her in a pro forma way, but they had no evidence, and she had no apparent motive. It's worth noting the police weren't privy to the information about Bob cheating on her."

"Once that came out, did they revisit the case?"

"It never came out. The private investigator was under no obligation to volunteer his findings, and Lisa wouldn't have shared the report with the authorities."

"Do I want to know how *you* acquired it?"

"Not really."

Kelly was aware that Benedetto was plugged-in and left it at that. "What can you tell me about Sydney's death?"

Benedetto referred to the documents on his desk. "She was murdered while Bob and Rachel were on their honeymoon. The site where her body was found yielded scant evidence. It appeared that someone wearing size eleven men's shoes had been lying in wait. The crime scene tech made a note that the stride length between footprints indicated a person approximately five foot five, whereas the average man with a size eleven shoe is between five ten and six two. They also found a few strands of red synthetic hair, presumably from a cheap wig."

Kelly had worn a synthetic wig when she met with Tommy Moretti. She was uncomfortable with the parallels.

Benedetto continued. "There was one witness who the police considered 'unreliable.' A transient who'd been illegally living in the park. He claimed to have seen a short, skinny man with shoulder length red hair and a black ball cap running from the area where the body was found."

"Was there anything helpful in the autopsy report?"

"Sydney's throat had been cut with an extremely sharp knife, and she died almost immediately. The slash was done from left to

88

right and the angle of the blade indicated that her attacker was standing in front of her, so he, or she, was left-handed."

Kelly's mind went from sharp knives to..."Lisa works as a sushi chef, right?"

"Yes, but it's a recent thing. Just the past few months. Sydney was murdered a year ago."

"Did the police look at Lisa for *this*?"

"She was never considered a strong suspect, although her reaction to finding out Sydney had been murdered was eerily similar to her reaction when Hattie died. The detective made a note that she was initially stoic, and a moment later she, and I quote, 'put on what looked like a theatrical display of grief.'"

"As if she lacked authentic emotion but realized how heartless that appeared."

"Exactly."

"The stories of women who've killed their children to retaliate against their husbands have been well documented," said Kelly. "It might be one of most depraved human acts there is. If Lisa is guilty of these crimes, she deserves punishment, but we don't know if she's guilty."

"Let's assume, for the sake of argument, that she *is* guilty. Guilty of not only killing Hattie and Sydney, but also of poisoning Bob's first wife, who died of a drug overdose. And then there's the attempt to blow up Rachel's car. If Lisa's behind all of this, which is quite possible, then it's only a matter of time before she acts out again. Which means that her daughter Emma could be in serious danger."

"That's too many assumptions for me."

"There's more. Bob recently got a promotion and is being transferred to Detroit. He plans to take Emma with him."

"And with Lisa's medical history and record of substance abuse, she'd have no chance of retaining joint custody."

"Precisely. He's already filed a petition for sole custody, and Lisa is protesting it. The person who requested the services of Gideon is extremely worried for Emma's safety."

"Who is it?"

Benedetto was taken aback. "Your father never asked. He didn't want his decisions clouded by the identities of the people at the other end of the assignments."

"I'm not my father. If this *is* something I consider, it'll be because I have a strong personal feeling about it. And for me to make that determination I have to know everything."

Benedetto took a moment to consider this, then revealed that the person concerned about Emma was her grandfather.

Kelly was surprised. "Bob's father wants someone to kill his ex-daughter in law?"

"Not Bob's father."

Kelly was momentarily speechless. Lisa's *own* father had put out a contract on her.

"Mr. Harrington has coped with his daughter's issues for years," Benedetto explained. "He knows she's unbalanced and dangerous. She showed signs early on, stealing from younger children and threatening them if they told. She was expelled from three different elementary schools. When Lisa was seventeen, she tried to kill her parents to collect her inheritance. Her father sent her to a private academy that specialized in dealing with troubled teens, but after she came at the headmaster with a cleaver, they shipped her home. Her father's convinced Lisa is responsible for the deaths of her daughters but has no hard evidence. He's afraid that when Bob takes Emma away, Lisa will fly into another murderous rage, and he feels it's his duty to protect his granddaughter in any way possible."

"Is this kind of thing…normal? I mean, did my father ever accept a contract on someone from a family member?"

"Once, unknowingly. I don't think it would have made any difference in his decision. The target was someone who was seriously unhinged and a threat to society."

90

Kelly was approaching another critical crossroad and was angry about being put in this position. The path of inaction could result in the death of a young girl. The other path would mean embracing the Gideon persona and taking a human's life.

It meant becoming a murderer.

Again.

17

While Kelly was wrestling with the question of what to do about Lisa Reynolds, Ron and Pete were traversing the SFSU campus. They entered the Psych class a few minutes before it ended with hopes that the student they sought would be in attendance and that they'd recognize her. They got lucky on both counts.

As the class was breaking up, they badged the blue-haired teen and asked if they could have a few minutes of her time. A wave of panic transformed her face from naïve to "she definitely knows something." She glanced over her shoulder, looking for a quick exit, but it wasn't to be.

Her name was Stephanie Geaghan, and she went by Stevie. She tried to beg off, pleading that she had a paper due and was meeting a few other students at the library, but Ron and Pete held firm, explaining they only had a few questions. They could either ask them here or at the precinct. Accepting the inevitable, Stevie's shoulders sagged. "Can we go someplace a little less, you know, in the middle of everything?" she asked.

They found a deserted bench outside the humanities building that provided some privacy. Pete pulled out his cell phone. "I'm going to record our conversation. Are you okay with that?"

"I guess."

"Great. Can you tell us where you were on Monday night? Around eleven?"

"Um, Monday? I'm not sure."

"Think hard. It's important."

Stevie's leg started twitching. "Do I like, need a lawyer or something?"

Ron shook his head. "Not at all."

Stevie's eyes darted back and forth between the two cops. "I was at the Social Club."

"Can you be more specific?" Pete asked.

"The Mission Social Club on 24th." Stevie's throat was dry and the nervous spasm in her leg became more pronounced. She couldn't shake the irrational images of being led away in cuffs, tossed into the back of a cop car, and carted off to jail.

Ron took over. "Stevie, relax. All we want to do is show you a few photos."

Her voice broke, "I really don't want to get involved."

Ron lightly placed his hand on hers. "We know you saw a shooting that night. You're the only witness we've got."

She violently shook her head back and forth as a powerful but groundless fear took root. "No. I...I was there, and I heard a loud bang, but I didn't see anything." The tears came.

"Stevie," Pete said, "there's nothing to be afraid of. Like my partner said, we only want you to look at a few pictures, that's all."

"What if he, that guy, finds out? He'd come after me, right? I just want to mind my own business. You can't force me do anything...can you?"

"We could bring you down to the station for questioning, but we'd like to avoid that."

Her face went ashen. "But I didn't do anything!"

"We know," Ron reassured her. "We need to find the man who was in that car, and you can be a huge help."

Her thin body shook like a leaf in a gusty wind.

"Breathe," said Ron. "Relax and breathe."

It's impossible to predict how witnesses to violent crimes will react. Some are happy to help; they feel it's their civic duty and are eager to work hand-in-hand with the police. Others have something of their own to hide and want to keep their distance from the law. Stevie fell into the third and most common category: the fear of retribution.

She finally gave in, knowing that one way or another, these two cops wouldn't stop until she gave them what they asked. "I'll look at your pictures, but that's it. I'm not going to sign anything or go to court, or anything like that."

Ron and Pete knew when the time came, the DA's office would call her as a witness, and she'd be forced to testify. Right now, that wasn't their problem.

Pete handed her a deck of six photos. Head shots of two Hispanics, one African American and three Caucasian males between the ages of twenty-five and forty. She slowly looked at the photos and when she came to the picture of Spencer, she had a sharp intake of breath. She glanced at the rest of the photos, then shook her head. "I don't see the guy."

Ron and Pete shared a knowing glance. She was clearly lying. "You don't have to be afraid, Stevie. Nothing's going to happen to you," Ron said. "Can you try to remember exactly what you saw the other night, and take another look?"

"He's not in there!" Her words barely came out between jagged sobs. "I've really gotta go."

She suddenly leapt up and bolted, dashing across the Quad.

Ron and Pete got their identification, even though it wouldn't stand up in court. They were convinced more than ever that Spencer was their man, but they needed tangible evidence.

Absent that, it would be time to put the squeeze on.

When Kelly arrived at the clinic, Ramona gave her a rundown of the morning's activity. It wasn't even 10:30 a.m. and they'd already treated a dozen patients. Three of them were brothers, aged six, eight and ten, who thought it would be cool to see if they could knock a beehive out of a tree with a football. It turned out they could. It also turned out to be a wasp's nest. Within moments, the boys felt their painful wrath.

Vik was treating an older man who'd severely sprained his knee tripping over his grandson's skateboard; Annie had her hands full with a twenty-five-year-old "party girl" who'd been brought in semi-conscious after a night of entertaining a couple of South African sailors, and the patient waiting in bay Three was suffering from nausea, migraines, and light-sensitivity.

"Where's Dr. Samuel?" asked Kelly.

"She had a phone call," said Sonita. "She said she'd be right back."

Kelly was on her way to her office when Alma Sanchez arrived with Diego. The young boy was clearly in agony.

"Doctor Kelly," Alma began.

Kelly raised her palm. "I'd like to hear from Diego first, *por favor*." She turned to Diego. "Tell me what's happening."

He wiped away his tears with the back of his hand. "It hurts worse."

"He needs something for the pain," pleaded Alma. "I give him Tylenol, but it's not helping."

Kelly gently examined the young boy's stump, and explained that she could give Diego another shot, but she couldn't prescribe stronger painkillers for him to take home because of his age. Even the lowest dose narcotics were too dangerous for children under twelve without medical supervision. The best thing would be for him to stay in bed and try to get some sleep. He needed to stop moving around, even on crutches, because every time he did, he risked chafing the stump and making it worse.

She turned to Diego. "You've been through so much in the last few months and you've handled it all like a boss. No one, especially a ten-year-old, should have to suffer like you have. It sucks. But if you can get past the next few days, your leg will feel so much better and pretty soon you'll be able to wear your prosthetic again. You're the toughest kid I know." She punctuated that with a smile and got a partial one in return.

As Sonita administered a shot to Diego, Kelly took Alma aside. "I can't give him any more pain injections after today. If his stump gets infected, you'll have to check him into the hospital so they can drain it and put him on an antibiotic drip."

The older woman shook her head. "Diego doesn't like hospitals."

"Fine. Then keep an eye on him. Tylenol every four hours and lots of fluids. And it would be best if he stayed in bed, so I'm giving you a plastic urine bottle."

"What about…?"

"If you can convince him to use a bedpan, more power to you. He can get up to go to the bathroom, but that's it." She put a hand on Alma's arm. "I know it's hard to see your child in pain, but you have to stay strong for both of you."

Ida was pacing in the tiny lounge, talking on her cell phone with her mother.

"Yeah, Mom. Everything here's good. You don't have to worry so much."

"Are you eating? When we did that Zoom thing last weekend, you looked so thin." Ida's mother had a soft Midwestern accent and the mien of a concerned parent.

Ida exhaled. It had always been like this. When she left for college, when she was at medical school, and now. The curse of being an only child to a clingy but caring mother. Especially one who'd taught third grade for twenty-five years.

"Yes, Mom. I'm eating. Three meals a day."

"How's Kelly doing? Your father and I think about her all the time. You'll tell her that, won't you?"

"Sure. Okay…I've gotta go…"

"She's such a lovely girl. And so nice to give you a job."

"I know, Mom. Listen, I'm at work and I have to hang up now." Ida was itching to end the call. There was a reason she moved halfway across the country.

"But your father's right here. Can't you talk to him for just a minute?"

"I'm sorry, but we've got patients backed up. He'll understand. I'll call you guys over the weekend."

"You sound tired. Are you getting enough sleep?"

"*Mom.* I'm eating, I'm sleeping. And before you ask again, I'm not dating anyone, I'm not drinking, and I'm not taking drugs."

Ida felt a headache coming on. She looked around to make sure she was alone then pulled the cylindrical pill holder from her pocket. She loved her parents, and the family had always been open and honest with one another. However, sometimes honesty was not the best policy.

"Gotta go."

Ida disconnected and rubbed her temples. She'd been suffering from a throbbing headache and chatting with her mother exacerbated the pain.

She unscrewed the top of the pill holder and shook out the contents. Three Dexedrine and two Valium. She popped one of the Valium into her mouth and dry swallowed. Twenty minutes from now, the troubles of the day would slowly evaporate.

Kelly had taken charge of the patient in bay Three; a fifty-eight-year-old named Cheryl Gartsman who worked as an executive secretary for an insurance company.

"How long have you smoked?" Kelly asked.

"Uh, forever. I started when I was about sixteen."

"How many packs a day, would you say?"

Cheryl shrugged and lied, as all patients do. "One-ish." Which meant two.

"And alcohol. It says here that you drink. How many per week?"

"I usually have a glass of wine or two at night."

"Every night?"

She hesitated, which answered that question.

Kelly continued. "Mrs. Gartsman, I'm not here to judge. We ask these questions because the responses help us determine the likely cause of your discomfort and how to treat it. I enjoy a glass of wine or two myself, so I completely understand."

Cheryl relaxed and inched closer to the truth. "Two glasses a night. Occasionally a third on the weekends."

"I'm going to give you a prescription to help with the migraines. We've seen some patients lately who share some of your symptoms, and it sounds like there may be a bug going around. In the meantime, I'd strongly suggest you refrain from smoking and cut back on your alcohol consumption. I know that's not as easy as it sounds but trust me, you'll feel a lot better if you do."

Kelly was back in her office, sorting through the mail and a stack of phone messages. Carter Dane had called twice to confirm she'd gotten his letter, and he was "at her service" to speak to her if she had any questions. As Kelly was trying to decide whether or not to shred messages, her cell phone vibrated. The call was from Peninsula Oaks.

It was Ingrid, relaying a message from Dr. Papadakis, asking if Kelly was available to come by in about an hour. Kelly pressed for more information, but Ingrid said it would be best for her to speak directly to the doctor, who was currently checking on other patients. Kelly hated being in the dark, even for an hour, and her thoughts immediately went to the worst-case scenario. She'd known too many doctors who played the "I'll tell you when I see you in person" card and it annoyed the hell out of her. She'd have to leave immediately to make it down the Peninsula in time.

As she was heading out of her office, she was intercepted by Ida, who'd seen Mrs. Gartsman's chart and had added her details to the growing list of patients who exhibited flu-like symptoms. The sample size was hardly sufficient to draw any medical conclusions, so she was going to contact the local hospitals and urgent care facilities to see if they'd encountered a similar uptick. Ida was optimistic, perhaps naively so, that she could pull together enough data to find the source of this new illness that had suddenly cropped up.

Kelly applauded Ida for her efforts and encouraged her to follow up with the other health care facilities in the city. But she cautioned Ida about stretching herself too thin.

"You look tired," said Kelly.

Ida nodded. "I was on the phone with my mom a while ago. She said the same thing."

"I once heard that behind every successful person is a mother who worried."

"Lemme guess. You heard that from a mother."

Kelly nodded. "My very own, in fact. How's your father?"

"Day by day, you know."

"Please give him my best."

"My mother said to give you the same."

"I've got to go check on Jessica. Let's talk later."

As Kelly was sliding into her car, she heard a man calling her name. She turned to see Carter Dane waving at her, heading across the parking lot in her direction. She wondered if she could fire up her car and back out before he closed the gap, but knew she'd only be postponing the inevitable.

"Doctor Harper. Did you get my messages?"

"I've been slammed. Sorry."

"No problem. I just wanted to make sure you got the new lease and wondered if you had any questions."

Kelly's only question was if Carter's company was a clan of heartless, blood-sucking ghouls, but she assumed that query wouldn't exactly endear her to her new landlords, so instead she simply shook her head.

"I got it and it was extremely clear. I've got an appointment that I can't be late for."

Kelly got into her car, revved the engine, and pulled away without another word.

Carter caught a glimpse of her face in the sideview mirror. He was extremely fortunate that looks couldn't kill.

18

Alexa's office on the thirty-eighth floor of One Market Plaza faced east, giving her a magnificent view of the Bay Bridge, Treasure Island and Berkeley. However, she rarely had the time or inclination to enjoy the visual splendor. The majority of her fourteen-hour days were spent in meetings with the partners, on conference calls with lawyers, or chatting with clients.

She'd printed out the financial statements from Kelly, and her desk was covered with Mission Street Clinic spreadsheets and contracts. Alexa was highlighting some of the entries when there was a knock on her door, followed a moment later by a tall, impeccably dressed man.

"You got a minute?" he asked in a resonant baritone.

Alexa smiled and waved him in. Gus Taylor looked like a cross between Sidney Poitier and Michael Jordan. At six foot seven, he had to constantly fend off questions about basketball. *Did he play in college?* No. *Why not?* Because he was more interested in how the business world worked than he was in putting a nine-and-a-half-inch leather ball through an eighteen-inch metal hoop. He preferred an MBA to the NBA.

Gus was the firm's forensic accountant and had a reputation as one of the industry's foremost experts when it came to uncovering financial fraud. It was he who spotted the irregularities that eventually led to the unravelling of Stefancsik's embezzlement scheme.

Gus flopped down in one of Alexa's guest chairs, his long legs dangling over the side.

"How's your damage control going?" he asked. "I know you've got four clients who lost money."

"I spoke to them yesterday. Their reactions ranged from shocked to offended to hysterical. When I explained the firm would be covering all the missing funds, everyone came back down to earth."

"I've been on conference calls all morning with lawyers and our insurance company. Financially, we'll be fine, but our rep is definitely taking a hit on the street."

Alexa shrugged. "A month from now, all will be forgotten."

Gus peered over at Alexa's desk. "New client proposal?"

"My friend Kelly runs the Mission Street Clinic, and I'm looking over her books to see if they might qualify for some kind of SBA loan or government grant."

"Is she the one whose father was killed in that hit-and-run a few months ago?"

Alexa nodded. "She's one of the kindest and hardest working people I've ever known. The clinic is bleeding red and she's scrambling to keep it going."

"If there's anything I can do, let me know."

"I may take you up on that. Kelly needs all the help she can get."

At that moment, Kelly was entering Jessica's room, and was surprised to find not only Dr. Papadakis and Ingrid, but also Sylvia Spiro, the facility director. They were clustered around Jessica's bed chatting amongst themselves and the mood in the room was light, bordering on festive. When they saw Kelly, they moved aside to give her a view of her sister.

Jessica's color had returned. In fact, Kelly couldn't recall a time since the accident that her sister looked so...alive.

As Kelly approached, Dr. Papadakis spoke, his voice tinged with pride. "I'm so glad you could come. I know you're very busy with your own patients and driving all this way is not particularly convenient, but I thought you'd want to see for yourself how well your sister is responding to the treatments." Kelly reached out and took Jessica's hand. In response, Jess slowly turned her head toward

Kelly. Her facial expression remained slack, but there seemed to be a slight glint of recognition in her eyes.

"We're all quite pleased with this development," chimed Ms. Spiro. Cynically, Kelly knew if there were any positive results, Ms. Spiro would trumpet them to the home office in Dayton, and they'd concoct a way to capitalize on them. Kelly didn't care. All she wanted was to have her sister back.

She sat on the side of the bed, clutching Jessica's warm hand. Dr. Papadakis droned on about testing levels on the Glascow Coma Scale, and even though it was early days, there was real potential for more improvement. Kelly tuned out the doctor's medical assessment. His voice became nothing more than background noise as her thoughts drifted to sweet childhood memories that she and Jess shared. The laughs, the pranks, the sisterly talks that went deep into the night.

It was far too optimistic to believe they'd ever share those moments again, but if Kelly knew one thing, it was that the future was utterly unpredictable.

19

Kelly had to see Lisa Reynolds in person. There was too much riding on this decision to make it in the dark. She was violating Benedetto's strict code of conduct when it came to a potential "assignment." According to him, the last thing she should do was engage in any kind of one-on-one with a target, as it could come back on her if there were a subsequent police investigation.

Kelly had crossed that line with Tommy Moretti. Thinking back on it now set off alarm bells: *surveilling Moretti from a coffee shop across the street...their eyes locking for a fleeting moment; bumping into him at a nightclub and him asking, "You here by yourself?"; ending up in his living room, being drugged and assaulted.*

Despite what should have been a cautionary lesson, Kelly was once again about to step into that danger zone.

The restaurant was called Kobudai. It was owned and operated by two women, and the entire staff, including the chefs, were female. The place got its name from a fish that is a sequential hermaphrodite; females of the species can change to male to breed. In other words, the females can take care of business on their own. The derivation of the restaurant's name was lost on most of their patrons, but those who understood its significance appreciated the symbolism.

Kelly intended to grab a table in the corner and observe Lisa from afar, but the dinner crowd packed the small eatery, and the only available space was at the counter directly across from one of chefs...a petite brunette with short, spikey hair. Lisa looked just like the surveillance photo in her dossier. Kelly thought about beating a quick exit, but that would mean making a life-or-death decision on a hunch.

Moments later, Kelly was seated at the counter. The first thing she noticed about Lisa was her intensity as she expertly sliced thin wafers of ahi and arranged them to form a perfect rose. The second thing she noticed was that Lisa was right-handed.

"Ahi sashimi plate!" Lisa's voice was unexpected. It was deep with a raspy edge and sounded like it belonged to an older, heavier woman with a smoke-damaged throat. A slim waitress with myriad piercings scooped up the fish and whisked it away. Lisa set down porcelain bowls of wasabi and pickled ginger in front of Kelly and smiled. Not only was the smile warm, but a partially chipped incisor gave Lisa a girlish quality and look of innocence.

Kelly had come expecting to find a frigid and brittle woman, and instead, found Lisa instantly likeable.

"What can I get you?"

"The ahi looks amazing. I'll have that and...what's a Kobu roll?"

"Salmon, scallions, pickled daikon topped with sesame and roe. It's delicious, but a lot of food for one person."

"Maybe I'll just stick with the ahi then."

"Do you like halibut? We got it in fresh this morning. I broke it down myself," Lisa said with a ring of pride.

"Sounds great."

Lisa called out, "Ahi sashimi and hirame at the bar!" and started on the dish. Her knife work was impressive.

"How long have you been working here?" Kelly asked in admiration.

"Only a few months. It's a three-year apprenticeship before they let you do some of the more complex dishes or present your own *omakase*."

"I've been to a lot of sushi restaurants and your knife skills rank right up with some of the best chefs."

Lisa beamed. "Thanks. I took lessons online before I got this job, and I practice all the time at home."

"You must eat a lot of fish."

"Fish, carrots, radishes. I'll slice up anything I can get my hands on."

The waitress reappeared and spoke to Lisa in hushed tones. "The guy on twelve wants to talk to the chef who prepared his Kubo roll. He's not happy."

For an instant, Lisa's mouth tightened and her face took on a hard edge. A moment later, she channeled some kind of inner chi and her anger was replaced with a spiritual calm. "What's the issue?"

"He says the fish is stale. Said it smells weird."

Lisa turned to Kelly with an apologetic smile. "Be right back." She ducked under the counter and strode over to a table where two men in their early twenties sat. They looked like typical tech bros, with their "I'm just an ordinary guy" Levi's, black T-shirts, Apple watches and three-hundred-dollar Maui Jims perched on their foreheads.

Lisa did an excellent job of keeping her emotions in check. Kelly hoped the conversation would escalate into a confrontation, because she wanted to see how Lisa would react. Suddenly, the unhappy patron loudly announced, "I'm not paying for this shit!"

Lisa stood her ground, allowing the asshole in blue jeans to vent, but when he swept his plate crashing to the floor, Kelly was instantly on her feet, shouting, "Hey!"

All heads turned in her direction. What was she thinking? This wasn't her fight. The absolute *last* thing she should do was attract attention, but she couldn't control herself. It was as if she was having an out of body experience.

Kelly stormed over to the table and let loose with, "What the hell's wrong with you?!"

The man was stunned. Who was this bitch and why was she getting involved? "What are you…?"

"You can't act like that in here!" Then it suddenly dawned on her. The abusive patron reminded her of Clarence Musselwhite…the man who'd killed her mother and bludgeoned Jessica.

The man's friend was crimson with embarrassment, quickly tossed a couple of bills on the table, then grabbed the asshole by the arm. "C'mon, dude."

On the way out the door, the man turned back toward Kelly. "Fuck you, you fucking dyke." He spun on his heels and stormed out.

The rest of the diners were stunned into silence for a moment, then abruptly broke into applause.

Lisa smiled at Kelly. "Thanks! I mean, I had it, but that was way cool."

Kelly was mortified. "I'm so sorry. I had absolutely no business doing that. He was just such a jerk, I couldn't help myself."

Lisa nodded toward the counter. "Let me finish making your dinner, which by the way, is on the house."

"No, that's okay."

"Are you kidding? I was about a minute away from turning that guy into sashimi." Lisa's grin suggested it was meant to be a joke, but the more Kelly would learn about Lisa, the more she'd wonder if Lisa's comment was literal.

20

Saturday

Sgt. Miguel Urbina was a former Sureño gang member who'd done a stretch in Ironwood Prison. While he was incarcerated, his sixteen-year-old sister was killed in a drive-by, and her death led him to reevaluate everything he'd come to believe. He left the Sureños, and when he was released from prison, he became a gang counselor. Years later he ended up with the SFPD, eventually overseeing the Gang Task Force. Besides working the streets and attempting to keep a lid on gang activity, the task force interfaced with the Homicide Detail when there was a gang shooting.

On this morning, Urbina was chatting with Pete when the scent of onions, chilies and chorizo wafted into the Homicide bullpen, followed a few seconds later by Ron carrying a bag of breakfast burritos. "Three Saturday Morning specials, extra jalapeños. Best way to jump start your day."

As they dug in, Urbina brought the inspectors up to date on what he'd heard about the Molina shooting. "No one knows who pulled the trigger on Gato, but the 24th Street Norteños are out in full force, looking for information. Supposedly, Molina was moving a heavy load that night, and when his body was found, the drugs were gone. Toro Echavarria wants his drugs back and the killer put in the ground."

"Are they still dealing the same high-grade brown?" asked Pete.

Urbina nodded. "They pride themselves on quality control. The dope only varies when one of their dealers gets entrepreneurial and dilutes the smack to make a little cash on the side. Two years ago, one enterprising Norteño hustler got into the habit of adding a few extra grams of baby laxative to his merchandise. His body was found in the trunk of a bullet-pitted Chevy Malibu behind a warehouse in Hunter's Point."

"Strong incentive to keep your hand out of the cookie jar," said Pete.

"If Spencer is our guy, he's sitting on a lotta smack," said Ron in between bites.

Pete chimed in. "Or he threw himself a hell of a party. I checked his Instagram, and he posted photos taken on his boat from Thursday night. Looked like he and a couple dozen ravers had themselves a good old time."

"You're telling me that after we brought him in for questioning, he left here, went straight out and partied, and then posted pictures to rub our faces in it? That is one brazen motherfucker."

"I spoke to the woman who manages the pier where Spencer has a berth," said Pete. "She wouldn't give me any information about him or his guests without a warrant."

Just then, Pete's computer alerted him to a new email. He clicked it open and smiled. "The DOJ just sent over a dealer's record of sale. Eighteen months ago, a Smith & Wesson MP9 was purchased by a Myles Middleton Spencer at a gun show in Turlock."

"MP9," said Urbina. "That's the make of gun that killed all three dealers."

"Why would Spencer tell us he doesn't own a firearm?" asked Ron.

"He probably didn't realize that gun show dealers are required to report sales."

"Or, maybe," Ron concluded, "he's a lying sack of shit."

Urbina chimed in. "Unfortunately, the MP9 is the choice of *cholos* everywhere. There are thousands on the street."

"So, we need to get ahold of Spencer's gun," said Ron.

"He knows the heat's on," said Pete. "It's probably at the bottom of the bay."

"Partner, how many times have I told you not to underestimate the profound stupidity of the bad guys?"

As they were discussing their next move, they were interrupted by Beverly Sanford, an officer from the Fraud Unit. She explained they'd busted a Russian hacker who was running a scheme to bilk retired folks out of their pensions by convincing them he was with the IRS and they owed back taxes.

"If he didn't kill someone, Bev, you're in the wrong department," said Ron.

Beverly gave Ron a tired courtesy smile. "This guy, Yegor Lukov, claims he has valuable information about a serial killer named Gideon."

"Great," said Ron. "I bet he can also tell us who really shot JFK."

"Hey, I'm just passing it along before we book him. He's looking for a deal and I heard that Inspector Ericson is the resident Gideon fanboy."

"Now, where would you have heard that?" asked Pete, directing his attention to Ron.

"Guys, I've got actual work to do," said Beverly. "Are you interested in meeting with Lukov to see what he's got, or do we decline his generous offer?"

"I'll sit down with him as soon as I get a chance," said Pete. "What can it hurt?"

Ron and Urbina shared a look. "Anglos. Sometimes there's just no explaining 'em. Am I right, Miguel?"

"Ever since they became a racial minority in California, I try to cut 'em some slack." Urbina smiled and took the last bite of his burrito.

As Kelly pulled up outside Benedetto's office, she checked in with the clinic. Ida had seen two more patients this morning who suffered from nausea, headaches and joint pains. She'd also heard back from some of the hospitals who reported a few cases, but nothing they found alarming. Regardless, she was determined to keep at it.

Moments later, Kelly was sitting across from Benedetto, recounting last night's events. When she finished, she got the reaction she'd expected.

"You not only engaged Lisa Reynolds in conversation, but you drew attention to yourself," Benedetto said. "Every person there will remember your face."

"Maybe, but I need to do things my way."

"I thought you might've learned from your interactions with Moretti."

"Seriously? Do you really think I don't relive those horrors every night?"

"And yet..."

"Yeah, I know, but like I said..."

Benedetto completed her sentence, "...you need to do things your way. I want to reiterate the danger of publicly associating with someone who may happen to die under suspicious circumstances in the near future."

"If there are suspicions about her death, that means I didn't do a very good job."

"Forget Lisa Reynolds. If you're still interested in a target, we can..."

"I'm not interested in a *target*! I'm not interested in being *a gun for hire*! If I do this, it's to save a young girl's life!" Kelly's ire was rising quickly. "Emma's already lost her sister. I know what that's like. She's the same age I was when Musselwhite destroyed my family. As painful as it was to move on, at least I had that opportunity. Emma deserves that opportunity as well."

"It's too risky."

"I read my father's journal. Seventeen kills. Eighteen if you include Musselwhite. Every one of them a risk."

"But he didn't come face-to-face with any of them beforehand, which mitigated the chances of being linked to their deaths."

"I'm not my father. He had his own set of rules. I have mine."

"And I have mine," Benedetto said. He paused, letting the temperature in the room drop a few degrees. "Kelly, if you're caught, not only is *your* life over, but what happens to Jessica? Take my counsel and walk away."

"What about Emma? What if Lisa *is* planning to kill her?"

"This is going to sound heartless, but it's not your problem."

"You *made* it my problem!"

She was right. For the first time, Benedetto had no response.

Kelly pressed on. "Would you have counselled my father to walk away?"

"Our relationship was different."

As Kelly digested this, the truth suddenly dawned on her. "You and I don't click because I'm a woman, is that it?"

"It has nothing to do with gender. It's about what drives you…emotionally and morally. You could say it's your working style. I'm not passing judgment. There's no right or wrong way to process critical decision making."

He paused to gauge her reaction, which was difficult to discern because Kelly's face didn't reveal any clues as to what she was thinking.

What Benedetto didn't know was he'd just lit her fuse.

Paul Johnson trudged into the Mission Street Clinic complaining of chest pains. It was no shock, given that he tipped the scales at a glazed donut under 350 pounds. He sat on the edge of a bed as Ida took his blood pressure.

"One sixty over ninety-seven."

"What's that mean in English?" Johnson had a nasal, country-boy accent.

"Do you have a history of high blood pressure, Mr. Johnson?"

He shrugged. "Sure. Just look at me. High blood pressure, high cholesterol and my wife tells me I snore like a chainsaw."

"Can you tell me what medications you're on?"

"A bunch of 'em, but I don't remember their names or anything."

"We can contact your doctor."

He shook his head. "He died last year. Don't have a new one."

"Where do you live, Mr. Johnson?"

"I got a poultry farm a little ways outside'a Greenwood, Arkansas. Me and some boys came out here to do some fishin' in the bay."

"I'm going to have you take off your shirt so I can get an EKG."

"I don't want no damn electrodes stuck on my body. I don't believe in that crap. Can't you just give me some nitro pills?"

"I'm sorry, but I have to collect some baseline information before I can prescribe any meds."

Johnson's voice doubled in volume. "I told'ya already! My chest hurts. Are you even a real doctor?"

Ida was quickly getting flustered. When she was in med school, she'd run into patients like this. People who were suspicious or fearful of standard medical procedures. Even things as non-invasive as an EKG. Most of these fears grew out of misinformation that was peddled on talk shows that were particularly popular in rural communities.

Ida tried a different approach. She pasted on a smile and said, "I'm from a small town too, and…"

Johnson suddenly reached for his chest and squeezed his eyes shut.

"Mr. Johnson. Why don't you lay back and…"

"Just gimme me some goddamn nitro!" he roared.

The curtain around the medical bay was flung open and Vik entered. "Do we have a problem here?"

"Yeah, we do! I got pain in my chest and she's refusin' to give me some pills to make it go away."

Vik turned to Ida. "Have you done an EKG, Doctor?"

"Mr. Johnson doesn't want one."

"Are *you* gonna give me nitro or not?!"

"I can give you a sublingual nitroglycerin," said Vik. "But once you take it, you'll need to remain here for at least thirty minutes so we can monitor your condition."

Johnson had a look of disgust as he got off the table. "Screw that shit. I got places I need to be."

And with that, he stomped out.

Ida was visibly upset. "I'm sorry, Dr. Danabalan. I tried to explain..."

Vik shook his head. "You did everything right. As one of my med school professors used to say, patients often lack patience."

"I worry that he's going to keel over from a massive angina."

"I don't doubt it for a second, but there's only so much we can do."

When Vik left, Ida pulled the cylindrical pill tube from her pocket. With shaking hands, she unscrewed the top and tipped it into her palm. Nothing came out. Dammit. She'd taken the last pill early this morning. Panic set in and her face grew flush. Her body craved medication.

Vik was already busy with another patient, as were Annie and Sonita, and the waiting room was full. Ida needed to pull her shit together, and there was only one way to do that.

She tapped in the code to the lock on the pharmacy door, slipped into the small room and went directly to the Valium. She popped one into her mouth, put two more in her pocket, then glanced over her shoulder. As long as she was there, she borrowed two Dexedrine as well. These would get her through the day, and on the way home, she'd get her prescriptions refilled. Tomorrow morning she'd replace the pills and no one would be the wiser.

Ida exited the lockup and headed toward the waiting room. She wasn't aware that Vik had come around the corner and seen her leaving the pharmacy. He waited a moment, then entered the drug lockup.

He hoped his suspicions were wrong.

113

21

Tomás watched the house from lengthening shadows. His mother worked for a caterer on the weekends, and tonight there was a banquet someplace downtown. The front door opened and Alma came out, dressed in a server's uniform. Tomás might've been embarrassed to admit that his mother worked as "the hired help," but the fact was, he didn't give a shit. Not about her, not about the family. The only person he cared about, beside himself, was his *hermanito,* Diego.

Alma climbed into her six-year-old Kia and headed out. Tomás waited a few minutes to make sure she wasn't coming back, then casually ambled across the street and entered the house like he belonged there.

"Yo D! *Dónde estás?* It's your favorite bro!"

"In the back, watching TV," came the voice of a tired but excited ten-year-old.

Tomás cruised through the kitchen, grabbing a handful of cookies along the way. A few crumpled dollar bills were on the counter, as if Alma knew he was coming and laid them out as a test. Tomás sneered at the money. Soon he'd be raking stacks, and his *madre* would still be living in this shithole, driving her crapmobile, and he wasn't going to toss her a dime. He would show her the same kind of consideration she showed him during his three years in juvie.

Diego was stretched out on a worn sofa, propped up on a few pillows, watching a recent *Spider-Man* movie. On the floor next to him was his plastic pee bottle. Tomás looked at it with disgust.

"Why you gotta use that?"

"Doctor Kelly says I gotta stay off my feet. I mean, my foot."

"So, you gotta piss in a jar?"

Diego was embarrassed, feeling like the cripple he was. Tomás saw this and changed the mood.

114

"What're you watching?"

"*Spider-Man.* Zendaya is hot."

"Which one is she?"

"The hot one, dude. She's like a bigtime movie star."

Tomás checked her out and nodded. "She's too old for you, but I could totally get with that."

"Yeah, right."

"Hey, when she sees my new whip, she'd be all like," Tomás spoke in a falsetto, "Hey homes. Love your ride. You wanna hook up?"

Diego burst out laughing. "In your dreams. She'd be all like," Diego raised his voice an octave, "Nice car. Where'd you steal it? You better go, 'cause my boyfriend Spider-Man is coming, and he's gonna kick your ass."

Tomás laughed. He loved this little guy, but that didn't mean he wouldn't use him, like he used everyone else. "Talkin' 'bout, Spider, he been around?"

"Me and Oscar don't talk much."

"I heard he got pissed at you 'cause you didn't want to be in the gang, or something."

Diego nodded, even though that wasn't the cause of the rift between him and Oscar.

"Fuck Oscar," said Tomás. "You don't want no part of him, anyway. Toro's gettin' tired of his bullshit, you know? I think *jefe*'s gonna knock him back down to being a runner, makin' loose change. Pretty soon, he be working' for me."

Despite his falling out with Oscar, Diego still defended him. "Toro wouldn't do that. Oscar's a good earner."

Tomás shrugged. "Word is Oscar's skimmin'."

"No way. He's loyal."

"Maybe. Maybe not. Anyway, there's new blood in town, little man, and I'm puttin' together my crew. You heard'a Luca?" Diego shook his head. Tomás smiled. "He's one scary motherfucker. He thinks he's all Luca Brasi from that Godfather movie, you know?"

Diego shrugged and Tomás continued. "Like an enforcer. Couple years ago, he caught a Sureño taggin' one of our murals and Luca used a pruning saw to cut off the dude's hands."

"For reals?"

"No shit. Now he works for me. Plus, I got some shorties, too. You know Hector Ibarra?"

"I thought Hector was a lookout for Gato."

"Was. Since Gato be in the ground, Hector hooked up with me. He knows it's a good opportunity for advancement. Once I get my piece of land and start pullin' in the green, there'll always be place for you. I take care of my boys, especially *mi hermano*, you know?"

"Thanks, but Mom would lose her shit."

"You not some mama's boy. You gotta grow up and get what's yours. Toro told me that the Sanchez family be next in line. Couple a years, we could be runnin' things, you know?"

Diego had a tiny smile. "Couple a years, you be working for me."

"Like hell," Tomás said with a grin. He tossed a pillow at Diego, who flinched. The sudden movement shot a bolt of excruciating pain up his leg, and he howled.

"Ah, bro! Sorry. I didn't know you were hurtin' so bad."

Tears ran down his face. "Stupid stump."

"Didn't the doctors give you meds?"

"Tylenol."

"Tylenol is for headaches." Tomás reached into his pocket and pulled out a small vial of pills. "Take one of these," he said, handing Diego a yellow pill.

"What is it?"

"Norco. Good shit."

Diego screwed up his face. "I don't know. Doctor Kelly said I'm too little to take strong drugs."

"Doctor Kelly's the one who's making you piss in a bottle, homes. Screw that bitch. You in pain and you don't got to be. This shit is safe, bro. Just take one and you be flyin' first class."

Diego was smart. He was a good kid. He obeyed his mother. But he was hurting big time. He washed down the pill with some Sunny Delight.

"That's it. Couple a minutes, D, and you gonna feel fine." Tomás shook two more pills into his hand, wrapped them up in a tissue, and gave them to his brother. "In case you need more tomorrow. Don't let your mama see them, or she'll take them for herself."

Diego slid the pills under his pillow.

"And what I told you about Oscar skimmin' is between you and me, bro. Just sayin', Toro got his eye on him. We gotta make sure you and me take care of ourselves, you know?"

Diego yawned, and his eyes were starting to droop as the opioids coursed through his tiny body. "Yeah, sure."

Alma was right. Tomás was a bad influence, and the trouble was only beginning.

On the way out, he snatched the two crumpled dollars off the counter.

22

Yegor Lukov looked every bit a Russian mobster wannabe. When he was booked and processed, he'd handed over his gold chains, faux diamond studs, and counterfeit Rolex Cosmograph, but that didn't affect his cocky attitude or the erroneous belief he'd be back at the Red Tavern eating cabbage rolls and drinking chilled Stoli Elit by dinner time. The fact that his feet were shackled to a bolt in the floor should've given him a clue that the SFPD took his crime seriously, but Yegor was monumentally clueless.

In his mid-thirties, he had a flat, too wide face topped with a thatch of unruly black hair that lacked any cohesive style. His most distinguishing features were the red hammer and sickle tattoo on the side of his neck and the large dark mole that sat slightly off-center between his bushy eyebrows. When he smiled, he revealed a set of crooked yellow teeth. Yegor exhibited the same disdain for dentists that he did for barbers.

Pete sat across from him, his laptop open. When Yegor spoke, the words came out in gushes, like he was in a hurry to impart his wisdom and catch a train. His command of English was adequate and his accent was thick, making him sound like Teddy KGB from *Rounders*.

"First off, I downloaded malware blocker into your computer, because places you need to go are filthy with bugs that attack hard drive. Program will make shitty little laptop slower, but be protected, like putting on titanium condom." He laughed at his very funny joke. "Now follow instructions I give. Even though you are not master hacker like me, let's see if you can make own way to promised land."

Pete was logged onto Torch, a Dark Web search engine with more than two million darknet platforms on their database. It was a different world...an anything-goes-world where the users were anonymous and completely unsupervised.

Yegor directed him to search "cartoons."

"Cartoons?"

"Will take you to a subsection, where you want to find message boards. From there, you look for 'Crazy Creatures Clubhouse.'"

Pete found the title, and when he clicked on it, he was immediately bombarded by an avalanche of ads, mostly for sex websites. "Holy crap."

Yegor laughed. "I told you, guy. These sick fucks plant shit everywhere. They take over computer, and then blackmail you."

"These 'sick fucks?' You do remember why you're shackled to the floor, right?"

He shrugged. "I was running sophisticated scam. These guys bullshit punks. Mostly in Pakistan or Romania. No pride in work. You know about Nigerian Prince who wants to move big money to United States for safekeeping? In return you get a big chunk of cash if you send very small transfer fee and bank account info. You hear about that one? That was me! Very successful operation."

"And you're proud of that?"

"Damn straight! It was world famous. You ever do anything make you world famous, guy?"

"Can't say I have. Then again, I haven't been arrested either."

The malware blocker did its job, and Pete was left staring at images of characters from Crazy Creatures, an animated kids TV series that ran for a few seasons. "I've got pictures of a dozen animals. I'm guessing they're characters from the show."

"You need find Garvin Guinea Pig."

"Seriously?"

"Hey, guy. I don't make this shit up. I just figure how to mine data. Click on pictures of guinea pig, scroll down, and read messages. Some are people who, for some fucking reason, have actual comments about TV show. Very strange why someone do that. But this is where info about Gideon is buried. When you find right thread, it will take you to another site. Some sites are behind paywalls, but not all."

119

"There are hundreds of posts here," said Pete.

Yegor nodded. "Once you get in, is like falling into bunny hole. Some roads take you to sexy and violent images. Some roads take you places with good info about Gideon." He sat back and smiled, flashing his stained canines. "So, guy. You tell police how I cooperate?"

"It depends on if this pans out or is just a bunch of bullshit."

"Is not bullshit!" Yegor was offended, as if his honor was being questioned. "Look for threads that mention Committee."

"What's Committee?"

"People who offer big reward to find Gideon. Millions of dollars. You read, and then will thank me. I give you some links to check out."

As Yegor dictated, Pete jotted down the instructions, realizing it was a hell of way to be spending Saturday night. But, if this could shine a light on the shadowy hit man called Gideon...and if Pete could actually prove he was real...it would be worth it.

Still, he'd rather be at *44 Degrees* with Kelly, having a glass of wine and a fancy dinner.

He wondered what she was doing.

Kelly was having a glass of wine, but her "fancy dinner" consisted of a bag of roasted almonds she'd found in the back of her pantry. They were stale, but they were healthier than the double chocolate Milanos, which she knew she'd devour later.

She'd drawn a vertical line down the middle of a legal pad, and unconsciously massaged the scar in her palm as she reviewed what she'd written. The left side was labeled *"WHY"* and the right side *"WHY NOT"*. The *"WHY"* column had only one entry: *Lisa might be planning to kill Emma.* Extremely compelling, but the single word *might* was too big a qualifier. The *"WHY NOT"* column was much more substantial: *Lisa's right-handed; there's no definitive proof she killed Hattie or Sydney; when provoked in the restaurant she kept her cool; taking this contract would be a huge risk; Emma's already had to deal with the death of her sister...it would be devastating to also have to suffer the death of her mother.* And finally, a personal note: *killing Lisa would violate what I vowed to never do again and would wipe out whatever progress I've made toward getting back a "normal" life.*

Upon reflection of that final item, Kelly wondered again if she shouldn't just forget this whole thing.

Alexa was also having a glass of wine, hers much more upscale. She too was jotting on legal pads, which sat alongside the spreadsheets from the clinic, and were now covered with notes and question marks.

Her pad was divided into columns labeled *"Consultations," "Speaking engagements," "Advisory Committee Honorariums,"* and *"Other???"* Down the left side she'd noted the dates of each payment made to David Harper for services rendered. The financials that Kelly provided only went back five years, and the payments had been rather consistent over that time. Outside revenue flowed into the clinic's coffer almost every month. Some months were blank, and other months had multiple deposits.

On a second pad, Alexa had written down the names of the organizations that had issued payments to the clinic on behalf of Dr. Harper: The Southwest Medical Association; St. Charles Surgery Center; Provident Alliance; Community Spirit; Mercy Health Systems; Ardent Resources...the list went on. Alexa wasn't surprised that she'd never heard of any of these medical groups, but what didn't make sense was how David Harper was able to do so much outside work and still spend fourteen hours a day, six days a week, running the clinic.

Alexa stared at her notes, something nibbling at the back of her mind. She absently reached for her glass and was dismayed to find it empty.

121

Kelly skimmed through the articles she'd saved on her laptop about mothers who murdered their children out of spite. A woman in Kentucky stabbed her two children so "her husband couldn't have them." A mother in Florida poisoned her five-year-son and then killed herself. She'd left behind a note to her husband who'd been having an affair: "I told you that you'd regret cheating. Now you can enjoy your life because nothing's stopping you. And never forget. This is all your fault." A lady in Oregon drowned her twin babies when she went into a rage after overhearing her husband asking his friend for the number of his divorce attorney. It turned out the husband was asking on behalf of his brother...but the damage had already been done. The woman ended up washing down a bottle of antidepressants with a fifth of Seagram's Peach Twisted Gin.

It was all extremely disturbing.

Her conversation with Benedetto replayed in her head.

"What about Emma? What if Lisa is planning to kill her?"

"This is going to sound heartless, but it's not your problem."

"You made it my problem!"

Kelly struggled with deciding how, or if, to proceed. As conflicting thoughts swirled around her head, the cycle was broken by the ringing of her phone. She glanced at the call screen and smiled.

"Why aren't you out having dinner with a handsome socialite at some overpriced, impossible-to-get-reservations-at restaurant?" Kelly asked.

"Because my best friend asked me to help her clinic from going bankrupt," Alexa replied.

"Lex, it's Saturday night!"

"Saturday nights don't mean the same as they did when we were in high school."

"True that. So, what's up?"

"I'm going through the clinic's books and noticed a lot of outside income."

Kelly's body temp seemed to plunge ten degrees. She had a hard time uttering, "Um, yeah. And?"

"It's amazing that your dad was able to juggle so many part-time gigs while putting so much time into the clinic."

"He *was* amazing. Worked himself to the bone, doing whatever he could to keep the clinic afloat." Kelly knew she was skating on thin ice.

"It's highly commendable the lengths he went to in order to provide medical care to the people in the Mission. I was thinking you should give some interviews to the local outlets, and let the public know how selfless your father was. Maybe it would motivate some wealthy patrons who want to guilt-wash their ill-gotten gains."

"That's an idea. I'll give it some thought." The absolute last thing Kelly wanted to do was draw attention to her father's extracurricular activities.

"Once I finish up my overview, I'll give you call, and we can discuss the next step."

"I hope you're at least having a glass of that melony wine."

Alexa burst out laughing. They knew each other so well...which made bringing Alexa into this a potentially huge mistake.

Chatting about her father triggered Kelly's recollection of his journal entry about Hope Miller. How he'd been offered a contract on a college student who was suspected of having engineered what was known as the *Middle School Massacre,* where twenty-five people were murdered. Kelly went back and read portions of what her father had written...

(David's Journal)

The target was a young woman named Hope Miller. A stunning brunette who was a senior at Kentucky Wesleyan University in Owensboro, Kentucky. KWU is a Methodist college with less than 800 students.

Hope was raised in Edgewood, Kentucky; one of the wealthiest cities in the state. She was an only child and was doted on by her parents. She wanted for nothing, and her success in life was destined. Head cheerleader, student body president, prom queen...they were all a given.

She attended Kentucky Wesleyan, partly due to her mother's urging and partly because she cherished the idea of being an orca in a tiny pond. It didn't take long for Hope to establish herself as one of the shining stars on campus, favored by her professors and longed for by all the males in school.

It turned out that Hope wasn't all she appeared to be; she had a deep-seated yearning to break out of the small town, pampered rich girl persona. She craved a walk on the wild side and soon found a like-minded partner in Larson Hobbes.

I didn't need to look far to find background information about Hobbes. His story dominated the news last year, after he shot and killed twenty-three students (and two teachers) at a Daviess County middle school. He spared the state the cost of a lengthy incarceration when he used his final bullet on himself.

Unlike many mass murderers, Hobbes didn't post nihilistic diatribes on social media or leave behind notebooks packed with satanic drawings, swastikas, or horrific "to do" lists. Authorities never found a reason why Larson Hobbes targeted that specific school. They did the usual round of exhaustive interviews with Hobbes' friends (of which there were very few), former teachers, his grandmother (who raised him), and of course, Hope Miller.

Hope swore she knew absolutely nothing about Hobbes' plans to go on a killing spree. After hours of questioning, the police affirmed her story. She was an innocent who had no information and no involvement in the incident.

The "Middle School Massacre" soon faded from the news cycle, as did Hope Miller. She was finally able to get back to a somewhat normal life at KWU.

Benedetto presented me with evidence that strongly indicated Hope was behind the Middle School Massacre. While she obviously wasn't the one who pulled the trigger, she'd driven Larson Hobbes to commit the deed. The question was, "why?"

Benedetto's tech wiz dug deep to find the reason but came up empty. Hope never had a bad day in her life. No humiliating experiences. No grudges against teachers. So again, why target schools? And why young children?

I agreed to fly to Kentucky to observe Hope Miller for a few days. I trusted my instincts. If she showed no signs whatsoever of psychopathic tendencies, I'd come home. If, on the other hand, I felt she was the epitome of evil, I'd take the contract.

I spent a week in Owensboro. After observing Hope for two days and getting a sense of her schedule and rhythms, I stepped up my surveillance. She went for a sixty minute run every morning at 5:00 a.m. through a densely wooded area that bordered the University. On day three, I entered her room and hid a tiny video camera in a light fixture.

Another few days went by. I watched and listened, but Hope showed no hints of being unbalanced. In fact, I was impressed by how diligently she studied and how generous she was with her time and money. She was quick to pay for things, ranging from pizzas for her study group to a few cases a beer for an upcoming coed softball game.

By day seven, I was ready to come home. Hope may have been a murderous puppeteer, but nothing I saw convinced me of that. I declined the job. If I were wrong, it would be the biggest mistake of my life. But if I was right, then I wouldn't be able to live with myself if I killed this intelligent young woman who had such a wonderful future ahead of her.

Benedetto took my decision in stride, completely understanding my reasoning. He had no emotional investment in the contracts. He appeared to get no satisfaction from the results. I believe he saw it as some kind of civic duty or public service.

Weeks went by, and all was quiet. I read the news every day from Kentucky, and there were no incidents. I'd made the right decision about Hope and thought about how close I came to snuffing out the life of someone else's daughter.

On March 19th, I got a call from Benedetto to turn on CNN. They were reporting on a deadly shooting at an elementary school in western Kentucky. Eighteen children were dead and seven were injured. The shooter took his own life before the police could do it for him. I was stunned. It had all the earmarks of the Middle School Massacre. What had I done? Or rather, what could I have stopped?

Later that day the shooter's identity was shared with the public: Khalid Nozari. It was immediately labeled an act of terrorism and the cry for revenge echoed from Frankfort, Kentucky to Washington, DC. The fact that Nozari was American born and had no ties with any terrorist groups didn't matter. People didn't care about the facts. They needed an enemy, and here was one that was tailor-made.

The perfect scapegoat.

Hope Miller had chosen well. I know it was her doing. My theory is that she got word that someone was trying to frame her with a ridiculous account that she was behind the Middle School Massacre. Hope laughed it off, but in reality what she'd done was shift gears. Hope picked up a new recruit, a Muslim no less, and accomplished her goal: a public outrage, the likes of which almost equaled that of 9/11.

It turned out I wasn't the only one who came to the conclusion that this tragedy was the work of Hope Miller. Two days later, while on her morning run, she was shot and killed. There were no witnesses, and the assailant was never caught. Her death made big news in Kentucky, but the rest of the country didn't have the time or interest to mourn the murder of a college coed. They were too busy focusing on the escalating rhetoric coming out of Washington about how America wouldn't sit by idly while terrorists came onto our soil and slaughtered our children. There was even talk about bombing strategic targets in the Middle East.

And all of this could have been avoided.

I'm only one man, and I know I'm not responsible for the actions of anyone else, certainly not for the heinous acts carried out by psychopathic serial killers. Having said that, I can't help but feel the yoke of judgment and inaction.

The case of Hope Miller was unique. It was the first time I had the opportunity to stop a mass murder. If I had killed Hope, would Khalid Nozari have ended up shooting those children? Perhaps, but it's highly unlikely.

David Harper had known in his soul that Hope Miller had been the mastermind, working behind the scenes to manipulate the shooter. He felt sick that he might've prevented the senseless killing, had he taken out Hope Miller a month earlier.

Kelly got up and poured herself another glass of wine, grabbed the Milanos, and stared at her legal pad. *"She might be planning to kill Emma."*

Kelly had to find out the truth, regardless of the risk.

She picked up her phone and called Lisa Reynolds.

23

Sunday

It had been two days since Kelly visited Jessica, and she was eager to see her sister's progress. It was encouraging how quickly Jess had responded to the new treatments, but Kelly had frequently witnessed patients show incredible turnarounds when beginning a new drug regime, only to rapidly peak and then regress. Ofttimes, they ended up worse than before.

Kelly kept her hopes tightly reined in.

She wheeled Jessica down a stone path dappled with early morning light as they made their way into the park-like grounds of Peninsula Oaks. Dr. Papadakis had encouraged Kelly to spend more time with Jessica and provide as much personal stimulus as possible: looking at family photographs, recounting stories of their childhood and sharing news about what was going on in her life. The intent was fine, but family pictures and recollections of happier times tended to remind Kelly of how both of their parents were brutally murdered. There wasn't much joy in reminiscing.

As for chatting about Kelly's life, what was there to say? That she had serious money issues? That her sometime boyfriend was sniffing at the edges of her darkest secrets? Or that she was possibly planning to murder a single mother who might be a homicidal sociopath?

In the past, Kelly had felt comfortable talking to Jess, sharing her sinister plans, and even admitting to killing two people. It was her method of confession, akin to her father keeping a journal. It was healthy for Kelly to release the pressure bubbling up in her mind and soul, specifically because Jessica lacked the ability to comprehend what she was saying.

Kelly had promised herself she would confide in her sister if there ever came a time when Jessica regained a sense of the world around her. However, as the light in Jessica's eyes shone a tad brighter and her gaze seemed to come more into focus, Kelly had second thoughts. It was impossible for her to determine Jessica's growing ability to process information, or her capacity to indiscriminately repeat parts of their conversations. The chance that Jessica would ever recover to that degree was extremely remote but results from medical trials were unpredictable.

Kelly and Jess arrived at their customary bench in an isolated part of the gardens. This was the very site where Kelly had told Jessica that she'd always be there for her and protect her…no matter what.

When Kelly took her sister's hand, Jessica looked into her face, wearing a haunting Mona Lisa smile. For a brief moment, there was a flicker of recognition in her eyes, and she squeezed Kelly's hand.

Kelly could barely speak, her voice choked with emotion. "Jess?"

It was as if hearing her name broke the spell, and the moment was suddenly over. The candle had been snuffed out and the lifeforce yearning to emerge into the light retreated into the depths of the empty shell. Regardless, Kelly pressed forward.

"I'm having lunch in Golden Gate Park today. Remember that area in Peacock Meadow where we used to hide from Mom? It's so peaceful over there. I'm going to have a picnic with a friend of mine."

Jessica was off somewhere in her lost world and didn't react to anything Kelly was saying. Kelly had no idea if her words were penetrating some tiny portion of her sister's consciousness.

"She's not actually a friend. Her name is Lisa, and I want to get to know her better." Kelly paused, considering how much to say, then continued. "The truth is, I *need* to know her better. She's, uh, complicated and may have done some very bad things. She might be planning to do something truly terrible, and if she is, I think I have to stop her."

As she had in the past, Kelly felt better after giving voice to her secrets. It provided her with a degree of clarity to speak aloud the deed she was contemplating. To her relief, Jessica's flat expression hadn't changed. No judging, nor any acquiescence.

The wind picked up, carrying the earthy scent of oak trees and the creamy almond aroma of lilacs. Jessica slowly turned her face to meet the fragrant air head on. After twenty years of being cloaked in a dense veil of oblivion, was the old Jessica stirring?

If so, how cognizant was she?

Ida Samuel's studio apartment was just shy of 300 square feet and her window overlooked a courtyard with weedy flowerbeds and a hedge that had taken on the look of a wooly mammoth. All of that for only $1,900 per month. Plus, she had a forty-five-minute bus ride to work. Life in the big city fell well short of her expectations.

She sat cross-legged on the floor, blurry eyed and exhausted, contemplating the charts on the wall behind her tiny sofa. She'd spent all night creating a tapestry of medical information, complete with patient contact data and brief descriptions of their symptoms. Tacked up alongside was a large street map of San Francisco covered with notations and dates. "Why can't I find the connections?" she pondered aloud.

She struggled to her feet and shuffled to the kitchenette, which consisted of a mini fridge, a compact range and a microwave. Ida had added a coffee pot and a blender, which took up most of the counter space. All in all, it was depressing as hell and she wondered, not for the first time, why she'd agreed to travel to San Francisco for work. She could've found a job in a smaller, homier, and much less expensive location. Someplace where she could ride a bike to the office, walk down the street and exchange greetings with the locals, and return home each night to a comfy little cottage with overstuffed furniture, a wood-burning fireplace and a kitchen large enough to turn around in.

The coffee pot was empty, which was just as well. Her acid reflux was acting up. Ida pulled a can of sugar-free Red Bull from the fridge and took a long swig. She felt the rush immediately and knew she was in for a head-splitting crash, but she was determined to spend a few more hours attempting to make sense of the patient map in front of her. There had to be a pattern. Something linked these people together.

Ida desperately wanted to unlock this mystery, but she suffered from a lack of confidence. All through high school, college and medical school, a tiny voice chirped at her that she wasn't good enough. Not smart enough. Not determined enough to make the cut. There were countless times when she was ready to give in to the voice and say, "screw it." Leave it all behind and not face the prospect of failure on a daily basis. But there were two things driving her forward; fear of not living up to her father's expectations, and drugs.

It was during her sophomore year at Hiram College. Ida had two papers due, and a midterm test in Anatomy, that she'd fallen very far behind. She saw no way out and decided that the only course of action was to quit school, slink home in utter shame, and see if she could find a job back in Sugarcreek. Maybe work at the Alpine Hills Museum or learn how to make primitive furniture from one of the many Amish craftspeople in town.

Ida's roommate offered another option. Dexedrine. Pop a couple of those babies, and by the end of the weekend, she'd be back on track. Ida had never ventured into the world of pharmaceuticals, but when she weighed taking a few orange pills versus moving back in with her parents, she figured "why not?" She had no idea at the time that Dexedrine would become an integral part of her life. And it was not long after that she started taking the occasional Valium to deal with her increased stress.

Uppers and downers. A dangerous chemical see-saw.

As Ida trudged back to her incident wall, her laptop chimed. She looked at the clock and saw it was 10:00 a.m. Damn. She'd forgotten that her mother had scheduled a Zoom call. Could she ignore it? Pretend she was in the shower, or maybe out on a Sunday bike ride with an imaginary friend? She knew if she chose to duck the call, she'd pay for it later with a heavy dose of guilt, followed by a double helping of her mother's disappointment.

Ida plopped down on the too firm sofa, positioned the laptop on the flimsy coffee table, put on a smile and logged in. A moment later, her parents' faces were in the room with her.

They exchanged morning greetings. It took maximum self-control for Betty Samuel not to make note of Ida's appearance. Her pasty complexion. The bags under her eyes. The overall look of someone who'd been up all night...several nights in a row.

Ida's father, Doc Joe, was looking equally unwell, but he had reason to. Lymphoma was eating away at him. He'd been a robust, cheerful and positive force, but as his life slowly ebbed away, it was too painful for Ida to see him like this. She wanted to remember her father as the man he was before he got sick, and so she avoided him, not realizing how much he looked forward to seeing her, talking to her, being part of her life. It was these interactions that kept him going.

Despite Joe's fatigue and constant pain, he radiated joy. He saw the notations on the wall behind the sofa and asked Ida what she was up to. She explained the sudden upswing of a bug that was going around San Francisco. So far, they hadn't been able to identify it or the source.

"Hold your computer up so I can take a look," he said. His voice was thin, wispy.

Ida placed the laptop on a few books and angled the screen so her father could see the wall in its entirety.

"Very impressive work, Doctor," he said with pride. "More contact points would be helpful. Have you heard from the hospitals?"

Ida shook her head. "Not many." If people were nauseous or dizzy, or had a few random pains, they didn't go to a hospital. Most simply took some aspirin and rode it out.

"What baffles me is the cases are spread all over the city," Ida continued. "You'd expect to find a cluster around a school, or an office complex."

"It's probably a seasonal thing that will run its course," said Joe.

"Something in my gut tells me it's more."

"Which makes you an excellent doctor."

Ida blushed. *An excellent doctor* was the last thing she felt like.

Betty couldn't hold it in any longer. "Sweetheart, you look exhausted. Can't someone else do this? Maybe one of the other doctors who's more familiar with the city can take this off your plate, at least until you get settled in."

"It's my *job*, mother" Ida replied. "I can handle it."

Ida was the new kid. The wet-behind-the-ears doctor from the sticks. She embraced this opportunity to prove herself. She may not have years of experience, and may not know the city very well, but she wasn't going to let that stand in the way of her showing Kelly and the others that she could pull her weight. That she belonged.

The conversation devolved into idle chat about the folks back home. Who was doing what with whom, and so forth. They managed to find enough mundane topics of conversation until the free forty-minute Zoom session expired.

Just before they signed off, Doc Joe said he'd give her medical problem some thought. "Two heads are better that one," he said with a small grin.

Ida completed their little joke, "Unless they're on the same body."

Smiles all around.

Ida barely got her laptop closed before she broke into tears.

24

Kelly laid out a stadium blanket on a grassy patch in a corner of the park. On top of the blanket, she placed a large wicker hamper. The moment she'd made the call she'd put herself at potential risk...again. Benedetto would be angry...again. Maybe even speechless, which would be a first.

Regardless, she had to play this out. As she waited, she ran potential scenarios in her head in the event she decided to go forward with the contract. A household accident? An exotic poison? A drowning would be ironic payback, but probably too difficult to orchestrate. Kelly was lost in homicidal scenarios when she heard a woman call her name.

Lisa emerged from a path through the trees. "I've spent a lot of time in this park, but never knew this little slice of heaven existed."

"It's away from the crowds, which is why I like it."

Lisa joined Kelly on the blanket and patted the picnic hamper. "What've you got in here?"

"Let's just say I hope you're hungry."

As Kelly started unpacking the hamper, Lisa laid out the containers. "You've got enough for a family of eight."

"Whenever I go to Molinari, I kind of lose control." The last items Kelly pulled out were two bottles of wine. Red and white. "I didn't know if you wanted wine."

"Drinking wine on the Sabbath is God's will," Lisa said with a mischievous grin. "I've also been known to have a glass at home after a tough day."

Kelly felt guilty about enabling a person with dependency issues, but she needed to know the truth. After spending two stints in rehab for drugs and alcohol, Lisa should've been firmly ensconced in "the program." That was clearly not the case.

Kelly tossed Lisa a corkscrew, which she deftly plucked out of the air with her left hand.

"Oh, you're a southpaw," said Kelly nonchalantly.

Lisa held up both hands. "Ambidextrous. I started out right hand dominant, but when I was nine, I broke my right wrist in three places and was in a cast for almost a year. We were learning cursive in school, so I had to write with my left. Since then, they're interchangeable."

One more piece of information to add to the list.

A short time later, their plates were piled with food, and they were onto their second glasses of wine. Small talk finally provided a segue for Kelly to causally mention an imaginary ex-husband.

Lisa perked up. "You too? What happened?"

"We were young," Kelly said. "Met during our residency. Long, brutal hours of work and hyper-passionate moments of release. We fell in love, or at least, what we thought was love. A few years later, I caught him with a pharmaceutical rep." Kelly shook her head with a sad smile. "Big Pharma intentionally hires hot young babes to push their drugs. I'm sure they did a study on doctors' afterhours habits and designed the perfect bait. One with long legs, a great ass and preprogrammed to say 'yes.'"

Lisa drained her glass and a moment later, it was full again. "It's like you've read the book of my life."

Kelly wondered if she'd gone too far with her fabricated past. Did she cleave too closely to Lisa's own history?

Lisa offered up her own story. "Bob, my ex, had an affair with a car dealer at a convention in Vegas. That was the first time. The next time was years later. I was out of town dealing with a family issue, and I came back to discover he was at it again with a different woman. There I was, going through a very difficult personal journey and he's banging some tramp."

"How do you guys get along now?"

"We don't. He married that tramp, and we only speak when it's about our daughter."

"Oh, you have a daughter. How old is she?"

"Thirteen. That wonderful age when they suddenly decide they're so much smarter than you."

"Does she live with you?"

"Right now, she's spending most of the time with her father."

"That must be hard."

"It's not that bad," Lisa said. "I adore having Emma around and everything, but I've gotta admit that being responsible for a kid full-time complicates the hell out of the dating scene." Lisa took a long pull on her wine and dabbed at her mouth. "That sounded really selfish, didn't it? I mean, I love Emma to pieces, but it's kind of nice to have a break once in a while."

"So, Emma's an only child?"

Lisa cocked her head, as if she were listening to the wind for answers. Her face was a mask of calm, but her mind was churning up memories she'd hoped would never resurface. Vivid memories of the horrific deaths of two children.

Lisa blinked a few times and came back to the present.

"Sorry, I kinda blanked there for a minute. What were we talking about?"

"I asked if Emma was your only child."

"Oh, right. She had an older sister. Sydney. Died last year."

"Oh my god," said Kelly. "That's horrible."

"That's why Emma is so precious to me. And to her father."

Just then, Lisa's phone rang. She checked the screen, and her face took on a stony demeanor. "Speak of the devil."

"Go ahead," urged Kelly.

Lisa shook her head. "I'm not going to let him ruin a perfectly nice afternoon."

Kelly shrugged. "It might be about your daughter."

Lisa reconsidered, then took the call with an icy edge. "Yes?"

Whatever Lisa was hearing, she didn't like. "This is bullshit, and you know it!" As she listened, her face bloomed with anger and her responses were terse. "No! That's not what we agreed on!" She ended the conversation with, "Damn right I'm calling my lawyer!"

Kelly tried to act like she hadn't been privy to this, but there was no way around it. Lisa saw her discomfort and apologized that she'd lost her cool. As she aggressively cranked open the second bottle of wine, Lisa explained that Bob had gone behind her back and filed for exclusive custody of Emma.

"He promised we'd be civil and work something out, but he was clearly playing me. Stalling for time. Cheating on me again. He wants primary custody of Emma because he and the new wife are moving to Detroit, and now he thinks he's taking *my* daughter with them. That's not gonna happen."

Lisa drank with a purpose. The more she drank, the more her façade crumbled. Behind the veil was a twisted creature full of venom and hate. Kelly felt a compassionate urge to step in and comfort this woman who was clearly in pain, but held herself in check. This is what she'd come for.

She'd hoped to catch a glimpse of Lisa's darker side.

What she got instead was a full-blown transformation.

Lisa's rage ran its course, and she was spent. Emotionally drained. She composed herself, apologizing again for her outburst. Her mood lightened when she mentioned that starting tomorrow, she had Emma all to herself for an entire week and was going to spoil the hell out of her, beginning with a Katy Perry concert tomorrow night in Oakland. In the meantime, she was going to contact her lawyer to get an injunction against Bob.

She reiterated that no one was going to take her daughter from her.

25

Kelly didn't know if Benedetto would be working on a Sunday, but decided to swing by and confess that she'd once again crossed the line with Lisa. Of course, Benedetto probably already knew where they picnicked, what they ate, and what they talked about. He had eyes and ears everywhere.

When she arrived at his office, she was surprised to be met by Cora Mathews and wondered if this poor woman ever got a day off. Cora explained that Mr. Benedetto wasn't here. In fact, she had no idea where he was.

"Is that unusual? Do you generally know his schedule on the weekends?"

A few minutes later they were seated in Benedetto's sumptuous office. "Mr. Benedetto is single and has no children," Cora said. "No brothers or sisters, and his parents have long since passed, so I'm the closest thing he has to family. Because of the unpredictable disposition of some of his former clients, I make it a point to check in with him on the weekends. I suppose it's a latent mothering instinct."

"I can understand a prosecutor being threatened, but why would a defense attorney have enemies?"

"There are always disgruntled defendants who are unhappy with how their cases were settled or have second thoughts about plea bargains. Some of them are prone to violence."

Based upon the story Benedetto related to Kelly days ago, "prone to violence" was no exaggeration.

Cora saw that in her face and continued. "Kelly, I think it's time for you to fully understand how much Mr. Benedetto confides in me." She exuded such proficiency and confidence it was easy to see why a powerful man like Benedetto would feel comfortable sharing information with her. But would he share *everything*?

"Trust is important in a good working relationship," said Kelly warily.

"Definitely. And I want you to feel you can trust me, too."

"I'm not sure what you mean."

"I know all about your father's outside interests, and yours as well."

Kelly played dumb as long as she could. "Outside interests?"

"Gideon."

Kelly was stunned. "I'm surprised Mr. Benedetto discussed that with anyone."

"It was unavoidable. I'm the one who gathers the information and prepares the dossiers."

"*You're* the tech expert? The hacker?"

"Surprising, I know. I have a skillset not usually found in women my age. I was there at the very beginning of the computer era and have kept up with the advancements."

Cora Mathews was extremely humble. Her *skillset* was extraordinary for any woman or man, regardless of age. She'd been a pre-teen math prodigy who'd gone on to become a computer virtuoso. The NSA recruited her out of college to write code that later became the basis for sophisticated worldwide surveillance. One would never know that behind her sedate demeanor was someone who'd suffered through a bad marriage and grieved for a daughter who took her own life.

"Why are you telling me this now?" asked Kelly.

"I've been unable to reach Mr. Benedetto since last night. That's not like him."

Kelly suddenly felt lightheaded. Was it the wine with lunch or the fact that Benedetto could be in jeopardy, which would have far-reaching consequences for them all.

"I've been monitoring dozens of message boards, as well as Dark Web sites, and when I get anything, I'll let you know. I don't want to alarm you, especially since you've got a lot on your mind, including what to do about Lisa Reynolds."

"The situation's awkward. Mr. Benedetto strongly advised me to drop it, but I couldn't just walk away. Not without knowing if she intends to kill her daughter."

"He told me about your conversation. That the two of you have disparate attitudes about operating procedures."

"That's one way to put it. He was comfortable dealing with my father, but not nearly as comfortable with me."

"Mr. Benedetto has a much greater sense of responsibility for your wellbeing then he did for your father."

"Because I'm a woman?"

"Because you're more emotionally vested. Some people would say that comes along with being a woman, but we both know that's a sexist generalization. You feel a need to get inside your target's head, which is dangerous, and that makes Mr. Benedetto nervous."

"How else can I determine if Lisa's a threat?"

"It's no easy task. Your father took on many jobs where the target was undeniably guilty of terrible crimes. In the case of Lisa Reynolds, it's not a question of punishing her for the deeds she may have committed, but specifically to protect her daughter."

"Even if I conclude Lisa's planning to kill her daughter, I'm not sure I could do what's necessary to stop her. I honestly don't know if I'm strong enough to deal with the psychological impact of committing another murder. Unlike my father, I find it impossible to rationalize taking a person's life."

"Regardless of the circumstances?"

"You're asking, if I had a daughter and the only way I could protect her would be to kill someone else? I'd have no choice."

"Let's say your daughter was murdered. Would you take revenge upon the person who committed the crime?"

"We're getting back to where this all began. My father killing Musselwhite. Were I in that same situation…no, I don't think I could kill strictly out of vengeance. Could you?"

"Yes." In fact, Cora had brought revenge down upon the man who was responsible for the death of her daughter, but that wasn't a story she was about to share. "I'll do some digging and see if there's anything more I can find out on Lisa."

"Thank you. And by the way, I'm glad you told me about your role in…all of this. It's nice to have a woman I can talk to. In fact, I was planning to confide in my closest friend…"

"Alexandra Russo."

"I shouldn't be surprised you'd know that."

"When Mr. Benedetto had me prepare a dossier on you after your father's death, it was extremely thorough. You said you were *planning* to confide in her. Have you?"

Kelly shook her head. "The conversation took a different turn, and it never came up."

"I'd suggest you reconsider mentioning anything. It could result in putting her in a compromising and potentially dangerous situation."

"I hadn't thought about that."

"When you need to talk, I'm here for you. I always have been."

"I appreciate that. And call me when you get anything on Mr. Benedetto. I'm worried about him."

"So am I."

26

The man was perched on a stool in front of a cigarette-scarred wooden bar top. He was rail thin, the skin on his face pulled taut, revealing the contours of his skull. His face was an olio of leftover parts: large wideset eyes, a delicate, tapered nose, small protruding ears and a thin-lipped mouth tightly packed with tiny white teeth that would've been more at home in the jaws of a child. His dishwater blonde hair was prematurely streaked with gray and slicked back tight to his scalp, which only served to accentuate his severe features.

Laid out on the bar was a ruler-perfect line of ten nickel-plated bullets. The man counted the bullets from left to right, silently mouthing the numbers from one to ten. He counted again, this time going right to left, which he found more challenging. His mind worked better when things were in their proper order. Left to right. Top to bottom. A to Z. He took a deep breath and began again. One, two, three…

A groggy voice behind him asked, "Where am I?"

The man stopped counting, his finger hovering above the cartridges. His annoyance at being interrupted was evident. He started anew. One, two…

This time, the question was louder, more forceful. "I asked, where am I?"

The man's focus stayed on the bullets. He finished his count, then carefully, slowly, loaded the ammunition into an empty magazine. When the mag was full, he brought it to his nose, taking in the scent of Hoppes gun oil. It was a smell he found foreign, and yet, it stirred something inside of him.

He picked up a 9mm Baretta from the bar and slid the mag into the handle until it clicked into place. He liked the sound of the pieces linking together. He liked the heft of the gun in his hand. It made him feel powerful. Important.

Perhaps, even normal.

He slowly turned and gazed around the room. Even though he'd spent many hours there in the past few days, every time he allowed his eyes to drift, it was like he was exploring his surroundings for the first time. Three beer taps collected dust. Glass shelves that once held expensive bottles of fine liquor were bare. A large flat-screen TV across from the bar was dark. And a well-dressed, but disheveled lawyer from San Francisco was sitting on a thin blanket, his left wrist handcuffed to a brass pole that extended from floor to ceiling.

The man pointed the gun at his prisoner. He sighted down the barrel, and blew out a puff of air, like he was taking target practice.

Benedetto had dozens of questions and went with the most obvious. "Who are you and why am I here?"

The man stared at his prisoner for a fleeting moment, then averted his eyeline, focusing on a spot near the ceiling. Eye contact made him uncomfortable. When he spoke, his voice came out a tad too loud, as if he were hard of hearing. "I want answers." His words had a flat intonation that made him sound almost robotic.

Benedetto, now more alert, took inventory of his situation. He gave the handcuff a tug. It held fast. He wasn't going anywhere.

He slowly got to his feet. "*You* want answers?"

The man nodded, exasperated. Didn't he just say that? "Answers. Yes, answers."

"How about *you* answer some of *my* questions, then I'll answer some of yours. Let's start with an easy one. Is this a stripper pole?"

The man was confused, which in turn made him frustrated. This was not how he planned it. Not how he'd scripted the conversation over and over in his head. Not at all. He needed to take charge, but he wasn't a take-charge kind of guy.

"The bar's there to keep you in place." As if the situation needed more explanation, he continued. "I'm renting this house. Just renting."

"And you've turned this man cave into a holding cell."

"Just renting!" His anger was quickly rising. Why did he have to repeat himself to his prisoner? He didn't like how this was going. He didn't like it one bit.

Benedetto looked around the windowless room. There was nothing to indicate where he was or the time of day. "How long have I been here?"

"Twenty-one hours, thirty-seven minutes." He didn't need a watch. Some things he just knew.

Benedetto was an expert at cross-examination in the courtroom, but he was swimming in uncharted waters here. In order to develop a strategy, he needed to gather as much information as possible.

"You're obviously an intelligent and resourceful man. The last thing I remember was walking down the street. How did I get *here*?"

"I've watched you for many weeks. You go to the same restaurant every Saturday. Same time. Walk home the same route. I'm very good at planning. Yes, I am. I had Mott steal a car and get a bottle of desflurane from a medical supply company. Desflurane is used in operating rooms. Knocks you right out. Yes, it does."

"Who's Mott?"

"My turn for questions."

Benedetto held up a cuffed wrist. "You didn't have to go to such lengths. I could've answered your questions over the phone."

"But you wouldn't. No way."

The man slowly shifted his line of sight to the other side of the room. "I'm a businessman. This is business. Yes. Answer questions, I pay you, you go free."

"You have a unique way of conducting business."

The man looked perplexed and asked in earnest, "Was that a joke?" Benedetto realized he was dealing with someone who was most likely on the autism spectrum.

"It wasn't meant to be a joke."

"Okay. Let's get to it. Yes, right to it. Who is Gideon?"

If Benedetto hadn't been mentally and emotionally hardened from years working as a criminal attorney, he might've flinched upon hearing the name. He'd dreaded this moment ever since David Harper had taken the life of Charles Crane; Gideon's first contract murder. Two months ago, Gideon's identity had been uncovered by Tommy Moretti and then shared with his cousin Anthony, but both were dead, and David's secret was buried along with them. Or so Benedetto thought.

"I have no idea what you're talking about," Benedetto said in an Oscar-worthy performance.

"No lies!" the man blurted. He swung up the Baretta, his hand quivering uncontrollably. "I have *good* information! *Very* good!"

Benedetto shrank back against the wall, unsuccessfully willing himself to get smaller.

The man violently shook his head back and forth, attempting to dislodge the rage that had overtaken him. He took three deep breaths and muttered something to himself. It was a mantra he'd learned to control his anger. It took a few, very tense minutes for him to eventually regain his stolid composure. "Next time, I want the truth. Yes. No more lies."

The man turned and headed for the door, silently counting every step on his way out of the room.

27

Pete sat in the corner of the bar nursing a fifteen dollar, locally brewed, small batch IPA. The Rialto was the latest trendy spot in the city. The luster would fade in a few months, but for now it was doing a brisk business, especially for a Sunday night.

Pete hadn't come to drink or to revel in the company of the too-hip patrons. He came to observe the table for eight where Myles Spencer was holding court. Spencer's posse laughed on cue at his crude jokes. A skinny, bespectacled groupie wearing a flat brim Blue Jays cap handed his Amex card to a swole, shaved head waiter who'd arrived with another round of bitter "hop forward" ales to keep the great artist happy.

Pete had no idea what he was accomplishing by being there, slowly going broke on overpriced drinks, but he was determined to stay on Spencer's ass until he could find the chink in his armor. Every criminal had one. Especially those that went through the day intoxicated or high.

The session with Yegor hadn't yielded anything concrete. Pete knew the whole notion of a mysterious hitman was most likely a total fantasy. However, it hadn't been a complete waste of time. Acquiring access to the underground message boards where drugs were traded, sexual liaisons were openly solicited, and the use of extreme force was offered in return for fair compensation, could potentially lead to a trove of valuable information pertaining to other cases in the future.

As he finished his beer, his thoughts drifted back to five days ago when he'd had drinks with Kelly. Their relationship had become increasingly strained since her father's murder, and Pete was afraid that what was once a blossoming romance was now withering on the vine.

He recalled what she'd said before she left that night: "*I know things have been strained between us. I've just got so much on my mind…*"

It was a shopworn blowoff line, akin to "It's not you. It's me." In Kelly's case, that line rang true. She'd suffered a serious loss when her father was killed, and now she was not only in mourning, but mired in a financial crisis as well. There wasn't much Pete could do to make either situation better. Shortly after David Harper died, Pete had toyed with the idea of asking Kelly to marry him. At the time, he wasn't sure it was a good idea.

In retrospect, it would've been a disaster.

As he fantasized about a brighter future for the two of them, the waiter swung by and dropped off a 'full-bodied dark stout.'

"I didn't order this."

"Compliments of Myles Spencer."

Pete looked over to Spencer's table to find him staring back, a sloppy, drunken smile on his face. Spencer gave him a salute that ended in the bird. Pete responded by slowly pouring the beer out into a large potted fern conveniently located next to his table, then fixed Spencer with a challenging glare.

Spencer's smile faded. Challenge accepted.

Spencer rose from his chair and started to make his way across the bar, unsteadily weaving his way through the obstacle course of four-tops.

His voice rose above the din. "Not very considerate, Inspector. Man buys you a beer, you should drink it."

Conversations in the bar faded as patrons were less interested in their own banter than they were in what was unfolding. Local hero versus some stuffy looking outsider who smelled like a cop.

Spencer's volume increased with each step. "Maybe thank him and even reciprocate. Instead, you told me to shove it up my ass."

Pete kept his cool as Spencer arrived at his table. "What the hell are you doing here? Why are you following me?"

"Settle down," said Pete. "I just came in for a beer."

"Bullshit. Never seen you in here before, and now you just happen to swing by 'cause you're thirsty?"

Pete hadn't anticipated a confrontation, but he wasn't about to back away from one. "Cool it, Myles."

"Fuck you. Don't tell me to fucking cool it."

Spencer's friends uprooted from their chairs and gathered around to cheer him on.

Pete stood, assessing the situation which had all the earmarks of something that could quickly escalate out of control. "Everyone relax," he said in a commanding voice.

"This guy's a cop," said Spencer, playing to his audience. "Tried to stick me with shooting some drug dealer, and now he's here to fucking harass me."

There were a few outbursts of trite, pre-packaged, phrases; "fuck him," "police harassment," and "that's bullshit, man." These days, there was no telling when even the smallest incident could snowball into something ugly, so Pete thought it best to take his leave.

Spencer had other ideas. As Pete attempted to make his way out, Spencer stepped in front of him, their faces almost touching.

"Stay the fuck away from me, pig, or I'll get you busted back to walking a beat."

"Really? And how exactly would you do that?"

"My family donates a shit-ton of money to the people who run this city. My old man's got the mayor on speed-dial."

"I don't care if he has the president on speed-dial. You're all talk, and from what I've heard so far, it's all lies."

Spencer turned away for a brief moment, then threw a roundhouse punch. Pete slipped the punch and wrapped Spencer up in an armbar. He pulled Spencer close and whispered in his ear, "I know you killed those dealers. Word is the Norteños are looking for the shooter. If they were to find out who pulled that trigger…." The repercussions didn't need to be verbalized.

148

Pete released Spencer. "I could file charges against you for assaulting an officer, but you're not worth the paperwork."

Pete shouldered Spencer out of his way and started to move through the crowd when a reflection in the front window caught his eye. He ducked just in time to avoid being clubbed by the wine bottle in Spencer's grasp. Pete instinctively reacted with a hard right cross that nailed Spencer on the bridge of his nose.

The artist collapsed to the floor like a suit of clothing that suddenly realized there was nobody inside. A puddle of dark red blood was already welling around his face.

Pete stood over him, thinking about the reams of paperwork ahead. He didn't know then that paperwork would be the least of his problems.

28

Monday

It hadn't taken long for the shit to hit the fan and cover Pete from head to toe. Myles had been carted off to the hospital, where an ER doctor reset his nose. A flurry of indignant phone calls were made, and by 8:00 a.m. Monday morning, Pete found himself sitting at a conference table with a bevy of dour-faced men, including his lieutenant, the precinct captain, Pete's union rep, and a pompous, triple-chinned liaison from the mayor's office named Toby Florence.

Refreshments were not served.

Pete was informed he'd be on administrative leave while last night's incident was investigated. He maintained his actions were strictly self-defense, but was interrupted by Florence, whose arrogance failed to cover up his insecurities. "Self-defense would've been protecting yourself from attack and subduing the subject. Sending him to the hospital with a broken septum, which may require reconstructive surgery in the future, falls squarely under the category of police brutality."

"The *subject* swung at me with a wine bottle. From behind."

The lieutenant spoke up, "Preliminary reports from witnesses indicate Mr. Spencer had picked up a wine bottle with the intention of pouring a drink. Not swinging it at your head."

"The witnesses are lying," Pete protested.

"Which is why we're investigating. Until then, you're on leave for conduct unbecoming of an officer."

Pete turned to his union rep. "Do I have any recourse here?"

Before the rep could chime in, the captain spoke up. "Inspector. Your actions have been noted by the brass downtown and by City Hall. We've been instructed to move quickly to minimize legal exposure and the inevitable negative PR."

The SFPD covered all their bases when investigating officer misconduct. It had more to do with managing public perceptions than it did with rooting out the truth. In this day and age of social media where one IG blast from Kylie Jenner could instantly hit 380 million followers, departments had to be extremely careful about staying ahead of negative PR, (and not pissing off Kylie). Myles Spencer was no Jenner, or even a Kardashian, but he still had over a hundred thousand followers of his own, so a few well-worded tweets and some pics of his displaced nose would spread like wildfire in less than an hour.

Pete scoffed. "Negative PR, because some drunk, entitled asshole got clocked for trying to assault a police officer."

"Pete," said the lieutenant, "that asshole's parents have powerful friends. At the very least, you can expect a civil suit. Plus, Spencer's lawyer says you threatened to tell Norteño gang members that he was the one who killed that dealer in the Mission, thereby putting a target on his back. If that's true, you'll be facing departmental discipline."

"Let me remind all of you that Myles Spencer is not some model, law-abiding citizen. He's been popped multiple times by this department for drug violations..."

"Alleged," interjected Florence.

"And," Pete continued, "is the prime suspect in the murder of Felix Molina, as well as the two other dealers who were killed..."

Florence interrupted again. "The mayor has spoken directly to Mr. Spencer's legal counsel, Deanna Frost, who made it clear that Myles Spencer has been unduly harassed by Inspector Ericson. And, I might add, this is not the first time the inspector has wrongfully targeted one of that lawyer's clients." He swiveled his chair to face Pete. "Do I need to remind you about Leonard Bach, who you attempted to frame for murder, and who the jury found not guilty?"

"I don't care what the jury said. He was guilty as hell."

"Not in the eyes of the law, Inspector. The same law that you are sworn to uphold." Florence smiled, having driven home his point.

Pete was about to say something he'd regret when the union rep grabbed his arm and shook his head.

The City Hall toady went on to say that Spencer's legal team had strongly considered filing suit against Inspector Ericson and SFPD, when the mayor personally got them to back off with the caveat that Ericson be suspended. In return, Spencer agreed to refrain from giving interviews or posting anything on social media regarding the incident at the Rialto until the department completed its investigation. "However," concluded Florence, "there is still the real possibility of a suit being filed in the future."

Pete couldn't stay bottled up for another second. "This is such bullshit!"

The union rep quickly cut in. "Inspector, at this time it's best to keep further thoughts to yourself. When we're done here, you and I will discuss your rights and what happens next. You've got nothing to gain by voicing your opinion on the matter."

Pete Ericson had a flawless record. His career had been on the rise. Not one complaint in his jacket. Until now.

If Myles Spencer wanted a war, he'd get one.

Alexa was an early riser and usually the first one in the office. This Monday was no different. She'd arrived at 7:00 a.m., armed with coffee, muffins and pages of notes regarding the clinic's financial records.

One of the details that caught her eye was that all the amounts paid to David Harper were under ten thousand dollars, which was the IRS threshold.

Alexa had compiled a list of the companies and associations that had paid David, and she'd begun cursory research into about half of them. They all had slick, professional-looking websites, but none provided anything more than the most generic details. She'd sent emails to a few and had yet to receive any responses. She was beginning to think she never would.

The next company on her list was Parkview Healthcare. She brought up their website and found the listing of corporate officers. The president and CEO was a man named Jacob Locke. She read his bio and noted that he received his MBA from Columbia. Her alma mater.

She dug around the internet, looking for more information on people named "Jacob Locke." A Google search yielded a contractor in Florida, a process server in Alabama, an engineering student at the University of Cincinnati, and a few others. No corporate CEOs who worked in the medical field.

Alexa picked up her phone and hit the speed dial for an old friend of hers.

"Columbia School of Business. Alumni relations. This is Milena speaking. How can I help you?" She sounded cheerful, which was fitting given that Milena Hayashi was the most upbeat person Alexa knew.

"Milena. It's Alexa Russo. How're you doing, girl?"

"Alexa! I'm fantastic. Wonderful to hear your voice. How are things on the Left Coast?"

"Earthquakes, fires and restaurant closures. The usual."

"You make it sound so glam. What can I do for you? Are you preparing to send us another incredibly generous check to add to your scholarship fund?"

"Not today. I'm actually looking for a fellow alum and hoping you can dig up his contact info."

"Definitely. I'm sitting at the computer right now."

"His name is Jacob Locke, with an 'e.' I'm guessing he graduated with an MBA in the early to mid-nineties."

Alexa heard Milena's fingers flying across her keyboard. It only took a few moments for her to come back with the answer. "He's not here. Let me try one other thing. We have a data base which lists people in the MBA program who either transferred or dropped out prior to graduation...and...he's not there either. You sure he's an alumnus of Columbia?"

"That's what's shown on the website. Maybe they made a mistake."

"Or maybe he graduated from some lesser business school, like Harvard, and was eager to impress," said Milena with a smile in her voice.

"That's probably it. Thanks for the information."

"So, when are you coming back out? There's a new head chef at Le Monde who's doing an insane seven course tasting menu. The Columbia Business School Alumni Association would be honored to pick up the tab."

"I'll let you know. Ciao."

Alexa disconnected, picked up her desk phone and punched in an extension. "Gus, it's Alexa. When you get in, can you swing by my office? I need your input on something."

She hung up, wondering what Dr. David Harper had been hiding.

29

Alma Sanchez had flown into a rage when she found Diego in a deep opiate-aided sleep and discovered the one remaining hydrocodone. She couldn't really blame him for using the pills to staunch the pain, but she sure as hell could blame Tomás for giving his little brother drugs that could lead to serious complications.

Alma had no idea how to get hold of Tomás, so she called Oscar. Even though he was still angry at his little brother, he went ballistic when he heard what Tomás had done.

Oscar arrived and explained to his mother that he was already looking for Tomás to settle a territorial dispute. All her sons, with the exception of Diego, had been in the gangs. She'd learned long ago she couldn't pull her older boys out, but she forbade them talking about their business in her house because she wanted to keep Diego as far away from their illegal dealings as possible. Before Tomás was sent to the Youth Facility, he'd accused her of being an *avestruz*, an ostrich with her head buried in the sand. Alma didn't care. Her house, her rules.

Now Oscar had even more reason to find his older brother. Alma didn't ask what he intended to do when he found Tomás. She didn't want to know. Maybe she was an *avestruz* after all, but that didn't mean she'd stop trying to guide her boys in the right direction.

"*Mijo*, it's not too late to get out."

"Get out? You mean the Norteños? That's crazy."

"I worry about you all the time. What's more important? The gang or *su familia*?"

"The gang *is* my family."

Alma was staggered. "How can you say that?"

"You and Diego are family too, but don't push me to decide which one means more."

The message was clear. If he'd be forced to make a choice, Alma would lose another son. She took his hand in hers. "Promise me one thing. Never repeat that to Diego. It would break his heart."

Oscar nodded and started to pull his hand away when Alma gripped it tighter. "And never let Diego be drawn into the gang. Swear it to me."

"*Lo prometo.*"

"*Gracias.* Now, go see your brother."

Oscar sat down on the sofa and brushed the hair from Diego's sweaty forehead. "How you feelin', D?"

Tears instantly swam in Diego's sleepy eyes. Oscar was the closest thing he had to a father figure, and yet Diego had betrayed him. He didn't blame Oscar for being mad, but Diego still loved him and needed him in his life.

"Tired, and my stomach hurts."

"You got any more of those pills?"

Diego groggily shook his head.

"Don't fuckin' lie to me."

"I'm not. I swear." The tears fell freely now.

Oscar cradled Diego in his arms. "Okay. It's cool. It's cool."

Alma watched from the doorway, tears rolling down her cheeks as well. She'd suffered so much pain and grief over the years with regard to her sons. It gave her a warm feeling to see them like this. And it gave her renewed hope that maybe one day Oscar would find his way out of the gang and go straight.

She truly was an *avestruz.*

The clinic was generally teeming on Monday mornings, packed with weekend warriors who pushed it too far, or revelers who pushed it too hard. For whatever reason, this Monday was light, which gave Kelly a few moments to duck into her office and do some reading.

Cora had sent over additional information on Lisa Reynolds. There was a thin file concerning Bob's first wife, Trish Reynolds.

Her autopsy showed she'd died from an overdose of Vicodin. An attached notation from the police detective who handled the case stated that Bob Reynolds swore his wife never took Vicodin, and as far as he knew, didn't have a prescription for it. A look at her medical records bore that out. Cora also included a copy of Lisa Reynolds's medical history that indicated she'd filled a prescription for Vicodin just a few days before Trish's death.

Again, barely enough to raise an eyebrow of doubt, but when you staked up all those coincidental facts, they formed a pointillist portrait of a potentially dangerous, sociopathic killer.

There was a knock on Kelly's door, which gave her time to stash the documents before the door opened and Ida leaned in.

"You wanted to see me, Doctor?"

"Come in," Kelly said. "Have a seat."

Ida had an uneasy feeling. She'd never been called to the principal's office, but she imagined it would feel a lot like this.

Kelly got straight to the point. "Talk to me about the Dexedrine and Valium."

Ida felt the blood rush to her head, her skin flushed with embarrassment and guilt. Ida wore her emotions, and her innermost feelings, like a vulnerable second skin.

"I'm so sorry." Despite all efforts, she began to tremble. "I, um, ran out of my meds and...I already replaced them this morning. I just needed to refill my prescription first."

Kelly fought the urge to come around the desk and take Ida in her arms, knowing this lesson would be critical to Ida's growth. Not only as a doctor, but as a person.

"Medications in the lock-up can never be used for personal reasons. *Never.* Not only is it a violation of our practice, but our pharmacy is stocked with the minimal amount of drugs projected to be needed to treat our patients."

Ida knew this. She also knew that she'd stupidly and irresponsibly bitten the hand that had reached out to give her a job. She was deeply ashamed and steeled herself for her punishment. At a minimum, she'd be fired. If Kelly wanted to press the issue, charges could be filed.

"Let's discuss your addiction. Besides Dexedrine, are you taking other stimulants? Adderall? Ritalin?"

Ida shook her head. "Just Dexedrine."

"When did this start?"

"In college. The pressure of school was too much for me. I fell behind and was totally overwhelmed. I was on the verge of quitting, but I knew it would crush my parents. One of my roommates convinced me to take a Dexedrine, and it helped me deal with the stress. It didn't take long for the drugs to become a crutch. The problem was the amphetamines made me dizzy and I had trouble sleeping."

"Enter Valium."

"Yeah." Ida hung her head in shame. "I wish I were stronger, like you, but sometimes I just feel like I need some…help." Ida struggled to hold back her tears. "I'm so, so sorry."

"Apologies accepted for 'borrowing' the drugs, but that can never happen again. As for your addiction, that's nothing to be sorry about. It *is* a problem, but one we can deal with. If you truly want help, step one is counselling."

Her voice quavered. "So, I'm not fired?"

"For being a bit fragile? No. What you went through is no different than a few hundred of my fellow students. Me included."

"You?"

"Medical school is grueling, and in my building, stimulants and anxiety drugs were passed around like candy. Every night was trick-or-treat. There's so much information to absorb and so much pressure to make it through. And then there's the whole issue of not wanting to disappoint your parents. Both our fathers were respected and admired doctors, and when we decided to follow in their footsteps, the bar was set pretty damn high…but not by them." Kelly smiled. "We do this to ourselves."

"I'm still doing it," said Ida.

"You know that recognizing the problem is critical to the first step of healing." Kelly didn't mention her own drinking. She wanted this to be a teaching moment, not a confessional. "You also know in your heart that your father, and your mother, don't have outsized expectations for your career. The most important thing to them is for you to be happy, and you can't be if you set unreasonable or unattainable goals for yourself."

"Is it unreasonable to want to make my father proud?"

Kelly laughed, "You're a *doctor*. A board-certified medical physician. Don't you think he's already beaming with pride? Cut yourself a little slack, Doctor Samuel."

The tears finally came, but they were tears of relief. Of joy.

There was a quick tapping on the door, followed by Annie leaning in. "It's getting busy, Doctors. Plus, Alma Sanchez is back. With Diego."

"Be right there," said Kelly. She turned to Ida. "We'll talk more about this later. Right now, we've got work to do."

A sluggish Diego lay on an exam table. Sonita took his vitals as an irate Alma told Kelly what had happened. "He was doing okay. He stayed on the couch all day. I give him Tylenol like you told me. He was still hurting, but he's such a brave boy, you know? And then his brother Tomás snuck into the house when I was working and gave him some pills."

Alma handed Kelly an oval yellow pill that was stamped "Norco 539."

"Damn it," Kelly muttered. "This is hydrocodone. These are extremely dangerous for a child."

"I know. He started throwing up and had trouble breathing, so I bring him here to you." Alma gently laid her hand on Diego's cheek. "Look at *mi angel*. He was getting better. Even excited to go back to school."

"Do you know how many of these pills Diego took?"

Alma shook her head. "I think maybe two, but I'm not sure."

Kelly looked over to Sonita. "What've you got?"

"Blood pressure is ninety-two over sixty-five. Pulse is slow. Temp is ninety-nine point eight."

"His vitals are on the low end. He needs rest, fluids and time for the drugs to flush from his system. We'll keep him here for a while and monitor his levels. If necessary, we can administer Narcan, but I'd like to wait on that."

"He'll be okay?" Alma asked hopefully.

"He'll be fine, but he can't be taking these drugs. I doubt Tomás knew how dangerous these are for a ten-year-old, but..."

Alma's rage simmered. "He probably knew. Tomás loves Diego, but he has an evil streak in him. He is cruel, and sometimes violent. Maybe he give his brother the drugs to get back at me for kicking him out of the house. Tomás can be *muy vengativo*."

Very vindictive. Great. As if Alma didn't have enough to worry about. Kelly felt her own anger begin to swell. She'd become quite attached to the Sanchez family over the years and cared for Diego like the little brother she never had. She'd been at his side when he was brought into the clinic with a gunshot, and then when his wound festered and his leg had to be amputated. She'd seen him through his recovery and helped him learn to walk with a prosthetic. She wasn't about to lose him to a deranged brother who thought it was okay to feed him opiates.

"Where is Tomás now? It might help if I can explain to him the danger of these drugs."

"He's hiding someplace. Oscar is out looking for him. Maybe he can talk some sense into his brother."

Kelly knew that Alma didn't believe that for a second.

30

By 10:00 a.m., the clinic was filling up with patients. While Sonita stayed with Diego, Annie tended to a four-year-old boy with head lice, which had run rampant at his daycare facility. Vik treated a recently single dad who'd badly burned himself attempting to iron his son's school uniform, and Kelly examined a homeless woman with a urinary tract infection.

Ida was treating an older man whose hands and arms were covered with itchy blisters. His eight-year-old Jack Russell had gotten loose and returned home filthy. The man didn't realize that the pooch had rolled around in the neighbor's poison ivy and was covered with urushiol oil. The dog was perfectly fine, but the man ended up with a puss-filled rash. Ida administered a prednisone shot and was completing her patient's paperwork when she spied Gretchen Sadowski coming through the doors. She was wearing dark sunglasses to protect her eyes. Her symptoms had gotten much worse.

Ida hustled Gretchen into one of the patient bays, where they were joined by Kelly. When Gretchen had come in six days earlier, she'd complained of neck pain, chills and nausea. Since then, her ailments had compounded. Her face was ashen, except her cheeks and forehead, which were flushed red.

"Tell me what's going on," Kelly said.

"My throat's killing me," she rasped, "and the sunlight is blinding. Plus, I've been having pounding headaches."

"Have you suffered migraines in the past?"

"I've had some whopper hangovers before, but not like this. Feels like my skull's in a vise. I've been taking Tylenol like the doctor said, but I've gotta have something stronger. I mean, I can't even go to work."

"You shouldn't *be* at work. You need to rest and stay hydrated." Kelly looked to Ida for her evaluation.

"I'd recommend Ms. Sadowski gets a full workup. Labs, blood culture, imaging and lumbar puncture for CSF," she said.

"What's a CSF?" Gretchen asked.

"Cerebrospinal fluid."

Gretchen recoiled, "That sounds painful."

Ida placed a reassuring hand on Gretchen's arm. "They numb the area, and all you feel is some slight pressure. It's over very quickly."

"What do you mean 'they?' Can't you do it here?"

"We're not equipped," said Kelly.

"If it's okay with Doctor Harper, I can take you to St. Francis and stay with you while they administer the test," said Ida.

Kelly smiled and nodded. Ida had a good heart and would develop into a wonderful doctor, once she embraced the fact that healing started with herself.

A short time later, Ida was helping Gretchen out the door to a waiting Uber. On the way, they passed Carter Dane, who was entering with an expensive bouquet of exotic flowers. He stopped at the desk and smiled at Ramona. "Could I bring these back to Doctor Harper?"

"The doctor's busy with patients, but you can leave them with me, or I can tell her you're here, but it's gonna be a while. We're swamped."

"I'll wait, thanks."

Carter squeezed into an empty chair between a gum-popping teenage girl whose hand was wrapped with an ice pack, and a young Latina mom holding a fidgety, crying one-year-old. Carter made them both for around sixteen years old. Other than that, their lives couldn't have been more different.

The girl with the ice pack explained that she was named the MVP of her soccer team, having stopped a game-saving shot-on-goal. It cost her two broken fingers, but her smile made it clear that it was totally worth it.

"Nice flowers," she said.

"Thanks. They're for one of the doctors."

"Girlfriend?"

"What? No. Just a little something to brighten her day."

"Nice move. Good luck with that." The girl may have only been sixteen, but she could see right through Carter.

The baby to his other side, reached out and grabbed one of the flowers. Her mother pulled the child away. "*Mija*! No!" That only served to make the baby cry louder.

Carter smiled at her. "It's okay."

"I'm so sorry. She's been up all night with colic."

The young mom looked like she'd been up all night as well. The bags under her eyes were better suited to a woman many times her age.

The whiney infant reached out again, and before her mother could pull her back, Carter extended the flowers in her direction. "Maybe these will make her feel better," he said.

As the baby took the flowers, she stopped crying. A tiny smile of wonderment crossed her face. The mother looked at the strange man next to her, and her face mirrored that of her daughter. It was a smile of gratitude, mixed with bewilderment.

The teenaged soccer player nudged him. "Class act, dude."

Carter, now flowerless, was at a loss of what to do. After an awkward few seconds, he stood up and exited the clinic. A moment later, Kelly entered the waiting room and glanced around to find a smiling infant holding a beautiful bouquet of flowers. Kelly shrugged quizzically and headed back to her patients.

31

Since Pete was sidelined from actual police work, he figured he might as well do something constructive. Following the instructions from Yegor, he logged onto Torch and navigated his way to the Crazy Creatures message boards. There'd been a sharp spike of posts of about Garvin the Guinea Pig a few months ago, but lately the comments had tapered off. He clicked on the most recent post which asked the question, "If Garvin were a person, what kind of cereal would he eat?" This inane query got twenty-eight responses. None of them had additional links. Pete sighed. This had all the signs of being a colossal waste of time.

For the next hour, he surfed the Garvin waves, which resulted in an endless cycle of wipeouts on unfamiliar shores. Several posts contained links, which he dutifully clicked on. One took him to a website that sold linoleum. Another boasted of a "doctor approved" apparatus that was guaranteed to enlarge your manhood or double-your-money back. It looked incredibly painful. Most of the links connected him to pornography. Porn of every imaginable variety, and a few he never cared to imagine. And as Yegor predicted, almost every site tried to worm its way into his computer with malware. Fortunately, the firewall held fast.

Pete followed another Garvin thread, this one concerning intricate designs for custom guinea pig cages. Most of the comments contained links to websites that sold elaborate modular pet pig abodes. When he clicked on the seventh link in the thread, his screen went dark. At first Pete thought his laptop had run out of power, but he still had plenty of juice. Next, he assumed a nasty virus finally penetrated the firewall. If that was the case, he'd be dead in the water.

A moment later, his screen came back to life. This website had no banner, no graphics, no frills of any kind. It was a long, ongoing thread dedicated to rumors and conjecture about Gideon. Finally.

Just about everyone on the thread had a theory on Gideon's identity, and no one was in agreement. The number of his possible victims ran into the hundreds, which was preposterous. Since Gideon's M.O. was making murders appear to be accidents, overdoses, or natural fatalities, it was easy to blame him for Uncle Murray mysteriously falling through a thin sheet of ice or Cousin Lorenzo suffering a heart attack. Ron was right…Gideon seemed about as real as a murderous Yeti.

Pete read about sightings, suppositions, and speculations. While none of the unfortunate people on Gideon's supposed "hit list" could be verified, their deaths all fit his nebulous modus operandi. And, according to the website, all of them had been involved in some shady practices…from accusations of illegal transgressions to outright criminal activities.

Before clicking on the "victims" tab, Pete perused the message board and saw several threads about something called "The Committee." He remembered Yegor mentioning it and thinking it was big deal. From what Pete could piece together, The Committee was a cabal of wealthy people whose relatives had presumably been victims of Gideon, and these folks were offering an enormous bounty for his identity. Some accounts claimed the payout was three million dollars, some said five million and the most recent mentions cited the figure at seven million. If Gideon *were* real, Pete would hate to be in his shoes. Seven million in cash must have unleashed an army of crazy bounty hunters who'd go to any lengths to track him down, not realizing they'd most likely be on nothing more than an elaborate snipe hunt.

Pete turned to the list of supposed victims, wondering if any of the names would ring a bell.

Richard Cody. Alleged enforcer for the Nardino Family in Newark, New Jersey. Died in an auto accident. His autopsy indicated he'd passed out behind the wheel due to an extremely high concentration of Nembutal (a sedative) in his bloodstream.

165

Andie Mikita. Ninth grade schoolteacher in Chico, California. Police records stated she sold Oxycodone to students. Died from a combination of morphine and scotch. Her death was deemed a suicide, but people who knew her stated she never drank alcohol.

Charles Crane. Professional bodybuilder, occasional stuntman and movie extra in Santa Monica, California. Rumored to be the Midnight Rambler...a serial rapist who terrorized women throughout Southern California. Died from a tainted batch of HGH.

John Berg. Firearms dealer in Tiburon, California. Specialized in illegal machine gun conversion devices. His body was found floating in Belvedere Lagoon. The police report stated that there were large amounts of Propofol (medical anesthetic) in his body.

Vern Johansen. Insurance salesman in Bozeman, Montana. Arrested on multiple counts of child pornography. One week after his release from prison, Johansen died from an air embolism in his circulatory system.

Miller Garfield. Ranch hand and rodeo clown in El Paso, Texas. Suspected of a DUI double homicide when his F150 slammed into a car driven by an elderly couple from Colombia. Claimed his truck had been stolen and he was never charged. Three months later, he died after being force-fed a poison dart frog. The dart frog is indigenous to Colombia.

Arthur Moretti. Businessman in San Francisco, California. Suspected of extortion, drug distribution and human trafficking. Electrocuted in his own home from a faulty wire in a lamp.

Arthur Moretti! Pete had gone into the Gideon treasure hunt with grave doubts about discovering anything of real value, but when he came across Moretti's name, this website suddenly took on some gravitas. Was it possible that Arthur Moretti was actually a victim of Gideon? If so, how about Tommy and Anthony Moretti? There were still questions swirling around both of their deaths.

Pete skimmed the remaining names, and one more leapt out. It may as well have been written in neon. *Clarence Musselwhite*. Pete knew all about the man who'd killed Kelly's mother and brutally attacked her sister. It was common knowledge that Musselwhite had died while in police custody. However, the information on the website told a very different story. Musselwhite was one of the earliest suspected victims of Gideon. In fact, it was speculated that Musselwhite's death may have very well been Gideon's first kill.

His origin story.

The entry on the message board was a bizarre account of how Musselwhite's death was faked and he'd subsequently been moved into witness protection in exchange for testimony against some unnamed mob boss. The thread went on to say that the mobster discovered Musselwhite's whereabouts and hired someone to kill him. A "leaked" autopsy report stated that Musselwhite died of a heart attack, but rumors persisted about exotic poisons.

Pete didn't believe it, but he could understand how weaving this tale accomplished what the website set out to do: ground the myth of Gideon in a quasi-logical set of facts that were more-or-less irrefutable. If a reader wanted to accept this as true, he could point to the information on the website and feel justified in that belief. It was far less outrageous than the websites that spun tales of Satan worshipping elites who ran a child sex ring, or those that "had proof" that NASA faked the moon landing.

The website raised more questions than answers, and Pete wondered if *any* of this was true. He'd set out to find information on a mythical hit man and had stumbled across a story about Clarence Musselwhite…the person who'd nearly destroyed Kelly's life. He couldn't trust the wild hearsay on a conspiracy theory website, but there was one source he had complete faith in.

It was time to pay him a visit.

32

Spider sat in the storeroom of a tiny bodega owned by Gizmo's uncle. He was cleaning a lightweight Ruger compact when Gizmo entered. Eighteen years old and bony, his red Jerry Rice throwback jersey hung off him like a king-sized sheet on a twin bed.

"What do we know?" asked Spider.

Gizmo turned toward the door and hissed to someone just outside. "Get your *pendejo* ass in here!"

Hector Ibarra skulked into the room. He'd been a lookout on Gato's crew, but since the untimely death of his boss, Hector had been adrift. Kind of.

Spider stared down Hector, who was trembling with fear. "*Que pasa*, Hector?"

"Not much, you know?"

"Not what I heard. What you doin' hangin' on my route?"

"What? Not doin' nothin', Spider. Just kickin' it, you know?"

"Don't give me that shit. I heard you workin' for Tomás. That true?"

Hector looked around the room, desperate for a way out.

"Boss asked you a question, *maricón*," said Gizmo.

"Yeah, I mean, nah, I ain't workin' for Tomás. He asked me to ring him if I see Five-0 around, but that's it. Don't mean nothin', Spider. I swear."

Spider shook his head in disappointment. "Means you lookin' out for him. Doin' him a solid. Sounds like work to me."

Spider walked over to Hector and tapped him on the chest with the Ruger. "Lemme do you a solid, Hector. Tomás will fuck you over every chance. Use you then toss you away like garbage. I'm gonna give you an opportunity to make things right, okay?"

Hector transformed into a bobblehead doll.

"You got any idea where Tomás is hiding?"

"I…I don't know for sure, but I might'a heard someone say somethin' about him and Luca holing up in some apartment over by Precita Park."

"Then here's what you're gonna do. You're gonna get your ass over there with the rest of the shorties, and you fuckin' find Tomás and call me. You got that?"

"Yeah, Spider."

Hector was frozen in place, too frightened to budge.

"Why you still here?"

Hector hurried out of the room. Spider turned to Gizmo. "Keep an eye on him. I don't trust that little fucker."

While the Norteños were searching the streets for signs of Tomás, Cora Mathews was searching the internet for signs of Benedetto. Cora's mastery, along with her bespoke equipment, allowed her access to almost any information sent into the ether. There were a few systems she never tried to crack, but then, she'd never had reason to. If she absolutely needed to hack into something like a nuclear power plant or a cryptocurrency exchange, she could deliver. It may not be before lunch, but definitely before dinner.

Cora had set up alerts on the most trafficked dark sites that had previously posted comments about Gideon. Years ago she'd built a backdoor into the site run by The Committee, and planted a *remora*; an undetectable program that allowed her real-time access to all the communications on their website, including private IMs hidden from visitors. There were no mentions of Benedetto, and no new activity regarding Gideon.

Nor was there anything concrete on "GIDEON WATCH," a service behind a paywall that existed solely to help subscribers suss out Gideon's identity to either collect the bounty from The Committee, or to seek revenge against the elusive hitman who might've ushered a relative to an early grave. The site contained threads linking Gideon to a plethora of "natural" deaths. In reality, of the dozens listed, he was responsible for only three.

169

Cora had a strong suspicion as to what happened to her boss. The law office and Benedetto's residence were side by side, and she'd meticulously gone through his home looking for clues. Nothing was out of place. No clothing or suitcases were missing. His car was in the garage, but his wallet and money clip were gone. So was the antique watch she'd given him for his birthday many years ago. There were no signs of a break-in, and the security company reported no activity at the residence. She'd spoken to the manager of Bishop's, the neighborhood bistro a few blocks from Benedetto's home where he generally dined on Saturday nights. The manager confirmed he'd been there, had his usual dinner at the bar, and left around nine o'clock.

Cora had hacked into the local CCTV cameras and watched as Benedetto exited the restaurant at 9:03 p.m., then strolled down the street without a care in the world. He turned a corner and poof...he was gone. There were some CCTV blind spots on the route between the restaurant and his house, and this tiny street was one of them. He'd been snatched off the street where a surveillance gap existed, which meant the kidnapper was either very lucky or very sophisticated. She suspected it was the latter, which was not welcome news.

She reviewed the footage again, this time focusing on any vehicles that may have entered or exited the street at the time Benedetto disappeared, but there were none. It made no sense. Was he hustled off the street into a building? That seemed highly unlikely. Something here didn't track.

Cora had pushed this enigma to the back of her brain, leaving it to gestate while she continued her sweep of the Dark Web, combing 4chan message boards and the most obscure websites. Suddenly, the answer dawned on her. She went back over the CCTV video. There was no time code, but she zoomed in on a digital clock in the window of a store on the corner. She went frame by frame and triumphantly registered the fact that the clock leapt from 9:06 to 9:10. Someone had gone into the CCTV system and erased four minutes of footage.

The footage that undeniably would've shown the vehicle that whisked Benedetto away.

She checked the other cameras in the nearby area and found additional gaps, effectively erasing any trace of the kidnapper's vehicle.

Cora loved a challenge, but not when her boss's life was on the line.

The man entered the room, slowly walking with his head down, measuring each step until he landed on the precise spot where he'd stood before. He snuck a peek at Benedetto, who was finishing a McDonald's cheeseburger.

"Thanks for this," Benedetto said. "I make it a rule to avoid fast food, but given the circumstances..."

The man didn't acknowledge Benedetto, but rather, glanced over at a behemoth who was sitting a few feet away. This was the aforementioned Mott, who had a .357 Desert Eagle on his lap, his sausage-like finger resting on the trigger guard, which explained why Benedetto had been given the leeway to eat and use the bathroom without restraints. Mott looked like an NFL lineman who'd played in the trenches for years without a helmet.

Benedetto dutifully held out his left hand and Mott snapped the cuff around it.

The man avoided Benedetto's eyes as he spoke. "Are you ready to answer my question?"

"I don't know who or what you're talking about. I've never heard of this Gideon person. I'm not saying he doesn't exist, but maybe, you've picked up the wrong guy."

"No. You are the *right* guy. You know Gideon, and you know he's an assassin. He kills people. Yes, kills. He has killed one hundred and nine people."

"If you say so."

The man cocked his head and looked directly at Benedetto for the briefest moment before averting his gaze. "I have spent much time, many, many months, researching everything about him. Almost everything is on the internet if you know where to look. I do. I am very good at planning and at using the internet. I found many lists of Gideon's victims. Some people say that he only kills bad people, but I know that's not true. Yes, that's a lie. I can name all his victims. Once I read something, it goes into the vault." He tapped his temple. "The vault. That's what my mother used to call it, because information goes in and stays safe, like it was in a bank."

The man began to tick off the names of victims, sounding like a schoolboy reciting state capitals. "A computer programmer in San Francisco, California. His name was Christopher Xavier Condit. A railroad leasing agent in Boulder, Colorado. His name was David MacLaren Edwards. A surgery nurse in Oakland, California, named Diane Nishikawa Salomon." He went on, using his fingers to count each victim.

After regurgitating the names of a dozen people, he suddenly stopped and began a different narrative.

"Twenty years ago, you represented a man named Dominic Vincente Bruno. He was a very bad man. Dominic Bruno was locked away, in a prison, because of secret testimony from another very bad man named Clarence Earl Musselwhite, Jr."

"That's all factual. I'm impressed," said Benedetto.

"I've spent almost all my money gathering information. Yes. Almost everything I had. Some information isn't available on the internet, even if you know where to look. But information can be purchased if you have enough money. It cost me so much money, but it was worth it. Definitely worth it. I found out many interesting things. Like Clarence Musselwhite was put into witness protection. His name was changed to David Richardson. He got a new driver's license and new credit cards and everything.

"I also found out that on April 5th, nineteen years ago, you visited Dominic Bruno at his prison. A supermax prison called Pelican Bay located in Crescent City, California. Two weeks later, Clarence Musselwhite was found dead. Completely dead."

172

"I'll take your word for it. I have no knowledge of what happened to Musselwhite after his testimony."

"The autopsy said it was heart failure. Just stopped working. But I paid someone so much money for a toxicology report that revealed Clarence Musselwhite had curare in his system. Curare is very dangerous poison."

Benedetto replied, "If what you're saying is true, and Musselwhite was murdered a few weeks after I met with Bruno, it's a huge leap for those two incidents to be even remotely connected."

"Wrong! Bruno paid you to hire someone to kill Clarence Musselwhite dead. You hired Gideon. He kills people. The connection is definitely there. Yes, definitely."

"Your presumption is ludicrous. I'm an attorney, not a conduit to an assassin. You've drawn conclusions using scant facts and faulty logic. I don't know this Gideon, and I'm not involved in some bizarre murder for hire scheme."

Benedetto watched as the man's face got increasingly redder. It was like a thermometer plunged into boiling water, the mercury threatening to shatter the top of the gauge and spray across the room. Three deep breaths, some muttered words of soothing, and the man slowly regained equilibrium.

"I had a twin brother. Raymond. Yes, twin brother. We owned a company. Cyber-security. Foreign governments hacked our elections and power grids and I created a program to prevent that. To protect America. Yes, America. My brother, Raymond, was good with people. We were fraternal twins. I turned out one way, and he turned out differently. Our mother told us I was more special, and Raymond was more normal. Much better with people. Our mother said he could sell ice cubes to Eskimos. I never understood why Eskimos would need ice cubes. I think it was a joke. I'm very good with planning and with computers, but don't understand too many jokes, and I'm not comfortable with people. No way. But Raymond was. We were going to sell our business for so much money when Raymond suddenly died. Completely dead.

"Raymond ran five miles every morning, each day, through the forest, along the river. One day, Raymond didn't come back. They found him, dead. Bitten by a snake. A rattlesnake.

"Raymond was my brother, my business partner, my friend. My only friend. When he died, the business died with him. Both completely dead. It was over. I couldn't do it by myself. No way. Didn't want to. I sold it for less than what it was worth. So much less. I was sad. Sad and angry. Mostly sad." The man uttered these sentiments stoically. They were statements of fact with no emotion attached to them.

"Then I got a call from the police. A call on my phone. They said the circumstances of Raymond's death were curious. Yes. That's the word they used. Curious.

"The venom in Raymond's body, the very dangerous poison that killed him, came from an Eastern Diamondback Rattlesnake. It's the largest rattlesnake in the whole world, but it's found in places like South Carolina and Florida and Alabama. But we don't live in any of those places. No way."

The man nodded several times, then hung his head. Deep breaths. Benedetto glanced over at Mott, trying to discern if this behavior was normal for his extremely abnormal host. Mott stared back at Benedetto, his face an unexpressive block of granite.

The man continued. "I'm good with planning and with computers. Very good. Not people, though. No way. I found a lot of information about Gideon. How he made murders appear to be accidents. Heart attacks, drug overdoses, poisons. Many kinds of poisons. Like rattlesnake venom. That's how Raymond died. Yes, died. That's why I need to find out who Gideon is. For Raymond."

Benedetto interrupted, trying to inject some logic into the conversation. "Why would someone hire this Gideon to kill your brother? Did Raymond have enemies?"

The man shook his head in confusion. Why was his prisoner asking questions? They were the same questions that the police asked. Why did people think he knew the answers to these questions?

174

"No more questions! All I want from you is a name. Gideon's real name. For Raymond. And because there are people who have formed something called The Committee. I don't know who they are, no way, but they will give me so much money when I tell them who Gideon is. Seven million dollars. I deserve that money. Yes. I deserve it."

"I'm sorry for your loss, but like I said, I have no idea who this Gideon person is." Benedetto rested his case, expecting a response. When none was forthcoming, he added, "So where does that leave us?"

"You need to make a choice. Yes, a choice."

"Between walking out or being carried out?"

The man shifted his eyes to look directly at Benedetto, then nodded.

Mott moved so fast that Benedetto never saw the massive fist before it slammed into his side with the force of a pile driver. The crushing impact of the blow was momentarily offset by the shock of the attack. It was the second punch, the one that cracked two ribs, that brought on the real pain.

33

Anders "Andy" Ericson bled blue. He was the son of a cop, the father of a cop, and had logged twenty years on the street before earning his gold shield. He worked the Homicide Detail until retiring two years ago at age sixty-eight. He'd been offered a job as consultant to get him to the magical fifty-year mark, but that meant sitting in an office, and Andy was no desk jockey.

He liked the action.

He'd witnessed the rise and fall of the Mitchell Brothers' porn industry in the Tenderloin; he'd been part of the task force that investigated the Zodiac killer; he was there when they arrested Patty Hearst and Wendy Yoshimura of the SLA; and he was only a block away when the Golden Dragon massacre went down in Chinatown. He'd had run-ins with Jimmy "The Hat" Lanza and Sergio Maranghi in North Beach. He'd seen the Castro District's transition into a gay mecca and had experienced the city, his city, evolve into a west coast melting pot of ethnicities and economic inequalities.

Andy was widely known as being tough but fair. He was one of the few old-timers who didn't see his constituency as black or brown, yellow or white. The stereotypical inbred biases that generally came along with being a cop had never defined him. His fellow officers learned early on to temper racist remarks around Andy. Either that or end up on his shit list, which was not a distinction anyone wanted. Andy had a wide circle of friends within the department, as well as throughout the city, and he'd fine-tuned the art of holding a grudge, so it was best not to piss him off.

Pete brought his father a fresh cup of coffee from the kitchen and nestled into the worn leather chair across from him. The den had been Andy's retreat when Pete was growing up. Someplace for him

176

to get away from the rigors of normal life after a twelve-hour shift of dealing with break-ins, battered spouses, and shootings.

Growing up, Pete had respected his father's sanctum and knew to tread lightly when he passed by the door to the den. Their relationship was best characterized as respectful. There was a military-like formality between father and son that left no room for overt expressions of love or emotion. Pete's mother, Roberta, was the glue that held things together, and her ebullience provided the family with warmth and caring.

After Roberta died, Andy spent more and more time in his den, often sleeping on the sofa. The bedroom felt empty, the living room hollow and the kitchen joyless. A cloud of cigarette smoke hung over the room, as Andy lit a fresh one off the glowing butt of the last one. He'd picked up the habit again the day of Roberta's funeral. Overnight, ten years of Nicorette gave way to two-packs-a-day of Camels. Pete never commented on his father's smoking or drinking. His dad was well aware of the medical implications of his habits and had no time for people who gave him unwanted advice.

Andy blew a stream of smoke toward the ceiling, sipped his coffee and nodded. "Thanks for the coffee. Haven't had a decent cup since your mother died."

"There's a coffee shop on almost every corner, Dad."

"I'm on a fixed income. Five dollars for coffee isn't in my budget."

Pete knew his father was financially set for the remainder of his days, even if he lived another sixty-eight years, but Andy was old school and wasn't about to change now.

"What brings you around?"

"Just wanted to see how you're doing."

Andy eyed his son. He could read Pete like an elementary school primer and knew he had some specific reason for being there, but Andy played along.

"Doing okay for an old guy."

"Have you been getting out on the bay?"

"Not lately."

"Maybe one of these days we could do that fishing charter again."

"Seriously? You were so seasick last time you spent the entire trip painting the side of the boat. I figured you'd never want to go out on the water again."

Pete smiled at the memory. "I was fourteen. I think it's time to give it another shot."

Andy nodded. "I'd like that. How about next weekend?"

Pete grinned. "That'd be great, Dad."

There was an awkward pause in the conversation that Andy stepped in to fill. "How are things with the doctor?"

"Kelly? It's complicated. She's got a lot going on in her life."

"I thought you were a big part of that. Weren't you talking about getting married?"

"That was before her father died. Things have changed since then."

"Sorry to hear that. So…you wanna tell me what's really on your mind?"

"Am I that transparent?"

"If I were you, I'd avoid high stakes poker games."

"Well, you're gonna think this is crazy, but…what can you tell me about Gideon?"

Andy snorted. "Seriously?"

Pete shrugged. "I know he's probably just a bogeyman, but I value your experience and opinion above everyone else's and wanted your take."

"Okay. I'll play along. The first whispers of some mysterious assassin started fifteen or twenty years ago. Nobody on the force ever gave them credence. It's an age-old story…someone dies of natural causes, and there's always one person who can't accept the truth, so they dream up a new one to validate their opinion. It happens in government every day. What do they call 'em? Alternative facts? I call 'em horseshit."

"Did anyone in the department ever seriously look into the possibility there could be a man who only..."

Andy interrupted his son. "...takes out the bad guys? A real-life Equalizer or Batman? In a word, no. There's never been a shred of hard evidence. Plus, the supposed vics all had it coming, so why rock the boat? If this guy *did* exist, he was doing us all a solid."

"Because this mythical executioner was killing bad guys, it was okay to look the other way instead of trying to find out if he existed and bringing him to justice?"

Andy stubbed out his cigarette and shook another one out of the pack. Pete gave him a look that he tried to make non-judgmental but failed. Andy laid the unlit smoke on the desk.

"There are enough *real* scumbags out there to keep the force busy 24-7. Is your case load that light you can spend time chasing shadows?" Andy returned the non-judgmental look. He was better at it.

"Alright, I get it. Moving on. Do you remember the Clarence Musselwhite case?"

"Of course. Rape, murder, assault with intent to kill. What about him?"

"The official word is he died in police custody, but I heard a rumor the other day he might've been put into the WITSEC program."

"That's a load of crap. He died during transport. I saw the coroner's report. Has this got something to do with the Gideon fantasy, or are you poking around a twenty-year-old case because Musselwhite killed Kelly Harper's mother?"

"Neither. Both. I don't know."

"Pete, drop it. It's a waste of time and, to tell you truth, running around and chirping about Gideon or Musselwhite is an embarrassment to our family name. Now, lemme ask you a question. What's the story with Myles Spencer?"

"You, uh, heard about that?"

"I'm still wired downtown. I know all about your suspension. Tell me about this guy."

"He's an artist from a family that's got some weight at City Hall. He got lucky and hit it big a few years ago, and now he scores drugs, throws parties, and last week, gunned down a dealer. Maybe his third."

"You sure about that, or is it your gut?"

"I'd say eighty-twenty."

"But the eighty's not enough for a conviction?"

"It might've been before I broke his nose."

Andy didn't hide his smile. "I heard about that too. Left hook or right cross?"

Pete couldn't help but return the smile. "Caught him with my right. Flush."

"You learned from the best. So, what's the play now?"

"I'm on leave. There is no play."

Andy finally lit his cigarette. His eyes twinkled, and his face came alive with thoughts of mischief and mayhem. "There's always a play. Son, you walk a straight line, and I couldn't be more proud of you, but sometimes you need to be morally flexible to get the edge. You know what I mean?"

Pete's response was guarded, "Go on."

"These days cops are like NFL defensive backs. The rules are stacked against us. There's a flag on almost every play. I'm not advocating violence, and you know where I stand on profiling, but there's so much public outcry and so many legal loopholes, that bringing the bad guys to justice is becoming almost impossible.

"In my day, policing in the city was like the wild west. Between the families in North Beach, the gangs in Chinatown, and the pervs in the Tenderloin, sometimes we had to color outside the lines."

Pete was nonplussed. He'd always believed his dad was a straight shooter. The idea that he cut corners took Pete by surprise.

"There were instances where I knew a perp was guilty, like caught them red-handed, but didn't have enough physical evidence to make the case a slam dunk. The system gave them certain protections unless we could tie things up with a fucking bow. In those situations, we occasionally provided what was needed to make the DA happy."

"You planted evidence?"

"We had access to a variety of…substances…that made the arrests more airtight. Plus, we always carried a throw down. Everyone in Homicide did back then. Saved my ass once or twice when it was questionable if a shooting was righteous."

This revelation rendered Pete momentarily speechless.

"I can see you don't approve."

"I'm just surprised."

"I never told you the story of Wil Zmak?"

"If you did, I don't remember."

"You'd remember this one. Willie Z was a hitter for a Croatian drug dealer named Niko Babić. The Croatians arrived in the early nineties and tried to elbow their way into the drug trade, which, like today, was controlled by the Latinos. Business in Ecstasy and GHB was starting to take off big time, and Babić figured there was enough room for everyone, but the Chicanos who hung out at Folsom Park weren't interested in sharing. Especially with some Eastern European punks.

"Babić gave Willie Z a list of names and turned him loose. Three of the Folsom Boys were found dead, their severed heads tucked between their legs. It didn't end there. Houses were burned to the ground with the families inside. The Croatians were a new kind of evil, and the Folsom Park gang knew they were overmatched.

"Javi Flores was running the Folsom crew and reached out to us. He offered to exchange information for a little assistance. The guys in Narcotics received names and routes of some mid-level drug suppliers, and in return, four of us from Homicide were assigned to 24-hour surveillance on Babić and Willie Z. The whole operation was strictly off the books.

"Two weeks later, Willie Z slipped through our net and took out four more of Javi's guys. The department, eager to get more information from Javi, made it clear to us that Niko Babić and Wil

Zmak were priority targets, and that everyone involved would be better off without the nuisance and complications of an extended court case."

"Meaning?" Pete asked, even though he knew the answer.

"Come on. You're no dummy. My partner and I worked the streets hard and got a tip that Babić and Willie Z were holed up in the back of a defunct Polish restaurant over on 22nd. Later that night, SFPD patrolmen found the corpses of Babić and Zmak, along with a dozen handguns, nine AR-15s, a few thousand pills and a footlocker full of cash. The remaining Croatians must've scattered because we never heard anything more about them."

Pete was astonished. "You executed them."

"Hard times call for hard measures. Does it really matter if you bend a few regs along the way to get the job done?"

"The regulations are there for a reason."

"To get politicians re-elected."

"I never realized you were this cynical."

"Then all these years, you haven't been listening. I never asked to be put on a pedestal. All I ever wanted from you, from anyone, was the respect I deserved, I earned, for serving my city. I don't have to tell you, it's a damn hard way to make a living, but the satisfaction you get from picking up the trash is worth it. At least it was to me. I'm proud of my service. My record. My commendations. And I don't have the slightest bit of guilt about the way I went about doing my job."

"You think I'm naïve."

"Not naïve. Idealistic. I've known a few cops over the years who insisted on going strictly by the book. Some were successful, most were frustrated. I'm not judging you or trying to talk you into anything. Just saying that every day the police are faced with doing a job that's difficult at best. Gaming the system doesn't make you a bad guy and doesn't make you morally corrupt. If you believe that Myles Spencer is getting a free pass because he plays the angles better than you, and that society would be better off if he was behind bars, then do something about it."

"And if I'm caught making a play?"

"You'd be fucked. You said this guy's family has connections. Depending upon the line you crossed, it could blow up and cost you your job. So, the question you've gotta ask yourself is, is it worth it?"

Pete suddenly found himself at a crossroads he never imagined approaching. Andy knew the signs all too well.

"If it *is* worth it, it's gonna need to be done right. I can help."

34

Kelly glanced at her watch. It was three minutes later than the last time she checked. She was too jittery to read, too nauseous to eat. She wanted a drink but needed a clear head tonight. Then again, maybe a glass of wine would help calm her nerves.

That was all the rationalization it took to convince herself that a drink was exactly what was required. As she poured, she wondered if she was turning into a full-blown alcoholic. Her consumption had noticeably increased since her father's murder. Prior to his death, she rarely drank during the week. The occasional shot with him after work, and the glass or two of wine with Pete, but otherwise, she'd kept her drinking to a bare minimum.

Now, each week there were more empty bottles in the recycle bin. Kelly cut herself some guilt-slack because of her grief, as well as the discovery of her father's alter-ego and the fatal events that followed, but it was time to get her act together and not use the tumult in her life as an excuse. She needed to take charge of her body and mind again. She had both the discipline and the desire.

She could do this.

As she raised the glass, she silently chanted the alcoholic's credo. "I'll start tomorrow."

The Chardonnay did the trick, and as Kelly relaxed, she reached for her father's journal. She needed a distraction and recalled an entry about his lone female target. She decided to read it again to see if it might give her some insight how to proceed with Lisa Reynolds.

Michelle Kettering-Adler is a thirty-seven-year-old widow who resides in a three-million-dollar estate on Mercer Island, Washington. She's outlived three husbands, each one wealthier than the last, and two stepchildren. She came to my attention because not only did she bury five family members, but it's strongly suspected she was responsible for their early demise. All of them.

Per usual, Benedetto provided me with in-depth background information on Mrs. K-A. She was the seventh child of Ralph and Carol Meadows, a blue-collar family from Henderson, Nevada. Her birth name was Misty. Misty Meadows. Her parents were evidently influenced by the billboards touting the strip clubs in nearby Las Vegas.

Misty steered clear of taking off her clothes in public but had no problem getting naked in private. It was during her stint with Executive Escorts that she met her first husband, Rolando Evans, a backup tight end for the Cincinnati Bengals. Rolando was in Vegas riding out a four-game suspension for violating the league's personal conduct policy. Misty and Rolando tied the knot at the Elvis Chapel. The marriage was extremely short lived, as was the groom. Two days after their nuptials, Rolando died of an overdose of Percocet that he'd been taking for a compressed disc. No foul play was suspected (at that time).

Misty helped herself to her deceased husband's bling, as well as his cherry red Bentley, and after a visit to her favorite pawn shop, she walked out with almost $75,000 in cash, got in the car, and headed north.

She ended up in Seattle, where she sold the car, adding another $100,000 to her stash, legally changed her name to Michelle (since her marriage to Rolando was so abbreviated, she hadn't bothered taking on the Evans surname), and set out to find another husband. Two years later, she married Sanford Kettering, this time in a Christian ceremony held in an extravagant backyard setting.

Sanford owned a string of very successful seafood markets and was considered one of the area's most eligible bachelors. The marriage lasted for precisely five years and ended abruptly when Sanford drowned in Elliott Bay. He and Michelle had been celebrating their anniversary on a sunset cruise aboard his vintage cabin cruiser. The police report stated that Michelle had gone below to the galley to prepare dinner and when she came back up, her husband was gone.

Sanford had been taking Flexeril to treat a pulled muscle in his back and had stopped drinking alcohol because the two didn't mix. However, since it was their anniversary, he purportedly skipped his meds so the happy couple could share a magnum of Moet.

When the coroner's report came back, it showed that Sanford had not only taken Flexeril that day, but also ingested an Ativan. Both were strong central nervous system depressants, as was the alcohol. It was little wonder he'd gotten dizzy, lost his balance and tumbled overboard. Sanford's doctor had no idea where his patient had gotten Ativan, or what would've compelled him to take it. Regardless, no foul play was suspected (at that time).

Michelle ended up a widow once again, except this time the payout was much larger.

In 2015, at age thirty-one, Michelle landed husband number three...a forty-seven-year-old biotech executive named Gabe Adler. This wedding took place at the Herzl-Nel Tamid synagogue on Mercer Island, which completed Michelle's wedding venue hat-trick. In attendance were Josh and Zack, Gabe's ten-year-old twin sons from his first marriage, as well as his ex-wife, Sarah. According to Benedetto's research, Gabe and Sarah had a very amicable parting and she was well taken care of in the divorce, getting half of Gabe's portfolio, which was valued at over eight million dollars.

Less than two years later, Gabe was en route to Sarah's house to drop the boys off for a long weekend. The Northwest was in the grips of a winter storm, and the roads were slick with black ice. No one knew (at the time) why Gabe's car spun wildly out of control, smashing into an overpass abutment before being slammed into by an eighteen-wheeler loaded with milled lumber. Gabe and the twins never had a chance.

There wasn't much left of the car, but the Seattle PD forensic lab was able to determine there'd been a leak in the brake fluid reservoir, which was completely drained at the time of the crash, rendering the brakes useless. Strangely, Michelle had brought the car in for servicing just a week earlier and everything had checked out fine. For the third time, no foul play was suspected. Not by the police department, anyway. However, someone in the family (Benedetto suspects it was Sarah Adler) had strong doubts, as well as a burning desire for vengeance.

If you ask enough questions, have enough money, and don't allow ethics to stand in your way, you can eventually locate someone who can point you in the right direction. In this case, Sarah was pointed to a Dark Web message board, which in turn got the attention of Benedetto. He had his tech expert compile a comprehensive dossier on Michelle Kettering-Adler, including police and autopsy reports, which was enough to convince me that the former Misty Meadows was indeed a Black Widow. In the words of Ian Fleming... "Once is happenstance. Twice is coincidence. Three times is enemy action."

I was initially hesitant to take on this assignment. Not because I thought Mrs. K-A was innocent, but rather, because I'd never killed a woman. Try as I might, I couldn't get the image of Mary's broken and violated body out of my mind, and even though I would never inflict that kind of depraved brutality on another person, the very thought of taking a female's life made me uncomfortable. If I were to move ahead on this, I had to be one hundred percent committed. Anything less would result in me lacking focus, which could lead to making mistakes.

I went back through all the reports, looking for something to tip the scales one way or the other. I reread the meticulously compiled background information on Michelle's life. What drove her to

become a murderer? Was it a simple lust for riches, or was there
something fundamentally rotten at her core? There were no
documented incidents in her early life to indicate she'd grow up to
become a serial killer. But did it matter? Sometimes life takes a
strange and unexpected twist, and you end up in a world you never
imagined possible. All I had to do to confirm that was to look in the
mirror.

When I reread the autopsy reports on Gabe Alder and his sons,
I came across a notation I hadn't seen the first time through. The
coroner determined that Gabe died instantly, as did Josh. However,
Zack's injuries were not immediately fatal. The autopsy stated that
he was probably alive and at least partially conscious for several
minutes before finally succumbing. This twelve-year-old boy had to
bear witness to the deaths of his father and twin brother.

I'll never know if Michelle intended to target only her husband,
or to take out her stepsons as well. However, I do know the following:
a) she didn't stop Gabe from driving the car that night; b) she
inherited a huge chunk of money and was sitting in a 4,000 square
foot house; and c) regardless of her sex, she deserved to die.

The first glass of wine had gone down easy. Kelly knew the second
glass would go down even easier, but she resisted. She needed to be
functioning at one hundred percent, both mentally and physically.
She still had time to kill.

She turned back to her father's journal.

(David's Journal)

I informed Benedetto of my decision, and the next day he told
me that Michelle was currently spending two weeks on the Big Island,
where her ocean front suite at the Four Seasons went for $3,000 a
night. She had no guilt about spending her ill-gotten gains.

Thinking of her in Hawaii, perhaps scouting her next mark,
gave me inspiration. In my travels with Doctors Without Borders,

I'd come across a multitude of poisonous reptiles, insects and plants. When I was in Zimbabwe, a two-year-old boy was brought in, suffering from severe nausea, vomiting and convulsions. The answer to his illness was found in his stool; he'd eaten some abrus precatorius beans (better known as rosary peas). Shiny red seeds with a distinctive black spot, commonly used to make jewelry and toys. Like so many deadly things in life, they're very pretty to look at, but highly toxic. I guess the same could be said of Mrs. Kettering-Adler.

Rosary peas contain abrin, a toxin similar to ricin, and is considered one of the most poisonous plants in the world. It just so happens that rosary peas grow abundantly in Hawaii. A plan was beginning to take shape.

Two weeks later, Benedetto arranged transportation (I traveled under a fake name, complete with all the required identification to back it up). I touched down at SeaTac in the morning. I had a single carry-on with my essentials and a return ticket for the last flight out that evening.

Three days a week, Michelle went to her personal trainer's studio. Keeping fit and having a tight body was a critical part of her "business plan." Finding a wealthy husband was hard work, but she was willing to put in the sweat equity if the payouts continued to be so lucrative. On her workout days, Michelle had a set routine. When she arrived home, she drank a protein shake on her back deck that overlooked Lake Washington and downtown Seattle. It was a good life, but all good things must come to an end.

It was a beautiful day, with a warm breeze drifting in off the lake. Michelle had left her kitchen windows open to allow the pine scented wind to fill her home. The screens pried loose without a fight, giving me easy access. I got her premade shake from the fridge, stirred in a half teaspoon of powdered abrin, and was back on the street again in a matter of minutes.

Roughly an hour later, Michelle returned home. I'd found a vantage point from where I could see her house and watched through my binoculars as she walked out on her deck, enjoyed the three-million-dollar view, and took a long drink of her poisoned protein shake.

The crushed rosary peas coursed through her system, and a few minutes later, she abruptly dropped her shake and clutched her stomach. She began to convulse as waves of pain rippled through her body. Ten minutes after that, it was over.

I returned to her house to create the necessary tableau. I washed down the deck, replaced the tainted shake with a fresh, unadulterated one, and set a small jar of rosary peas on the table, along with two handcrafted rosary pea bracelets, a DIY bracelet kit, and a few partially crushed peas, as if they broke while she was working with them. I then dipped her fingers in the powdered abrin.

The police would see a woman who'd recently returned from Hawaii, bringing home a jar of shiny red seeds to make bracelets for her friends. A few of the seeds had broken open, the dust got on her hands, and she'd absently wiped her mouth.

By the time I'd gotten back to San Francisco, there was a text message from Benedetto saying that the trip was a success.

As I write this, I realize I have no sense of heightened guilt as a result of accepting a contract on a woman. Her actions were truly despicable, and she didn't get a free pass due to her gender. If anything, the fact that she killed her stepchildren made her all the more deserving of dying at the hands of Gideon.

Kelly reread that last paragraph again. Is there a more heinous crime than the murder of innocent children? Could there be anything more debauched than taking the lives of your own offspring?

Kelly returned the journal to its hiding place behind a row of hardcover novels. Her father's entry filled her head with ideas. Thoughts so dark they had no place in the mind of a normal, law-abiding person…a description that no longer applied to her.

35

Pete sat in a red vinyl-covered booth in the corner of Rockin' Johnson's, a diner crammed with rock and roll relics that looked like they came from a Planet Hollywood yard sale. The uneaten burger and fries on his plate were getting cold, and his beer was getting warm.

He felt like a voracious parasite had worked its way into his body and was gnawing at his stomach lining. He'd gone to talk to his father about Gideon and ended up discovering that Inspector Andy Ericson, that paragon of virtue, had cut a lot of legal corners, including violating the basic rights of the people he'd sworn to protect and serve…not to mention gunning down a suspect or two. Pete didn't ask how often his father had forsaken the moral code he'd promised to uphold in order to make a "righteous" arrest. As far as Pete was concerned, those questions had been best left unasked, and the answers best left unspoken.

It took him a moment to realize that someone was talking to him. He looked up from his food to see a middle-aged waitress standing next to the table.

"Sorry," he said. "Did you say something?"

"I asked if there's anything wrong with the food."

"Oh, uh, no. I just don't have much of an appetite."

"Did you want me to box that up to go?"

"No, I'm good. Thanks."

"Okay," she said as she placed the check on the table. "Take care of yourself."

Pete left a two twenties on an eighteen-dollar tab and headed into the night.

He walked the streets, having no idea where his feet were taking him. It didn't matter. His thoughts were turbulent as he tried coming to grips with his father's nonchalant admission of killing Niko Babić and Wil Zmak. And then there was the offer of assistance if Pete chose to circumvent to law. Pete got the distinct impression his father was encouraging him to follow in his crooked footsteps. He'd always wanted to make his dad proud, but never dreamt it would entail breaking the law. If he took that route, would he ever be able to find his way back?

Andy's voice echoed in Pete's head, "...*it could blow up and cost you your job. Is it worth it? If it is, it's gonna need to be done right.*" 'Doing it right' meant not getting caught.

Pete pondered this conundrum. All the while, the creature inside him continued to chew.

Kelly was pondering her own conundrum. Unlike Pete, she'd already traveled that dark path, so breaking the law was no longer her issue. The issue was whether to take another life. Tonight's expedition would be the determining factor.

She was deep in thought when a knock on the door startled her. "Who is it?"

A few minutes later, Pete was sitting in Kelly's cozy living room, a scotch in his hand...a second glass of wine in hers. She wondered why he'd shown up out of the blue, and she soon found out.

Pete recounted the series of events that resulted in him being put on administrative leave. When he got to the part about breaking Myles Spencer's nose, Kelly was stunned. She'd never known Pete to be rash, especially when it came to his job.

He finished his story, and she could tell something else was bothering him. Something that weighed heavier and was more personal. It didn't take much to coax it out of him.

"I spoke to my father today and discovered some things I never knew," he said. "It turns out, Dad went rogue a few times when he was in the department."

"I don't know what that means, exactly."

"Planting evidence. Covering his ass with false reports. Using a stash of drugs skimmed from busts to pay off snitches."

"All I know about police work is what I've heard from you and what I've seen on TV. None of this sounds particularly shocking."

"The drugs could be overlooked. What's harder to overlook is that he and his partner raided a Croatian hideout and gunned down two people."

"You make it sound like murder. How do you know what happened? Maybe your father and his partner were involved in a shootout and…"

"He told me flat out. They went in with one specific purpose. To kill. It was nothing more than an execution."

"Why'd they do it?"

"Because the Croatians were trying to muscle in on the city's drug trade and had killed a half dozen Latino gangsters and their families."

"Their *families*? Have you considered that maybe your father's actions were justifiable?" she asked. "That killing these gangsters was the best outcome all around?"

"That's the problem. I think if I were in him, I'd have done the same thing. And that's what bothers me. You and I…we've always been on the right side of morality."

Kelly forced a smile that felt as hollow as a campaign promise.

Pete continued, "As far as I'm concerned, the law is black and white."

"I know," she said, her heart pounding.

"My father spent a lot of time in gray areas and convinced himself that occasionally breaking the law was worth the end result."

"And you think he might be right."

"I never did before. But now I'm not so sure, and that's what's haunting me. For the first time I'm not only wondering if I'd consider bending the law, but how far I'd be willing to go." He stopped, looking like a child who was suddenly lost and afraid.

Kelly had never seen him so vulnerable.

Without even thinking, she crossed over and threw her arms around him. It felt good. It felt natural. As they clung to each other,

Kelly thought there might be a sliver of hope that she and Pete could possibly have a strangely twisted future together.

An hour later, Pete rolled out of bed and picked up his clothes that were haphazardly strewn on the floor. Their lovemaking started out awkwardly. Kelly hadn't been intimate with anyone since being violated by Tommy Moretti, and she had to put her mind and body on autopilot. She and Pete soon got into a familiar groove, but the aftermath was filled with an undercurrent of confusion about the status of their relationship. Had they bridged an emotional chasm, or was this the grand finale?

Kelly cast a surreptitious glance at the clock. She needed to leave soon and didn't want to say anything that may encourage Pete to think spending the night was an option. Fortunately, he had places of his own to go to.

"So, how long is your suspension?" she asked.

"Could be a few days. Could be a week or more. All depends on what the brass considers best for our public image."

As Kelly slipped into her clothing, she asked, "What're you doing in the meantime?"

Pete considered taking Kelly into his confidence but decided against it. She was the most ethical person he'd ever met, and he couldn't bear the look of disapproval on her face if he told her that he was strongly leaning toward going off the reservation to bring down Spencer.

"I'm reviewing some old cases. In fact, one of them involves Tommy Moretti."

"Moretti? The man who killed my father?" She knew that wasn't the truth, but it was the official conclusion by the police, and Kelly had no intention of setting the record straight.

Pete nodded. "Remember I mentioned there was a dark-haired woman with Moretti at a club the night he overdosed? And that we found a few strands of synthetic hair at his house?"

"Vaguely," Kelly said. Given that Kelly had been that dark-haired woman, she dreaded what was coming next.

"We have a new tech in the department who can do miracles with video. I gave him the footage from The Patch, and I'm hoping I can finally get a look at the woman's face. If we can ID her, maybe we can fill in the missing pieces of the puzzle and figure out what really happened that night."

Kelly flashed back to 'that night' at The Patch: *Moretti and another man fighting; Kelly slipping drugs into Moretti's drink; Kelly suddenly growing dizzy; Moretti saying "Sofie? You coming?"*

Pete's voice brought her back to the present.

"I don't know if anything will pan out," Pete continued, "but it's worth a shot. I'd like to finally put that case to bed. In the meantime, and you're going to think this is crazy, I'm trying to chase down information on a phantom hit man."

Kelly's only option was to play naïve. "Phantom hit man. What's that even mean?"

"For years there have been stories about a mysterious contract killer who only takes out the bad guys."

"Sounds rights out of the tabloids."

"It might be."

"Why are *you* interested in him all of the sudden?"

Pete was about to mention the rumored connection between Gideon and Musselwhite but thought it best to keep that to himself. "Many of the deaths attributed to him are located in the Bay Area. Ron thinks I'm spinning my wheels, and my father says the guy's an urban myth, but I've got the time, so I figured, why not?"

Kelly managed to utter, "Huh." She suddenly felt lightheaded and sat back down on the bed.

Pete turned. "You okay?"

"Yeah." She forced a smile. "I think our gymnastics caught up with me."

Pete misinterpreted her smile and was optimistic their lovemaking was the first step in their relationship getting back on

195

track. Kelly, on the other hand, was fairly certain it was the last time they'd share a bed.

As the front door closed, Kelly collapsed onto her sofa. Pete's casual throwaway revelations were earth shattering. He had no idea he was on the verge of inadvertently exposing Kelly's deepest secrets. She wondered how he'd feel if he knew he'd just had sex with "the unidentified dark-haired woman" *and* "the mysterious contract killer."

Kelly couldn't worry about that now. She had other things on her mind.

36

Lisa Reynolds's house was located on a quiet cul-de-sac of ranch style homes that, thanks to their proximity to San Francisco, had steadily increased in value over the last decade. She could've sold the house and made a sizable profit, but it was the only thing of value she had.

It was just after 9:00 p.m. when Kelly cruised the block. The house was dark, as were the homes on either side. They rolled up the streets early on Monday nights in Millbrae. Unless Lisa's plans had changed, she and Emma would be at the Katy Perry concert for another two hours, which gave Kelly plenty of time.

She parked a few blocks away in the lot of the Skyline Terrace Apartments, her sedan blending in with a dozen cars just like it. Ten minutes later, Kelly stood in the darkened doorway of Lisa's house and rang the bell. If Lisa was home, Kelly had a readymade excuse, along with a bottle of wine in her backpack. After the second ring went unanswered, Kelly pulled the electric lock pick from her pack. Cora had noted that despite the security company sticker on the front window, Lisa had cancelled the service months ago. Also, based upon Lisa's purchases in the past six months, there were no indications she owned a dog. As Kelly slipped the lock pick into the door, she hoped that Cora was right on both counts.

After a few anxious moments, the tumblers lined up and the door swung open. Kelly eased inside, closing the door behind her. She wasn't searching for anything specific. She was looking for validation. She longed to answer the question, *"was Lisa a real threat to Emma?"*

The house was single story with a basic floorplan. Living room, small formal dining room, and a kitchen that opened into a den. The furniture was dated and worn. The carpeting was getting thin in spots and the walls bore years' worth of nicks and scrapes. Housekeeping wasn't a big priority for Lisa.

The hallway fed into three bedrooms and a bathroom. Kelly slipped on a pair of latex gloves and went to work.

The farthest room was stark and yielded no indications that anyone had ever lived in it. The walls were bare, as were the dresser top, the desk and the nightstands. The drawers were empty, and the closet was home to a dozen plastic hangers, sans clothing. Many parents who lost children kept their rooms intact…either as a shrine, or in the sad expectation that one day they'd miraculously knock on the front door and walk back into their lives as if nothing happened. Lisa, on the other hand, had dealt with her grief, or guilt, by scrubbing the memory of Sydney completely out of existence.

Kelly couldn't imagine the depth of pain that a mother felt when her child was snatched from this life, especially in such a horrific way. Nor could she imagine the degree of depravity of a mother who would murder her daughter in cold blood.

She desperately needed to know which end of the scale Lisa occupied.

Kelly quickly searched the next room, which belonged to Emma. It looked like that of typical teenager, albeit an extremely neat, upper-middle-class teenager. Her clothing was hung with precision and her shoes were perfectly aligned. The iMac on her desk was flanked by a word-of-the-day calendar and an iPad in a rainbow-colored leather case. The dresser top was home to a half dozen bottles of perfume aligned by height, a jewelry box that housed what looked to be a few expensive rings, and four identically framed photos of Emma posing with friends. Kelly made a mental note that none of the photos included Sydney.

The last bedroom belonged to Lisa. It was a mess. Her bed was unmade, and clothes were haphazardly tossed onto a chair in the corner. Next to the chair was a laundry basket of towels and sheets waiting to be folded and put away. Dresser drawers were ajar to reveal tangles of socks, bras and underwear. The top of the dresser was cluttered with a random scattering of face creams, an array of colorful gemstones and crystals, a few prayer candles, a brass incense burner and a well-thumbed book entitled *Interpreting The I Ching*.

The rooms were a perplexing juxtaposition, and Kelly wondered if Emma was a classic type A personality (if so, it was a trait she'd inherited from her father), or if it was a way for her to find order amidst the chaos of her life with her mother. The other explanation was that an overbearing Lisa forced her daughter to maintain her room like army barracks.

Kelly stared at the overflowing dresser in front of her and considered rummaging through the drawers, but to what end? What could she hope to find? A bloody knife? A guilt-ridden letter admitting to murder? She was beginning to believe this was a fool's errand.

She headed into the garage, which was a cacophony of cardboard boxes. The idea of digging through them in less than ninety minutes was daunting, and didn't hold much promise, but Kelly was determined and took on the challenge.

Many of the boxes were marked with post-it notes signifying they were bound for the Salvation Army. There were old books, outgrown children's clothing, and mismatched kitchen implements that had long since been replaced. One box was a trove of men's clothing. Doubtlessly items that Bob left behind. Kelly was ready to move on when she suddenly had a thought. Digging through the box she found two pair of men's shoes. Size eleven. Neither had mud or dirt in the treads, but they were the same size as the footprints near Sydney's corpse.

She turned her attention to a stack of smaller boxes and quickly sorted through them. Time was getting tight, but Kelly was on a mission, and she pushed harder. It was almost 10:30 p.m. when she came across a plastic crate of photographs. Everything from school pictures to Polaroids snapped at holiday parties. Kelly couldn't go through all of these, but she'd come to get a sense of Lisa and her relationship with her daughters. What better way than to look at family photos?

There were a few dozen envelopes, each labeled on the outside. Most of them contained pictures of Emma growing up. Emma as an infant, her first day of school, starring in a third-grade play, front and center in a soccer team photo. Emma's early life had been well-chronicled, and Kelly assumed that many more recent pictures were stored digitally.

Pictures of Sydney, on the other hand, were glaringly absent. Lisa had been thorough in expunging the memory of Sydney from her life.

Kelly came upon an envelope labeled "Christmas." It held random pictures of a festively decorated tree surrounded by brightly wrapped packages, as well as a yellow Lab wearing a Santa hat, and an eight-year-old Emma dressed like an elf. The last photo in the envelope had been ripped in half. The remaining portion showed Emma sitting on Lisa's lap. Kelly imagined the missing half featured Bob and Sydney.

She slipped that photo into her backpack and checked her watch. She allotted ten minutes to peruse the remaining pictures. It turned out she only needed half that. When she unearthed a photo of Lisa and Bob at a Halloween party, she stopped and stared. Lisa was having a grand old time, dressed like Poison Ivy and sporting a long, red wig. Kelly recalled Benedetto's words, "...*one witness claimed to have seen a short, skinny man with shoulder length red hair and a black ball cap running from the area where the body was found....They also found a few strands of red synthetic hair, presumably from a cheap wig.*"

Kelly was suddenly assaulted with flashing images. Images of events she hadn't experienced firsthand but that lived in her head like violent movies: *a person with long red hair emerging from a grove of trees and slashing a young girl's throat; Clarence Musselwhite swinging a weighted bat and clubbing Jessica over the head; Emma Reynolds screaming in fear, realizing she was about to die.*

Kelly jolted back to reality and was left reeling from the visions. She looked back at the photo, focusing on Lisa's laughing face framed by the red wig. Kelly felt a sudden upswell of anger and indignation. As far as she was concerned, all the evidence taken together tipped the scale of uncertainty. Kelly was now convinced Lisa murdered Sydney, and she no longer had lingering doubts that Emma would be next if she didn't intercede.

Kelly's instincts told her to run. To get the hell out of the house before she got caught. But she couldn't leave yet.

Not without a plan.

She slipped this photo into her backpack as well and hurried into the main house.

She went into the kitchen and quickly leafed through a stack of printouts on the counter that described different cuts of fish and how to prepare the more exotic and artistic sushi dishes. Next to the printouts were three partially consumed bottles of wine: a fruity Pinot, a light Rosé and a dark, heavy Cabernet. Kelly assumed the varietals were on hand to match Lisa's moods. Next to the stove was a rack of knives. Beautifully crafted Dalstrong Shogun sushi knives, honed to a lethal edge.

Drawing inspiration from her father, an idea was coming into focus. Kelly photographed each knife and took a dozen pictures of the kitchen.

This would be Gideon's canvas.

Just then, the front door swung open. Kelly had been so engrossed in her thoughts she hadn't heard the car pull up. She frantically looked around, but there was no place to hide.

She was screwed.

"Mom! I left my backpack in the car."

Lisa responded, "The car's unlocked."

As Emma dashed back out to the car, Lisa made a beeline for the bathroom down the hall. The moment the bathroom door closed

Kelly bolted out the rear door into the backyard. A few seconds later, she heard the car door slam, followed by the front door closing.

Kelly quickly made her way down the side of the house and out to the street. It wasn't until she was almost a block away that she remembered to breathe.

Earlier that night, about the time Kelly had been sorting through boxes in Lisa Reynolds's garage, Pete had been casing Myles Spencer's building. He knew Spencer was out on his boat for another of his infamous "dinner, drugs and debauchery" cruises, and took joy in the fact that the fucker's nose was too busted to snort coke.

Spencer's penthouse loft was located in the easternmost of three conjoined six-story buildings that shared a common lobby as well as a rooftop patio. The lobby was staffed by a security guard, which meant Pete couldn't simply stroll in. Instead, he waited by the rear door of the western building and casually entered as a tenant exited. He took the stairs to the roof and was lucky that the frigid San Francisco fog was keeping most people inside for the evening. One couple was huddled around a gas fire pit, braving the cold with the help of a bottle of Schnapps.

Pete stayed in the shadows as he traversed the rooftop, then silently made his way down a fire escape. He pried open a large window that led into Spencer's living room and slunk into the loft.

Not much had changed in the four days since Pete and Ron had rousted Spencer. Other than the ashtrays being emptied, and the beer cans and wine bottles cleaned up, the place still looked and smelled like a frat house. Pete passed through the living room and into what could best be described as a bachelor's wet dream. That is, if the bachelor had too much money, not nearly enough taste, and the maturity level of a college freshman.

One wall was dedicated to a massive flat screen monitor connected to a Klipsch sound system. A floor to ceiling shelving unit held an Xbox, a PlayStation and a Nintendo Switch, along with a full complement of game cartridges. Another wall was home to the obligatory bar, that was stocked better than most hotel watering holes, complete with a 150-bottle wine fridge.

Two classic pinball machines sat side-by-side in the corner. One featured Indiana Jones, and the other, the Loch Ness Monster. Pete figured they were valuable but had no idea he was looking at over $30,000 worth of wiring boards, flashing lights and rubber flippers.

A massive painting of a reclining nude woman dominated the room. Pete thought she looked vaguely familiar, maybe a B-level actress, and wondered if she'd been one of Spencer's frequent guests in this den of iniquity.

Pete peeled his eyes away from the rich boy's toys and got down to business. He had years of experience tossing residences, looking for weapons and illegal substances. Pete had no doubt that locating drugs in Spencer's loft would be easier than finding eggs at the White House Easter Egg Roll, but he wasn't interested in stealing pills or dope.

He was here to make a deposit.

The baggie in his pocket held two grams of Mexican Brown, which had a street value of about eight hundred dollars. It was identical to the heroin that the Norteños were currently slinging and would chemically match the stash taken from Gato Molina.

"Borrowing" drugs from the police evidence lockup wasn't easy, even for a homicide inspector who had access to the room. Drugs and weapons were kept under a separate lock, and every cop's entrance was logged. The fact that Pete was currently on suspension made access for him impossible. However, Andy Ericson's network of contacts still ran deep and ran wide. An hour after Andy had placed a call, the heroin was dropped off at his house. No questions asked. Pete didn't know if the drugs came from a police lockup somewhere in the city or from a Norteño delivery boy. He didn't need to know.

He didn't want to know.

The heroin had to be stashed someplace organic, where it wouldn't be too difficult to find, and yet, wasn't accidently consumed by Spencer or his buddies. From experience, he knew most users kept their best stuff in the bedroom, readily accessible when they lured a companion into their web.

Pete moved on to Spencer's bedroom, did a quick sweep, and found a few grams of coke in the top drawer of a bedside chest, along with a pipe, a small amount of meth, and a set of works. He decided to stash the dope somewhere a little more exclusive.

He slid open the bottom drawer, which was home to sex toys. They looked recently used, which was a disgusting thought. As Pete slid the drawer back into place, he realized something was off. The drawer didn't extend all the way to the rear of the chest. He pulled it back out, gingerly removed the paraphernalia, and felt around until he located a lever. He flipped the switch, and the drawer slid all the way out of the chest, revealing a four-inch-deep secret compartment in the back.

Nestled inside was a gun.

Pete plucked a pen from his pocket and fished out the gun, a Smith & Wesson MP9, with hand-carved handles and gold inlay on the barrel.

This changed everything.

It was a night of revelations all over the city. Kelly had found confirmation, Pete had found damning evidence, and Hector Ibarra had found Tomás Sanchez. Tomás was said to be hanging out in a duplex that belonged to Luca's brother, who currently resided in Cell Block C at San Quentin. Word got to Spider that Tomás would be on the move working the streets until midnight, which gave Spider time to tool up and roll out.

The duplex was across the street from Precita Park, which provided Spider a place to hang without attracting attention to himself. The moment Tomás showed his face, Spider planned to confront him.

204

As hour one stretched into hour two, the wet mist wrapped its clammy fingers around Spider's lean body. He was about to call it a night when Tomás emerged from the darkness, a smug look on his face. "I wondered how long you were gonna keep your skinny ass in the park."

"You knew I was here the whole time, huh?"

Tomás grinned. "I got *ojos* everywhere."

"Building your own little army. Toro's not gonna be happy about that."

"Toro thinks he got everythin' wired, you know, but he's old school. These young *soldados* are hungry, and they like my style."

"You plannin' on makin' a move on him?"

"I'm gonna be *jefe* eventually, so why wait? What you come to see me about? You pissed about my boys on Cypress? Cause' last I heard, that property's up for grabs."

"Yeah, well, we be grabbing it back. I came to tell you to stay the fuck away from Diego. That shit you gave him? You coulda killed him, asshole."

"Just tryin' to ease the pain. Fuckin' doctor wants him to take aspirin or some shit. Anyway, I thought you two weren't even talkin'."

"Ancient history, *hermano*. Just like you."

"That's where you're wrong, Oscar." Tomás spit out his brother's Christian name like a bug that had crept into his mouth. *"Soy el futuro."*

"Whatever. Just keep your fucking distance from Diego. And while you're at it, you better rethink your moves, 'cause it's not gonna end well."

"Finally, we agree on something, *hermano,*" Tomás said as he brought up his gun and shot Spider in the chest.

Five minutes later, Tomás and Luca hurried down the rear steps of the building, cut through a neighbor's yard, and moved from shadow to shadow, listening for the sounds of police sirens that never materialized. Luca was no fan of Spider but wondered if Tomás hadn't been a little too trigger happy. Gunning down one of Toro's street bosses was a declaration of war, and they weren't ready for that. They had to recruit more men, which meant taking more risks. They also needed money and product. Luca might be unhinged, but he had no death wish, and right now, Tomás was looking more like a liability that an asset.

Tomás grinned like a man whose life had finally turned the corner. For the first time, things were going his way. Sure, he'd just shot his brother and left him bleeding on the cold, damp pavement, but he had a plan. Tomás always had a plan. It was the only way to stay one step ahead of everyone else. First, he'd get word to Toro that he shot Spider in self-defense. The story being that Spider and Gizmo had been stealing, selling short bags, and stockpiling horse so they could go into business themselves. Tomás, being a good soldier, confronted Spider about it, and his fucking brother drew on him. His own flesh and blood. Tomás had no choice. He was just taking care of gang business. His allegiance to Toro was greater than to his own family.

Second, he had to bag the asshole that killed Gato. Tomás had a half dozen shorties on the street looking for information. They'd heard the killer was a *blanco*, but that was all they had. However, dangle enough dope around town and eventually someone who knew someone would offer up a name. The fallback option was simple: if Tomás couldn't uncover the actual shooter, he'd deliver Toro a random body and claim this was the guy.

Once Tomás got Toro on side believing this shit, he'd let him get comfortable. Wait until Toro's guard was down and then take him out. Make it look like a Sureño hit, or maybe just disappear his ass out in the mudflats. That would be Luca's job, and Tomás knew he could convince him it was a good play.

Luca never liked Toro anyway.

With Toro out of the way, Tomás would be *El Jefe*, and Luca, his *numero dos*, his enforcer, just like that Luca-fucking-Brasi in the movies. The two of them would take over that sweet clubhouse and live the life. Money, *mujeres*…whatever they wanted whenever they wanted. Tomás glanced over at Luca and saw the look of concern and doubt in his otherwise dull eyes. "It's all good, *amigo*. I got it all worked out. Trust me."

Tomás wanted Luca to trust him? Luca wasn't particularly bright, but didn't the snake in the garden say something like that to Adam?

And Tomás wasn't called "Culebra" for nothing.

37

Tuesday

The early morning sun was fighting a losing battle against the Colma fog that shrouded the cemetery in a layer of dense air. It seemed fitting that the ambiance was something out of a gothic novel.

At this hour, Kelly was the only visitor in the cemetery. She wove her way past the ornate monuments and mausoleums, taking the same path she trod every time she'd visited her mother over the last twenty years.

David Harper believed a person's final resting place should not be ostentatious, and the simple granite headstones which marked her parents' graves reflected that. He was also adamant about not adorning graves with flowers. It wasn't a money thing. It was seeing countless graves with dead or wilting flowers, that he found extremely depressing. Kelly heeded his wishes, and in lieu of flowers, she brought a small silver flask filled with single malt Clynelish.

She unscrewed the cap and poured a healthy shot onto his burial plot. Despite the extremely early hour, she knew that Dad hated drinking alone. She took a small sip before she tucked the flask away.

Kelly spent the next few minutes bringing her parents up to date on the latest news: the incredible progress Jessica was making with the new drug trial; the fact that the clinic was busy as ever and continued to be a beacon of light in the neighborhood (she neglected to mention the impending financial problems); how well Ida Samuel was working out (she left out Ida's inability to handle pressure without the assistance of drugs); and finally, that things with Pete were wonderful as ever (David had been so happy when the two of them became a couple and she saw no reason to dispel that notion).

Kelly had no idea why she was lying to her parents. If they were alive, she'd tell them the truth. She always had. Now that they were gone, why was she being deceitful? Was it because she wanted them to believe that everything was fantastic? Or was it because she didn't want to admit aloud that her life was spiraling out of control?

She finally got around to real reason she'd come.

"Dad, I went to see Matthew Benedetto the other day. It was the first time I'd been there since…well, in a few months. We talked a lot about you, of course, and then he mentioned a job. *A contract.* I was stunned, and to be honest, pretty pissed off. I'm so proud to follow in your professional footsteps. The other thing, I want no part of, and Benedetto knows that.

"But…it turns out there's this girl. Her name is Emma. She's only thirteen, and she's in real danger from her mother. If someone doesn't step in, Emma could be dead in a few days.

"Last night, I was ready to cross that line, but this morning, I have second thoughts. I could really use your advice on this. You'd probably tell me to walk away. That I'd be crazy to even consider it. On the other hand, I'm pretty sure you'd do whatever's necessary to protect her. The problem is, Emma needs Gideon, but Gideon's dead…right? I honestly don't think I've got what it takes to…"

A motor started up nearby and Kelly turned to see a groundskeeper in a compact excavator digging a new grave.

She was suddenly overcome with horrific images: *a casket being lowered into the hole; Bob Reynolds tossing dirt into the grave; Lisa Reynolds looking on, alligator tears flowing down her cheeks.*

Kelly reeled from the vision and steadied herself. She kissed her fingers and touched them to both headstones. "Love you guys."

She turned and walked away, knowing that she needed to make a decision, and make it quickly.

Kelly and Cora had agreed to meet at 8:00 a.m. and Kelly insisted she'd pick up coffee and pastries. After all the meals Benedetto had provided, it was the least she could do. Ironically, Benedetto himself wasn't there to enjoy the reciprocation.

Cora scanned in the photo of Lisa from the Halloween party and ran it through a program that restored the Polaroid picture to a brilliant, richly digitized image. The police report from Sydney's murder was on a second screen. Cora scrolled to the photos of the evidence collected at the scene and clicked on the thumbnail of the red polyester strands bagged by the crime scene techs.

Kelly considered herself capable with computers, but she marveled as Cora blew up the side-by-side images and did an intricate color analysis.

"It's a match," Cora announced.

"Now that we have this piece of evidence as well, can we pull together everything we've found and bring it to the police?"

"That's problematic on many levels. How would we explain where it all came from? Especially the information I obtained illegally. And then, there's the question of the provenance of the Halloween party photo. We couldn't prove it was found at Lisa's house and that it wasn't a fake. Plus, the police would want to know why we were interested in Lisa in the first place."

Cora was right. Even if they could convince the police where the photo came from, it would neither be admissible or compelling evidence. Just because Lisa wore a red wig, it wouldn't place her at Sydney's murder scene. There were probably hundreds of thousands of identical red wigs coming out of the same factory in China.

Kelly's aggravation was evident. "So, even though we're convinced that Lisa killed her daughter, there's not enough to convince the authorities."

"You just verbalized the very reason Gideon came into existence. Mr. Benedetto and your father were certain beyond a shadow of a doubt that every one of their targets were guilty. However, if there'd been enough evidence for the authorities to arrest and convict the suspects, they never would've been on Gideon's hit list."

"It's so frustrating."

"Your father expressed that exact sentiment when he was starting out."

"I'm not starting out. I'm not *starting* anything here. After this, I'm done."

"Kelly, you've been in turmoil since your father died, and I'm not sure it's a good idea for you to add more turbulence to your life. *If* you go through with this, all the progress you've made toward healing in the past two months will be washed away and you'll likely take a massive step backwards."

"I don't see that I have a choice. I'd rather deal with my own demons than with the knowledge that my inaction resulted in the death of a thirteen-year-old girl. I wish Mr. Benedetto never told me about Lisa Reynolds, but I believe it was meant to be. Maybe it's fate's way of balancing some cosmic scorecard. I put Jessica in grave danger, and now I have a chance to save Emma."

"Do you have a timetable?"

"Lisa has Emma for a week, and based upon what Lisa's told me, she's got every moment planned with mother-daughter activities right up until Emma flies out."

"Pampering Emma until she takes her life. That's perverse."

"We're dealing with a sociopath. I'm assuming Emma will be safe for a few days, which will give me time to pull things together."

"If you need anything at all, call me."

As Kelly was heading to her car, she got a call from Vik informing her that Oscar Sanchez had been shot and taken to San Francisco General.

Ten minutes later, Kelly rushed into the hospital to find a grieving Alma. Usually a compact force of nature, she looked frail and defeated. Her head hung low, her focus on a set of well-used rosary beads she fingered while intoning a continuous prayer for her son.

"Alma," Kelly said quietly.

Alma looked up and burst into tears at the sight of her friend and confidant. She rose and fell into Kelly's arms. Kelly rocked this woman who'd been through so much in her lifetime. Fleeing the horrors of the South American cartels for the safety and freedom that the United States offered, only to have her sons get pulled into the gangs. One was dead. One was in prison. One was permanently maimed, and now one was in the operating room fighting for his life.

And then there was Tomás. Maybe the smartest of them all. Definitely the most evil.

"What have the doctors told you?" Kelly asked.

"Nothing!"

If Oscar had died, they would've notified Alma immediately, so no news was good news. But the question was, how bad was the "good news."

"I'll speak to the doctors. Do you need anything?"

Alma shook her head. Her tiny body trembled as Kelly helped her back to her seat. "It'll be okay."

"Doctor Kelly, I hate this life *por mi hijos*. Oscar may have done some bad things in his life, but he doesn't deserve to die. When I think back to losing Chavo, it makes me appreciate *todos mijos.*" Alma slowly shook her head when she admitted, "Even Tomás. I couldn't stand to lose another child. No mother could."

Kelly knew the pain of death, having lost both her parents. She hoped to never experience the death of a son or daughter.

The doctor who operated on Oscar was between surgeries and he brought Kelly up to speed. The bullet had missed the heart and esophagus but had shattered two ribs and punctured his lung. There could also be some damage to Oscar's spine. The ER doctors had intubated him, suctioned the blood from his chest wall and re-expanded his collapsed lung, before repairing the gunshot wound.

They were waiting on an orthopedic surgeon to arrive to do a spinal evaluation.

The odds were fifty/fifty that Oscar would walk again.

When Kelly finally arrived at the Mission Street Clinic, she found Ida manically adding more information to the tracking chart, which had been relocated from her apartment to a wall in the tiny breakroom. Kelly took Ida aside and asked how she was feeling. Ida assured her she was flying strictly on adrenaline and espresso.

Kelly stepped over to give the map a closer look. "How's this going?" she asked.

"The connection escapes me, but there *must* be one," said Ida.

Kelly tapped on the map. "What's this? An office building?"

Ida checked her notes and nodded. "One of the cases, a Mrs. Hartung, is a vice president at a bank in the lobby."

"And what about this?"

Ida consulted her notes. "That's a strip mall with a dry cleaner, a salon, a yoga studio and a liquor store. There were two cases in this area."

Kelly took a step back to get a broader picture. "We assume this is being spread by airborne contagions, or personal contact, but the patients don't appear to have any kind of communal point. It *could* be that the point of contact is mobile."

Ida's eyes lit up. "Like an Uber driver? Or a delivery person?"

"A lot of these people work in office buildings or strip malls. Where do most of those folks eat these days?"

Ida shrugged. "I don't know enough about the city to venture a guess."

"Food trucks."

Ida took a step back and joined Kelly for a less myopic view of the map. Her face lit up. "A food truck! Of course!"

Over the next hour, Ida left word for every patient she'd seen, desperately hoping that one or more would confirm they ate from the same truck in the past few days.

As her determination grew, her energy flagged. Out of sheer habit, she reached into her pocket and retrieved the cylindrical pill holder. It beckoned to her. A single dose and she'd be good to go for another few hours.

She asked herself the question…what was more important right now? Kicking her habit or finding that food truck?

38

Pete met Ron for an early lunch. Like thousands of hungry diners who had limited time and budgets, cops were food truck junkies. New trucks were coming into the city every month and Ron heard about one that was rumored to have the best tamales in town; spicy *lengua* covered in tomatillo habanero salsa. The problem was, that truck, like many others, didn't have a permanent spot so it was a crapshoot to stumble upon it at lunch time. Once a patrol car found one of those roaming gems, they sent the word out over the "black and white network" and uniformed officers would converge like ants at a bake sale. SFPD inspectors were left to fend for themselves.

Pete and Ron settled for prewrapped sandwiches from a corner deli and sat at one of three small tables in front of the shop, overlooking a street badly in need of repair that nevertheless teemed with traffic, which described almost every street in the city.

Pete offhandedly mentioned his Dark Web exploits, and Ron humored him. "Garvin the pig?"

"Guinea pig," Pete corrected. "He was a cartoon character, and now, he's the gateway to info about Gideon."

"Those crazy hackers and their alliteration. You know this is a complete waste of time, right?"

"Maybe, but once you get into the darknet, there's some interesting stuff."

"Other than porn?"

"You've got a one-track mind. There's a group of people called The Committee who are offering seven million dollars for proof of Gideon's identity."

"Sure, there is. I wonder how much they'd pay to find out how the Joker really got those scars."

Pete considered telling Ron about Arthur Moretti and Clarence Musselwhite, but decided it was better to keep that under wraps and

215

run with it himself to see where it might lead. He changed the subject.

"Have you heard anything on my situation?" Pete asked.

"They're keeping a tight lid on. What's your rep have to say?"

"Be patient, don't talk to the press, stay far away from the Molina case, and even further away from Myles Spencer."

"That shouldn't be so tough."

Pete's poker face failed him again.

"Oh, fuck," said Ron. "I know that look."

Pete never realized just how transparent he was. That could end up being a problem.

Ron continued. "You've been on suspension for twenty-four hours and you've already crossed the line?"

"Crossed what line?"

"Shit, you did. Tell me you didn't talk to a reporter."

"Of course not."

"Good thing. The department would take your shield and put you on permanent assignment walking a beat in the Tenderloin. So, you've been sniffing around Spencer." It was a statement. Ron already assumed the answer, fully aware that Pete wouldn't accept a suspension without doing everything possible to prove his innocence.

Pete didn't know if he could convince his partner of the veracity of his tale, but everything was riding on it. He channeled his father, and the lies began to flow.

"I went to the marina last night. Checked out the berth where Spencer keeps his boat and spoke to a few people who have boats nearby. He's known as the king of the booze cruise. Most nights, his fifty-foot Hatteras is a floating rave, complete with unlimited party favors."

"Other than potentially piloting a vehicle under the influence, it's not illegal."

"The drugs are. Especially the Mexican tar."

"If he had any on board."

216

"I got the name of a guy who was out with Spencer two nights ago. I tracked him down, and he claimed Spencer was dishing out packets of brown smack. I remember hearing that Narcotics busted a Norteño dealer last week. If we could get our hands on even a few grains of heroin from Spencer's boat, the lab could run a comparison."

"Which would require doing a sweep of his boat."

"True. I'm guessing he doesn't bring in a cleaning crew, and junkies aren't too careful when they're brewing a fix, especially if they didn't pay for the product. There's got to be all kinds of stray powder on that boat."

"How am I supposed to get a warrant? No judge is going to sign off on this unless I've got a pretty strong argument, and you've already pissed off the DA's office, not to mention our own brass."

"I can put you together with the guy who was on the boat."

"This person would be willing to sign a statement that he was partying on a boat where people were doing blow and shooting up? Why would he do that?"

"Because he walked in on Spencer screwing his girlfriend."

Pete could see Ron's wheels turning. Ron was well-respected in the department, as well as downtown, and if he pushed on this, he could make it happen. "It might work. Jealousy is a powerful motivator. I'd probably have to cash in a few favors."

"Yeah, so? What are you saving them for?"

"For when *I'm* on the receiving end of a department fuck-fest and need all my chits."

"If we can close the Molina case, and the other two dealer homicides, you'll stack up more goodwill, and I'll get this bullshit rap expunged from my jacket. Plus, we both know Spencer's guilty. This is our best shot to put this scumbag away."

"Maybe. Let me make a few calls, test the waters. In the meantime, give me the details on this witness."

217

Pete handed Ron one of his cards with the witness's info written on the back. Ron smiled and shook his head. "Always prepared. You're a fucking Boy Scout."

The Boy Scouts don't give out merit badges for lying, breaking-and-entering, or planting evidence.

39

The clinic was operating at capacity, a revolving door of gashes, fractures and allergic reactions. The myriad patients included two more people exhibiting symptoms similar to Gretchen Sadowski. Ida excitedly questioned both, but neither recently ate from a food truck or knew anyone who had. However, both reported coming into contact with people who were suffering from nausea and terrible headaches. Ida gathered as much information as she could, certain that whatever illness was making its way through San Francisco would continue to build steam.

The patient flow finally tapered off. Ida was writing up notes on her last patient when she got a call from a nurse at St. Francis. Gretchen Sadowski had experienced a series of petit mal seizures and was admitted to the hospital for observation. Her partner was with her now, and the attending physician expected to get the results from Gretchen's spinal tap any minute.

As Ida hung up, another call came in. This one from Shannon Casey. She confirmed she'd eaten some food truck tacos last week and still felt terrible. She couldn't remember what day it was or the name of the truck, but it was run by a young Latino couple who spoke halting English.

Meanwhile, Kelly took a call from Cheryl Gartsman, who said she'd gotten lunch from a truck called Tico's Tamales the day prior to feeling sick. Three other people in her office were out sick with the same symptoms. They'd all eaten from Tico's.

Ida and Kelly compared notes and realized they may have found their Typhoid Mary (who, ironically, was a cook) in the form of a Mexican food truck. The problem was Tico's truck could be anywhere in the city.

Ida began the search with the Public Works Department, which regulated the food trucks in the city. A harried woman answered, "Public Works. This is Darlene. Please hold."

"Wait, wait, wait." said Ida. "This is a medical emergency."

"Then you've called the wrong number. This is Public Works. I've got three people on hold and…"

"I understand. Really, I do. My name is Doctor Samuel, and I desperately need information on a food truck."

Darlene's patience was stretched to the limit, and she didn't hold back the attitude, "Listen, *Doctor*. I've got people who have actual business with this department, so…"

"Let me explain," Ida said in a rush. "There's some kind of epidemic going around, and we're pretty sure it's being spread by a food truck. Every minute that goes by without shutting the truck down, puts more people's lives in jeopardy."

There was momentary pause on the line. When Darlene spoke, she sounded like she was slowly coming around. "How do I even know you're a doctor?"

"Darlene, please. My name is Ida Samuel. I just started working at the Mission Street Clinic, and I really need your help. I'm sorry that I'm not used to dealing with big city bureaucracies, so I'm hoping you can cut me a little slack."

"Huh," Darlene was beginning to thaw. "I'm a small-town girl, myself."

Ida switched tactics and took on a more conversational tone. "Where are you from?"

"A one-light town I'm sure you've never heard of. It's a tiny dot on the map called Frazeysburg."

"Shut up! Home of the world's largest apple basket!"

"What? How in heaven would you know that?"

"I grew up in Sugarcreek."

"Oh, my goodness," said Darlene. "George and I stopped there once on our way up to Cleveland for a Browns game. I love those little Amish shops, and that giant Cuckoo Clock! Now here we both are in San Francisco. Such a small world. I guess I can spare a few minutes for a fellow Ohioan. Gimme the name of that truck."

Kelly smiled as she watched Ida cajole the woman into looking up Tico's Tamales. It was the first time Kelly had seen Ida come out of her shell and allow her natural personality to shine through.

After a short delay, Darlene informed Ida that they had no such truck in their system. It was either brand new, or more likely, one of a dozen gypsy food trucks that operated around the city without a permit. Darlene apologized that she couldn't help but did mention that her social calendar was wide open and would love to grab a drink and talk about home.

Ida hung up in frustration. They were so close to nailing down the probable source of the outbreak, and yet it remained just out of reach. Every hour that went by would result in more cases, and Ida was at a loss on how to proceed.

Annie and Vik had joined the conversation, and he offered up an idea. Annie knew a lot of policemen, having dated her fair share of beat cops in the past few years. Maybe she could make a few calls. As it turned out, she was currently in an on-again, off-again relationship with a patrolman who had only two things on his mind: sex and food. He liked them both extra spicy and was constantly on the prowl.

"Annie, you've gotta call him," Ida said.

"I've kinda been avoiding him lately. He keeps hinting at playing house, and I'm not looking for a roommate."

Ida gave her an understanding smile but wasn't going to let her off that easy. "Annie, we've got patients who are quite ill. It's our duty as healthcare professionals to…"

Annie acquiesced. "I know. I know." Her part-time booty-call answered immediately, his hopes rising. When she explained what she needed, he was slightly subdued, but figured he could parlay information for something more substantial. He'd heard about a tamale truck from some of the guys on the squad. He thought he *might* be able to get a line on it if he put it out on the radio, but….

He let the offer dangle out there, fishing for a quid pro quo. Whatever Annie whispered into the phone must've worked because he said he'd call her right back.

She hung up, shaking her head. "If the public only knew the sacrifices we healthcare professionals make on their behalf."

Ida's cell buzzed. It was the nurse from St. Francis. They'd just gotten the results on Gretchen's lab work. As Ida listened, her expression grew progressively grim. She ended the call and turned to the others. "We've got an outbreak of bacterial meningitis."

Bacterial meningitis, an acute inflammation of the membranes covering the brain and the spinal cord, was transmitted through droplets of respiratory secretions. Kissing, sneezing, or coughing were the most common ways of spreading the disease. It was easy to imagine a cook coughing or sneezing into food.

If left unchecked, meningitis could be fatal.

Ida continued. "It took longer to diagnose because it's a mutant strain. The doctors at St. Francis believe it's more virulent than common meningitis and spreads faster."

Annie's phone chirped, and she read the text from her cop friend. "No one's seen the truck since this afternoon. The police think it only does lunch, which means it'll be tucked away until tomorrow. That'll buy us a little time."

Kelly said, "I'll contact Public Health and have them put out a bulletin. Ida, call the hospitals and let them know what we're dealing with." She turned to Annie. "We need to get in touch with our patients and have them go to the nearest hospital immediately for testing and antibiotics. And tell them they're going to need a list of any family members or other people they've been in close contact with."

Kelly's next call was to the Captain of Field Operations for the SFPD. He assured her that first thing tomorrow morning, they'd issue an APB on Tico's Tamales with an order to quarantine the truck and the operators.

As Kelly wrapped up her conversation, she got a call from Ingrid at Peninsula Oaks. Dr. Papadakis requested she swing by so they could discuss Jessica's recent response to the drug trial. When Kelly asked if everything was alright, Ingrid replied there was nothing to worry about. The doctor would fill her in when she arrived. How soon could she get there?

Kelly squelched the desire to reach through the phone and throttle Ingrid for a straight answer. She had guarded optimism when it came to Papadakis' medical knowledge but resented his theatrics and self-aggrandizing manner. She wished he were less P.T. Barnum and more Jonas Salk, but every doctor had their quirks.

Kelly was a living example.

At the same time Kelly was pulling into the parking lot at Peninsula Oaks, a nondescript white sedan was pulling into the parking lot at the San Francisco Marina Harbor. An older man got out, carrying a small tool bag and wearing a windbreaker with a Pacific Security logo. He looked at his watch and casually walked west. A nattily dressed couple in their early sixties were strolling in his direction. They carried a cooler and were headed to one of the expensive yachts for a dinner cruise.

The security guard smiled and stepped aside for them to pass. The woman brushed up against the guard for the briefest moment, apologized for her clumsiness, and the couple continued on, stopping to peer out at Alcatraz arising from the choppy bay waters.

"Did you get it?" the man asked in a low voice.

The woman slid her hand into her coat pocket and came out with a piece of paper that contained a six-digit numerical code. She nodded, then checked her watch. "Two minutes."

Meanwhile, the guard had arrived at an electrical junction box labeled "Pacific Security." He glanced around as he opened his toolkit and pulled out what looked like a radiator hose clamp connected to a coiled wire that extended down into the tool bag. He

223

secured the clamp around a thick wire running out of the electrical box, then reached into the bag and flipped a switch.

The jaunty couple arrived at a three-sided security gate. The woman punched the six-digit code into a touchpad and the gate buzzed, then unlatched. The couple ambled through the gate and picked up speed as they headed toward one of the yachts.

They had exactly twelve minutes.

Thirty miles south, Kelly entered Jessica's room to find her propped up in bed. A video camera was set up to capture the events that were unfolding.

A portable meal tray extended across Jessica's lap and on top was a child's wooden shape-puzzle. A blue triangle, green oval and red rectangle were snuggled into their respective places.

Kelly was speechless. Just one week ago, Jessica was lying in the same bed, her life slowly wasting away in a netherworld. And now, she had the mental acuity to comprehend basic shapes. Dr. Papadakis might be unconventional in his methods, but no one could argue with these jaw-dropping results.

"Jess?" Kelly crossed the room, not wanting to disturb her sister's concentration, but at the same time, feeling a desperate urge to be near her. With a nod from Dr. Papadakis, Ingrid switched off the camera.

Jessica slowly raised her eyes, seemingly noted the presence of Kelly, then went back to the task at hand.

"Incredible, isn't it?" Papadakis sounded like a proud father, crowing about his child taking her first step. In a sense, she had. Her first step toward cognizance in over twenty years.

"It's amazing."

He beamed. "It's a *major* breakthrough. No MCS patient who's been in a near vegetative state for twenty years has ever regained this level of responsiveness."

Kelly couldn't stop staring in awe at her sister. Jessica managed to fit the blue triangle into the correct slot, and let out a breath, as if the effort was overwhelming. She glanced up at Kelly, and her lips formed the faintest smile.

It was the most beautiful smile Kelly had ever seen.

Tears formed at the corners of her eyes, and Kelly let them flow. It had been a long time since she'd cried tears of joy, and as they trailed down her cheeks, Kelly was awash with a sense of positivity and happiness that had been lacking in her life since the death of her father. Maybe this was the beginning of things turning around.

She turned to Dr. Papadakis, "What's next?"

"We'll continue with the overall course of treatment. I believe we can achieve an even greater degree of lucidity." Dr. Papadakis radiated with the near certainty that a Nobel was finally within his grasp.

"Could I have a few minutes with my sister?"

"Of course, of course." He motioned to Ingrid, and the two of them left the room, quietly closing the door on their way out.

Jessica seemed to ponder the yellow wooden square in her hand, as if she didn't realize until now that it was there. She slowly opened her fingers and the piece clattered to the tray.

"Jess," Kelly said quietly. "How are you doing, sweetheart? How do feel?"

Jessica slowly raised her head. She looked at Kelly and blinked several times, trying to bring her sister's face into focus. It was a chilling moment for Kelly, as she wondered what, if anything, was going through Jessica's mind.

"It's me," she whispered. "It's Kelly. Your sister."

Jessica held her gaze for five seconds. Those five seconds felt like an eternity and filled Kelly with questions. Did Jess recognize her? Did she have any idea where she was, or how long she'd been there? If she continued to make progress, and eventually achieved a modicum of awareness, how would she react to the fact that the world had moved on without her?

Jess finally broke off her look and settled her head back onto her pillow. Her color was good, but she looked drained. The time she'd spent back in the real world had taxed every fiber of her being.

As Jessica closed her eyes, Kelly felt a swell of optimism. Jess would never fully recover, and it was highly unlikely she'd achieve the capacity to stand up and walk out of the facility, but if she could navigate her way to the surface once in a while and be mentally present, even for a few precious moments, it would be nothing short of a miracle.

40

Matthew Benedetto hoped for a miracle of his own, however he'd accepted the grim reality that "hope" was a dim notion, getting fainter by the moment. Try as he might, he couldn't imagine a scenario where he'd walk free.

When he'd regained consciousness, he'd attempted to stand up. Even that small movement resulted in excruciating pain. An agonizing reminder that Mott was fast and dangerous. Benedetto wondered how badly he was injured, and then wondered if it even mattered.

Alone in the room, he bowed his head and spoke in hushed tones, "Caucasian, average height, extremely thin. Ash blonde hair going to gray. Bodyguard named Mott..." Benedetto stopped when the man entered the room, counting his steps, a bottle of vodka in one hand and a file folder in the other.

"How do you feel?" the man asked without a hint of empathy. The fact that he didn't look Benedetto in the eye made the question all the more rote.

"Like I was hit by a truck."

"I'm sorry about that. Yes, sorry." He held up the bottle of vodka. "I don't drink alcohol, no way, but maybe you would like this."

Benedetto was tempted to take a shot to help dull the pain but thought it best to have all his brain cells humming at max capacity. "I'll pass."

The man was offended that his offering wasn't accepted. "My mother said it was rude to turn down gifts, even if you don't want them."

"Your mother sounds like a wise woman," said Benedetto, "but I don't drink alcohol either."

"Liar! I watched you drink wine when you eat dinner at Bishop's on Saturdays. Every Saturday night. I have photographs. You eat at the bar, and drink wine. Sometimes white. Sometimes red. So, you are lying. That's why I can't trust what you say. You lie about everything!"

The man put the vodka down on the bar, then dragged a folding chair over and motioned for Benedetto to have a seat. He pulled up a second chair for himself. Even though the two of them were face-to-face across a low coffee table, the man turned his head slightly so as to not look directly at his prisoner. "No more lies. Only truth. Okay?" He paused, waiting for a reaction from Benedetto. When none came, the man looked perplexed. "Okay?"

Instead of another denial that would engender more outbursts of anger, and undoubtedly more physical punishment, Benedetto decided on a different tack. "How exactly is this going to work? After kidnapping me and holding me prisoner for days, you're just going to let me walk out of here?"

The man nodded. "And give you money. Cash. For information."

"Information about this supposed assassin..."

"He's real, and you know him. Yes, you do."

The man opened the file folder to reveal a stack of eight by ten color photos of various people as they arrived at Benedetto's office. He laid the pictures on the table, squaring the edges. "Eleven months and ten days ago, I had a micro-camera installed on a street sign across from your office. There are many, many photos. One thousand, four hundred, fifty-two. I haven't looked at all of them yet. No way. I concentrated on people who showed up multiple times. Like Cora Mathews. She's there every day. Yes, every day. You must like her."

The man flipped to the next photo. "This is Sadhana Greenberg, a law student at the University of California. The one in Berkeley, California. I looked her up on LinkedIn. She works for you sometimes."

Benedetto suddenly felt naked and exposed. He'd assumed that one day someone would discover Gideon's identity, and then follow the breadcrumbs from David Harper to Clarence Musselwhite to Dominic Bruno and finally end up at Benedetto's doorstep with a gun. He hadn't imagined the trail would play out in reverse.

The man laid out more photos. "These other people aren't Gideon," he said matter-of-factly. "They're too young, too old, or they're invalids. Gideon is not a cripple. No way. He started killing twenty years ago, so he must be between forty-five years old and sixty-five years old. That narrows it down."

The next photo was of a stocky, bearded man in his fifties. "Thomas Edward Abel. He's an electrical engineer and also has a degree in biology from the University of California. The one in Los Angeles. He's very smart and knows about all kinds of things. He has been to your office many times but has no arrest record, so he doesn't need a lawyer." As the man recounted these facts, he seemed to take pride in his ability to not only have amassed this information, but also to have arrived at his Holmesian deductions. "He could be Gideon. Yes, he could."

The second photo showed a pale, lean man in his sixties. "William Cuzner Leetham. He's a professor of zoology at the University of San Francisco. He teaches entomology, which is all about insects. His fiancée was killed by a drunk driver many years ago. The man who drove that car died a year later while he was camping outside of Tucson, Arizona. He was bitten by a Bark scorpion. The Bark scorpion is the most poisonous scorpion in the world. Yes, the entire world. That sounds like Gideon. Maybe William Leetham hired Gideon. Maybe William Leetham *is* Gideon."

The third and final photo showed David Harper. "Doctor David James Harper. His wife, Mary Farnsworth Harper, was murdered by Clarence Musselwhite. Murdered dead. This makes David Harper the most obvious person. Yes, so obvious. Especially if he found out that Clarence Musselwhite didn't die in police custody. If he were told that Clarence Musselwhite was in witness protection, then

David Harper would kill Clarence Musselwhite for revenge. For sure. David Harper came to your office many times."

Benedetto shook his head disdainfully, as if the idea was utterly ludicrous.

The man continued. "At first, I was sure that David Harper must be Gideon. It made the most sense. Yes, it did. But he died two months ago, and there have been more victims since then."

Benedetto cut in. "Do you really think if I was acting as a middleman for an assassin, I'd meet with him in person, in my office?"

The man nodded. "Yes. Just like us. You and me right here. Now."

"This whole thing is ridiculous," said Benedetto.

"Why were you meeting with Doctor David Harper? He doesn't need a defense lawyer. He has no criminal charges against him. No way."

"You're an intelligent man so I'm sure you're aware of a thing called attorney-client privilege."

"I don't care about that!" The man's hands began to shake with a fury that was enveloping him. He bowed his head and breathed deeply, intoning his mantra. Time crept by slowly as he struggled to turn back the tide of rage.

He abruptly gathered up the photos into a neat stack and slid them back into their folder. "I think Mott had the best idea. Yes, the very best idea." The man suddenly lashed out and struck Benedetto in the damaged ribs with a surprisingly powerful punch.

Benedetto slid off his chair, gasping in shock, tears of pain welling up in his eyes.

"More lies mean more pain. Yes, more pain."

"Fuck you," Benedetto muttered through clenched teeth.

Their eyes met, and in that moment, Benedetto could see the undeniable reality of his situation. There was one way, and one way only, he'd ever get out of this hellhole alive.

Cora had three computer screens open, running string searches for different keywords that might provide a clue to Benedetto's situation. Years ago, she'd hacked into the computer systems at the city's local hospitals, as well as the ten SFPD precincts. The databases confirmed that Benedetto hadn't been admitted as a patient anywhere in the city, nor had he been booked by the police. Additionally, there were no incident reports involving any "John Does" who matched his description.

Just then, the center screen emitted a chime signifying she'd gotten a hit. A few simple keystrokes and the screen displayed a short thread from one of the hundreds of message boards that hid behind layers of obfuscation and complex firewalls. For Cora, these were as readily accessible as Google. The thread that popped up referenced The Committee, and a user posted, "On verge of positive ID. Expect confirmation w/in next 24 hrs. Yes, one day."

She attempted to trace the origin of that post, but the user had signed off and left no electronic footprint behind. Whoever this was had some serious electronic protection. All of this led to a single, chilling conclusion: Benedetto was in deep trouble and the clock was ticking.

41

Benedetto wasn't the only one having a bad day. Oscar Sanchez was in traction with a tube sticking out of his chest, running from his pleural cavity into a suction bottle, which slowly filled with blood and other fluids. Twin IVs pumped painkillers and antibiotics. His breathing was shallow, and his eyes twitched under heavy lids as he floated in a morphine-induced haze.

Diego, now recovered from his own opiate fog, was allowed to briefly look in on his brother. He limped into the room on crutches, and with each step, felt increasingly worse about letting Oscar down. Diego reached out to gently touch his brother's face and Oscar's eyes fluttered open. He managed a tiny nod to acknowledge Diego's presence.

"How you doin', Oscar?" It was a silly question, but Diego didn't know what else to say.

Oscar blinked a few times then parted his lips. Nothing came out but a puff of dry, stagnant air. Seeing his brother in such a frail state, Diego felt a panic rising up from his chest. Oscar was his rock and his best friend. Diego felt like he'd lost Oscar two months ago when Oscar stopped talking to him. The thought of losing him for real was too much to bear.

Oscar focused his gaze and tipped his head to the left. Diego took that as a signal to lean in. He put his ear near Oscar's mouth. Though strained, Oscar was able to form words that came out in halting whispers.

As Oscar spoke, Diego's eyes grew wide in disbelief.

Traffic on the 101 was heavy, and Kelly's drive home from Peninsula Oaks was stop-and-go. When her cell buzzed, she assumed it was Pete, calling about getting together for a drink and an encore of last night's hookup. The thought of doing either was exhausting. She decided to let it go to voice mail and deal with Pete tomorrow, but when she glanced at the screen, she was surprised to see Cora Mathews' name.

Kelly picked up immediately.

"I've been monitoring Bob Reynolds's email," Cora explained. "He just received confirmation from Delta for three passengers flying from San Francisco to Detroit, departing in two days. The third passenger is Emma."

"Lisa said she had Emma for an entire week."

"It appears her ex has a different agenda."

"When she finds out, she'll come unglued. I need to accelerate my plans."

"Are you prepared?"

"The closer I get to actually doing this, the more trepidation I have."

"We've already had this conversation, but you don't have to go through with this, Kelly. There's a chance Emma will be just fine."

"There's a better chance that in the next thirty-six hours, she'll be dead." Then, almost as an afterthought, she asked, "Have you heard anything about Mr. Benedetto?"

"There's been some chatter on the message boards, but nothing definitive." There was no reason to alarm Kelly with her suspicion that Benedetto was in serious trouble. "I may be completely wrong about this entire situation. It's possible he just wanted to get away for a while and he'll show up tomorrow like nothing ever happened."

Cora knew her wishful thinking was just that.

Kelly arrived home to find Alexa's BMW parked in front of her building. Ten minutes later they were in Kelly's living room reviewing the clinic's financial situation.

"My co-worker Gus Taylor got in touch with several doctors who actively consult with hospital groups around the country. None of them were familiar with the medical associations that hired your

233

father over the years," Alexa said. "Kel, I don't know what to make of that."

Kelly shook her head. "Neither do I. Dad never talked to me about his side gigs, other than to say that he was going to be out of town for a few days to do some consulting." Kelly hated to lie to her best friend, but Alexa had unexpectedly gotten much too close for comfort. Kelly should've known that Alexa would go to great lengths to help her out, which meant turning over every conceivable stone.

"I'm worried your father may have inadvertently gotten involved with some questionable people."

That's an understatement, thought Kelly. "You know what? Let's just forget this whole thing. I'd hate for something to come to light that could potentially smear his reputation."

"I understand, but what if it was illegal? I'm not suggesting that your dad was knowingly doing something against the law, but if this money is dirty, it could put the clinic at risk. It also might end up being a problem for you."

"Can't we just let sleeping dogs lie?"

"I'd feel a lot better if we could figure out exactly what's gone on so we can get ahead of this. Is there any way I can get in touch with your former accountant? Maybe she's got some answers."

Kelly shook her head. "She's on a cruise ship somewhere in the Pacific. Or maybe the Atlantic, I don't know, but she made it clear she'd be unreachable."

"Then I'd recommend we give everything over to Gus. He's the smartest forensic accountant I've ever known and..."

"I wish you hadn't brought him into this."

"He just made a few calls. Trust me. Gus deals with confidential information every day, and whatever he discovers stays between him and his clients. He's under no obligation to report any irregularities to the officials."

"I don't want him involved in this, okay?"

Alexa was surprised at Kelly's tone but chalked it up to the myriad pressures she was facing. "I get it, Kel, but understand that you're not going to be able qualify for any grants or loans with these financial statements."

"Then I'll have to think of another way to come up with the money."

Alexa was at a loss. She knew Kelly was fiercely protective about her father's memory, but there was something else at play here.

Something Kelly wasn't sharing.

42

Four 1000-watt halogen lights on tripods cut through the night and illuminated Myles Spencer's craft from stem to stern. Ron Yee supervised three forensic techs clad in white coveralls who methodically combed through the boat. They'd already collected several bags of suspicious substances, which fueled their desire to find more.

While the techs concentrated on the particle level, Ron's focus was the larger picture. The warrant gave them unlimited access to the entire vessel, including those spaces secured with locks. Before the officers had descended upon the boat, Ron attempted to contact Spencer to inform him of the warrant and acquire the necessary keys. Predictably, Spencer hadn't answered his phone or responded to the patrolmen who went to his loft. It was just as well. They'd done their due diligence, and now they were free to use whatever force was necessary to gain access. The twelve-inch steel pry bar Ron carried did the trick nicely.

He searched the living quarters, where he found a crack pipe, sexual bondage gear, and a pair of women's lace panties, all of which went into evidence bags. He also came across an SOG tactical folding knife with a four-inch blade. The blade was open and had a dark residue along one side. It appeared to be dried blood. Had Spencer used the knife to stab someone or to cut his steak? They'd find out soon enough. It went into a bag.

Ron headed topside, handed over his finds to one of the techs, and began to explore the deck area. He came to a storage room door and was about to pop the lock when a woman, amped up on nicotine, caffeine, or both, angrily called out, "What the fuck are you doing?"

Ron turned to see Deanna Frost striding in his direction. While he could've extended her the courtesy of notifying her of the search, it wasn't required. Her presence would only slow things down. Plus, she was haughty, rude and a general pain in the ass. After an already long day, it was the last thing he needed. Even so, he put a smile on his face. Not because he was happy to see her. Because he knew it would piss her off.

"What brings you out on this fine evening, Counselor?"

"You know damn well what brings me out. Fortunately, I've got a contact in Judge Campagna's office who informed me of your little raid. Has my client been notified?"

"As per our warrant, we made every attempt to reach Mr. Spencer, but got no response. Since this isn't your first rodeo, you're well aware we have total access to the boat." Ron punctuated this by yanking back on the pry bar and snapping open the storage room door. A long strip of the door frame splintered off and landed at Deanna's feet.

"I don't know how you convinced the judge to issue this bullshit warrant. As far as I'm concerned, this search is not only unnecessary, but is all part of the department's attempt to further slander my client. You've been unable to locate the real shooter, so you're doing everything in your power to fabricate a case. I promise you it's not going to stick."

"Inspector?" Ron and Deanna turned to see one of the forensic techs holding up a clear evidence bag. In the bag was a 9mm pistol with gold inlay on the barrel. "We found it in the engine compartment, tucked behind the intake valve."

Ron looked over at Deanna, failing to keep the tiny grin off his face. "I believe this case just got a little stickier."

In the next two hours, Deanna Frost logged at least a mile as she paced back and forth across her $25,000 dollar Mashad rug. She left four urgent messages on Spencer's phone…one call every half hour. When he finally returned her call, he sounded drunk and clearly annoyed that she was harshing his buzz. Deanna could feel countless hours of cognitive behavioral therapy being pushed to the limit as she explained to Spencer that he was in a boatload of trouble…no pun intended.

He sobered up quickly when she informed him the police found a 9mm pistol on his yacht and wanted him for questioning. Spencer swore he knew nothing about a gun on his boat.

"That's total bullshit! Either the nine belongs to someone else or the fuckin' cops planted it!"

"They also found what looked like traces of coke and heroin," Deanna said.

"So what? They can't prove its mine. Anyway, who gives a shit about leftover powder? Any decent lawyer can make that go away with one phone call. Take care of it, or I'll find someone who can!"

"*Relax…See the sun, smell the pine…*" she muttered to herself before coming back to reality. "Myles, listen to me. The police are doing a spectrum analysis on the heroin and comparing it to samples they have from a recent Norteño bust. If it matches, and if the ballistics on the gun indicate it was the one used in the shootings of those dealers, the circumstantial evidence will *strongly* suggest that someone on your boat was responsible for the murders."

"It wasn't me!"

"Fine. Then go to the station now and I'll meet you there. If you're not in shape to drive, I can pick you up."

"I'm not at home."

"I'll come get you wherever you are. It'll go a lot easier if you come in voluntarily than if the police have to drag you in." She resisted the urge to add, "Like last time."

"No fuckin' way I'm doing that. It's a set up! I walk into that station, I'm never walking out again!"

"Myles…"

"Do your goddamn job!" he screamed into the phone.

He clearly hadn't attended the same anger management seminars.

"Myles! Listen to me…" The line went dead. Deanna looked at the cell phone in her hand like it was a traitor. A tsunami of indignation swelled up inside her and she was about to violently hurl her iPhone 14 across the room, when it chimed. She had a voice message.

It was Inspector Yee, informing her that officers had gone back to her client's home and he still wasn't there. Had she spoken to him? Did she have any idea where he might be? The sooner they brought him in, the sooner they could begin the process of resolving the situation, one way or the other. The inspector left his number and urged her to call him.

Deanna cursed her colleague at the law firm for taking maternity leave, then cursed her again for getting pregnant in the first place. Who in their right mind would voluntarily bring a kid into the world these days? She tried to calm down using guided imagery, but when she pictured herself in a verdant field of spring flowers, Myles Spencer came charging out of the nearby woods with a maniacal look on his face, firing at her with a 9mm with a gold inlayed barrel.

Screw it. She called Ron Yee to say she'd spoken to Spencer, had no idea where he was, and feared that he'd gone into hiding.

"We have some very talented bloodhounds in the department. If he's still in the city, we'll ferret him out. But the longer it takes, the worse it's going to be for everyone."

Deanna hung up. A moment later, the cell phone flew across her living room, making solid, crunching contact with the hand-painted Pavoncelle tiles around her fireplace.

43

Wednesday

The fish markets on Pier 45 opened early. Kelly, wearing a black hoodie and red-framed faux glasses, entered the market farthest down the pier and spoke to the fishmonger. He didn't carry what she was looking for and suggested she try one of the other seven fish dealers that dotted the pier.

Kelly struck out at all eight markets and was about to call Cora to see if she could help, when an Asian teen said he'd overheard what Kelly wanted. He knew of a shop in Japantown that carried a wide selection of exotic sea creatures. The problem was the owner of the shop didn't speak English. The boy pulled a notebook out of his backpack, jotted down some kanji characters, then tore out the page and handed it to Kelly. She knew she was leaving behind a trail, but it couldn't be avoided…and she was running out of time.

She found the unmarked fish stall, wedged in between an incense shop and a mochi donut stand. The man behind the counter looked ancient and frail. He pulled off a rubber glove covered in fish scales to reveal a wrinkled hand. Kelly gave him the note and the man's eyes went from the paper to Kelly's face. His expression was impossible to read. She thought he might balk at her request, but instead, he turned and dug something out of a battered cooler.

A few minutes later, Kelly walked out with her purchase neatly wrapped in newspaper.

Pete's reinstatement came with no fanfare. No apologies. No formal recognition that he'd been right about Myles Spencer or that the department had been too quick to pass judgment on one of their most decorated officers. No one other than Ron was aware that Pete was instrumental in providing the information that led to the search of the boat. That fact would never be revealed for fear it would taint the case. And there was another reason for keeping Pete's involvement under wraps…Ron wasn't convinced his partner was being straight with him. If *that* were true, it presented its own set of complications.

Pete was sitting at a small table outside Beloved Cafe when Ron emerged holding two coffees. "This is your official welcome back. Congratulations on serving the shortest admin leave in the history of the force."

"We caught a break," said Pete.

"Yeah," Ron agreed without revealing a hint of skepticism. "Finding a witness willing to give us a sworn statement about the drugs on Spencer's boat was a major stroke of luck."

Pete nodded, sipping his coffee.

"And then stumbling upon the potential murder weapon. No one saw that coming."

"Like I said, we caught a break. It's not like we don't deserve to occasionally get dealt a good hand."

"I'd say we got a straight flush, especially if the ballistics are a match."

Pete smiled. "I've gotta believe they will."

Ron appraised his partner, wondering if and when he was going to come clean, but Pete remained unwavering. After a long, cold moment, Ron broke the tension with, "I know I'm the one who's always going on about how fucking stupid most criminals are…."

"But…?"

"But keeping evidence that can tie you to three murders? I mean, I understand finding traces of drugs, but why would any moron purposely bring a murder weapon onboard a boat, take a cruise out to the middle of the bay, and, as you said yourself, not pitch the gun overboard?"

Pete shrugged. "Maybe he wanted to show it off. Be a big man. Was there anything special about it?"

Ron eyed his partner. "It's a custom job. Fancy grips and some gold inlay on the barrel. Probably cost him a grand, but Spencer's got the cash to buy a hundred more just like it."

"You've met him. He thinks he's above the law." Pete sipped his coffee and redirected the conversation. "Has the DA's office issued a warrant for his arrest yet?"

Ron shook his head. "Waiting on prints and ballistics."

"Damn. We've gotta move on this before he leaves town, if he hasn't already. Any word from his attorney?"

"I left another message for her this morning. When I spoke to her last night, she had no idea of his whereabouts."

"I don't trust her," said Pete with obvious disdain. "It feels wrong."

"I've gotta tell you, partner. There's a whole lot about this case that feels wrong."

Pete tried to keep his response neutral, but a whiff of caution crept into his voice. "What's that mean?"

"It means I'm not entirely comfortable how the pieces of this investigation conveniently stacked up."

"Let's not sell ourselves short. We've been working this murder hard. How many times have you seen a case where once the right domino falls, the rest tumble in order?"

"A few, but you've got to admit the chain of events appears less like solid investigation and more like...I don't know...dumb luck. You *happen* to interview a guy who *happened* to know a guy on the party boat who *happened* to walk in on Spencer boning his girlfriend."

"Ron, I respect the hell outta you, but I don't like where this is going."

Undaunted, Ron continued. "This guy provides information about evidence, evidence that may come back and bite him in the ass, which leads to a search warrant where we find the gun that may have been used to kill Molina and the others. You understand why I'm a little hesitant to accept all of this as luck."

Pete could no longer bottle his frustration. "If not luck, what then? Are you accusing me of something?"

"Just pointing out the obvious, partner. The same thing any good lawyer's going to do when this goes to trial. If I recall, once Ms. Frost gets people on the stand, she takes no prisoners."

"That's a cold fucking shot, *partner.*"

"Something else came to my attention this morning. There's a surveillance camera on the pier where Spencer's boat is docked. The feed inexplicably went dead yesterday afternoon from 5:51 to 6:03 p.m."

"And, what? You want to know where I was at that time? Meeting with my union rep, in his office. You can check with him if you need to."

"No. I believe you."

"But that's the problem. You don't."

"Let me explain something. We're partners. The only way that works is if we have each other's back. No secrets, no lies, no going off and playing Lone Ranger."

"Ron...I swear I..."

Ron held up his hand. He wasn't done. "If you do something stupid and, say, plant evidence, or convince someone to fabricate stories to help move a case along, not only will that get you bounced, but it'll stick to me as well. I'm not asking if you did anything illegal or unethical. I'm telling you that our partnership is based upon trust. If at any time I find out that my trust in you isn't justified, or that you've done something to put my career at risk, I'll personally make sure you go down. If you think I'm being too harsh and want to request a new partner, I'll understand."

From that moment on, Pete knew he had to tread with extreme care. Everything he'd said was a lie. He could only hope that Ron never found out that their witness was a CI for one of his father's cop buddies. He *had* been on the boat, but the story he concocted about Spencer and the girlfriend was total bullshit. Ron could also never know that Andy Ericson's cronies were the ones who supplied the Mexican brown; leaned on a guy who owned a boat moored at the harbor to get the code to the electronic gate; posed as a security guard and used a video jammer to disrupt the feed from the surveillance camera at the pier; and, planted both the drugs and Spencer's weapon onboard the boat.

"No," said Pete. "I'm cool. I've always walked the line and always will."

"Great. Then let's go see if the lab has processed the weapon. Hopefully, we've got what we need to pick up that piece of shit."

44

The report from forensics was concise and damning. The prints on the Smith & Wesson belonged to Myles Spencer. Ballistics were a match between the gun and the casings found at the three murder scenes. The heroin collected from the boat was chemically identical to a sample recently obtained in the arrest of the Norteño dealer, down to the percentages of baking soda and Miralax used to cut the tar. The DA's office had all they needed to charge Myles Spencer with the three murders, but before they could arrest him, they needed to find him.

Pete had spoken to Deanna Frost, and she swore she had no idea where her client was. Pete could hear in her voice that she was rattled, and he had no reason to doubt her. The last thing she needed was to be found lying to the police to protect a client charged with three counts of murder.

To further complicate matters, Sgt. Urbina informed Ron and Pete that the Norteños had Spencer's name. Evidently, there'd been a temp working inside the DA's office who overheard that the police had identified Molina's shooter. The temp's roommate was the sister of a Norteño street boss. And just like that, the gang put out the word that the *blanco* named Myles Spencer was worth a lot more dead than alive.

As far as Pete was concerned, life would be a whole lot easier if the gangbangers got to Spencer before the police did. Taking this case to trial and getting grilled on the witness stand by Deanna Frost was not something he looked forward to, especially given the reality of how the evidence had so conveniently stacked up.

Spencer had seemingly vanished. Nobody had the slightest idea of his whereabouts. Nobody, except for a pale, anorexic, part-time squeeze named Belinda, who was sitting cross-legged across from him at a chipped coffee table, snorting cocaine and chasing it with a bottle of Boone's Farm Strawberry Hill. Belinda had been stunned to see Spencer standing in her doorway last night, and despite not having heard from him for over a year, she still kinda crushed on him. Very few people knew about Belinda (she was strictly an off-the-books skank), and the fact that she lived in a dingy one-bedroom apartment in a sketchy part of town made this an extremely unlikely hidey-hole for a man of Spencer's wealth and fame.

Spencer listened to the most recent message from his lawyer about how the police had his prints on the gun used to kill the dealers, and that an arrest warrant had been issued. Deanna urged him to turn himself in as soon as possible.

"Fucking cops!" he roared, startling an already frightened Belinda, who tightly hugged her skeletal legs to her chest. "It's that cocksucker Ericson. I know it! He planted that piece on my boat! I'm gonna sue the fucker!"

Belinda feared Spencer would take out his anger on her. He'd always scared her, especially when he was loaded. Plus, he liked his sex rough and often left her bruised or worse. But there was the money he'd leave on the dresser, and the quality drugs he had in endless supply. And more importantly, he was Myles Spencer. He was famous. And rich. And every once in a while, for a few hours, he was hers.

"What?" he bellowed. "You got something to say?"

Spencer was wired, balancing on a razor's edge. The last thing Belinda wanted to do was set him off by pointing out that he couldn't hide forever. Even if he skipped town, they'd eventually find him, and when they did, it wouldn't end well.

"Spence…maybe it *would* be better to, like, turn yourself in."

"Are you fucking crazy, bitch? Once they got me in that cell, I'd be good as dead. They'd strangle me with a bedsheet and claim it was suicide. Happens all the fucking time."

Belinda bit her lower lip. Trying to talk to Myles when he was sober was a losing proposition. Attempting it now was a complete wasted effort. However, she sensed he was on the verge of doing something incredibly stupid, so she gave it one more try.

"Babe, you got money. Your family's got connections. If you need an alibi, I'll swear you were here with me. I do whatever you need. Whatever it takes."

Spencer stared at Belinda as if she were some kind of alien lifeforce, jabbering away in a nonsensical foreign tongue. But something she said snuck past his fried synapses and flipped a switch in his brain. His anger suddenly fell away as a wild notion took shape into an action plan. A glimmer of a smile appeared on his face, and Belinda returned the smile. Finally, she'd gotten through to him. Maybe this could lead to a something real. Maybe even a relationship.

"You're right, babe. Whatever it takes." He grabbed his phone and made a call to one of his posse.

He spelled out exactly what it would take.

Kelly was in her office along with Ida, watching as the spokeswoman for the Department of Health conducted a televised press conference, notifying the public that San Francisco County was experiencing an outbreak of meningitis. She went on to describe the symptoms, as well as how the disease was passed (both airborne and via personal contact). While she didn't mention Tico's Tamales by name (since no one was certain it was ground zero), she did say that one potential carrier could be a food truck (which provoked an outcry from the mobile food vendors throughout the city). The Department strongly urged anyone experiencing symptoms to immediately contact their doctor. The press conference ended on a foreboding note, informing the public that this strain of meningitis, if not treated early, could lead to permanent brain damage, and in some cases, death. It would take a massive effort to keep this outbreak from spreading further.

The police department wasn't having any luck locating the truck. Either it hadn't hit the street yet, or worse, Tico had decided to take his business across the bay or down the Peninsula.

If that happened, there was no telling how far and how quickly the meningitis would spread. The talking heads on the morning shows told their viewers that hospitals around the city were setting up tents in their parking lots to handle the throngs of people with symptoms. They also made it clear that the diagnostics and antibiotics to treat meningitis were only available at hospitals. And yet, some people didn't have the inclination to deal with the inconvenience that came along with hospital care, and instead turned to neighborhood clinics for whatever relief they could provide.

One such person was Susie Wall, a twenty-four-year-old food blogger who was sitting on an exam table at the Mission Street Clinic, being gently poked and prodded by Ida.

"Any discomfort here?" Ida asked running her fingers along Susie's neck.

"Yeah. It's tender."

Ida made a notation and then shined her penlight in Susie's eyes, causing her wince. "Light sensitive."

She nodded and swallowed, trying to lubricate her scratchy throat.

"You're showing all the symptoms, I'm afraid. You'll need to be tested."

Susie couldn't stop tears from forming. "Is it really meningitis? I mean, how serious is that?"

"We caught it early enough. I'll call over to San Francisco General and ask that they see you as soon as you arrive. They'll be able to treat you, and in a few days, you'll be good as new."

Despite her fears, Susie managed a tiny smile of thanks.

"Did you, by any chance, eat Mexican food in the past week from a truck called Tico's Tamales?"

Susie brightened. "Tico's? I wrote about it in my blog! But it's not Mexican cuisine. It's El Salvadoran. It's the most authentic Central American food I've ever had off a truck."

Something about El Salvador sparked Ida's memory, but the recollection was vague, and she couldn't quite get a handle on it.

"I talked to the owners," Susie continued, "Tico and Lucia. A totally rad couple from a town called Aguilares. They only arrived here like a month ago. Their *pupusas* are killer, and so is the fried yucca. They even make *gallo en chica,* which is rooster meat. No way you'll find that on any other trucks in the city. You should definitely check it out."

Suddenly the memory crystalized and Ida had to tamp down her excitement. "Thank you. That's a tremendous help."

Susie hopped down off the table and before she was even out the door, Ida was logging into the file of Abelino Lopez, one of the first wave of patients to have meningitis symptoms. He'd listed his emergency contact as his cousin, Tico Alvarez. It had to be the same person. There was no home address or phone, but Ida recalled Abelino worked in a Peruvian restaurant on the Embarcadero. She called the restaurant and got an answering machine.

There was no time to waste.

As Ida left to track down Abelino, Kelly was on the phone with Lisa Reynolds, casually mentioning she'd love to stop by the restaurant for dinner.

"When we spoke yesterday you were hoping to get off early and spend the night with Emma, but I thought I'd check to see if that all worked out. If not, I'm craving your tuna sashimi."

"I'm only on 'til six, then heading home for a quick dinner before I pick up Emma at her friend Jordyn's house. We're going to make ice cream sundaes and binge a new series on Netflix. I can save a seat for you at the bar if you swing by before I leave."

Kelly heard the joy in her voice and assumed that Lisa wasn't aware that Emma would be flying out with her father and stepmom first thing in the morning.

"Thanks," said Kelly, "but I'll be at the clinic until seven or eight."

"Well, let's get together in a couple of days after Emma goes to Detroit with her father."

If everything went according to plan, a couple days from now Lisa wouldn't be getting together with anyone.

45

Pete and Ron swept Spencer's loft looking for clues as to where he might be holed up. Ron marveled at the game room, and Pete did his best to act blown away, as if he was seeing the elaborate setup for the first time.

They did a thorough search of Spencer's bedroom. His closet and dresser were overflowing with clothes, the medicine cabinet in the bathroom was brimming with prescription drugs and toiletries, and they found a few ounces of grass along with an eight-ball of coke. Spencer had either bolted in a hurry, or more likely, hadn't been home when he heard the police were looking for him.

Next, they headed to the marina, where Spencer's boat was festooned with yellow police tape and patrolled by two uniformed cops. Ron questioned the manager of the marina, while Pete went to the small security shack to meet with the guard who monitored the cameras placed around the marina.

The buttons on the corpulent security guard's uniform were holding on for dear life and the place smelled like capicola, peppers and onions.

"Do you know why the cameras weren't working yesterday afternoon?" Pete asked.

The guard wheezed when he spoke. "The main office said the signal was temporarily jammed, but they haven't been able to figure out how or why."

"Were you on duty yesterday when the outage occurred?"

The guard shook his head. "Nope. That'd be Omar."

"What's the standard protocol when the video signal drops out?"

"We contact the office, and they check it from their end. They usually transmit a reset signal, and the cameras go back online."

"And if it doesn't?"

251

"We're supposed to do a manual inspection of the electrical junction box. It's down the street, about a block away."

"And did Omar do that?"

"I doubt it." The guard glanced around and lowered his voice. "Omar's not exactly by-the-book. He's more interested in experimenting with new varieties of ganja, looking for what he calls, 'the ultimate righteous high.'" The guard suddenly remembered he was talking to a cop. "Oh, shit! I shouldn't have said that. You're not gonna bust him, are you? Dude really needs the job."

"I'm not with Narcotics."

"Cool. Thanks, man. You should reach out to Marianne at the home office. She's our tech expert, and any time there's even a tiny dropout, she's all over it. The company's real big on promoting itself as '*reliable, all day, every day*,' so they take even the smallest hiccup seriously. A few negative Yelp reviews can really put a dent in the bottom line, or so they tell me."

"Got it. Thanks."

Ron and Pete met back at the car. "The manager doesn't know anything," said Ron. "Any luck with the guard?"

Pete shook his head. "He wasn't on duty. He said the main office was aware of the dropout, but since the signal came back on a few minutes later, no one thought it was a big deal. Where to next?"

It was lunchtime when Ron and Pete entered The Rialto. Many of Spencer's buddies from Sunday night were dining together at a large table. Pete nudged Ron and nodded in their direction. "Spencer's entourage."

As they started over, one guy recognized Pete. "Look who it is. Mr. Sucker Punch." That got a laugh, followed by a round of whispered snarky remarks about Pete and the SFPD in general.

"Any of you guys seen Myles around?" Ron asked.

They all swore they'd had no contact with him.

"We've got a warrant for his arrest," said Pete. "If any of you are lying or worse, like harboring him at your place, you'll be booked as an accessory."

The skinny guy with the Blue Jays cap spoke up. "Accessory to what? That's bullshit."

The others chimed in, talking about police strongarm tactics, and how their boy Spencer was being framed. Ron and Pete considered dragging the whole lot down to the station for questioning but decided it would be a waste of time.

As they were leaving, Ron turned to Pete and muttered loud enough for all to hear, "I wonder if the Norteños are having more luck than us. If they get to Spencer first, we're gonna have another homicide on our hands."

Ida found Abelino washing dishes in the kitchen of the Peruvian restaurant. He looked flushed and in obvious pain. He'd had no choice but to continue working, despite the real possibility he was infecting everyone around him. Abelino confirmed that Tico and Lucia operated the food truck in question and agreed to take Ida to the tiny apartment where they all lived.

Thirty minutes later they arrived to find Tico Alvarez lying on the sofa, suffering from a headache and a raspy cough that came from deep in his chest. Ida gave him a quick once over, and it was clear Tico was suffering from advanced stages of meningitis. He needed immediate medical attention.

While Ida called for an ambulance, Abelino explained the situation to his cousin. The police were out looking for the truck, and the lady doctor was going to take them to a hospital.

When Ida got off the phone, Abelino informed her that Lucia had left with the truck about an hour ago.

"Does your cousin know where she went?"

"He thinks she went to a school. The kids buy food after class."

"Which school?" Lucia could already be infecting a whole new group of people. They had to move fast.

Unfortunately, Tico had no idea where Lucia went, and since she didn't have a cell phone, there was no way to get in touch with her.

Ida made another call, this time to the police department.

46

While the police were scouring the city for the food truck, and Ida was escorting Abelino and Tico to the nearest hospital, Kelly had her own, much more personal, agenda. She was on her way to Lisa's house, and as she drove, she reevaluated every detail of her plan, scrutinizing it for any potential stumbling blocks. She was so fixated on her "to-do list" that when the disposable cell rang, it startled her, and she nearly swerved into oncoming traffic.

Only one person had that number. The person who provided the phone.

"Cora?"

"I'm checking in to see how you're doing."

"I'm fine, all things considered." Kelly hesitated for a moment, then naively asked, "Is there any way this call can be traced or recorded?"

"No, the line's secure. Kelly, for the next few hours, you've got to put every other thing in your life, even the smallest possible distractions, into a box, seal it up, and tuck it into the farthest corner of your mind. The only thing that's important right now is the task that awaits."

"Understood," Kelly said. "You know, you're much better at this than Mr. Benedetto."

"I'm not better. Just more hands-on."

"Any word on him?"

"Nothing new." Cora once again decided not to share her concerns that Benedetto's situation was looking dire. She wished Kelly the best of luck and disconnected.

Despite Cora's attempt to assuage her, Kelly was definitely concerned. If Cora couldn't find any traces of Benedetto, he was clearly in trouble. Was his disappearance connected to Gideon? Kelly conjured up mental images of jumper cables being applied to his chest. Or his testicles. Fingernails savagely removed with rusty pliers. The greater his imagined pain, the more jittery she became. Her post-traumatic stress disorder kicked into high gear, her breathing quickened, and her forehead was suddenly damp with a sheen of perspiration.

Kelly pulled off the road and parked. Overwhelmed with anxiety, she began to question every element of her game plan. There were so many variables that could go wrong. A tiny mistake here, a random encounter there. Fate could intervene at any moment and screw up the most foolproof scheme. Suddenly, this seemed like a terrible idea, and Kelly had a sinking feeling that something would go horrendously sideways, and she'd end up getting caught.

Images flashed through her mind: *a headline-grabbing trial, a dank prison cell, Jessica crammed into a four-person room of catatonic patients.*

Kelly's hands shook uncontrollably, and her heart pounded. She hadn't experienced a full-on panic attack like this before and she needed to get her act together. She had to focus and fully commit to her plan of action.

As she slowly regained control, she took Cora's advice and compartmentalized the rest of her problems. Tomorrow she could worry about Benedetto, about the clinic's finances, about Jessica's future, about the spread of meningitis. Today she could only have one thing on her mind.

Killing Lisa Reynolds.

Gus Taylor strode into Alexa's office, a look of consternation on his face.

"What did you find?" she asked.

Despite Alexa's agreement to "let sleeping dogs lie," she worried that Kelly didn't fully grasp the ramifications of receiving funds from potentially illicit sources. If the IRS ever did a deep dive into the clinic's financial records, Kelly, as the sole proprietor, could be liable for a massive fine, or worse, could end up incarcerated. Alexa wouldn't allow that to happen.

"What we both suspected. All these associations and companies are SPVs (Special Purpose Vehicles). I don't know what the good doctor was up to, but his outside revenue stream came from sketchy sources." Gus referred to his notes. "Provident Alliance, Community Spirit, Ardent Resources... they're legal in that they've been set up according to lawful guidelines, but none of them appear to be in actual operation. They are no records of seminars, board of directors' meetings, or any kind of ongoing consultations."

"All dummy shell companies."

"'Fraid so."

"Damn."

Gus nodded.

Alexa picked up her cell, steeled herself, and made a call.

Kelly entered Lisa's house and went directly into the kitchen, where she discovered that two of the three wine bottles were gone, leaving only the Cabernet. She'd been ready to adulterate multiple bottles, but this made things less complicated.

She slipped on some thin latex gloves, then gently worked out the cork, careful not to spill any wine on the white countertop. From her pocket, she pulled out a small vial which contained a milky liquid called tetrodotoxin. The poison found in puffer fish. The toxin was extremely potent and more deadly than cyanide. She poured the liquid into the wine, gave the bottle a shake, and replaced the cork.

Next, she took what looked like a ring box out of her backpack and opened it to reveal a tiny nanny cam nestled in foam. The camera broadcast audio and video and had an adhesive backing. She pressed a button and a green light flashed twice, then went dark. The camera was active.

She stood on a stool and affixed the camera to the arm of one of the four angled spotlights that hung from the ceiling. Even if you were looking for it, you'd be hard-pressed to find it.

Kelly brushed off the stool and slid it back into place. She gave the kitchen a quick visual once-over and was satisfied it was just as she found it, with the few modifications. Phase one of her plan was complete.

Now it was up to Lisa to do her part.

47

Pete wandered around the Gang Task Force conference room, looking at the organizational charts pinned to the walls. The Mission was home to Norteños and Sureños, and both were divided into geographic sets. Every gang had a *jefe*, or Big Homie, a lieutenant or two, as well as street bosses, dealers, runners and lookouts. The size of the gang was dependent upon how much territory they controlled. The boundaries were constantly in flux, as every gang's goal was to expand. These days, the gangs' territories were shrinking and becoming more fragmented due to the constant gentrification taking place throughout the city.

While individual Norteño sets tended to respect each other's territory (the same was true of the Sureños), there was inevitably one *jefe* who felt it was time to make a move, even if it meant stepping on the toes (or spilling the blood) of his fellow bangers. Blue-on-blue, or red-on-red crime was a reality in the streets, and as a result, no one completely trusted anyone outside their immediate gang.

Or, as was the case with Tomás Sanchez, sometimes even your own homies were not to be trusted.

Miguel Urbina entered the room and asked, "Where's your partner?"

"He's meeting with the homicide inspectors from the other precincts to coordinate a citywide dragnet. Spencer's become priority number one."

"I heard the Sureños and MS13 are looking for him as well. Put a bounty on his head."

"How much is a dead Myles Spencer worth?"

"Ten grand, or the equivalent in product. The streets are crawling with trigger-happy bangers looking to make a score and a name."

"That can't be good."

"There's also unrest inside the Norteños. Did you know that Oscar Sanchez was shot?"

Pete was stunned by the news. "Oscar? Did he survive?"

"So far. He's in SF General with a chest wound. I'm surprised your girlfriend didn't mention anything."

"Kelly? How's she involved?"

"I heard she went to the hospital to see Oscar. A favor to the mother."

"Any idea who the shooter was?"

"Rumor is Tomás Sanchez."

"His brother? Was he making a play?"

"Don't know. I haven't seen him since he got back into circulation. I seem to recall he was a real piece of crap. My guys are out looking for him now. I'm gonna bring his ass in and have a little come-to-Jesus chat."

"I saw him last week, and your assessment is spot on. I'd be happy to sit in if you want."

"Thanks, but I want to spend some quality one-on-one time with him. See if he needs a refresher course in the ways of the world."

Pete was headed back to his desk when he spotted Charlie Thongsuk waiting in the hallway outside the Homicide bullpen. A few minutes later Charlie was at Pete's desk, firing up his laptop.

"Sorry it's taken so long, Inspector, but they've piled on the requests and cut back on my overtime."

"Don't worry about it. The whole department's understaffed. Every politician claims he's the 'law and order' candidate, but that never translates into more hours, more cars or more bodies."

As Charlie cued up the video, he explained the visual wizardry he'd accomplished. "I went through all the security footage from The Patch. There's only one camera angle of the table where the woman was sitting. The footage they had was too dark, and when I tried to boost the gain, the image totally washed out. I went down to the club and discovered there was another camera angle that catches a reflection of that table in the glass wall."

"Fantastic."

"Would be, except they didn't send those images over to you and that drive was wiped clean a long time ago."

"Damn it."

"I know. They've got a dozen cameras around that place, and because of the low lighting, most are totally useless. Clubs generally install security cams for show, not function. Plus, the noob who runs their video surveillance is some clueless high school AV burnout."

"So where does that leave us?"

"I contacted the company that installed the system and found out they'd put in a cheap backup that stores six months of low-res video. The forty-watt at the club didn't even know it was there. I went back and was able to find a few seconds where the woman's face is revealed. I'll run it from the start."

The security footage played. The image was pixelated, but Pete could make out Moretti and the brunette in question sitting at the table. Her face is obscured by his shoulder. A moment later, a man in a black T-shirt interrupts them, and a fight quickly ensues. When Moretti leaps up from the table, there's an instant where the woman's face is visible, but she's still in the shadows. Charlie paused the video there.

"This is the only decent angle. If these guys would've taken their fight deeper into the club, we'd have a clean shot of her, but they blocked the camera. I tweaked it the best I could."

Pete watched as the image of the woman slowly went through several passes of video manipulation. "I boosted the contrast, adjusted the black levels and removed the video noise. Then I applied an algorithm that extracted all the usable information and filled in the blank spaces with AI elements to create the most probable likeness."

As the image of the woman became clearer with each pass, Pete experienced an uneasy sensation that started in his gut and wormed its way up his spine to his brain. His mouth was instantly dry, and there was a faint ringing in his ears.

Charlie glanced up at him and saw that he looked pale. "Are you okay, Inspector? I heard on the news that something was going around."

Pete pried his eyes away from the screen and snapped out of his trance. "Oh, uh, yeah I'm good."

Charlie nodded at the attractive dark-haired Goth woman on the screen. "Does this help?"

Pete shrugged. "Maybe. I don't know. Can you give me a copy of this?"

"I dropped it onto a stick." Charlie handed Pete a flash drive.

"Thanks. You should delete this from your computer. I'm taking a flyer here, and if it doesn't pan out, I don't want you catching any flack for doing unauthorized work."

"No problem. Hey Inspector, if you do ID her and she's local, maybe you could get me her number. She's a total babe."

Pete forced a smile. "That's not entirely kosher, but I'll see what I can do."

"Cool. Let me know if you need anything else."

Ten minutes later, Pete plugged the flash drive into his computer. He glanced over his shoulder to make sure he was alone and brought up the photo of the woman. He only needed a few seconds to confirm what he already knew. He closed his computer, slipped the drive into his pocket and made a call.

"Kelly. It's Pete. I think we've IDed that dark-haired woman who was with Tommy Moretti. Call me as soon as you get this."

48

Kelly parked around the corner from Lisa's house. She would've liked to have been someplace less conspicuous, or at least farther away, but the range on the nanny cam was limited. A six-inch screen sat on her lap, and she glanced at it sporadically, trying to appear nonchalant. She felt exposed, and exposure could lead to serious problems down the line.

She wondered if her father had faced the same doubt in moments like this, or if he was more resolute. She wished she could call him and ask. Of course, were that possible she wouldn't be sitting here now, waiting for Lisa Reynolds to walk into her kitchen, drink a glass of spiked wine, and suffer an excruciating death.

There was something about Lisa that was nibbling at Kelly's subconscious. Being sociopathic, she was extremely difficult to read. After years of hiding her true self, Kelly wondered if Lisa even knew the real her. Kelly thought back to the conversation they had in the park. *"I adore having her around and everything, but I've gotta admit that being responsible for a kid full-time complicates the hell out of the whole dating scene. I mean, I love Emma to pieces, but it's kind of nice to have a break once in a while."*

There could no room for doubt. Emma had to be protected.

Lisa had to die.

Just then, a noise came through the tiny speaker built into the screen. A key turning in the front door lock. Kelly checked her watch. Something was wrong. Lisa wasn't due home for another half hour. Had her plans changed?

A teenage girl said, "It's in my room. It'll just take a minute."

It was Emma! Why was she home? Had Lisa picked her up early? This was a disaster! Kelly imagined how it would unfold: *a happy mother and daughter making plans for the evening; Lisa pouring herself a glass of wine and raising it to her lips, a smile on her face; moments later, Lisa writhing on the floor in the throes of death, with Emma looking on in horror.*

How could Kelly stop this? As she desperately ran through options in her mind, a sixteen-year-old boy appeared on the screen. He looked around the kitchen and headed directly to the wine bottle on the counter.

This situation had just gotten much, much worse.

"No, no, no, no…" Kelly exclaimed. "Don't drink that!"

The teen grabbed the bottle, checked out the label, then cast a glance over his shoulder.

There was no time to get to the house before he would swallow a lethal dose of poison. All Kelly could do was sit and watch in stunned, horrified silence.

He pulled the cork and raised the bottle toward his lips when someone shouted, "Dude! What are you doing?"

Emma's friend Jordyn had entered the kitchen. "Put that back!"

The boy held the bottle firm. "Why? Just a little shot. Not like anyone's gonna find out."

He raised up the bottle again. Kelly froze. Her heart pounding. She wanted to look away, but she couldn't. This was her doing.

Emma burst into the kitchen from the hallway. "Liam! Put it down! My mom knows like every drop of booze in the house!"

"Fine," Liam said, putting the bottle back on the counter and tapping in the cork. "Whatever. It probably tastes like piss anyway."

"You're such a loser," said Jordyn.

Kelly sat motionless, glued to the small screen as Emma, Jordyn and Liam exited the kitchen. A moment later, the front door was locked, and the house was quiet.

Kelly leaned her head back and closed her eyes, letting out a long breath.

She'd been moments away from murdering an innocent teenager.

Benedetto was facing a life and death situation of his own. He was beyond exhausted, but this was no time to rest. He needed to act quickly and decisively before his captor concluded Benedetto was of no use to him.

The door was flung open, and Mott entered, followed by the man, who had a strained facsimile of a smile plastered on his face. Benedetto envisioned him practicing in a mirror for hours, trying to replicate the appearance of happiness.

"I looked through the images from the past sixty-four days," said the man. "You know what I found. Yes, you know." It was statement, not a question.

"I have no idea what…." Benedetto's denial was cut short when Mott's ham-sized hand slapped him in the temple with a Mjölnir-like blow that left his head ringing and eyes watering. Mott sat down and placed the Desert Eagle on his lap, just in case Benedetto needed another reminder of who was in charge.

"Tell the truth, or I will leave you alone with Mott. He will teach you a lesson. My mother sometimes had to teach me lessons. When she spanked me with The Paddle, she said it hurt her more than it hurt me. I don't think that's true, but she said it every time. Mott won't need a paddle. No way. He has very big hands."

Benedetto took a moment to consider his options, then nodded his head. Sadness and defeat were etched on his face. His ribs screamed, his head throbbed, and a trickle of blood seeped from his ear where Mott had thumped him.

He was a broken man.

"I'm ready to talk."

"If you tell more lies, Mott will hurt you. Badly. And then he will hurt Cora Mathews. Yes, Cora."

"Yeah. I got it. You think before we do this, I could use the bathroom? It's been hours."

The man looked vaguely in Mott's direction, then nodded. Mott faked a lunge toward Benedetto, causing him to flinch. Mott enjoyed Benedetto's fear, almost as much as he enjoyed inflicting the pain that caused that fear. As he rose, he set his gun down the coffee table then stepped over and undid Benedetto's handcuff.

"I know the truth," the man suddenly crowed. He couldn't keep his excitement reigned in a moment longer. "I know how Doctor David Harper, aka Gideon, killed from the grave. His daughter Kelly Harper took his place. Yes!"

With each passing minute, Kelly's acid reflux had gotten worse and the throbbing in her head went from a faint backbeat to a full-on drumline. The reverberating lows of the tympani were joined by the shrill rat-a-tat-tat of a taut-skinned snare. She had a sudden rush of juices in her mouth…that terrible sensation one gets just before regurgitating everything they've consumed in the past twenty-four hours. Kelly was about to open her door and splash the street with the stale coffee and grilled cheese she had for lunch, when there was movement on her screen.

The light in the kitchen came on.

Lisa was home.

Kelly swallowed hard. This was no time to be sick.

She watched an agitated Lisa stride into the kitchen.

Benedetto suppressed his reaction to the man's proclamation, but inwardly chided himself for being sloppy. He never should've met with David or Kelly in his office. If he somehow got out of this predicament, his first order of business would be to figure out how to permanently erase all traces of his association with Gideon. Cora would know how to create a credible strawman.

And then there was Kelly. Her time as Gideon was definitely over. This harrowing experience finally convinced him it was far too dangerous. If she needed money, he'd give it to her. Funding the clinic and paying for Jessica's medical bills was the least he could do in return for convincing her to risk her career, her future…her life.

"You're wrong about her," Benedetto said, rubbing his badly chafed wrist.

"No way."

"I can see how you'd come to that conclusion, but it's not Kelly. She wouldn't hurt a soul."

Lisa grabbed a wine glass, reached for the bottle on the counter, then changed her mind, and opened the cabinet over the refrigerator. She pulled out a bottle of Blue Ice vodka.

Kelly's eyes bugged. "Vodka?" she muttered. This would ruin her entire plan. Everything hinged on Lisa drinking the wine. Kelly shook her head in frustration, berating herself for such a flawed idea.

She watched as Lisa poured the vodka into her goblet. The yield was less than an ounce before the bottle was exhausted. "That's just fucking perfect!" Lisa slurped down the clear fluid and turned back to the cabinet to find the backup.

Kelly prayed she didn't have another bottle. Or that she didn't opt for other hard spirits for the rest of the night.

Kelly's prayer must've reached Bacchus because Lisa closed the cabinet and reached for the wine. Kelly sighed in relief.

The train to Poisontown was back on track.

The man's expression remained slack, but he clearly wasn't convinced, so Benedetto pushed harder. "You said no more lies. Fine. You wanted Gideon, you have him...standing right in front of you."

Benedetto launched into the most important closing argument of his life. "You were correct earlier when you said that Dominic Bruno hired me to take out Musselwhite. That was the spark that started everything, and it was easy to fan the flames to create the myth. All the requests for Gideon's services came to me. I've got the information encoded on the computer in my office. I can take you there, show you the proof, and you can give it to The Committee and get your money."

267

The man was intrigued, but not persuaded. "Why would *you* kill people?"

"Because I got sick of helping scum go free to be released back into the world. They needed to pay for their sins. I couldn't rationalize doing it any longer, and I used the guise of Gideon to repay my debt to society."

"By admitting this, you put yourself in danger. Yes, so much danger."

"You haven't left me much choice. Besides, I'm tired and ready to walk away from it all. I just want to disappear."

"You can't hide from The Committee. No way."

"I'll take my chances."

Benedetto could see the man was considering his tale, so he pushed harder. "Like I said, I've got all the evidence you need back in my office. Mott can come with me, look at my correspondences, my notes on where and how I carried out the hits. It's all there."

Lisa uncorked the bottle and poured. "He thinks he can take *my* kid? Him and his whore wife?" She filled her glass to just below the rim. She meant business.

"Well, fuck them." A smile crossed her face as she raised up the glass in a mock toast. "To Bob and Rachel. This time next week, you'll be burning in hell."

Kelly was staggered by Lisa's utterance.

Lisa wasn't planning to kill Emma. She was going to kill Bob and Rachel.

Kelly's sole reason for taking this assignment was to protect a teenage girl from a vindictive and bitter mother. Kelly had considered all the facts, critically analyzed all the evidence, and along with Benedetto, had drawn several conclusions: 1) Lisa was psychotic, perhaps schizophrenic, which made her extremely dangerous; 2) the events in her past strongly suggested she'd murdered Sydney, probably Hattie, and maybe even Bob's first wife;

268

3) Bob was whisking Emma thousands of miles away, which would set Lisa off; 4) based upon her history, there was every reason to believe that Lisa would kill her daughter to spite her ex-husband...as she'd done twice before.

However, both Benedetto and Kelly had come to the wrong conclusion regarding Lisa's intention. Had Kelly known the truth, she never would've taken this assignment.

Unfortunately, that was now a moot issue.

Lisa chugged the wine. She barely had time to set the glass down before the effects of the powerful tetrodotoxin kicked in. She was rapidly overcome with paralysis and her diaphragm was shutting down.

Breathing would quickly become impossible.

A darkness had crept over the man's face. Benedetto's admission was an unexpected curve ball and distracted the man just enough for Benedetto to make his move.

Mott was caught completely off guard when Benedetto swung the dangling handcuff at the big man's face, ripping a gash in his cheek. In the midst of the chaos, Benedetto grabbed Mott's gun and fired a shot that punched a hole through his thigh. Despite the blood spouting from Mott's femoral artery, he charged, wrapping his massive arms around Benedetto's chest. The gun roared again, this time tunneling through Mott's sternum. No man, regardless of how large or strong, can survive a .357 dumdum to the chest fired from point blank range. Mott staggered backwards, hit the wall, then slid to the floor amid a rapidly expanding puddle of blood.

Benedetto spun around to find a compact Beretta pointed at his heart.

The man was literally vibrating with rage, and the gun shook in his hand. He wasn't incensed by Mott's death, but rather by the shocking turn of events, the gruesome mess, and the sheer inconvenience of having to deal with the aftermath. He looked directly into Benedetto's face. "Why did you do that?"

"I don't plan to spend the rest of my days running from The Committee."

"They aren't interested in you. They want Gideon. Yes, they want *her*."

Benedetto whipped up his gun and a shot was fired. The dark TV screen was spattered with blood, bone and blotches of human tissue.

Kelly watched as Lisa lie on the floor, her mouth opening and closing like a fish on dry land. Kelly might have appreciated the analogous, sardonic image if she hadn't been overwhelmed by the fact that she'd just committed another murder.

49

Pete was twisted into emotional knots about the revelation that Kelly was likely the last person to see Tommy Moretti alive. Would her prints match those found at Moretti's apartment? Did she have sex with him? If so, was it consensual? Was she there when he overdosed? Was it an accident or did she have something to do with his death? The possibilities were mind-numbing and unimaginable. Pete thought he knew Kelly, but he was quickly coming to the conclusion that she was a total mystery.

And worse, a potential murderer.

There was another explanation. A much more plausible one. That the woman at The Patch wasn't Kelly at all. It was simply someone who resembled her. Charlie said the computer program created an image based upon partial data. A case of mistaken identity made much more sense, if not for the undeniable coincidence of a Kelly doppelganger being with Moretti on the night he died.

Pete resolved not to jump to conclusions. He'd speak to Kelly first, then compare her prints to the ones found at Moretti's. If they didn't match, he'd finally let the case go. If, on the other hand, the prints did match Kelly's…

The intercom on Pete's office phone buzzed. It was Officer Molly Chang at the front desk. There was a caller on hold who asked for him, intimating he had information about Myles Spencer. Pete picked up immediately.

"Inspector Ericson."

The voice on the line was hesitant. "I'm uh…I'm a friend of Myles Spencer." The man had a slight accent that Pete couldn't place, but that didn't matter right now. This could be the break he was hoping for.

Pete slow played it, not wanting to seem too eager. "Can I get your name?"

The man ignored Pete's question and continued. "I talked to Myles a little while ago and he's freaking out."

"What do you mean by that?"

"He swears he's innocent and this whole thing is a setup."

"If he's innocent, he should turn himself in. He'll have his day in court."

"Yeah, well, he thinks if he surrenders to the police, they'll beat the shit out of him for what happened between you and him at the bar."

"I can assure you if he gives himself up, nothing like that's going to happen."

"Dude, I watch CNN. It happens all the time."

"Sir, do you know where Mr. Spencer is right now?"

There was a long pause on the line. Finally, "Maybe."

"Look, I understand why you're being cautious, but we just want to get his side of the story. If he's nervous about coming to the station, I'll go to him, wherever he wants to meet. Tell him he can record the whole thing on his phone. That'll ensure nothing questionable goes down."

"Yeah. Record it. That sounds good."

"Great. What did you say your name was?"

There was another pause. Pete realized he pushed too hard and was on verge of blowing this opportunity. A moment later, the man said, "1417 Donner Avenue. It's an old roofing supply warehouse in the Bayview. He uses it as a studio." Before Pete could get any additional information, the man hung up.

Pete had a fleeting thought about following protocol, which was to notify the lieutenant and call for a team of uniforms to back him up. But then he harkened back to the conversation he'd had with his father two days ago.

He was going to handle this on his own.

Depending upon how the situation played out, it would be better if there were no witnesses.

Pete was contemplating committing murder. Kelly was a step ahead of him.

She stood in the doorway to Lisa's kitchen, surveying the scene as she pulled a pair of latex gloves from the backpack slung over her shoulder. As she crossed over to Lisa's body, she snapped on the gloves, then crouched down and pressed her finger to Lisa's neck.

Lisa's eyes suddenly flew open.

Kelly instinctively lurched backward, bumping into the kitchen island.

There was a momentary look of recognition in Lisa's eyes. She was too far gone to draw any rational conclusions as to what was happening to her, or why Kelly was there, but a glint of hope gave Lisa a miniscule surge of strength.

Her lips parted and she struggled to form a single word. *Help.* Kelly immediately flashed back to Angelo Moretti's oxygen-starved face smashed up against his window, mouthing the word *help.*

The next few seconds felt like an eternity as Lisa's body bucked one last time, then finally gave out. The toxin had done its job.

Kelly again pressed a finger to Lisa's neck. This time there was no pulse. She lifted an eyelid and shined a penlight into her pupil. There was no reaction.

Kelly's heart was racing. She had to gain control of her rampant emotions so she could focus on the tasks that awaited. As she'd learned from her father's journal, setting the tableau was critical. She stuffed the wine glass and bottle into a garbage bag, then pulled out a Ziplock that contained a partially butchered puffer fish.

She carefully laid the fish on Lisa's cutting board, then took a razor-sharp sushi knife out of the knife block. Kelly ran the blade through the fish a few times. The critical thing was to "accidentally" puncture the liver, which released the deadly toxins. With that complete, she pried open Lisa's right hand and carefully wrapped her fingers around the handle, then dropped the knife to the floor near Lisa's body.

Next, Kelly dipped her finger into the fish and scooped up some of its natural oils. She rubbed the poison onto Lisa's left hand and wiped some on her lips as well.

Kelly peeled off her slimy glove, slipped on a new one and added the final piece of "set dressing," which was a computer printout entitled "How To Safely Prepare Fugu." The scene told the story of a diligent, novice sushi chef who wanted to impress her employers with her ability to tackle the most challenging dish, but sadly wasn't up to the task.

Emma was surprised when she got a text message from her mom explaining that their plans for tonight had changed and that her father would be picking her up. The message went on to say that Lisa would make it up to her next time she came to visit. The text ended with three heart emojis, which Kelly had noticed in Lisa's earlier texts to her daughter.

Moments later, Bob Reynolds received a text from Lisa saying her schedule had changed, and he could pick up Emma at Jordyn's house.

Kelly placed Lisa's phone on the counter and silently made her way out, resisting the urge to look back one more time to confirm her death.

She didn't need to.

50

Ron entered the precinct and was headed to the elevator when he was intercepted by Officer Chang.

"Hey, Inspector. Did your partner get hold of you?"

Ron shook his head, then checked his phone. There were no missed calls.

"Why? What's up?"

"I thought he might've contacted you. He got a call from some guy who said he had information about Myles Spencer, and then he blew out of here. I know your department has an APB out on Spencer, so…" she trailed off.

Ron was certain Pete had pulled some behind the scenes bullshit while he was on admin leave, and now Pete was keeping Ron in the dark about Spencer. Once they had Spencer locked up, the two of them would have a very serious conversation about protocol.

Then he'd request a new partner.

Fortunately, the department logged and recorded all incoming calls and stored them for forty-eight hours. Ron stepped over to Officer's Chang's desk, and she played back the call.

"Sir, do you know where Mr. Spencer is right now?"

"Maybe."

"Look, I understand why you're being cautious, but we just want to get his side of the story. If he's nervous about coming to the station, I'll go to him, wherever he wants to meet. Tell him he can record the whole thing on his phone. That'll ensure nothing questionable goes down."

"Yeah. Record it. That sounds good."

"Great. What did you say your name was?"

There was a pause, followed by, *"1417 Donner Avenue. It's an old roofing supply warehouse in the Bayview. He uses it as a studio."*

Ron told Officer Chang to dispatch a unit to the warehouse and then rushed out the door.

Pete approached the rundown building with caution. He knew it was incredibly foolish to come alone, but he wasn't thinking rationally. The image of Kelly sitting at the club with Moretti had him rattled and angry. He channeled that anger toward Myles Spencer and wanted the satisfaction of personally taking him down...one way or the other.

The front door was ajar, which put Pete on alert. He pulled his service gun and inched the door open with his foot.

"Spencer?"

Pete cautiously moved deeper into the cavernous, gloomy warehouse. There were no signs of canvases or paints. This didn't feel right. "Spencer! SFPD! Come out, hands up!"

His order was met with silence.

Pete's senses were on edge. He'd put himself in an extremely dangerous situation and suddenly his cop instincts kicked in, superseding his hunger for vengeance. He decided, then and there, that Spencer would be brought in by the book.

He pulled out his phone to call for backup when a pigeon burst from its roost in the rafters. Pete turned, gun raised, his heart pounding, and he spied a person in the shadows with his arm extended straight out...a gun in his hand.

Without hesitation, Pete snapped off three quick shots.

The person exploded into a thousand fragments.

Before Pete could process what had happened, a voice behind him called out.

"Ericson!"

As Pete turned back, Spencer fired.

The bullet struck Pete in the head. His body spun around, and he collapsed to the floor.

Pete had severely underestimated Spencer. In his fervor to prove himself right, he'd gamed the system…but in the end, he'd gotten outplayed.

Spencer emerged into the dim light, a short-barreled pistol in hand. He was semi-delirious from a combination of drugs and loathing. He had a distorted, ugly grin on his face as he walked over to Pete's body, aimed the gun at his chest.

"Fuck you, asshole!" He gleefully pulled the trigger. Nothing happened. He pulled again and again, but the cheap pistol was jammed.

"Piece of shit!" He angrily threw the gun into the inky alcoves of the warehouse, giving no thought to fingerprints. His mind wasn't operating with any degree of coherence.

His anger blossoming, he kicked Pete's prone body in the ribs. Once. Twice. He was intent on stomping Pete until there was nothing left but a bloody pulp, and he would have if he hadn't been interrupted by the sound of the approaching sirens.

51

Kelly arrived home shortly after 9:00 p.m., and barely had the strength to push open her door. The stressful events of the evening had repeatedly pumped adrenaline into her bloodstream, and now she was tapped out and running on fumes.

She poured herself a glass of wine, giving no thought to the fact that she'd just used a glass of wine as a vessel to carry out a murder. She retrieved her cell phone and saw she had three missed calls.

The latest one was from Vik. *"Doctor Harper. This is Vik. I hope everything went well with your meetings this afternoon. The rest of the day here was relatively uneventful. We had two more patients with meningitis and sent them to General. The couple who owns the food truck are both there as well, along with their cousin, Abelino. Ida put the doctors in touch with the local hospital in El Salvador, to get more information about this strain of meningococcus. I am locking up and will see you in the morning."*

The second call was from Alexa. *"Kelly, we need to talk about the clinic's revenues. I did some more research, and I'm really worried that you're walking through a legal minefield. I have no idea what your father was into...I'm not suggesting he knowingly broke any laws or anything...but I'm afraid he's left you with a very suspect financial situation. Let's get together as soon as possible and talk about where to go from here. I love you, sister and I'll do whatever I can to help clean this up. Call me."*

Kelly bowed her head in defeat. It was one thing after another. She didn't know how much more she could take before she simply curled up into a ball and quit caring altogether.

But that wasn't an option. Not while Jessica relied upon her. Not while she still had an obligation to the clinic, to the people of the Mission, and most importantly, to her father's legacy. He died as a result of doing what he felt was right, and she owed it to him to do everything in her power to overcome whatever obstacles life tossed into her path.

In the morning, she'd contact Cora, and hopefully Benedetto himself, and talk to them about the money they deposited in the clinic's account. Just how clean was it? Would it stand up to scrutiny from the IRS?

And then there was the question of what to say to Alexa. Should Kelly continue to lie to her best friend, or was it time to admit everything and bring her into the circle of trust?

As these thoughts ricocheted in her head, she remembered there was a third message.

It was from Pete. Her initial inclination was to skip the message, but with everything going on, she resisted that urge and hit play. *"Kelly. It's Pete. I think we've IDed that dark-haired woman who was with Tommy Moretti. Call me as soon as you get this."*

Kelly was dumbstruck. Just when she thought this night couldn't get any worse, it took an unexpected, dangerous turn. She heard it in Pete's voice.

He knew.

She stood motionless, the phone in her hand, trying to process the sudden overload of information. The phone vibrated, startling her.

"Hello?" she said tentatively.

"Kelly, it's Ron Yee."

She immediately knew something was terribly wrong. "Is it Pete?"

"He's been shot. I'm at General, and the doctors are working on him as we speak."

"Where was he hit?"

Ron had never been one to mince words. "The bullet struck him in the head."

Kelly audibly gasped. "Oh my god...."

"The doctors have no idea what he's gonna be like when he wakes up. If he wakes up. I'm hoping you could come down here and talk to medical staff."

"Ron, how'd this happen?"

"I'll explain when I see you."

Ron paced outside the Emergency Room doors, growling into his cell. "I don't give a shit if they're backed up. Tell Forensics I want the ballistics on the shell casing and the prints on that gun first thing in the morning. And ask around and see if someone can track down where that fucking mannequin came from."

"Ron!"

He turned to see Kelly striding in his direction. Her face reflected her fatigue and concern. "Anything new?"

He shook his head. "Waiting for the doctor."

"What happened?"

"Has Pete told you about Myles Spencer?"

Kelly had feared Pete would do something stupid, or at least careless, when it came to Spencer. It appeared he had. "He mentioned the situation and his suspension."

"Pete got a call at the station. A tip from an anonymous source claiming to know where Spencer was holed up. Pete went alone, hell-bent on bringing Spencer in by himself. It was a dumb move. He ran headlong into a trap."

"I can't believe he'd do something so reckless."

Ron shook his head. "He wasn't thinking straight. When he was put on leave, he took it personally. To be honest, he's been a different guy the past few days. I don't know what he thought was going to happen when he confronted Spencer, but I've got a feeling that only one of them was going to walk out of that place."

Kelly knew Ron was right but managed to conceal her reaction. Fortunately, the moment was interrupted by the approach of a slender blonde doctor wearing scrubs. Her facemask hung loosely around her neck.

"Emily?" Kelly asked.

The doctor nodded with a tired half-smile. "Hi, Kelly. I was going call you later. I'm glad you're here."

Kelly turned to Ron. "Doctor Emily Wommack. We're friends from med school. Pete's in the best hands possible." She looked to Emily. "How is he?"

"It's too early to tell. We staunched the blood flow, stabilized his BP and oxygen levels. Inspector, did you recover any shell casings from the scene?"

Ron nodded. "And a gun. A Pathfinder .22. Short barrel. We're fairly certain it's the weapon in question."

"The short barrel explains why the bullet entered with such low velocity," said Emily. "Inspector Ericson's lucky the shooter wasn't using a more powerful gun."

"If you can call getting shot in the head lucky," Ron said.

"I'm not making light of his situation, Inspector, but it's all relative. A bullet penetrating a skull with low velocity means there were limited shock waves to the brain, which is a positive sign. The CT scan showed a hematoma, and we've called in a neurosurgeon to do an emergency craniotomy to evacuate any clots and remove whatever debris or devitalized tissue might be present."

Kelly picked up the narrative, explaining to Ron that the craniotomy would relieve pressure inside Pete's skull, but it was likely the surgeon wouldn't attempt to remove the bullet, since that would only cause more bleeding and damage to the surrounding tissue.

Emily added, "There was one other thing. The Inspector was not only shot, he was kicked repeatedly in the torso. He's got a broken rib and substantial bruising."

Ron seethed. "That son-of-a-bitch Spencer is gonna pay."

"Emily, do you have any idea when I'll able to see him?" Kelly asked.

"His condition's touch-and-go. I'd suggest you both go home and check in with us tomorrow for an update. Inspector Ericson will be in the ICU for several days."

Ron asked the question that Kelly was pondering. "What are the odds he'll fully recover?"

"This isn't Las Vegas. We don't deal in odds. I understand your concern and appreciate your questions, but brain injuries are extremely complicated and we're not able to predict his recovery. He may end up with some physical impairments; he could lose other functions such as memory and speech. He might be able to walk out of here in a week like nothing happened, or it could take months, even years, for him to recover certain cognitive processes. At this point, there's just no way of knowing."

Kelly headed out. Waiting at the hospital would accomplish nothing, other than depriving her of much needed sleep.

On her way to the parking lot, she ran into Andy Ericson. At first, she didn't recognize Pete's father. Kelly had met him once a year ago at a family wedding, and their paths hadn't crossed since. She remembered him being a bull of man, tall and broad chested, overflowing with confidence. Now he seemed smaller, more withdrawn and cloaked in sadness. What she didn't know was that Andy was wracked with guilt. If he hadn't convinced Pete to take the matter of Spencer into his own hands, he wouldn't be lying in a hospital, his life hanging in the balance.

"Kelly," Andy said, taking both of her hands in his. "Have you seen him?"

"No one's allowed in. I spoke to the doctor, and they've called for a neurosurgeon."

Andy's face drooped. "That doesn't sound positive."

"Actually, it is. The attending physician is excellent, and she'll take very good care of Pete. It's going to be a while before they know anything."

"I saw him just the other day. We made plans to go fishing."

"You still can. It just may have to be postponed a bit."

A tiny smile crossed Andy's face. "I can see why my son's crazy about you."

Kelly felt her face redden. "Pete's a very special guy. They're going to do everything they can to get him back on his feet."

"I'm glad you're here," Andy said. "I know he can sense your presence, and I'm sure it means a lot him."

Kelly had no response to that.

While Kelly drove home, her brain was still firing on all cylinders, trying to process everything that had happened. She'd had no time to decompress between murdering Lisa...finding out that Alexa was doing a deep dive on her father's past...learning that Pete had discovered the identity of the "dark-haired woman"...and capped off by the biggest shock of the night...Pete getting shot.

She didn't speculate on the possibility that Pete might die, or that his injury could result in a memory loss. Even though the latter would be a bizarre twist of fate, she'd never wish that upon him. She still loved Pete and only wanted the best for him, even if it meant her being implicated in the murder of Tommy Moretti.

Her mind went to Lisa, lying on the floor in excruciating pain, but still holding onto life. The pleading in her eyes. The instant when her breathing finally stopped. What had Kelly felt? Pity? Guilt? Relief? She didn't recall.

The aftermath of staging the scene: sending the text messages; slinking away into the night. Suddenly, Kelly was struck a nagging pang of doubt. What was it? Had some part of her plan had gone awry? Did she fail to cover her tracks? She quickly ran through her checklist: the wine, the fish, the knife...and then it hit her. The nanny cam! She'd forgotten it! Panic engulfed her. Had she touched it without gloves? Did it just transmit images, or did it record as well?

Kelly had to get back there immediately. It would be risky, but she had no choice. If the police found the camera, they might be able to track it back to her. Even if she hadn't left fingerprints, the fact that someone had planted a camera in the kitchen raised all kinds of questions. It potentially turned the house from an accident scene to a murder scene.

Less than an hour later, she pulled to the curb, a block from Lisa's house. The neighborhood was quiet, and Kelly hurried forward, eager to get inside the house as quickly as possible, but at the same time, not attract undue attention.

She went around to the rear of the house and levered open the patio door, which slid without a sound. Kelly slipped into Lisa's kitchen, closing the door behind her.

The moon provided ample illumination for her to confirm that Lisa's body was where she'd left it, as were the knife and sliced fugu.

So far, so good.

Kelly quietly positioned a stool beneath the spotlight, climbed up and felt for the nanny cam. A quizzical look crossed her face.

She pulled a Maglite mini out of her pocket and shined the beam on the overhead fixture.

Her expression morphed from quizzical to alarmed.

The nanny cam was gone.

52

Thursday

Kelly spent a sleepless night agonizing about the world falling apart around her, and particularly about the missing nanny cam. Who would have known it was there? Why would they have taken it? And the biggest issue was, whoever entered Lisa's house to retrieve the camera would've seen her corpse. Did the person call the police? None of it made sense, but one thing was certain.

Kelly was compromised.

She owed Alexa a call, but she didn't know what to say. She had to bring Cora up to date on everything, but that could wait. First and foremost, Kelly needed to swing by San Francisco General and get an update on Pete's condition.

When Kelly passed through the waiting room, she found Alma, stretched out across two seats, gently snoring. Someone had draped a hospital blanket over her shoulders. Kelly let the poor woman rest.

On her way to find Dr. Wommack, Kelly ran into Oscar's attending physician, who explained they'd repaired his lung and removed bone and cartilage fragments from his chest cavity. However, the surgeons decided it was too risky to operate on Oscar's spinal cord until his lung and chest had a chance to heal further. It would be a few more days before they scheduled exploratory back surgery. Until then, they were keeping him stabilized.

Kelly tracked down Emily and got an update on Pete. His craniotomy had gone well; they relieved the pressure in his skull and were able to evacuate two clots. As Kelly suspected, they left the bullet in his head. Pete would forever carry around a memento of his encounter with Myles Spencer. He was still unconscious, but his vitals were strong and the general outlook was positive but guarded. He was in the ICU if Kelly wanted to look in on him.

She decided she'd rather wait until he was conscious. Seeing Pete lying in bed hooked up to myriad machines was not a picture she needed to add to the rest of the horrific images that had taken up residence in her brain.

Ron had already been to the hospital and was now sitting at his desk, replaying the phone call between Pete and the friend of Spencer's who'd called in. He listened to the call repeatedly, concentrating on the background noises, knowing that even if he heard a car honk or a train whistle, it wouldn't help much. Spencer was in the wind, the caller couldn't be IDed, and Pete was lying in Intensive Care.

Miguel Urbina walked into Homicide to find an angry and frustrated Ron Yee.

"I just heard what happened. Really sorry, man. Anything I can do?"

"Yeah. Tell me the Norteños found Spencer and killed the motherfucker."

"Not yet. No leads on where he might be?"

"Someone knows, but I can't figure out who," said Ron.

"You lost me."

"A guy called in and gave Pete the address of that warehouse. He's obviously in touch with Spencer. I've listened to the call a dozen times, but I've got nothing."

"Lemme hear it."

Ron played the call over the speaker, and Urbina nodded. "Once again."

Halfway through, Urbina held up hand. "Right there. Guy's trying to hide a Canadian accent."

"Canada? I don't hear it."

"I worked with a guy down in San Jose who was from a town outside of Toronto. We used to give him shit about the way he pronounced stuff like "dramma" and "passta." Anyway, your boy's picked up an accent. My guess is he's not born and raised. Maybe went to school there or something."

Ron suddenly flashed on an image of Spencer's buddies at The Rialto. Specifically, one wearing a Blue Jays cap. "Cocksucker!"

"I take it that wasn't directed at me," said Urbina.

Ron leapt to his feet and slapped Urbina on the shoulder. "I owe you, amigo."

"Hey, I just finished night shift and need to burn off some energy. Want some company?"

Ron and Urbina pulled into a no-parking zone across from The Rialto, and Ron left his business card on the dash so he wouldn't get towed. The place wasn't open for business yet, but their loud and persistent knocking drew the attention of the musclebound bartender from Sunday night who was setting up for the day. Ron and Urbina showed their badges and were ushered inside.

"We're looking for some information on one of your regulars," said Ron.

The bartender sported an intricate tattoo of a fire breathing dragon running down one arm, a scorpion running down the other, and a look of disdain on his face. "What kind of information?"

"A name."

"The owners make it a practice not to divulge any personal information about our clientele."

Back when Urbina ran with the Sureños, the first thing he learned was how to intimidate. He'd excelled in his lessons. He stepped in real close and tapped the bartender's chest. "This is a bar, not a law firm. I don't think 'the owners' want to get on the wrong side of the SFPD. You really want us doing nightly spot checks for underage customers?"

The bartender knew when to fold 'em. "Who you looking for?"

"One of Spencer's pals," said Ron. "Skinny guy with glasses and the Jays cap."

The bartender not only offered up a name but a place of business and an Amex receipt.

53

When Kelly arrived at the clinic, she was intercepted by Ida who, despite her fatigue, was beaming. She gave Kelly a full rundown on yesterday's events...starting with finding Abelino and ending with setting up a conference call with the doctors in Aguilares, who provided information about treating this strain of meningitis.

Kelly lavished Ida with praise, complimenting not only her passion but her perseverance, and the concern she showed for every one of her patients. Kelly marched Ida into her office and placed a call to Doc Joe and his wife Betty. Ida was beet red when she heard Kelly tell her father how his daughter "almost single-handedly" staved off what could've become a widespread, deadly epidemic.

After Kelly was done extolling Ida's work ethic and success, she handed the phone to Ida, then headed out of the office, quietly closing the door behind her. She heard Ida's gleeful voice through the door. It was the nicest thing Kelly had heard in quite a while, and it brought an unexpected smile to her face.

Cora, on the other hand, had nothing to smile about. She was on day five of digging through convoluted Dark Web sites that took her into the most morally repugnant corners of the internet. Suddenly, a chime alerted her to a search hit. She opened a new window that took her to SFPD's real-time incident reporting. The site was updated every few minutes and listed police activity around the city, from traffic stops to homicides. Cora had set the site to ping her if there were any hits on the key words "Caucasian males," "ages forty to sixty," and "unidentified victims."

There were three reports that fit her search parameters, and she quickly scrolled through them. When Cora got to the last one, she was gripped with dread.

She grabbed her keys and hurried from the office.

The Mission District was only three miles south of the Marina, but it may as well have been a different country. While Cora was exiting Benedetto's multi-million-dollar building, Tomás was at the Norteño clubhouse, pacing on a threadbare carpet, attempting to weave a believable tapestry of lies. His audience was a very dubious Toro.

"I never heard nothing about Spider skimming," Toro said. He and Tomás were alone in the gang's hangout and the air was thick with stale smoke and tension. "*Tu hermano* has always been a good soldier and strong earner. How do I know this ain't bullshit?"

Tomás was twitching on Adderall and trying hard to keep his focus. He'd need it to pull off his story. "*Jefe,* it's no secret me and Spider didn't get along so great, but no way I'd draw down on my own blood unless he pulled on me first. For reals. You can ask Luca. He saw everything happen just like I say."

"Luca's your boy. I can't trust what he say, so I'm gonna check around on my own. Maybe pay a visit to Spider and get his side, you know? In the meantime, I gotta problem. I lost a good dealer when Gato was taken out. Plus, I lost of load of quality merchandise. Now, I'm down a lieutenant because you put him in the hospital. That's a lotta lost revenue, and I'm not in this for my health. So, tell me, homes, how the fuck you gonna make that up to me?"

"First of all, that *cabrón* who killed Gato? I'm gonna bring you his head."

"I already got guys on the street looking for that piece of shit. How you gonna find him?"

"Trust me."

"You see right there? I don't know if I do trust you. But you find him, you waste him, that'll help, you know? So, what about the money you owe me?"

That one caught Tomás off guard. "Owe you?"

"Like I say, Spider was a big earner. One of my best. You shot him, you need to cover his weekly take. Five Gs. When you gonna be bringing that around?"

"Gimme one week on his corner."

"By then, it'll be up to ten."

"I'll get it to you, Toro. I swear."

"You better hope so, homes. You brought this on yourself. You deliver or I find someone else who can. *Comprende?*"

Tomás hadn't anticipated his brother surviving. If he'd only pulled the trigger a few more times, he'd be in the clear. Maybe he could talk Luca into taking out Spider before Toro got to him. Wasn't there a scene in that Godfather movie where some guy kills some other guy in a hospital? Luca would love that shit.

With that problem solved, Tomás felt a lot better. He plastered on a cocky grin and hoped it didn't look as phony as it felt. *"Comprendo, jefe."*

Meanwhile, across town Hector Ibarra was coming out of a minimart with two Slim Jims and a liter of Mountain Dew when he happened to see a strung out *blanco* exiting a barber shop across the street. He kind of looked like Myles Spencer, but in the photos that Tomás had passed around, Spencer had bushy hair. This guy had a buzz cut.

Hector needed to be certain before he dropped the dime. He couldn't afford to fuck this up. He sauntered across 24th, trying to look as casual as a thirteen-year-old who was on the verge of shitting his pants could look. He stopped on the corner and feigned he was lost, turning his head in all directions trying to get his bearings. A moment later, buzz cut walked by.

It had to be him.

Tomás promised a big reward to anyone who spotted Spencer. This would elevate Hector in the gang. Maybe even impress the *chicas* that hung out at Garfield Square.

He watched as Spencer turned the corner and headed up to a second-floor apartment above an abandoned storefront.

Even though he was afraid of Spider and Gizmo, he was way more intimidated by the idea of having to face Tomás and Luca. He weighed his options, then made the call.

Tomás was grateful for the info and said he'd take care of Hector after he dealt with Spencer. Before Tomás hung up, he made Hector swear not to tell anyone else.

Hector agreed. No problem. Except there was a problem. Tomás was a snake. A backstabber. Hector had heard that he was the one who shot Spider. Suddenly, Hector got nervous and decided to cover his ass.

He made one more call.

54

Kelly finally had a break in her day and decided she couldn't put things off any longer. Her first call was to Cora, and she was surprised when it went to voice mail.

"Cora, this is Kelly. Things last night took a very strange turn." Kelly suddenly realized that leaving a message detailing the events of the evening was an extremely bad idea. "I'll, uh, explain when I see you, which I hope will be soon."

The next call was to Alexa, and it went to voice mail as well. "Lex, it's me," Kelly said somewhat relieved. "I've been crazy busy, but I got your call and agree that we need to sit down and go through everything. Thanks again for having my back. Talk soon. Love you."

Kelly leaned back in her chair, wondering when the next shoe would drop.

Unfortunately, it would be sooner than she thought.

Ron and Urbina came up the walk of a three-million-dollar fixer-upper. A bright metallic green-yellow Porsche Cayenne was parked at the curb, and the Regal Realty sign in the yard confirmed what the receptionist at the real estate office had told them. This was the exclusive listing of Jerry Waterston…aka the guy with the Blue Jays hat…aka the douche who set up Pete.

Ron knocked on the heavy oak door, and Jerry answered, a smile plastered on his face to greet more potential buyers. When he recognized Ron, the smile immediately wilted.

"What do you want?" he asked brusquely, which was not a well-advised move when confronting two very pissed off cops.

"Myles Spencer," said Ron. "Where can we find him?"

"I have no idea." Jerry tried to keep up a tough façade, but it was crumbling around him like a sandcastle on a fault line.

"Mister Waterston?" called a woman's voice from deeper in the house. "Can we see the backyard?"

"Absolutely," he called back. "Be right there!" Jerry turned to Ron and Urbina. "Look, guys," he said, beads of sweat magically appearing on his forehead, "can you give me a few minutes here? I've been trying to unload this place for months and finally have some interested buyers. Maybe thirty minutes, and then we can talk. What do you say?"

"Thirty minutes?" said Ron. "You don't have thirty *seconds*."

"Oh, come on…"

Urbina stepped in. "The last thing you should worry about right now is selling this house. We've got your voice on tape. You cooperate, and we'll mention it to the DA after we book you."

"Book me? What are you…?"

Ron grabbed Jerry by his $250 Brioni necktie and yanked him forward so they were face-to-face. "You set Inspector Ericson up. You're already an accessory to assault with intent to kill. If my partner dies, you'll be implicated in his murder. And a cop-killer in prison?" Ron shook his head. "You'd be better off getting into that hideous chartreuse Porsche and driving it off a really high cliff. Am I being clear?"

Jerry wrenched himself free and attempted to straighten his tie, but it was hopeless. As was he.

"Myles is hiding out with an old girlfriend named Belinda. She lives over on 24th and Alabama."

"Be more specific," Ron growled.

"It's on the corner, over an old bakery. Apartment C. Can I go now?"

Ron and Urbina shared a look of disbelief. Jerry Waterston clearly had a misguided idea of how the world worked.

Ron spun Jerry around, slamming him into the doorframe, as Urbina cuffed him, ratcheting the metal until it bit deeply into Jerry's wrists. "I'll call for a patrol car."

"Mister Waterston," the woman called as she entered the hallway. She stopped when she saw the scene playing out in front of her. "Oh my god!"

Ron pulled back his coat to show his badge. "Mister Waterston no longer has the exclusive listing on this property. And you might be interested to know this house has a substantial termite issue."

Spencer was on the phone, desperately trying to make arrangements to get out of town. Far out of town. "You know I'm good for the money. I've just gotta get someplace where I can chill for a while until things calm down." He listened to whomever was on the other end of the call and didn't like what he was hearing. "No, dammit! I'm not gonna hide out in some motel in Visalia. I'm talking about Cancun or Rio. Maybe Havana. Can Americans get into Cuba these days? And I've gotta fly private. I can't risk going…" The doorbell rang, interrupting Spencer's itinerary planning.

What the hell? The bell rang again. Spencer yelled for Belinda to get the fucking door, but there was no response. Goddamn it! Where was she? Had she snuck out? She was such a pain in the ass.

The bell rang twice in rapid succession. Motherfucker!

Spencer growled into the phone. "Someone's at the door. Hold on." He crossed to the door and angrily yanked it open. "What the fuck do you want?"

The answer came in the form of two .38 hollow points. Spencer was dead before his body hit the floor.

Tomás pulled out his cellphone and snapped a few pictures. He'd make sure everyone knew he was the one who took out the *blanco* that gunned down Gato Molina.

As Tomás pounded down the stairs, he heard sirens. He wasn't concerned. Police cars, fire engines, and ambulances were forever headed someplace in a hurry and sirens were part of the city soundscape.

But these were getting louder, and closer.

Tomás couldn't imagine they were coming for him, but he wasn't about to take a chance. He ran.

All the sudden, the sirens seemed to be converging from multiple directions. Shit! Maybe they *were* coming for him. How could they respond to the shots so quickly? The police would box him in unless he could figure a way out in the next minute.

Just as Tomás made it to the corner, a chopped Buick Skylark four-door screeched to a halt in front of him. Tomás didn't recognize the car, but when the driver's window went down, he saw Gizmo behind the wheel. It was Tomás's lucky day.

"Gizmo! My man! We gotta get out of here now!"

As Tomás lunged for the door handle, the back window lowered, and the barrel of a black matte 9mm spit out a bullet that ripped a hole through Tomás's throat. The second shot finished the job.

The gun was a knockoff of a Sig Sauer Micro-Compact. It's small size, light weight and minimal recoil made it perfect for Diego Sanchez's tiny hand.

Gizmo slammed the gas pedal to the floor, and the Buick peeled away only moments before the SFPD arrived to find a bizarre double murder scene that would take some time and imagination to piece together.

Toro Echavarria was seated at a long wooden table, piles of tens, twenties and fifties in front of him. Off to one side were rubber-banded bundles…the payouts to his crew. Sitting across from him were two hulking, battle-worn lieutenants and Luca, all of whom were enjoying the finest tequila and smoking the smoothest chronic. The week's haul had been better than usual, and the mood was celebratory.

Toro's phone buzzed, and he picked it up.

"*Sí.*" He listened for a beat, his face stoic. "*Muy bien.*"

Toro disconnected, laid down his phone, then gave an almost imperceptible nod across the table. The lieutenants sprang into action; one wrapped a beefy arm around Luca's neck while the other grabbed Luca's wrist and drove a six-inch hunting knife through the back of his hand, pinning it to the table.

Luca roared in pain, writhing back and forth, but Toro's boys held firm.

"I saw that Godfather movie, homes. I really liked that scene in the bar when Luca Brasi got whacked."

Luca's eyes grew large. He tried to struggle, but the vise-like forearm around his neck was cutting off his air.

"Tomás is dead. I know you two were planning to make a move against me." Toro let out a small chuckle, which turned into a scowl. "I mean, what the fuck, Luca?"

Luca's voice came out as a raspy whisper, "*Jefe, por favor…*"

Toro shook his head. "I treated you well, and in return you pull this shit? *Lo siento,* Luca, but I gotta make you an example, you know?"

The banger behind Luca squeezed harder, his arm like a boa constrictor. Luca's eyes bulged and his face grew red.

"*Nadar con los peces, cabrón,*" said Toro.

As Luca thrashed, Toro went back to counting the cash. Moments later, Luca slid from his chair, his hand still pinned to the table.

55

It had been a long, stressful week for the staff at the clinic. The meningitis outbreak had resulted in an added crush of patients, and everyone was exhausted, so Kelly made an executive decision and did something she'd rarely done. She closed early.

Sonita scrounged up a half dozen mismatched glasses. A tiny shot of Scotch was poured into each. Vik, Annie, Sonita, Ramona and Kelly raised their glass.

"To Doctor Samuel," said Kelly. "In the past week, she's come to embody the foremost canons of the Hippocratic Oath. *I will apply, for the benefit of the sick, all measures that are required. I will not be ashamed to say, "I know not," nor fail to call in my colleagues when the skills of another are needed for a patient's recovery.*"

Ida blushed from the beautiful tribute, as Kelly continued. "And finally, *I will prevent disease whenever I can.*" Kelly fixed her eyes on Ida and raised her glass high. "We are truly happy, and fortunate, to have Doctor Ida Samuel as a member of our staff, and our family. On a personal note, I'm very proud of how far you've come in such a short time. We're all here for you."

"To Doctor Samuel," said the others. Scotch was downed.

Ida was speechless, but her tears of joy spoke volumes.

Kelly was reaching for the bottle when her cell buzzed. It was Ron Yee.

She excused herself and took the call in her office.

Ron's words came out in gushes. "...and when we got there, Myles Spencer was dead. After I cleared the scene, I came to the hospital. They let me see Pete for a few minutes so I could tell him what happened. I don't know if he heard me, but he opened his eyes."

Kelly froze.

"The doctor thought it'd be good idea if you came by. See how reacts."

How *would* he react? How much would he remember? The identity of the dark-haired woman? The investigation into Gideon?

"Kelly? You there?" asked Ron.

"Uh, yeah. I'm, um, just wrapping things up the clinic, and then I'll come by."

"I'm sure he'll be happy to see you."

Ron's words couldn't be further from the truth.

An hour later, Kelly arrived at the hospital and found Dr. Wommack. Kelly needed to know what she could expect before facing Pete.

"He's made a surprising recovery, all things considered," said Emily. "However, he's on heavy meds and fading in and out. I wouldn't put much hope in him being able to converse."

Which is exactly what Kelly had hoped. "Is Inspector Yee still here?"

Emily nodded. "He asked if he could sit with Pete for a while."

This was not welcome news. *If* Pete was awake, and *if* he recognized Kelly, and *if* he happened to remember his revelation about the dark-haired woman.... It was a lot of "ifs" but at the same time, possible. Kelly had two choices: either leave, or confront this head-on, which meant she really had no choice at all. She took a deep breath and entered the ICU.

Ron looked up from his phone as Kelly slid back the curtain and stepped over to Pete's bed. Ron smiled at her. "Thanks for coming. He's been sleeping off and on, but when he's awake, he seems to know what's going around him."

"That's great," said Kelly with an ersatz smile.

She stood silent, taking a medical inventory of the person lying in bed. His head was encased in gauze, his face only partially visible. Monitors measured every conceivable bodily and brain function. Pete looked like death warmed over, which was a fairly accurate description of what he'd gone through. He was lucky to be alive.

Kelly felt intense pity for this man. Only a few days ago they'd shared a bed. So much had happened since then.

298

Pete's eyes fluttered open, and Kelly gasped. He blinked several times, trying to focus on the person standing before him. Was it a doctor? A nurse? A shimmering memory teased his damaged brain. Who was it?

"Pete, it's Kelly."

The words drifted around Pete's subconscious. *Kelly.* What did it mean? And that voice? Was it someone he knew? He couldn't remember.

She touched his hand and whispered his name. He stared into her eyes, and Kelly felt goosebumps along her arm. Pete slowly moved his lips, but no sound emerged. He took in a breath and tried again, but the effort was too much.

"I think that's enough for tonight," said Emily as she walked in. "He needs his beauty sleep."

Pete's eyes closed, and a moment later, he was out.

Kelly deeply sighed, and Ron put his hand on her shoulder. "It'll all be fine, Kelly."

He had misread her sigh. It wasn't sorrow.

It was relief.

Ida walked into her cramped apartment and flopped down on the sofa. All she wanted to do was sleep for a few days. She couldn't remember a time when she was so physically and mentally drained. After a grueling week of chasing the outbreak and then experiencing the incredible rush of uncovering the source, she felt hollow. She'd run the race, crossed the finish line, gotten the accolades for her accomplishment, and now...what?

She closed her eyes and replayed parts of Kelly's tribute in her head, "*In the past week, she's come to embody the foremost canons of the Hippocratic Oath...We are truly happy, and fortunate, to have Doctor Ida Samuel as a member of our staff, and our family. On a personal note, I'm very proud of how far you've come in such a short time. We're all here for you.*"

Would Kelly feel *truly happy* to have Ida around if she knew the truth?

Ida pulled the pill container from her pocket and dumped the contents onto the coffee table. Three Dex and two Valium. She stared at the drugs for a long moment, then plucked up a Valium and popped it into her mouth.

As she laid back on the sofa, she hoped no one noticed the pills were missing from the lockup...and then she realized, she didn't really care.

While Kelly was visiting Pete, she'd gotten a call from Dr. Papadakis. He sounded quite animated and asked her to call him back as soon as possible.

When Kelly connected with him, he asked if she was able to come see her sister.

"Tonight?" Kelly feared Jessica had taken a turn for the worse. "Is everything alright?"

"Everything's wonderful," he replied.

"How about tomorrow morning, then. It's been a long day and..."

"She spoke. Jessica said your name."

Kelly was stunned. The hits just kept coming.

Papadakis continued. "Jessica is more alert than we ever thought possible. If she could see you, I think it would help tremendously."

Kelly subconsciously equated Pete's condition to that of her sister. Two people she loved, both wavering in and out of the here-and-now. She desperately hoped both would recover and that one would forget the past, and the other would miraculously remember it.

"I'm on my way," Kelly said.

Visiting hours at Peninsula Oaks ended long ago, and the facility was quiet. As Kelly walked down the hallway, the only sounds she heard were the faint haunting moans that emanated from patients in the middle of the night.

She pushed open the door to Jessica's room to find her sleeping, the head of the bed raised. Dr. Papadakis was there, along with the omnipresent Ingrid. They greeted Kelly warmly, and Papadakis began boasting about this 'miraculous medical achievement.' He was a man who loved the bright lights, and he could already feel the warmth of their glow. Visions of Nobels danced in his head.

"...and I've contacted the New England Journal of Medicine, which has requested a synopsis of my findings, as well as the documentation. They also asked if they could use Jessica's name. I know it's an unusual request, but in this case..."

Kelly raised her palm. "Doctor, let's take it one step at a time, alright?"

Kelly sat next to the bed and lightly touched Jessica's face. "Jess," she said, "it's Kelly." For the second time this evening, she was attempting to reach someone who existed in a nether world.

Jessica slowly opened her eyes. She glanced around the room, and her gaze finally landed on Kelly.

"Hi, sweetheart," said Kelly. "How are you feeling?"

It appeared as if Jessica was processing the question and attempting to arrive at a conclusion. Her face was passive, but her eyes were clear and focused. For the first time since Jessica's violent run-in with Clarence Musselwhite, she exuded an air of being present.

Kelly squeezed her hand, and Jessica's fingers responded with miniscule pressure. The touch was lighter than a feather, but Kelly swore it was intentional. They were communicating. It was more than Kelly had allowed herself to expect. Tears sprang to her eyes as the realization began to take root. Her sister might, against all odds, resurface.

Jessica closed her eyes and parted her lips. It was an immense struggle for her, but she managed to utter, "K...K..."

Papadakis broke out in an ear-to-ear grin. "There! She's saying your name!"

Kelly shot him a withering look, and Papadakis took a step back, giving the sisters a modicum of privacy.

"That's right, Jess. It's me. Kelly."

"K...K..."

Kelly put her ear to Jessica's lips. It had been twenty years since she'd heard her sister speak.

Jessica's voice was almost imperceptible. "K...kill."

Kelly must've misheard. It sounded like Jessica said...

"Kill," she whispered again. "Killer."

Kelly recoiled, looking at her sister in a totally different light. Jessica opened her eyes, and Kelly saw something in there that froze her to the core.

She saw fear.

Jessica turned away and started shaking uncontrollably.

"Doctor," said Ingrid. "Her BP is rising."

"Get her a sedative," he said. He turned to Kelly. "I don't know what caused that. I suspect all the excitement was overwhelming. Or perhaps it's a latent reaction to her medication. Either way, there's no cause for alarm."

Kelly knew different. There was every cause to be alarmed. In the past two months, Jessica had heard Kelly's confessions. The words had been locked away somewhere, and now those admissions of guilt, of murder, had surfaced in her consciousness.

She knew Kelly was a killer. And it scared the hell out of her.

Twenty years in a cocoon of oblivion, and when she finally emerged, she was afraid of her own sister.

Kelly was devastated.

56

It was after midnight when Kelly arrived home. She was bone tired but knew sleep wouldn't come easy.

She lit a fire and poured a glass of wine, her hand trembling as she raised it to her lips. She couldn't stop seeing the recurring image of the terror in her sister's eyes and hearing the whispered word, *killer.* That moment would torment Kelly forever.

The dark journey of the Harper family began some twenty years ago, and the motivation for Kelly to assume the mantle of Gideon lay at the feet of her father. While he wasn't to blame for Kelly's decisions, she would have never taken that path were it not for the journal he'd left behind.

She was surprised that her glass was empty, as was the bottle. Kelly rectified that situation with a new bottle, refilling her glass and taking a drink before removing the journal from its hiding place. She contemplated turning to a random page to hear his voice once again, but suddenly had an acrid burn in the back of her throat. She sniffed the wine, wondering if it had turned. It smelled fine. She sipped. It tasted better. It wasn't the wine that left a bad taste in her mouth.

It was the contents of her father's journal.

She stared down at the leather-bound book wondering how in the hell she'd gotten to this moment in time. Benedetto was missing. Pete was lying in ICU. Jessica was waking to a new set of horrors. A nanny cam that could tie Kelly to Lisa's murder was missing.

As she stared at the fire, her head was pounding, and her heart was palpitating. She couldn't take anymore. It was time to reassess every aspect of her life. The clinic would run out of funds in a month and shut its doors. She'd have to find a job. Probably sell the condo. She had no idea what to do about Jessica.

One thing was certain. The killing had to stop.

Gideon was through.

She needed a clean slate, and she knew where to begin.

The pages ripped out of the journal without putting up a struggle. She fed them, one by one into the fire. As each page turned to white ash, her father's voice got fainter and fainter. She felt as if she were saying goodbye to him all over again. Her eyesight was blurred by the unending flood of tears, but she wouldn't allow that to deter her from her task. If she stopped to even wipe her face, she feared she may lose her nerve and save a few pages of the journal as a keepsake. Something to clutch to her chest on those nights when she missed her father the most.

No. She needed a total and complete break. Getting rid of the journal would never erase the truth she knew about her father, about Gideon, but it was a start. It would eliminate the temptation to relive his homicidal recounting, and if Pete did recover and suspect Kelly of being involved in the Moretti family fatalities, burning the journal would eliminate an extremely damning piece of evidence.

It became increasingly difficult to toss the pages into the hungry flames, watching as her father's distinctive handwriting went up in smoke. She held the final journal entry in her hands and second thoughts crept in. Surely, saving these final few pages would be okay. She could conceal them inside one of her medical books. Or stash them away in a safe deposit box.

To what end? Kelly was determined to find closure. It began here and now.

She slid the final pages into the fire and felt a weight lifted from her chest. She hadn't realized before that the journal itself was such an emotional burden.

Kelly raised her glass and made a silent toast to her father. As she finished her wine, she was startled by someone urgently knocking. Who'd be outside her door at this time of night? Alexa? Maybe Benedetto?

When she looked out the peephole, she was taken by surprise. Kelly opened the door and ushered Cora in. She'd never seen Cora appear so spent. Arriving at her doorstep after midnight was undoubtedly a harbinger of more bad news.

Cora perched on edge of the sofa. Despite looking frail, her voice was tinged with an anger that gave her a sense of strength and purpose. "The police found Matthew's body. He'd been shot, and his corpse dumped in the bay."

Even though Kelly had anticipated the worst, she wasn't prepared for this. Of all the things she'd been through in the past few hours, this hit her the hardest. She wasn't sure why. She hadn't known Matthew Benedetto for long, and their relationship was extremely abnormal. Truth be told, she didn't really like him. So why did his death move her so deeply? Because he was the last link to her father? Or was it because he'd known her secrets, and as such, could see into her soul?

Kelly was out of tears but badly shaken. She sat down with Cora and took her hand. "I'm so sorry. I know how much he meant to you."

"He was a kind man. Generous to a fault. He was very complicated, but one of the smartest and most compassionate people I've ever known. He cared deeply about your father, and about you as well."

"Do the police have any idea who killed him?"

"None."

"Do you think it had anything to do with Gideon?"

"I know it does."

"How can you be so sure?"

"When I discovered the police had pulled a man in his fifties out of the bay, I immediately went down to the station. I explained my relationship to Mr. Benedetto, and they asked if I could provide a positive identification. It was him. And he was wearing this." Cora reached into her purse and took out Benedetto's watch. The crystal was cracked, but the watch was otherwise intact. "I gave this to him on his birthday ten years ago."

"I remember seeing that watch and recall thinking that it was rather plain for a such a wealthy man. No offense."

"It is plain, for a reason. When I was working in the government, there was a tech who loved gadgets. We jokingly called him Q. When I left the agency, he gave me this watch as a going away present. I never wore it, but I got a more masculine band, had it engraved and regifted it to Mr. Benedetto. He was rarely without it."

"I don't understand. How does this watch tie the killer to Gideon?"

"It does more than tell time." Cora pulled out the watch stem and suddenly a man's voice came from a minute speaker built into the bezel. The sound quality was tinny, but the words were clear.

"This is business. Yes. Answer questions…you go free."

The next was an exchange between Benedetto and presumably his kidnapper.

"…unique way of conducting business."

"Who is Gideon?"

Cora stopped the playback. "The mechanism was damaged in the water, so the recording is spotty, but still extremely informative."

Kelly had suffered so many unforeseen blows in the past few days that she barely had enough energy left to react. This revelation simply left her numb. Numb and terrified. Benedetto was kidnapped days ago. If he'd been tortured, how much pain would it have taken for him to reveal her identity?

"What did he tell…?"

"Hear for yourself." Cora started up the playback. The unidentified man was speaking.

"…an assassin…he kills people…one hundred nine people."

Kelly held her breath as the playback continued.

"…Bruno…two weeks later…Musselwhite…found dead. Completely dead."

Kelly blanched. "He made the connection."

There was a long stretch of static, then, *"…called The Committee…seven million…deserve that money…"*

Benedetto can be heard saying, *"no idea who this Gideon person is,"* followed by someone being struck and grunting in pain. A second blow resulted in an agonizing wail.

Benedetto had been defiant. But for how long?

"It's just a guess, but I think this next part of the conversation took place a day later," said Cora.

The man was speaking again, *"...his wife Mary...murdered dead...Harper the most obvious...died two months ago, and there have been more victims since then."*

"He knows," Kelly whispered. She was suddenly enveloped in a frigid embrace of fear. Her teeth began to chatter.

Cora reached over and gently grabbed Kelly's hand. "Do you want to hear the rest?"

Kelly braced herself and nodded.

More static, followed by someone gasping in pain. Benedetto being subjected to more torture.

"... lies mean more pain. Yes, more pain."

Benedetto responded with complete disdain, *"Fuck you."*

In that moment, Kelly's admiration for Benedetto soared. "He stayed strong."

There was a pause in the recording, followed by Benedetto saying, *"I'm ready to talk."*

Benedetto had broken after all.

The other man responded, *"...more lies, Mott will hurt you...then he will hurt Cora Mathews...I know how... Gideon killed from the grave...daughter Kelly Harper..."*

Kelly's shoulders slumped. Her secret was out. Her life was in danger, again. She turned to Cora. "I don't blame Mr. Benedetto, but still..."

Cora interrupted. "There's more."

Benedetto was talking again, *"wrong about her...not Kelly...wouldn't hurt a soul."* And then, *"Gideon ...standing right in front of you."*

Kelly was stunned by Benedetto's admission.

307

More static and garbled voices, followed by Benedetto saying, *"evidence… in my office…where and how I carried out the hits…"*

Kelly was startled by a loud gunshot. "Was that…?"

Cora held up a hand. Wait…

Benedetto spoke again, *"spend the rest of my days running…."* The last voice on the recording was the man, *"…aren't interested in you. They want Gideon. Yes, they want her."*

A moment later, there was another gunshot.

Cora looked at the watch in her hand, then tucked it back into her purse.

"I don't understand what happened," said Kelly.

"I've listened to this many times. My assumption is there was a third person in the room. A person named Mott. He was probably holding a gun on Matthew. Somehow, Matthew managed to get the gun away from him, shoot him, and then turned it on the kidnapper, but was a fraction too late."

"He risked his life trying to protect me," Kelly said.

"Protect both of us. Unfortunately, the person who killed Matthew knows about you."

Kelly slowly shook her head, running her hand across her face. She couldn't remember a time when she felt so drained. So utterly defeated. "I can't go through this again."

"Matthew gave his life for us. I think we owe it to him to find the man who murdered him."

"You're talking about a revenge killing. That's how this all started twenty years ago."

Cora nodded. "You've come full circle."

"Cora, I appreciate what he did and what he meant to you, but I just…I can't."

"You've been through hell, and I know how much it weighs on you, but this man not only killed Matthew, he knows who you are, which means either he, or The Committee, or both, will be coming after you next."

"I wouldn't even know where to begin. Plus, there have been some added complications."

Kelly ticked off the potentially disastrous issues that recently cropped up: the missing nanny cam; Pete discovering that Kelly was with Tommy Moretti at the club on the night he died; and Alexa's probe into the clinic's finances.

Cora listened calmly and without judgement, then responded, "The nanny cam will no doubt surface, and when it does, we'll figure out the best way to deal with it. Until then, there's nothing to be done. As for Inspector Ericson, that's another case of wait-and-see. As you said, there's no predicting what his condition will be when he eventually recovers. Finally, don't worry about the apparent financial irregularities. While the companies may appear to be questionable, all of them are legitimate, and there is no way for anyone to track the initial source of the money. The best thing you can do is convince Alexa to move on. I'm sure she has better things to do with her time...as do we."

"Avenging Mr. Benedetto."

"It's not just that. Your life is in danger."

"You're saying that Gideon has more work to do."

"Is there really any choice?"

Kelly looked over to the fireplace at the pile of ash sitting at the bottom of the dying embers. She'd thought they represented the end of Gideon.

She'd been wrong.

EPILOGUE

Pete had been experiencing a fitful sleep when he suddenly opened his eyes. He wasn't sure if he'd had a bizarre dream or if his memory was surging back.

He woke knowing the identity of dark-haired woman. The last person to see Tommy Moretti alive.

He pressed the nurse call button. He needed to talk to his partner right away.

And then he needed to talk to Kelly.

To be continued...

ACKNOWLEDGEMENTS

Once again, my eternal thanks to my wife Marjorie for her constant encouragement and invaluable input.

The diverse voices of my three daughters; Laura-Lee, Elizabeth and Megan, helped to shape the myriad female characters throughout the novel. I thank them for being there for me, and for being so wonderfully unique.

I'm in debt to Dr. James Guadagni and Dr. Emily Wommack who helped me immensely with the medical details. Any errors in that area are strictly mine.

A special thanks go out to my agents, Laurence Becsey and Emma Alban at Intellectual Property Group, who continue to provide both keen guidance and staunch support.

Much thanks to Dave Richardson and Christopher Condit who read a very early draft and helped set me on the right track.

And finally, everlasting thanks to my parents, who gave me many gifts, not the least of which was being born and raised in San Francisco.

Made in United States
Troutdale, OR
07/11/2023

11161825R00179